TWISTING THE TRUTH

STEVEN SUTTIE

Twisting The Truth

Copyright © Steven Suttie 2020

Published by Steven Suttie 2020

Steven Suttie has asserted his rights under the Copyright, Designs and Patents Act 1988 to be identified as the author of this work.

This novel is a work of fiction. Names and characters are the product of the author's imagination and any resemblance to any persons, living or dead, is entirely coincidental.

This book is sold subject to the condition that it shall not, by way of trade or otherwise, be lent, resold, hired out or otherwise circulated without the publisher's prior consent in any form of binding or cover other than that in which it is published and without a similar condition including this condition being imposed on the subsequent purchaser.

Cover design by Steven Suttie

Cover photograph:
Strangeways, the panopticon of light © Nick Dunn, 2016

Font type Calibri Light

P/B 1st Edition – published 18th May 2020
Kindle 1st Edition – published 18th May 2020

Thank you to Professor Nick Dunn of Lancaster University for kindly allowing me to use his superb photograph, "Strangeways, the panopticon of light" for the cover of Twisting the Truth.

Also, happy 50th birthday to Dorothy Smart! I hope you enjoy the book, which I scheduled especially to coincide with your big day!

Chapter One

FRIDAY

Clare Miller was walking quickly through the primary school's gates, keen to get back to her car and get on with the rest of her day following the morning from hell. The twins, Leo and Molly had definitely got out of bed on the wrong side today. They'd been arguing and crying, refusing to eat their breakfast and had even made a big performance of getting dressed. Leo had hidden his school uniform behind the toy box and when he'd finally agreed to get dressed, he had put his jersey on back to front and suffered another meltdown when Molly began laughing hysterically at his mistake. It had all culminated in them now being late for school, and then refusing to go inside because they were scared of everybody looking at them.

It was fair to say that the twins had come close to driving Clare crazy today and it was only five past nine. She didn't feel the slightest bit guilty that she was glad to see the back of them as they stomped and huffed through the school doors, still squabbling as they went.

Clare thought that the terrible twos had been bad, but the trying threes and then the frantic fours had been incrementally worse. Now, the twins were going through the stage that she called the fucking horrific fives. She loved the twins dearly, they were her whole world. But right now, after all of this morning's tears and drama, she was delighted that they were going to be out of her hair for the next six hours and fifteen minutes.

Clare was suddenly jolted from her thoughts as a figure appeared from the shadows of the path which runs along the side of the school railings. The hooded male barged into her as she neared her car, crunching into her shoulder.

"Oh... sorry... I didn't see you..." Clare raised her hand to rub her shoulder, that had really hurt.

"Watch where you're going, you stupid bitch!"

"What... I'm... wait, what did you just call me?" Clare Miller had just ranged through a whole spectrum of emotions in the past half-second. At first, she had been shocked and alarmed, then apologetic and embarrassed. Now, she was absolutely furious that this awful young man was talking to her in such a disgusting and unprovoked manner.

"You know what I said. You heard me, you cock-eyed bitch." The youth was talking with the fashionable black accent which for some reason, they thought made them sound cool. He was far from black. Despite his hood being up over his head and a black scarf covering the bottom half of his face, his pale complexion was obvious around his eyes and forehead. He looked like he was on something, he was definitely a druggie, thought Clare. Her adrenaline was racing but she knew better than to take this little bastard on. She pressed the button on her key fob and rushed around to the driver's door, all she could think about was getting away from this obnoxious, nasty bastard.

"Oh, I get it yeah. You think cos your husband's a big noise in the po po that you're better than me, yeah?" The youth was staring straight at her, his eyes were filled with hatred. Clare suddenly froze at the side of her car, the utter shock of this extraordinary exchange had become too much and she was struggling to fully comprehend the situation. Her voice wavered as she spoke, she was trying desperately to make some sense from this unbelievable situation.

"You…you… know my husband?"

"Yeah, I know your husband. And I know you now, and your two little kids. Now if you don't want me to stab you in the face, you had better fuck off now yeah, you get me?"

Clare got in the car, quickly pressing the door lock as soon as the door was closed.

The youth walked to the front of the car and stood there staring at her over the bonnet. After several seconds, he pointed at his eyes, then pointed two fingers directly at Clare. With that, he turned and began walking casually away down the pathway by the side of the school from where he had appeared less than one minute earlier.

Chapter Two

SCIU Offices, MCP HQ

"Honestly, I've never met a single person who doesn't like cheese on toast!" Exclaimed DC Peter Kenyon.

"What, so you've asked every person you've ever met?" Asked DC Helen Grant.

"Yes, I have actually. And every one of them said they fucking love it!"

"Well you've led a charmed life Pete, you've obviously never met anyone who is lactose intolerant."

"Shush, gaffer's coming," said DS Jo Rudovsky out of the side of her mouth. "He looks like he's in a mood."

Detective Chief Inspector Andy Miller had a cautious look on his face as he approached his officers. "Good morning team."

"Morning Sir!" Came the familiar, cheerful chorus from DCI Miller's small team of officers.

"Listen, today's shit joke is cancelled I'm afraid."

The team applauded and cheered enthusiastically but Miller didn't laugh. He looked quite stressed. "I'm afraid we've had a new case handed our way this morning, the guy who was stabbed yesterday in the city-centre didn't make it through the night... so we've been back-heeled the murder investigation."

The inevitable mumbles and groans commenced but Miller continued talking over his officers. "We need to start this morning's briefing with a strategic overview of our current case-load."

This was not a good start to the daily team brief. Miller's team were currently working in pairs on separate cases which were all showing signs of positive progress. His announcement meant that at least two of his officers would be taken off their case with immediate effect, which was the worst possible scenario for maintaining a positive outlook in the department. The complaining continued, most noticeably from DS Jo Rudovsky who couldn't see why the team were constantly being disrupted.

"I know, I know, it's a pisser Jo. But it's been on the news all night and loads of people have been sharing video footage of the aftermath when the paramedics were working on the victim. That footage has now gone viral and as usual, the public believe that this is the only crime in the city."

Miller's team knew the scenario, it had happened many times before. Running the most senior crime detection department in a city of almost three million people, with a tiny staff team of just seven full-time officers often meant that case-loads had to be juggled around.

"It's not all bad, we will have city central CID at our disposal, so it's more a case of managing them and making sure they are on-the-ball. We just need to be seen visiting the crime-scene this morning…"

"All of us?" asked Rudovsky with an unmistakable expression of irritation.

"Yes, afraid so Jo. And then at least two of you will be joining me in running the investigation. Shit news, I know, but we'll get there in the end."

Miller was the MCP's most recognisable detective and his department were widely known as the elite of senior detectives in the Greater Manchester area. It was common for him and his team to be wheeled out for high-profile investigations as the Manchester City Police Force tried to reassure the public that they were throwing everything at the most public cases. Miller's success throughout a long list of high-profile investigations had earned him a solid reputation as a safe pair of hands in the media's eyes. As such, this fine accolade had a rather dubious aspect, as the MCP senior officials tried to get Miller and his team involved with every major investigation, purely to keep the press on-side. It was a nice gesture on the one hand, but this tactic wasn't sustainable.

DC Peter Kenyon had his hand in the air. Miller nodded to him.

"Sir, why do you always say 'we'll get there in the end' whenever you tell us something shit?"

This cheeky remark received a good laugh, and Miller was pleased that the frosty mood had thawed a little.

"We will Pete, we will..." Miller looked down at the desk as he noticed that his phone was lit up. It was Clare, his wife. The unusual situation threw the DCI slightly as Clare very rarely rang him when he was at work. He began to feel a little panicked as he realised that it was five past nine and Clare knew that he had his team brief between nine and ten, making this call even more unusual.

"Just a sec guys, sorry..." Miller pressed the green phone icon on his handset and held it up to his ear as he turned his back on his team. "Hi Clare, what's up?"

Miller froze as he heard his wife crying down the phone. This was not normal and his mind suddenly began racing with all manner of terrible scenarios. Had she had a crash? Had she run someone over? Was it the kids? His adrenaline had kicked in and his heartbeat was suddenly racing at such a thunderous pace that he felt slightly faint. "Clare, talk to me love. What's happened?"

The SCIU team members all looked at one another, they too felt concerned. Clare Miller was well known to all of them and they knew that she wasn't a drama queen. Whatever she was calling their boss about, they knew just from Miller's voice and body-language that something very serious had happened.

"Clare, listen... calm down. Take a deep breath. Right?"

"Yes."

"Right, calm down, just calm down."

The SCIU detectives all felt very uncomfortable, it almost felt as though they were intruding.

"Right, Clare, tell me what's happened..." Miller turned to face his team, his face was bright red and he looked scared.

"I've just been threatened..."

"Threatened? What do you mean... Where? By who?"

"I don't... I don't know. I was coming back to the car after dropping the twins at school..." Clare's voice sounded weird and Miller picked up straight away that she was in shock. "...I was just near the car and this young bloke shoulder-barged into me and then started saying really horrible things to me. He said he was going to stab me... in the face..." Clare had been doing really well in explaining the situation but now her voice was starting to break up as the sheer terror of the situation came flooding back.

"What, Clare, this doesn't…"

"He said he knows what my kids look like now…"

"What?" It was Miller's voice which faltered this time.

"He said he knows you." Clare began crying again and her words became inaudible. Miller felt like he needed to sit down and walked unsteadily across towards the nearest empty chair and sat down. His detectives watched on, desperate to know what was going on, desperate to be able to offer some support to their boss. Miller grabbed a waste-paper bin and vomited into it. It was at this point that his team knew that something was very seriously wrong.

Chapter Three

"Good morning, Worsley Green Primary School." The school secretary Mrs Maher had a very soft and friendly telephone manner.

"Ah yes, hello, good morning. I hope you can help? I'm just trying to confirm something." The man who was phoning sounded very well-spoken and confident.

"Yes, I'll certainly help you if I can."

"Great stuff. I'm just trying to confirm that the children of DCI Andrew Miller attend your school?"

Mrs Maher was stunned by this extraordinary question. She felt her heartbeat quicken as a dozen questions began running through her mind. "I'm sorry but we are not in a position to provide any such information about any of the school's pupils." It was clear from her voice that this utterly bizarre question had unnerved the experienced staff member.

"Oh, of course, GDPR and all of that... but it's right that the Miller twins attend your school?"

"No, what... it's got nothing to do with GDPR. I'm sorry, but who am I speaking to?"

"I'm afraid that I will remain nameless. However, I have some information which is extremely important and I need you to listen very carefully. Do you understand?" The initial friendliness and warmth was disappearing from the man's voice, a cold, threatening edge had crept in.

"Okay..."

"If this *is* the school that DCI Miller's twins attend, I must warn you that some very, very bad people are planning to punish DCI Miller, by hurting his children."

"Oh... my..."

"I have been made aware of the plan and let's just say that I am completely uncomfortable with this situation in every sense. So, I am risking my own personal safety in making this call. I am warning you now that there are plans for a very disturbing incident to take place at your school at any moment. I suggest that you inform the police of this conversation, and you make arrangements for DCI Miller's children to be removed from the premises with immediate effect."

"What... is... is this..."

"I'm being deadly serious, you need to phone 999 right now and request the immediate presence of an armed response team. I can assure you that there is an immediate threat to life."

Mrs Maher's hand was trembling as she made notes on her pad. The telephone line went dead.

Chapter Four

"Clare, listen… listen… I need you to calm down again. Just take a big deep breath and hold it. Right, now blow it out very slowly through pursed lips, as though you're trying to whistle." The emotion and stress in Miller's voice was shocking for everybody who was witnessing this astonishing scene. Andy Miller is widely acknowledged as the calmest and most laid-back police officer in the city. But not today, he was falling apart in front of his team's eyes.

"Right, that's it, you're sounding a bit better now. Where exactly are you?"

"Outside school."

Miller's head snapped up and he locked eyes with his number-two, DI Saunders. "Keith, can you get on to Salford's Inspector and tell him that I need an urgent police presence at Worsley Green Primary School right now?"

"Sir."

"Right, Clare, stay in the car, keep it locked. If anybody approaches you, you need to drive away as fast as you can… but police officers will be there in a few minutes if not sooner. I'm coming down there now."

"Okay…"

"Keep taking those deep breaths. I'll be ten minutes max."

Miller hung up and leapt up out of his seat. "I need to go, somebody's just threatened to stab Clare and the kids."

"What?" Said Rudovsky, holding her hand to her mouth as the rest of the team looked at their boss with shock and panic etched on their faces. They had all realised that something shit was happening but none of them had guessed it was anything as alarming as that.

"I've got to go…"

"Do you want us to come boss?" asked Rudovsky.

"No… no… cheers… right, shit, gotta go."

Miller ran out of the office, tapping his pocket to double-check he had his car key as he went. Saunders was relaying the message to the Duty Inspector at Salford and began running after Miller as he saw his boss racing out of the office.

"Yes, every available patrol in the area, right now. Thanks." Said Saunders as he hung up and put his phone in his pocket as he raced down the stairs after Miller.

"Sir, hang on, I'll drive. You call Clare back."

Miller accepted the offer of help and threw his car-key to his DI. Saunders thought he saw tears as their eyes met briefly.

Within seconds, Miller's unmarked silver Insignia was racing through the city-centre streets with its siren blaring and the blues and twos lights revolving. Just minutes later the car was bouncing over the speed bumps on Chapel Street as the vehicle raced through Salford towards the East Lancs road where Saunders stepped on the accelerator and drove the screaming police car at 80mph towards Worsley.

"Hi, are you okay?" Asked Miller as the call reconnected to his wife's phone.

"God Andy, I think I'm having a panic attack."

"Just keep taking those deep breaths. We're on our way, just coming onto the Lancs now. Keith's driving."

"The police are here, a car turned up about a minute ago and there's another van just pulling up behind me now."

"Brilliant. Good, you'll be alright."

"Why the hell did he say that Andy? About knowing what the kids look like?"

Miller had an idea why, but he couldn't possibly say anything about this to his wife, their mother.

"Just try and stay calm. He'll just be some scrote-bag. I'll soon find him and he'll wish he'd never been born when I do."

"The way he was staring at me though. It was really scary Andy. It's like he hates me."

"Can you describe him?"

"No, not really. Just a scally, hoody up, something covering the bottom half of his face. He looked evil though, evil eyes. It was horrible."

"Yes, a little coward, hiding his face and threatening a

woman. Threatening to... Just try and stay calm Clare."

"Okay."

"So, what else did he say?"

"Nothing really. He was just calling me a stupid bitch. He was talking in that weird way, you know, like a yardie."

"But he was white?"

"Yes, just looked like a spice-head. No older than twenty-five. I swear to God I did nothing wrong Andy, I was just walking back to the car, minding my own business."

"I know you didn't Clare. Honestly, I'll soon get to the bottom of this. Listen, we're just on Worsley Road, we'll be with you in less than two minutes. Okay?"

"Okay. The policeman is standing next to the car, I think he wants a word."

"Right, well, let your window down and explain everything to him. I'll see you in a minute."

Chapter Five

The headteacher of Worsley Green School was called into the school office and was informed of the terrifying telephone call as Mrs Maher relayed the details to Manchester City Police. The school secretary had not wished to waste valuable time explaining the story twice, so Mrs Hughes, the forty-three-year old headmistress was learning about this unthinkable situation at the same time as the police call-handler.

Mrs Hughes raised her hand to her mouth as the full, shocking revelation came to its conclusion, specifically with the details regarding the need for an armed-response unit at the school and the immediate threat to life. This was such an extraordinary situation for the headteacher, but one which she was fully trained and briefed in how to cope with. The "teacher-training" and "in-set" days which most parents assumed were just extra holidays for the staff, were the invaluable training days when school staff were taught how to deal with threats to the school community, amongst many other scenarios. So far, Mrs Maher had followed the text-book perfectly.

Worsley Green Primary is an old, red-brick, traditional looking primary school. Built at around the time that Queen Victoria died, it was one of few surviving "old-fashioned" primary schools in the city of Salford. Most of the older schools had been demolished and rebuilt since the second world war had ended, replaced with cheaper and more modern facilities. It was the historic look of the school which added to its charm. Worsley Green is widely acknowledged as one of the best primary schools in the city, not just for its "outstanding" OFSTED rating, but also because it was the school which serves several local personalities children. A Manchester United star's daughter attends the school, as does the grandchild of the local MP. A well-known Coronation Street star's son also attends the school, and these details have added to the school's excellent reputation locally. Worsley Green is the first choice for every parent within its three mile-radius.

Mrs Hughes snapped-out of her initial shock at this

chilling situation and set about her work, as Mrs Maher began clarifying and repeating details of the conversation to the call-handler at MCP headquarters. Her first task was to lock the internal doors at the school entrance, which meant that any intruder would have to break through two sets of doors to gain entry. Next, she sounded the school bell with four short blasts, informing all staff on site that the school was entering the well-rehearsed and trained-for DEEP drill which was an acronym for "Domestic Emergency Evacuation Procedure." This was the emergency procedure which needed to be implemented in the case of an external threat to the school's community, effectively evacuating the children and staff to a location within the school building which was safest, away from windows and immediate sources of entry from outside.

This was the first time that the DEEP drill had ever been implemented for real. On every training day, instructors advised teachers that the drill would probably never be required to be carried out. But, they had cheerfully advised, it would save lots of lives if ever it was needed. The shocked expressions on all of the staff member's faces as they stepped out onto the corridor confirmed that they had never thought they would be carrying out this drill for real.

The children were quickly led from their classrooms and escorted in single-file along the corridors into the school hall, where they were instructed to sit down for a special assembly. As her staff took their pupils to the hall, Mrs Hughes did a sweep of each classroom along the corridor, ensuring that every last child had left. She checked every nook-and-cranny in the school, the toilets, the sick-bay, the cloakrooms, the storage areas where the gym equipment was stored. Mrs Hughes knew all too well that her pupils could often be found in the most random of places.

Just a couple of minutes after she had blasted those four short bursts of the school bell, Mrs Hughes entered the school hall. She was confident that the school had executed the DEEP drill faultlessly. The children all looked excited and happy about this impromptu assembly, which reassured her that they had not been given any cause for alarm or panic. It looked as though the protocol had been carried out perfectly.

"Good morning children."

"Good mo-orning, Mrs Hughes," cheered the 140 boys and girls in unison, sitting on the shiny floor with their legs crossed before them.

Just as soon as the good morning greetings had been completed, Mrs Hughes noticed the sound of police sirens in the distance. It was the most reassuring sound that she had ever heard in her life and it made her feel a little light-headed. She turned to the school's secretary Mrs Maher, who was also the school's pianist for assemblies.

"Let's start this special assembly with a few songs, children please say good morning to Mrs Maher who is going to start us off with All Things Bright and Beautiful."

The children responded to the instruction instantly with a very cheerful welcome to Mrs Maher. It was clear from the look which the secretary and the head exchanged that they both understood one another. Mrs Hughes wanted the children occupied and distracted noisily from the sound of the emergency services vehicles arriving outside. The school secretary sat down at her piano stool and began hitting the keys immediately, the sound of the introduction to the popular school song sounded a little off-key as Mrs Maher tried to overcome her nervousness and anxiety following that utterly chilling phone call less than five minutes earlier. As soon as Mrs Maher paused for a second to prompt the pupils to start singing, they did so with great enthusiasm.

"All things bright and beautiful, all creatures great and small. All things wise and wonderful, the Lord God made them all...."

Chapter Six

As Saunders screeched the car to a dramatic halt by the side of Clare's car, both Miller and Saunders were relieved to see several other police vans and cars pulling up, albeit with similar haste fifty yards away in the opposite direction.

"Fucking hell, they've sent an ARU as well," said Miller as he waved through the passenger window to Clare who was talking to a police officer who was standing beside the car. Clare didn't look relieved to see that her husband had arrived and that she was no longer vulnerable to the horrible lad who had given her such an intimidating shock. She had a grave look on her face as the uniformed officer continued to talk to her.

"Right, nice one Keith. I'll sort Clare's head out and I think we'll take the kids out of school for the day. I'll probably take them all out somewhere. Blackpool or Chester Zoo or summat, I think she needs chilling out. Are you alright to hold the fort?"

"Course." Said Saunders.

"Right. Cheers. I'll give you a buzz in a bit, I'm going to have to find out who this little bastard is and see what he's trying to achieve by upsetting my wife.

"Go on boss, see to Clare. We'll get to the bottom of it Sir, try not to worry."

"Yeah, cheers Keith. Thanks mate."

Miller got out of the car and Clare gave him a peculiar look through the car window as another police car came screaming to a halt outside the school gates. Miller looked up and saw that yet another Armed Response Unit was pulling up at the side of his own car.

"Bloody hell, I didn't think they'd send armed units! Are you alright love?" Miller smiled reassuringly at Clare as he joined the uniformed officer who had been talking to her.

Clare's eyes were filling with tears. "Andy... do you not know..."

"What?" Miller's face contorted as a sudden fear hit him low in the stomach, making his bowel twitch.

"I was just informing your wife, Sir... there has been a threat made against the school. The armed response officers are doing a sweep of the area."

"What?" Miller's face drained of all colour as he stood there open-mouthed.

"That's why so many units are in attendance. The school is on emergency lock-down."

It was clear from the look of sheer disbelief on Miller's face that this was new information. "What kind of threat?"

"I don't know the specifics Sir. But all units were sent on a code red, literally a minute after we'd received the first call to attend."

"Everything's secure?"

"That's not been confirmed as yet, Sir. Armed Response are in the process of making those checks as we speak."

Chapter Seven

Mrs Hughes moved slowly along the side of the hall, smiling widely at her children's rendition of All Things Bright and Beautiful. She moved slowly but steadily, passing each of her staff members as they retook their registers, checking that every child who had been present in the classroom was accounted for in the hall. Mrs Hughes finally reached the final row of pupils and inched her way out of view of the school community. As she reached the back of the hall she slipped out of the door and back onto the corridor, pleased that the children were completely oblivious that the school staff were carrying out a very scary and stressful internal evacuation.

As she sprinted along the corridor, she realised that she had never felt so relieved as she was feeling right now at the sight of several armed police officers standing outside the school entrance, with several other officers jogging across the school yard towards the doors. It was the most reassuring thing that she had ever seen. Suddenly, with this excellent response from the police, she began to feel the enormity of the situation catching up with her.

"Is everything secure inside the school?" Shouted the leading officer, displaying a machine-gun across his chest.

"Yes, yes, the school is completely locked and the pupils are evacuated." Shouted Mrs Hughes through the double-doors.

"Good. Let us in please, but the children are to remain in the evacuation zone." Barked the armed officer.

The headmistress followed her orders, typing in the passcode into the lock on the first set of doors, before nervously jangling her keys, looking for the correct key to open the external set of doors. The police officers who were waiting outside had very serious and menacing looks on their faces, which made Mrs Hughes feel even more nervous as she fidgeted with the huge bunch of keys. Finally, she found the correct key and opened the doors.

"Thanks. My officers will need to do a thorough search of the school. Can you please go back to your evacuation zone with this officer and stay there until further notice?" The armed officer had sergeant stripes above his breast pocket, and was shouting the information to Mrs Hughes, which was both alarming and reassuring at the same time. Another armed officer stepped inside and said, "come on, Miss," in a much quieter tone.

Within seconds, Mrs Hughes and the armed officer were inside the school hall as Mrs Maher segued seamlessly into the opening chords of Lord of the Dance. Mrs Hughes stood nervously at the back of the school hall with the armed response officer by her side. The children were unaware that she had even left, let alone had reappeared in the hall with a policeman who was holding a semi-automatic weapon. But it was only the children who were oblivious. All of the staff members who were standing at the edge of each class line along the side of the hall were acutely aware of the machine gun, the sight of which came as an overwhelming relief to them all.

Chapter Eight

Ben Clayton had been walking to his work at the Bridgewater Hotel when he began to become disturbed by the amount of police cars and vans which were screaming past him at high-speed. It wasn't unique to see and hear police vehicles racing through the streets of Salford, but it was certainly uncommon to see so much police activity around here, the posh part of the City of Salford. Perhaps in the neighbouring towns of Swinton and Eccles this kind of thing was quite normal. But it certainly wasn't normal here in leafy Worsley and the sheer numbers of blue-lighted vehicles which were passing Ben at break-neck speeds sent a chill through the young man's bones.

Every few seconds another police vehicle came flying past with its sirens wailing. Whatever was going on, he knew that it was something of a very serious nature. He counted a tenth vehicle, a police van, zooming past him and tried to recall how many had passed before he'd started counting. This area wasn't far from the motorway junction and Ben assumed that there must have been a hell of a smash on there to require this many coppers. But there hadn't been any ambulances. Ben was thinking of different scenarios that might require such a huge number of police officers.

It wasn't long before Ben neared the corner and began to see that this incident, whatever it was, was taking place just down the road. It looked as though the police cars, vans and Range Rovers were stopped close to the primary school. His heart was beating high in his chest as he began to realise that whatever this was, it was very serious indeed. He broke into a jog and headed down the road, eager to find out what the hell was going on. He had friends and colleagues whose kids attended Worsley Green primary school and he felt stressed and panicked by this extraordinary police presence outside the school's gates. As he jogged quickly towards the school, another police car whizzed past, it looked like the armed response Range Rover.

"What the fuck is going on?"

As Ben neared the school, he was stopped by a policeman who was walking across the road. He was fixing police tape from a lamppost on the other side and was unrolling the remaining tape as he walked.

"Sorry mate, the roads closed, you can't get through here." Said the officer as he reached the pavement and began tying the tape around the final section of the school's railings. A car pulled up as it reached the cordon line.

"What's going on?" Asked Ben.

"We're dealing with an incident. Can you turn around and head back in the direction you came from please Sir?"

"Wait, what's the incident?" Ben looked frightened. The lady who had been driving pulled on the handbrake and got out of her car to ask the same question. The scene beyond the policeman looked very serious indeed.

"I'm afraid I can't comment but for your own safety you are advised to vacate this area immediately and head back in that direction." The copper nodded beyond Ben's shoulder and continued tying the tape.

"Come on officer, what's going on?" Ben was pleading with the police constable but he received no further feedback.

Ben tutted and looked at the lady who also had a look of alarm and distress on her face.

"This looks bad. Do you know what's happened?" She asked. Ben shook his head as he looked at the activity which was taking place beyond the cordon line. The police vehicles were all parked haphazardly in the middle of the road and most of the police officers were standing by their vehicles or standing in small groups, they all had concerned looks on their faces. It was a very worrying sight. Ben took his phone out of his pocket and clicked on the Facebook icon. Within seconds, he was broadcasting live on the "Salford Online" group. He held his camera up and began transmitting the scene before him to the group's twenty-five thousand members. As his broadcast began, the unmistakable sound of the police helicopter began to get louder overhead as it neared the location.

Ben's voice sounded stressed and emotional as he gave a commentary to accompany the alarming video. "Hello everyone, just walked into this on my way to work. I'm standing at a road-block outside Worsley Green Primary school, Worsley Road. There are about twenty police cars and vans all blocking the road and this police tape is not allowing anybody through. Don't know what the hell is going on and I've asked this copper but he won't tell me anything. Just thought I should let everyone know that something very serious is going on here this morning and if you've got kids at the school, I bet you would want to know."

Ben stopped talking and started zooming his phone's camera in on the police vehicles and the groups of police officers standing in groups. The officers were talking to one another with very serious expressions on their faces. Ben panned his phone around to the vehicles, zooming in further to demonstrate the sheer numbers of hi-visibility police cars, vans, dog-vans and ARU vehicles which filled the road. The roar of the helicopter was becoming deafening as it circled the area. After a moment or so, he zoomed out and panned around to the policeman who was standing at the cordon line.

"Why won't you tell me what's going on? This video is live on Facebook. Everyone in the area is watching it. Come on, tell us what's happening at the school."

"As I've explained Sir, I am not permitted to divulge any information other than to explain that we are dealing with an incident and that this road is currently closed until further notice."

"Thanks for nothing, officer." Ben moved his camera away from the copper and pointed it up to the sky, trying to catch glimpse of the helicopter which was adding further tension and drama to the situation with its almighty, relentless roar. Ben couldn't catch sight of the aircraft as the huge oak trees above obscured the view from his position.

This shaky-handed amateur broadcast sparked a sense of deep terror in every local parent and grandparent who saw it. Instantly, frantic comments from terrified mums, dads, grandparents and members of the public began appearing beneath Ben's video.

"Is this happening now?"

"WTF?"

"I'm phoning the school now, it's ringing but nobody's picking up. Anyone got any more information?"

The Facebook broadcast was quickly picked up by local journalists who began calling the police's press office for some more information, desperate to get an official explanation for this alarming scene outside the school for 4-11 year olds. But they were in for a disappointment if they wanted a quick overview of the situation. The only information that the press office were prepared to reveal only heightened the sense of alarm.

"This is a live ongoing incident and any information on the nature of the police operation is currently embargoed. Further details will be released once the incident has concluded. Until that time, members of the public are advised to stay away from the location."

Chapter Nine

Gemma Taylor was feeling overwhelmed with the amount of work that had loaded onto her handheld computer.

"Is this taking the piss?" She asked a colleague with a look of hatred on her face. Gemma had only just arrived at work after dropping her kids off at school. Her job at Experte Logistics on Wardley Industrial Estate in Swinton was arguably the shittest job on planet earth. It consisted of walking around the gigantic warehouse with a shopping trolley, picking the shitty items that her little computer thing told her to. If she didn't tell the computer that the item had been picked and packed within the time frame it allowed, the computer froze and told her to "seek support." Crucially what seek support actually translated to was "go find a manager and get a fucking good bollocking for taking the piss you absolute shit head."

The mysterious little items that Gemma had to pick and pack were used in the Conservatory industry, so it wasn't as if she even had anything exciting to say whenever anybody asked her what she did for a living. "I am an IT led operative within the home-improvement, building and insulation industry" was the easiest answer, she'd realised over time. It also sounded a lot better than the truth which was that she "was a picker packer in a freezing cold factory near the East Lancs."

Gemma hated this job more than anything else and was attending college at night to try and improve her prospects for something a little less brain numbing. Always keen to look for positives, Gemma realised that having this shitty job had been the kick up the arse she needed to improve her CV. Plus, the money came in handy now that the father of her kids had effectively left her as he was working as a holiday rep in Cyprus although he never sent any money home.

Gemma set off on her first rotation of the gigantic factory floor which was set out like the most depressing supermarket in the world. The aisles were filled with millions of clips, connectors and nuts and bolts. The only drama to be had here was when one of the products was out of stock, which was very rare. It really was the shittest job ever.

As Gemma grabbed her trolley and smiled angelically at the managers, she felt her phone vibrate in her pocket. She set off with her little computer terminal attached to her trolley and entered the first aisle which was out of sight of the managers and supervisors. At the first opportunity she got, she took her phone out of her pocket and held it inside one of the plastic tubs which held all the products, so that it was out of sight of the CCTV cameras which monitor every move that the staff make. Gemma's heart started racing as she read the message. It was from her mate Jodie.

"Gem, don't know what's going on but there's millions of police at school, armed cops, choppers up, road-blocks, everything. I'm going up there now, I'll keep you posted hun X"

Gemma could feel the colour draining from her face as she stared at the phone screen. She felt the sudden urge to be sick and held her hand over her mouth as she began running back towards the managers and supervisors. As she got closer to them, she couldn't fight the feeling of nausea and vomited on the floor, before standing up straight again and running as fast as she could towards the factory doors.

"Gemma! Are you okay?" Shouted one of the supervisors, but the question was met with the sound of the factory door slamming shut behind her. The supervisor looked at the floor and saw the vomit, before looking towards another picker packer. "You! Stop picking and clean this puke up. I'll pause your terminal."

Gemma was racing down Worsley Road, as fast as her legs would carry her. Tears were streaming up her face as she went. All the cars were stopped and some of the drivers were stood beside them, others were beeping horns whilst others were performing aggressive three-point-turns and racing off in the opposite direction.

"What the fuck is going on?" Said Gemma as she continued to sprint towards the primary school. All she could think of was her two kids, 6 year-old Poppy and 4 year-old Karl. She was praying that everything was going to be alright, that her beautiful little kids were safe. "Please God, please God," she repeated breathlessly as she continued to race past the cars, vans and trucks which were all stuck along the road.

Gemma could hear the roar of the police helicopter up above, it seemed to be staying still at one spot above the school, and there was another helicopter above it, much higher, which seemed to be circling the area. Normally, Gemma couldn't run across a road without getting a stitch but today, she was sprinting towards the school like Jessica Ennis going for gold. She was still half a mile away from school but there were rows and rows of police cars and vans all parked up on the kerb, deserted on both sides of the road. As she reached the bend and could finally see the school, the tears became even heavier and were stinging her eyes. There was a huge crowd of people being held back by all the coppers who'd dumped their cars.

"What the fuck... please God, please..." she pleaded to the heavens as she continued to run towards that terrifying, confusing cordon line, with everything she had.

Chapter Ten

The police incident in Worsley was like nothing the local community had ever seen before. It looked as though every officer in Greater Manchester was in attendance, people were commenting that there were over a hundred emergency services vehicles in attendance, parked along the roads up to a mile away from the school, in all directions. Whatever it was that was going on at this school, it was something major. The roads all around Swinton, Eccles and Worsley were becoming gridlocked as people tried to make their way down to the school to see what was happening or to collect kids from the school. This was an unprecedented incident which the police were struggling to manage, their work was not helped by the insensitive news crews who were jostling in amongst the crowd with their TV cameras and microphones.

Hundreds of people were gathering at each end of the police cordon lines, many of whom were local people who'd come down to have a nosey. The vast majority of them were parents, anxious for official information about what was going on, desperate to retrieve their kids from the school and take them away to safety.

All kinds of rumours were being spread at both ends of the cordon. There was talk of an unexploded bomb from the second World War being discovered beneath the playground. Another theory which was circulating and creating even greater panic was the constantly repeated rumour that a terrorist had broken into the school and was holding the children hostage. Other rumours were circulating too, and it was creating a pressure cooker environment at the cordon lines. Mums and dads were screaming at the police officers to let them through and pick their kids up from school. The police officers in attendance were now creating a fluorescent yellow barrier between the public and the school.

"You better fucking let us get our kids!" Shouted angry parents, some of whom were becoming physical with the police officers as the sheer terror of the situation took hold and created more and more panic.

More police officers were being sent to this job, from every corner of Greater Manchester. As two new officers arrived at the scene to support their colleagues at the cordons, ten more frantic parents arrived to collect their kids. The duty Inspector from Salford was trying to instruct his officers to retain the cordon but he was becoming desperate for even more officers to support this complicated and increasingly volatile situation.

"Everybody stay back or you will be arrested!" Barked the Inspector into his megaphone, but the crowds could barely hear him over the noise of the chaos which was all around, most notably the sound of pure anger from the parents, grandparents and guardians who had come to collect their children and get them as far away from this place and whatever the hell was happening, as soon as possible.

Dozens of people were recording the scenes on their phones, some of them were broadcasting live on Facebook which in turn was creating even further panic in the wider community.

The Facebook story which Ben had posted on the Salford Online group had gathered the most momentum and was still creating panic and hysteria throughout the city. Those that had seen it on the Facebook group had shared it onto their own timelines and as a result, the entire community were made aware of these disturbing scenes from Worsley Green Primary School. Ben's video had gone viral for all the wrong reasons.

The comments underneath the video weren't doing anything to reassure the parents and relatives of the children who had been dropped off there within the past half-hour. Facebook user's names were being dropped into the comments, along with thousands of people expressing fear and shock beneath the video, adding extra gravity and alarm to an already terrifying situation.

Most parents who had been alerted to the commotion outside school had already got into their cars and were speeding towards the school, desperate to know what had happened. Desperate to collect their children, God willing, safely. There were so many appalling acts being carried out around the world, the affected parent's minds were filled with hundreds of terrible thoughts as to what might have happened at the school. Thoughts of bombs, shootings, a hostage situation... there was literally no end to the terrible thoughts and theories inspired by the completely unbelievable scenes in the Facebook video.

The roads all around the area were jammed and many parents had dumped their vehicles and raced on foot to the school when they'd finally realised that the traffic was at a stand-still. Vehicles had been abandoned on kerbs, down side-streets and even in bus stops. The only vehicles that seemed to be getting anywhere were the dozens of police cars and vans which were still negotiating through the traffic chaos with their sirens blaring.

Journalists were also making their way to the school, reporters from the local TV news channels and local radio stations such as Salford City Radio, as well as the Manchester Evening News and various other online news gathering platforms in and around Salford. It was clear to every single newsperson who had seen the footage from Worsley Green – whatever was going on was likely to be a major news story. The police response was of a level that is only reserved for major incidents.

Sky News, the national rolling news channel had been informed of the Facebook footage and had ripped the video from the internet and after their initial enquiries had been confirmed by MCP's press office, they went live with the story, complete with their BREAKING NEWS banners.

"And some news which is just reaching us from Manchester in the past few moments. It appears that police in Salford are dealing with a major incident at a primary school in Worsley, in the west of the city. Our North of England correspondent Paul Mitchell joins us on the line. Paul, can you tell us what is happening?"

As the Sky News correspondent started talking, Sky's viewers were provided with the video which had streamed live on Facebook just moments earlier.

"Yes, well, we are aware that there is certainly

something happening at the school, but at this moment in time we are unclear as to what exactly this incident is. I'm on my way there now, but as the footage which is currently playing out on the screen shows, this looks to be a major incident which Manchester City Police are currently dealing with."

"What is happening at the school, as you understand it, Paul?" Pushed the newsreader, clearly disappointed with the vagueness of the correspondent's explanation.

"At this moment, nobody knows. What we do know is that there is a significant police presence at the junior school in the leafy suburb of Worsley on the edge of the city of Salford. I've been contacted by numerous parents of children who attend the school, some of whom are currently outside the school where police have set up a cordon line and are not allowing parents to proceed anywhere near the building."

"In terms of police presence, Paul, what can you tell us?"

"Well, as I say, I'm still making my way to the scene of this incident so much of what I know is being fed to me by people at the scene. One mother sent me a Tweet just a few moments ago saying that she thinks that every police officer in Greater Manchester seems to be at the school, hundreds of officers and dozens of police vehicles have arrived and many more are currently making their way to the school. Another Twitter user contacted me to ask what is happening as she has never seen so many police vehicles racing through Manchester with their sirens and blue lights on. As you know, this kind of police activity is very rarely seen, in fact it is only ever seen when a major incident is declared. Quite what that incident is, at this stage, nobody seems to know except those police officers who are attending."

"Paul Mitchell in Manchester, we will come back to you soon, but we are joined on the line right now by Lisa Ledger who is a local journalist who lives close to the school in Worsley, Greater Manchester. Lisa, can you tell us what's happening there?"

"Yes, well, I'm struggling to hear you properly with all the sirens and the police helicopter which is directly overhead.

Can you hear me okay?"

"Yes, we can hear the noise in the background but you are coming through loud and clear, Lisa. Tell us, what's happening?"

"Well, to be honest nobody seems to know what's going on. Some people are saying that a body has been found in the school grounds, whilst other people are saying that somebody has planted a bomb in the school. Its just so confusing, nobody really knows what's happening. People have asked the police officers who have set up a road-block and are stopping the public from getting anywhere near the school, but they are saying that they aren't allowed to say what's going on."

"And tell us about yourself Lisa, are you a parent of a child at the school?"

"No, fortunately mine are a bit older now and attend high school. But this was their primary school and I know most of the staff, so it's all very concerning."

"And you are close to the scene?"

"Yes, my house backs onto the school playground. I was working in my office when I heard some shouting outside and when I looked out of the window, I saw several armed officers surrounding the building, others were looking in the bushes and down the grids. One of them was on the roof, I have no idea what he was looking for. I went outside to try and find out what was going on and I got caught up in all of this."

"You say there was shouting, did you hear what was said?"

"No... no... it was, it sounded like 'clear' or something which was when I looked outside and then another officer was shouting at a man who was walking his dog near the railings, telling him to move back."

"It must have been very unnerving for you Lisa?"

"Well, yes and no really. I'm more concerned about what's going on. Something is very seriously wrong here."

"What time was it when you heard this commotion outside your window?"

"Oh, it would have been, what about twenty minutes ago now. Since then, more and more police cars and vans have been arriving, I'm... I really didn't know that there were this many police vehicles in Greater Manchester, it's all you can see in all directions."

"And apart from the emergency vehicles, what do you see in front of you right now?"

"Well, I'm standing at the cordon line which is at the bottom of my street and there are dozens, if not hundreds of people here, all pleading with the police officers to let them through to pick their kids up. The mood is getting very angry because nobody is being told anything."

Chapter Eleven

Clare Miller was being comforted by her husband and a police constable in the back of a police car close to the school's entrance on Worsley Road. As far as Miller and his wife were aware, there had been a threat against the school and that was as much as they knew. Miller knew that he could quite easily turn the volume up on his radio to find out the specifics, but he'd reasoned that this would be a foolish move. Firstly, anything he heard, Clare would also hear and if it was something dark, then it would do nothing to keep her, or himself, calm. Secondly, Miller had seen that most of the city's ARU officers were in attendance and they would be much more useful than he ever would in any potential confrontations.

Miller had decided to sit tight and let the professionals do the work that they are trained for and spend the time trying his best to keep Clare calm and positive. It was no easy task, his wife had already been in pieces regarding the unexpected confrontation at the school gates. Now, this talk of a threat against the school only meant one thing as far as she was concerned. The threat was against Leo and Molly, her innocent little kids that she couldn't wait to push into the school just half an hour earlier.

"Listen, love" said Miller, holding Clare's trembling hand. "The very best people in the city are here and are dealing with it. You've got to remember that."

Miller was trying his best, and it was coming from a good place, Clare knew that. But he was really irritating her, repeating the same stupid shit over and over again. She couldn't care less if it was Superman and the Teenage Mutant Ninja fucking Turtles in there, she just wanted to know that her kids were okay and Andy's constant rabbiting on was really doing her head in.

The police van door slid open and the Millers were greeted by the Inspector who had been running the scene.

"Mrs Miller, Sir." He said, he looked stressed and slightly awkward.

"What's happening?" Pleaded Clare.

"Can you come inside the school please, we can explain everything."

"I'm not going anywhere until you tell me what the fuck is going on!"

Miller appeared shocked at his wife's outburst, Clare rarely swore, she certainly didn't do it in front of strangers.

"The children are fine, all of the children are fine," Said the Inspector. His words caused Clare Miller to break down. This was all she had wanted to hear since this nightmare situation had begun thirty or so minutes ago. It took a minute or so for Clare Miller to compose herself and step out of the police van. She began running towards the school, with Miller running after her.

Mrs Hughes was waiting by the doors with several armed officers.

"Hello Clare, Andy," said the headteacher. She looked as though she had seen a ghost, her usually olive complexion had turned an unhealthy tinge of grey.

"What's been happening?" Asked Miller of the ARU sergeant who was standing beside the head.

"Sir, there has been a threat made against the school, by telephone. The specific target of that threat was your children."

Clare's legs buckled as the armed policeman's words sank in.

"Named?" Asked Miller, desperate to hear that there was some exaggeration going on.

"I'm afraid so, Sir. The caller asked if your children attend the school. And it went from there."

Clare was sobbing openly as she listened intently to what was being said.

"What kind of threat was it?" Asked Miller, a look of anger was heating up his complexion.

"The threat," interrupted the sergeant, "was that the Miller twins need to be removed from school immediately as they are in grave danger from an imminent attack."

Clare looked as though she was about to break down

completely, but somehow she found a strong and assertive voice.

"Bring me my kids. I need my children here, now."

Mrs Hughes wasted no time. She nodded and turned on her heels and disappeared into the school hall immediately. For the brief second that the door was opened, both Andy and Clare noticed how happy and contented the children looked. It was a bizarre and surprising scene, under these extraordinary circumstances.

The sergeant lifted his radio to his mouth and began speaking. "I need the transport for the family asap. Come right up to the school entrance and we'll load from the back. Escort vehicles standby. Over."

Miller looked at the sergeant, he knew him quite well. It felt strange to be part of this twilight world of being treated like more of a civilian than a DCI.

"So, what's happening now?"

"No idea Sir. Our priority is to get you off site and then repatriate these children with their parents."

"And presumably, there was no valid threat?"

"Negative Sir. We've done a complete search of the building and the grounds, the place is clear. It's unlikely that anybody would approach this area with bad intentions now, Sir. We're happy that any threat has been neutralised."

"Yes, but..." Clare was about to add some extra details to this confusing picture but she was stopped in her tracks.

"It's okay Mrs Miller, we're aware of the exchange you had outside school. It will be a different department who deals with all of this from this stage, as I'm sure you'll understand. Normally, I'd have thought it would fall to you, Sir." The sergeant had a kindly look in his eyes as he spoke. It was obvious that he sympathised with the two parents standing before him, but he had no more answers to any questions. His and his team's work here was done.

Chapter Twelve

The children of Worsley Green Primary School were totally ignorant to the drama which was taking place outside the school hall. This great big room is very familiar to them all as their assembly hall, dinner-hall and PE hall. They were having a lovely time, the singing had stopped now and one of the ARU police officers was standing on the tiny stage, giving a talk to the children about his job in the police service, his weapon was being looked after by his partner who was hidden behind the curtain a few feet away.

Molly and Leo Miller were sitting together, as always, with their arms folded and legs crossed, listening intently to the policeman, both were wondering if he might be a friend of daddy's.

The police officer found some inspiration for this impromptu talk to the school via the police helicopter which was thundering above the school.

"And can anybody tell me any other things that the police helicopter can help us with?"

All of the hands in the school assembly hall shot up in the air at once.

"Yes, you there," said the policeman, pointing enthusiastically into the sea of infants and juniors.

"Is it... you know when... like if a boat crashes and all the people fall out?" Asked a little girl near the front.

"Yes, that's a very good answer! Police helicopters can help to rescue people in the sea, or if they are lost in the mountains or in the countryside. We also use our police helicopters to help a very special person once a year, on Christmas Eve. Does anybody know who that special person might be?"

The hands all shot up in the air again, and the police officer looked as though he might just be starting to enjoy this bizarre start to his shift.

"Father Christmas?" Yelled the kids, particularly those nearer the front. Most of the ten and eleven-year olds towards the back were playing it cool.

"That's absolutely right! On Christmas Eve, our police helicopter has to follow Father Christmas and his reindeers as they deliver all of the presents around this area, it's a new health and safety thing that has come out in the last few years. And do you know, boys and girls, this is the only night of the year that the police helicopter doesn't make any sound at all. Can you all hear it right now?"

"Yes!" Shouted 160 kids with deafening excitement.

"And can you hear it on Christmas Eve?"

"No!" They shouted once again.

"Well, there you go."

Just as the policeman asked if anybody else had any questions, Leo and Molly were tapped lightly on their shoulders by Mrs Hughes. As they span around, they heard their headteacher whisper into their ears. "Can you follow me please, children?"

Molly and Leo looked a little disappointed that the exciting talk by the policeman was being interrupted, but they stood silently and followed the head as she negotiated her way back through the line of crossed legs on the shiny wooden floor. Within seconds, the Miller twins were outside the school hall, being hugged by their parents. It was clear on their faces that they were both completely confused by this unusual situation.

"Are you alright? Molly? Leo?" Clare Miller's eyes were streaming with tears, she was trembling as she hugged the kids as tightly as she could without hurting them. Andy Miller was rubbing her shoulder and smiling at his twins. He looked sad and suddenly, the twins began to feel spooked. They sensed that something strange was going on.

"What's wrong mummy?" asked Molly, wiping her mother's tears away with her hands.

"Okay, if we can get you all outside and into the vehicle by the doors please, as we discussed?" Said the AR Sergeant, without any pleasantries. His objective was to get the targets of this threat away from the school as soon as possible. If that meant hurrying up one of the most senior detectives in the force, then so be it.

"Come on guys, we're going for a ride in a police van!" Said Miller, as though suddenly snapping out of a trance.

"A police van? Really?" Said Leo, clenching his fist in excitement.

"Yes, come on, if we ask nicely they might even put the siren on!"

The Miller twins cheered as they were carried to the huge Tactical Aid van which had been reversed right up to the school's entrance. The Millers literally took one step into the schoolyard before they were negotiating the steps into the van. An armed officer was sitting near the front, his weapon concealed, but his uniform told Miller that he was an ARU officer and it brought him peace of mind.

As soon as the seatbelts were fastened, the van began pulling away from the school entrance. Miller looked ahead, through the windscreen and saw that an ARU Land Rover was leading the way. Dozens of police officers were standing by the school gates as the vehicle turned onto the main road which was completely jammed on both sides with police vehicles. The Tactical Aid vehicle driver sounded the siren as he negotiated the huge dark blue van around the abandoned police cars, vans and motorcycles and headed towards the cordon line.

"Everybody back, get out of the road right now!" Said the ARU driver up ahead into his Tannoy system.

Despite the fear and confusion on all of the faces, the people followed the line of police officers who had been holding them at the cordon and stepped away towards the pavements on either side of Worsley Road. The ARU Vehicle began speeding up through the parting and the TA van driver stepped on the accelerator as well. "You might want to bob down in your seats at the back, I think there are some press photographers up ahead."

Andy and Clare both followed the advice, holding their children as they ducked below the windows. The crowds outside were shouting but it was hard to make out what they were saying as the siren was drowning the external noise. Within just one minute of stepping inside the vehicle, the Miller family were zooming away from the school and were heading towards

Astley. Miller looked around over his shoulder and saw that another ARU vehicle was following them.

"This is so cool!" Said Leo and Molly laughed loudly at her brother's quip. It was clear on her face that she agreed.

Miller and Clare exchanged a look which was the polar opposite of the twins reaction to this terrifying ordeal.

Miller unclipped his seatbelt and fixed it around Leo before walking up towards the cab and sitting next to the armed officer.

"Where are we going?" He asked.

"No idea Sir, we're instructed to follow the ARU ahead. I think the idea is to get you all as far away as possible and then swap vehicles."

"Any idea what's going on?"

"Nothing one hundred per cent yet Sir, but no threat was detected in the school or grounds. Looks like a hoax call."

"A hoax?" Miller had heard the officer but was repeating the answer for his own benefit.

"As I say Sir, it's a very confusing picture at the moment. I'm sure you'll be privy to more of the finer details than we will."

"Okay. Well, thanks."

"Sir."

Miller stood and negotiated his way back towards his family. Clare was in floods of tears but the twins hadn't noticed, they were busy looking out of the windows, thrilled to be having such an exciting day. Miller sat down and began rubbing his wife's shoulder. After a few seconds, he was left under no illusion that his gentle attempt at comforting Clare was annoying her, as she shrugged his hand away.

Chapter Thirteen

Detective Chief Superintendent David Dixon had arrived at the school as things were beginning to calm down. At least things were very calm within the building. Outside the neat little primary school, it was a different matter altogether.

The police officers were having a hell of a time trying to calm the parents and keep order. This was no normal job, these officers were all very experienced and worked all around the UK on crowd control jobs at football matches, political rallies and Royal visits. It was one of the few over-time perks in the police service, most of the time these jobs simply involved bringing a visual presence to proceedings. But none of the officers present this morning had ever tried to manage crowds of terrified, angry and emotional parents before. Some of the mums were feral, their only objective was to get into the school to their young. It was certainly a major challenge and a number of unpleasant skirmishes had broken out. As yet, no arrests had been made as the duty Inspector at the scene felt that any such action, despite being fully justified, would only inflame matters.

Dixon's first objective was to try and reassure the parents who were stuck at each end of the cordon line which was being manned by the police officers who were coming under constant verbal attack by the anxious and stressed out parents. It was completely understandable, these people had no idea what was going on and were furious that they were being obstructed from advancing any further towards the school and their children.

As the most senior police officer at the scene, Dixon decided to go the cordon line with the most parents and try to calm them all down. With a megaphone in his hand, he walked urgently towards the lines of police officers.

"Attention!" He shouted and a sudden, obedient hush came over the boisterous crowd of several hundred people, they were all desperate to hear what this senior looking copper had to say. "Thank you. Please keep quiet whilst I give you all an update on this incident. First of all, I want to reassure you that all of your children are safe and they have absolutely no knowledge of this incident, they are all very happy inside the school, they've been singing in a special assembly and have been completely distracted whilst all of this has been going on."

A sudden noise disturbed the quiet, it was an unsettling, eery sound of dozens upon dozens of parents crying and weeping with relief.

"Please, everybody, stop worrying and I will give you a further update in a few minutes, as soon as I've relayed this same message to parents at the other cordon line." Dixon dropped his megaphone to his side and turned, before walking briskly up the road, in between all of the police vehicles which were parked haphazardly on both sides of the carriageway. Behind him, the parents who had been screaming blue murder just moments ago were hugging one another and crying, some were smiling and laughing with relief.

At the other cordon line, to the east of the school, Dixon walked into the exact same situation that he had encountered a minute earlier. With each step forward, the noise and chaos, the pushing and shoving seemed to subside dramatically. Dixon lifted the megaphone and repeated his good news message, witnessing the same emotional reaction. It felt good, being the bearer of such reassuring news. He had no idea what these poor parents had been going through for the past half an hour or so, but he imagined that their minds would have wandered to the most horrific, darkest of places as they'd stood here amidst this chaos and confusion.

The police officers were also glad of this news, not just for the obvious reasons, but because they could finally have a breather. Nobody really knows just how exhausting a job it is holding back crowds of people unless they've done it themselves. Not one of the police officers here today had ever experienced such power from a crowd. They all felt that Dixon had come out just in the nick of time with this reassuring news. They had all felt that there was going to be a major problem containing this amount of terrified parents, things had definitely been about to kick off.

Dixon lifted his megaphone and continued into the

second part of his message. "If I can just have your attention for a couple more seconds, please. I understand that you are all eager to collect your children, and Mrs Hughes is currently making arrangements for this to happen, class by class, starting with the younger pupils. In a few minutes, we will reopen the road and all parents who wish to collect their children will be asked to stand in the playground and school staff will instruct you all on the procedure. Thank you."

Dixon dropped his megaphone to his side and turned to walk away and repeat this message to the parents at the other cordon. But one of the parents had a query.

"Hey, just a minute. Aren't you going to tell us what in God's name has been going on?" It was a young dad, relieved that Dixon had brought such favourable news, but still concerned that there was no information.

Dixon stepped back towards the line and lifted the megaphone once again, so nobody missed anything that he said.

"I'm afraid that the school received a threatening phone call shortly after nine am. As you can see, we take such matters extremely seriously and my officers have carried out a full inspection of the school and the surrounding area. It would appear that this was a very sick hoax call and we will now focus our efforts on tracing the person responsible."

Chapter Fourteen

Paul Mitchell, Sky News' north of England correspondent was standing in a long line of news reporters. Besides TV representatives, there were journalists from newspapers, online news agencies and several local radio stations who had all congregated along the perimeter fence of Worsley Green Primary school. The TV news presenters were standing with their backs to the school railings, allowing the camera lenses to frame the reporter, the school building and the lines of emotional parents who were standing in the school's playground.

ITV Granada, BBC North West and Sky were the biggest players here, but their numbers were small in comparison to the amount of people who were standing near the same vantage point, broadcasting live onto Facebook and other social media sites using their mobile devices.

"And so, as these emotionally drained parents wait patiently to collect their children from this school following what a senior police officer has described as a very sick hoax call, there is a great deal of anger and confusion at this place right now."

"Paul, is there any information regarding the children, and the experience that they have had this morning?" Asked the Sky News presenter from the London studios.

"Well, that's quite a remarkable thing actually. From what we understand, the pupils of this school were completely unaware of the activities taking place here, which is testament to the professionalism of all of the staff members here. We are hoping to speak to the headteacher, Mrs Hughes a little later, but as you might imagine, she is quite busy at the moment coordinating this early finish today."

"Well, its extremely good news all round Paul. We'll check in with you a little later once the police have said a little more on the situation."

Chapter Fifteen

Strangeways is one of the oldest and most famous prisons in the UK. Built in 1868 on the outskirts of Manchester's city centre, the category A jail has been in the news regularly throughout the years. Most recently, it made headlines for holding the disturbing record of having the most suicides amongst its inmates. It has also been in the news in recent times for having "freezing cold prisoners" as the heating system doesn't reach all of the cells.

But, Strangeways is probably best known for being the scene of the longest running prison riot that Britain has ever seen. Inmates took control of the jail on April Fools Day 1990 and kept control for almost a month, ripping off the roof and throwing the slates and coping stones at any prison officers or police officers who tried to re-enter the Victorian building. Over the following 25 days, the rioters practically dismantled the place, causing so much damage to the prison that it cost 55 million pounds and took 4 years to put right. The public inquiry headed by Lord Woolf concluded that conditions at Strangeways had become "intolerable" for inmates and the infamous protest led to major reforms in all of the prisons in England, Scotland and Wales.

Upon its rebuilding in 1994, the Grade II listed building was renamed HMP Manchester, but it is still known as Strangeways amongst its inmates, the staff and practically everybody in Greater Manchester. It is a very imposing place, situated just a few hundred yards from Manchester Arena on the fringe of the bustling city centre, the red brick prison and its 71 metre tall ventilation tower are a very well-known local landmark.

Behind the 16 feet thick "impenetrable walls" of Strangeways, 44 year-old Tommy McKinlay was lay on his bed, watching Sky News on his tiny TV screen. He had a huge grin on his face as he watched the rolling-news channel's reporters trying to make some sense out of the confusing situation which was unfolding just a few miles down the A6, in one of the wealthiest parts of Greater Manchester.

Tommy had told the prison guards that he wasn't feeling well enough to work in the laundry today. It was the first day's work he'd missed since he had been remanded in custody, awaiting a trial date. Tommy preferred to get out of his cell for the six hours a day and have a bit of crack with the rest of the lads. But today, he knew that he was going to be kept occupied enough following the news. He was quite surprised to see Sky News broadcasting it live though. He thought that it would be BBC Radio Manchester and a couple of the community radio stations covering the story. He hadn't expected it to attract national broadcasters, nor had he anticipated such a massive turn-out from the police, either. All in all, it had been an excellent effort from all concerned.

Despite only being a resident for a relatively short-time, Tommy is one of Strangeways best known prisoners. He is viewed as more of a celebrity and a VIP in the jail than a con. As a result, he is treated differently to the rest of the prison population. Despite this, none of the other inmates would dare to pass comment. Tommy McKinlay is a completely different kettle of fish to the rest of the Strangeways population, and everybody in there knows it, whether that's the cons or the staff. The way that screws talk to him is different, the way he casually swaggers around the place as though he is just visiting is unsettling for the rest of the inmates. Tommy McKinlay treats this place as if he owns it, and nobody dares to bat an eyelid. Tommy even has one of the few cells in the Victorian prison which boasts a decent view of Bury New Road and Manchester city centre. On a clear day, he can see the huge power-station at Fiddlers Ferry in Runcorn. It may not sound too luxurious, but most of the prison's 1200 population have a view consisting of nothing more than mouldy old walls and razor wire, that's if they can see anything out of the ancient glass panels which have been scratched and etched into for the past 150 years or so. But this issue didn't affect Tommy McKinlay, the small panes of glass in Tommy's cell had been replaced after he had complained that he couldn't see through the scratches and smears. This is without doubt preferential treatment, but nobody dares to say anything.

Prison is a weird place. It does weird things to people. Anybody who is serving any length of time becomes completely preoccupied by the day to day politics within the place, nothing else matters. If somebody was issued with a new mattress, there was always the potential for riots, because everybody wants a new mattress. It may seem odd, trivial almost, but prisoners don't have a great deal else to think about. Something which may seem so inconsequential and mundane really does have the potential to create serious problems for the prison service staff. Such is the attention to minutiae of people in prison, the tiniest thing in the world can become a major issue when you have nothing else to occupy your mind.

But Tommy McKinlay was above all of this, normal, activity and his three-inch thick panes of glass were replaced without any comment. People knew not to worry about anything concerning him, because it would inevitably end in tears if they did.

Before arriving at HMP Manchester, Tommy had enjoyed a charmed life. He'd been something of a local celebrity and was well known as a friend to some major sporting figures from the worlds of boxing, football and rugby. Just 12 months before he was imprisoned, Tommy's business empire had been the subject of an ITV documentary series entitled "The Private Police." Over the course of the six episodes, camera crews followed Tommy's security business empire across the north-west, documenting his success in resolving disputes which the ordinary police would not or could not, get involved with. The programme attracted impressive viewing figures of between 4 and 5 million per week.

Most people who watched the programme were captivated by this northern charmer's ability to bring sworn enemies to the table, help them to resolve their differences and shake hands at the end. There were plans for a second series to be made when Tommy was arrested. Those TV viewers who were a little more savvy sensed that the television show was a very watered-down look at Tommy McKinlay's business dealings. Where the TV screens showed an affable, often hilariously funny man helping to resolve matters which had been going on for years, the more cynical viewers had a sense that Tommy McKinlay didn't resolve all of his company's issues with a slice of cake and a good old natter. But none of these perceptive TV viewers were foolish enough to make their thoughts public via Twitter or Facebook. They kept their thoughts firmly to themselves. Tommy McKinlay has something which is hard to describe, it is like an aura that forewarns people — his very presence seems to send off a danger signal to everybody that he comes into contact with.

And this was a major part of Tommy's success in business and in life. He was an incredibly intimidating character, even through a television screen, people instinctively got the impression that this was a man that you wouldn't want to cross under any circumstances. For all of the wise-cracks and the charming banter which had made his TV series so endearing, it was clear that there was another, far more sinister side to this man's character.

It had been a big news story when Tommy McKinlay had been arrested and remanded into custody. Although he denies all of the charges against him, it seemed that the newscasters and journalists who reported the story were unsurprised. The viewing public were also quite matter-of-fact about the arrest, too. There were no shocked expressions or dramatic gasps as the news was revealed. It all just seemed like something which was bound to happen, sooner or later.

Tommy McKinlay never gave anybody the impression that he was mithered about being in Strangeways. He just got on with his day, working in the laundry and playing football in the exercise yard. To every other prisoner in the place, Tommy McKinlay was the ultimate person to look up to. They all knew that if they could become friends with him, they'd never have any problems to worry about.

As the news story from Worsley Green Primary School began to repeat itself, Tommy became a little bored and switched his TV off. He was happy with the morning's eventualities, it seemed that everything had gone very smoothly and it was superb to see that the media had made such a big deal of it.

"Slow news day!" Remarked Tommy as he stood on his bed and looked out through his fresh panes of glass, looking across the rooftops of Lower Broughton in the direction of Salford, the place that any criminal with half a brain would have been busy in today, taking advantage of the lack of police resources. He smiled widely, it felt incredibly empowering to see how easy it was to get every police officer in the region running about like headless chickens because of one prank call. Tommy laughed loudly and began to feel an excitement build within him.

"Seconds out, round two!" Said Tommy as he jumped off his bed and began shadow boxing around his cell, the look of delight on his face was unmistakable.

Chapter Sixteen

TEA TIME

Miller was sitting in the hotel room, trying to absorb the shocking start to the day. The twins, Leo and Molly were quite content with the TV on, completely absorbed in the disagreement that Dennis the Menace was having with Softy Walter. Clare was lay on the bed, still shaking uncontrollably from the shock of everything that had happened, and the disturbing realisation that all of this was somehow directed at her husband. It was such an horrific, overwhelming situation to be at the heart of, knowing that somebody was making threats to kill her children, but feeling completely powerless and at the mercy of whoever this person, or these people were. Clare was too exhausted to talk, too stressed to switch off, she just lay on the bed, staring through the window at the sky above.

Miller was sitting in the armchair, feeling completely helpless. His immediate removal from duty had seemed logical at first. But now, as the hours had wound on, he was beginning to feel frustrated that he had been sent here, miles away from home, and told to sit tight whilst the police officers that he was employed to manage, tried to make some sense of all this horror without him. It was a hard position to accept and Miller was chewing hard at his fingernails, desperate for some news.

Finally, Miller's phone began ringing. He snatched it off the table and looked at the screen. It was Dixon. Miller answered the call and said "one-sec Sir," as he walked out of the hotel room and stepped out onto the corridor, past the armed officer who was guarding the door.

"What's happening?" Asked Miller as he closed the door behind himself.

"Hi Andy, there's been a development." Dixon sounded stressed and anxious.

"What?"

"Well, if this is what I think it is, we've got a major problem on our hands..."

"Sir, for God's sake, can you get to the point?" Miller

was far too tightly wound-up to put up with Dixon's flowery language. He just wanted to know what the fuck was going on.

"We've had a phone call from HMP Manchester. A certain prisoner has phoned the top-floor saying that he needs to speak urgently with you."

The top-floor that Dixon was referring to meant the direct-line of the MCP Headquarters most senior department. The top floor was the location of most of the senior police officials, the Chief Constable, the Deputy Chief Constables as well as the most senior departmental heads, including DCS Dixon.

"Who's the prisoner?"

"Tommy McKinlay."

This was news. The line went silent a moment. Miller knew all about Tommy McKinlay, the notorious Manchester gangster who had been remanded in custody towards the back end of the previous year, a trial date still hadn't been set which suggested that there was still plenty of work to do for the prosecution.

"What does he want with me?" Miller's voice was cold and he sounded confused. Miller had played no part in McKinlay's down-fall, the whole case had been handled by the National Crime Agency, a major aspect of their "County Lines North" operation which had smashed a number of significant drug gangs throughout the north of England during the major NCA operation which had been live for almost two years. Miller had had no involvement in the case whatsoever and he had never even met Tommy McKinlay.

"We don't know what he wants, Andy. But it seems quite the coincidence that we suddenly find ourselves with this morning's issues and then the most powerful con in Strangeways is requesting an urgent chat."

The line went silent again. Miller was trying to make some sense out of all this, but there was none to be made. Why would a key gangster want a word with a detective that he had never had any dealings with? The north's prisons were full of men that Miller had put away. Why would one that he hadn't put away request a meeting, under these completely terrifying circumstances?

"Andy... are you there?"

"Yes... yes, just trying to work it out. What exactly was said?"

"He said that he needs to speak to you urgently..."

"Was that it?"

"No... he said that you have to come alone and that it would be extremely unwise to wear a mic."

"What?"

"He said that he has some extremely sensitive information that he wants to share with you."

Miller exhaled loudly and Dixon could hear that Miller was still struggling to calm his adrenaline. "So in con-talk, he's saying that he's the one who is behind the threats today and he wants to see my expression when he explains what it's all about?"

"That is certainly my interpretation of the situation, Andy."

"When?"

"I don't have any further details. But I'm sure that we can arrange something with the Governor at a moment's notice."

"But what about Clare and the kids? I can't just leave them here on their own and come back to Manchester. Aww, for... this is a fucking nightmare."

"Listen, it seems to me that the sooner we know what the situation is, the better for all concerned. Speak to Clare, see what she thinks and then get back to me."

"Okay. But I don't think it'll be today, she's in no fit state to be left."

"Well... like I say, talk to her. She'll probably be just as eager to hear what all of this is about as you and I are. Besides, she's at a secret location with armed officers by her door. She's literally never been safer in her life."

Miller exhaled loudly and an uncomfortable, prickly silence filled the line before the DCI finally spoke. "Right. I'll phone you back in a bit."

Chapter Seventeen

Tommy McKinlay was an extremely well-known north-west character both inside and outside the forty-foot prison walls. Long before the success of his TV series, he had attracted a great deal of attention as a bare-knuckle fighter in the mid 1990s and had quickly gained himself a notorious reputation for being one of the hardest men in the country, if not *the* hardest. McKinlay wasn't a particularly big man, but he was well known for his extraordinary strength and his complete and utter refusal to ever give up. Defeated fighters admired his incredible ability to keep going, earning him the comical nickname "Rock Hard Tommy."

Early in his illegal fighting career, he had fought the very hardest and most brutal men and won, shocking the fighters, organisers and spectators with his meteoric rise through the rankings. McKinlay spent less than two years taking down the biggest, strongest and fittest fighters through sheer determination and a stubbornly obsessive refusal to give up. Some people thought that cocaine was a major part of Tommy's firepower, but there were no rules in these types of fights and that liberal attitude extended to the misuse of drugs. In some cases Tommy's fights had lasted as long as ninety minutes, McKinlay's total refusal to give up quickly became his trademark. It hadn't taken very long for him to become the number-one fighter on the UK's underground bareknuckle circuit.

These fights were not for the faint hearted, the sport was popular mainly because of its utterly ruthless nature and over the course of the past twenty years it has become much more widely accessible, although admittedly watered-down, with its reinvention as cage-fighting. The sport has become a global, multi-billion-pound industry and Tommy McKinlay is recognised as one of the fighters who had increased so much interest in the sport during the dot com era, that his name is invariably linked to enabling the sport that we have today.

But winning money for fighting wasn't everything that Tommy McKinlay was interested in. He was also well known as the best person to speak to about any problems that needed resolving in his local area. He managed to build up a very lucrative security company in Rochdale, the district in which he had grown up. It had all started out as a very casual enterprise, Tommy would be asked to "have a word" with certain people who were making a nuisance of themselves in the area. It quickly transpired that Tommy had a natural gift for making problems go away, extremely quickly.

The first such encounter had happened quite by accident. Tommy was only 22 at the time and was still in the process of rising through the bare-knuckle rankings. He had visited his local corner-shop, the My Mum's Supermart on Oldham Road one dark, wintery night and had noticed that the owner, Mr Patel, a lovely, kind-hearted man who Tommy had known since being a little lad, looked quite stressed and wasn't his usual, happy-go-lucky self.

"Hey, what's up with you Mr P? You seem a bit down in the dumps." Asked Tommy as he placed down his grocery basket on the counter.

Mr Patel looked down at the floor momentarily, before trying to bluff his way out of the awkward question. The aging shopkeeper returned his eyes to the younger man. "Oh, no, nothing wrong with me Tommy. What's wrong with you? Are you scared I'm going to beat you up again?" Mr Patel laughed loudly, but it seemed forced, where normally this kind of banter would feel perfectly natural and Mr Patel would be quite at ease whilst teasing his customers. Tommy smiled warmly, but he knew that something was wrong.

"Listen Mr Patel. I've known you all my life and I've never seen you looking so stressed out. What's wrong with you?" Tommy's cheeky smile and warmth disappeared, he had a look of deep concern on his face. Mr Patel had behaved like a family member when Tommy's dad had died in a road accident when he was a little lad, he'd even given Tommy's mum a significant amount of money to help with the funeral costs. After that, he'd given her tick in the shop and whenever she came to settle up, he pretended he'd lost the chitty and told her not to worry about it. He was a diamond of a man and was very well loved in the local community, especially by the McKinlay family.

"Come on Mr Patel. Somethings up with you. If it was summat and nowt, you'd have told me by now. What's the matter? I'm not going until you tell me." Tommy had adopted his most intimidating stare, quite by accident. But it worked. Mr Patel's bottom lip began quivering and his eyes began filling up. Eventually, he began to speak, a deep, unmistakable stress disguised his normally laid-back, care-free voice.

"Well, okay. I've been getting some trouble Tommy."

"Who's giving you shit Mr Patel?" Tommy's face began heating up.

"It's the racists lot, all the National Front lads from the top estate. They keep coming in my shop and taking whatever they want from my shelves. The ciggies, the booze, you name it. They tell me that if I say anything to police, they'll burn shop down. Now, they're coming every day, and taking more stuff every time." Just saying this, just recalling the threat and the terror he felt was too much and Mr P, as he was affectionately known amongst the local community, broke down and his shoulders started heaving as his emotions took over. Tommy walked around the counter and placed his hand on the shopkeeper's shoulder.

"Do I know them?" He asked quietly.

Mr Patel shook his head slowly. "I don't know."

"Have they been today?"

"No. Not yet. That's why I'm so distressed. I don't know what they will take today. They know that I can't do anything so they are becoming more courageous each time. They bring more people every time. It's not fair, Tommy."

"Right, listen Mr P. I'm gonna go and sit on the stairs and I'm not moving 'til they've been. Right?" Tommy gestured towards the staircase which ran up to Mr Patel's stockroom. He guessed that these people would be coming, there was no way they'd take a day off from looting a shop of its stock.

"No, no Tommy, you don't need to be involved in trouble."

"Bollocks. This stops today, and these people will pay you back every fucking penny they owe you as well. So wipe your face and start working out what they've taken and how much they owe. I'll be sat right behind you on the stairs. As soon as they come in, you just say that you don't want any trouble. Okay?"

"Yes. No trouble."

"As soon as I hear that, I'll know what's happening."

"Yes."

"Put your keys in the door so I can lock them in. Right?"

Mr Patel looked up at Tommy. He looked sad that he was involving him in his problems.

"Seriously, if you don't say right straight away, I'll start going down to Cellar Five from now on!"

Mr Patel smiled briefly. "Alright. Alright Tommy. If you insist. And thank you."

"No problem. Right, where's the keys?"

Mr Patel's hands were shaking as he lifted the huge bunch of keys from under his counter.

"Good, now put them in the door. Right?"

"Message understood Tommy. Thank you."

"Is that the button for the shutters?" Tommy pointed at the big red knob close to the shop's door.

"Yes."

"And what do you do to bring the shutters down?"

"Just turn the arrow for up or down and keep hand on the button."

"Sorted. Right, see you in a bit." Tommy patted the shopkeeper's shoulder as he stepped past Mr Patel and out onto the staircase, closing the door to as he went. He took a seat on the second step and felt his anger start to rise as he considered the kindness that Mr Patel had always shown to people. And now some arseholes had decided to take the piss out of him and bully the old man.

The shop was always busy, the beep of the door opening and closing was non-stop for the following hour as people from the local community came in to buy their bits, have a quick chat with Mr Patel, and then the beeper would sound again as they left.

Finally, the beeper was followed by the words that

Tommy had instructed Mr Patel to say.

"I don't want trouble!"

Tommy leapt up from his step and inched towards the tiny gap between the door and its frame to get a look at Mr Patel's adversaries. There were six or seven that he could see, all aged between sixteen and twenty. He knew one or two of their faces but wasn't familiar with their names.

"Ha ha ha! Have you heard yourself? You don't vant trouble? Shut up you fucking smelly old paki. I don't vant people like you taking over our shops. I don't vant your sort in this country. But I do vant all your cigarettes so start emptying them shelves into bags or I'll put you to sleep."

Tommy was watching silently. The shop door was closed now and he was quite satisfied that every member of the gang were inside the shop. He opened the door that he'd been hiding behind and jumped over the counter, locking the shop door before any of the young men knew what was happening. He took the keys and put them in his pocket. Suddenly, the lad who'd been threatening Mr Patel had stopped talking. Tommy pressed the big red button beside the door and a heavy, grinding noise filled the silence as the steel shutters began rolling down outside the shop.

"Just a second lads, I'll be with you as soon as you're all locked in and there's nowhere for you to run away to." Tommy had a crazed look in his eyes as he stared at each one of the lads, a weird smirk on his face added even further menace to the proceedings.

"Is that Tommy McKinlay?" Whispered one of them as the grinding sound continued. Finally, the bottom of the shutter crashed against the pavement outside with an intimidating crunch which made all seven of the young men jump visibly.

"Right, Mr Patel. Do me a favour mate, you go off upstairs and have a cup of char while I sort these little shit cunts out. I don't want you seeing what happens."

Mr Patel nodded nervously and did exactly as he was told, he was a gentle soul and was relieved that Tommy was excusing him from this horrendous situation. The elderly shopkeeper stomped slowly up the stairs and Tommy smiled as he heard the door close upstairs. He walked across to the lad who had been taking the piss out of Mr Patel's accent, who was now cowering with a hand up in front of his face. "Don't!" Was all he said in a whimpering, feeble voice.

"What's your name?"

"Johnny... Pritchard..."

"Rubber Johnny shit bag, more like. Look at the fucking state of you." Said Tommy, standing close to the pathetic young bully.

"Don't!" He whimpered again, cowering down even further as the anticipation of pain became overwhelming. Two of the younger members of the gang were crying as they stood by, trembling.

"So judging by your response, I take it you all know who I am?" Asked Tommy. The sad, scruffy group of delinquents all nodded. Tommy smiled sarcastically. "But the thing you didn't know, I'm guessing, is that Mr Patel is one of my oldest friends. He's been like an uncle to me, since I was about this big." Tommy put his right hand by his hip.

As Johnny glanced at his hand, he was struck by an almighty punch from Tommy's left hand, which sent the young man flying backwards into one of the shop's shelving units before flopping out-cold on the tiled floor. Johnny lay there unconscious, as a tin of beans which had been dislodged from the impact fell down and bashed off Johnny's head with a hollow thud before rolling off along the floor. Tommy began laughing loudly, he found the spectacle hilarious. The six remaining young racists were even more petrified now. They all knew that Tommy McKinlay was the worst person to cross on this side of Greater Manchester. He was well recognised as one of the hardest young streetfighters in the UK. And here they were, having crossed him, and he was laughing his head off.

"Right well, how are we going to sort this out?" Asked Tommy of the six gang members who remained standing. None of them answered.

"It's a bit embarrassing this. You've all walked in here like heroes, as though you are all proud that you can rob and bully an old man. You were all thinking you were something else... and now look at the fucking state of yous all."

"Sorry..." Said one of the lads. He was dressed in the generic clothing of the day, an Adidas tracksuit and Nike trainers, with the look completed with a Nike cap. It is a fashion style which has barely altered in the twenty years since this infamous incident occurred.

"You *will* be sorry lads. You're going to be very fucking sorry. You picked the wrong elderly shopkeeper to steal from, racially abuse and humiliate. Didn't yous?"

"Yes!" Chanted the six lads.

"You know what? I've got a mate who works at a hospital. Can any of you mongs guess what his job is?"

The pale, terrified looking lads all shook their heads.

"His job title is an 'Incineration Operative.' Do any of you fucking spackers know what that means?"

They all shook their heads. It was pretty clear that they were as thick as pig shit.

"It means he's in charge of burning all the stuff they don't need anymore. The arms and legs the surgeons have chopped off. One day he might only have a gammy foot to burn away. Other days, he has legs and tits and lungs and ears. And some days, if he's asked really nicely, he burns entire bodies away. Do you all understand the point I'm making?"

Once again, the six teenagers chanted "Yes!"

"He can only do one at a time though, the amount of smoke a full person creates is shocking so its best if it's a windy day, all the smoke fucks off really quickly. Anyway, its gales tomorrow so everything is looking good. So now, you're going to have to choose which one of yous my mate's going to burn off. And don't fucking say Johnny just because he's asleep you tight cunts!"

Tommy walked around the six young men, grinning at them all. Not one of them dared to look him in the eye.

"But I suppose if its gales, he could do the lot of yous. I could snap all your necks now, then chuck your bodies in the back of Mr Patel's van and drop it off for my mate to sort out. Burning you all away so your mums and dads will never know what happened to their fucking horrible entrails."

Three of the group were crying. Tommy laughed loudly as he saw that another had pissed in his pants.

"Or, there's another way I could deal with this… wait a sec…" Tommy walked away from the tragic group of friends and headed up a different aisle in the shop. He whistled as he browsed the shelves. After a minute, he'd found what he was searching for and casually walked back around towards the counter, clutching a roll of cling-film. "This is the stuff. It's 79p. Anybody got 79p on them?"

One of the lads rummaged in his tracksuit pocket and pulled out a pound coin and held it out for Tommy. His hand was shaking violently.

"Good man. Go and put it on Mr Patel's counter." The lad stepped forward and placed the coin down. As he did so, Tommy began opening the cling-film box and placed the cardboard on the counter beside the coin. He then tutted as he struggled to find the end of the cling-film.

"Fucking thing. I can never find the end." He said to himself, ever so casually. Once he had unravelled it, he stepped towards the lad who had offered the £1 coin and began rolling the transparent plastic around his face.

"This is the coolest way I've ever seen somebody die. If you start at the top of the head, and slowly work your way down with each new rotation of the roll, it gets more and more terrifying."

Tommy was smiling wildly as the boy's friends watched on in horror. The unmistakable terror on all of their faces told Tommy that he was making his point. "Once this cling-film gets down over his nose and mouth, wait until you see how red his head goes as his lungs are starved of oxygen. It's amazing."

The lad just stood there as Tommy continued rotating the roll around his face. As the thin, transparent plastic covered his airways, Tommy laughed loudly as the rest of the group looked down at the floor, all five of them were openly crying. "Look, your mate is dying for a breath!" Tommy laughed again as the young man's legs buckled and he began collapsing to the floor. Tommy let him fall and as he landed, the suffocating racist began trying to pull the cling-film away from his mouth.

"Fucking hell, he's literally seconds from death. Do one of yous want to save him?" Asked Tommy. The five youths looked panicked and unsure of what to do. "If one of yous doesn't make him an air-hole pretty sharpish his hearts going to stop."

Suddenly, the lad who'd pissed his pants dropped to his knees and stuck his fingers through the cling-film. A loud gasp for breath made Tommy laugh loudly once again. He looked as though he was really enjoying this.

Johnny, the lad who had been knocked out a couple of minutes earlier seemed to be coming around a bit now as his legs began twitching on the floor.

"Ah! Rubber Johnny! You've woken up! I thought I might have to chuck you off the motorway bridge, let all the trucks squish you up."

The mood inside Mr Patel's shop was becoming even more tense. None of the seven young men had any idea what Tommy was likely to do next. One thing was becoming increasingly clear though, he was enjoying himself putting the fear of God into them and he didn't look like he was getting bored yet.

"You've just saved your mates life. Because he could die for me, I couldn't give a fuck. I'll tell you one thing though... if one of you ever upsets Mr Patel, or anybody else in this town again, I will fucking kill you, and you will be cremated with a bag of cancerous human organs and infected limbs. Do you understand me?"

All seven members of the gang said "Yes!" once again and Tommy nodded as he stepped over to the shop's counter again. "Right, you all write your names, addresses along with your mam and dad's names and your phone numbers down on this." Tommy took Mr Patel's biro from the little tub next to his till and placed a scrap of paper on the counter. "QUICKLY!" He shouted, making them all jump with fright.

"Right, while you're doing that, I'll get Mr Patel down here and you can all apologise to him and we'll work out what's going to happen next." Tommy walked around the counter and opened the door to the stairs. "Mr Patel, have you got a minute please?" He shouted up very politely. There was some shuffling around upstairs before the elderly shopkeeper responded.

"Just coming down now, Tommy." Said Mr Patel as he began to make his way slowly down the creaking staircase.

"All sorted here Mr P. These boys know that if they ever cause any more upset, I'm going to make their mams beat their dads to death in front of them, and then I'm going to beat their mams to death and I'm going to make them all bury their mams and dads in their back gardens. I'm going to make sure they never upset anybody ever again, I'm determined about it."

"Oh, thank you Tommy." Said Mr Patel as he reached the bottom step and walked behind the counter. He looked apprehensive as he made eye contact with the seven people who had been making his life a living hell for the past few weeks. But he needn't have worried. They all looked like they were traumatised by whatever had been going on down here in his beloved shop.

"Not a problem, it's my pleasure. I just wish you'd come to me about it, I'd have sorted it out the day it started."

"Oh, well, I don't like to be a pain."

Tommy looked away from the shopkeeper and stared once again at the sorry bunch of losers before him. "Tell you what, if any of you lads can go on to become ten-per-cent of the man that this fellah is, you'll be doing alright. I don't think you'll find a better man than this one in Rochdale. Have you all got something you'd like to say to Mr Patel?"

"Sorry." They said in chorus. Mr Patel nodded and accepted their apologies with good grace.

"How much do they owe you Mr P?"

The shopkeeper reached under his counter and pulled out a book. He had followed Tommy's instruction earlier and to the best of his ability had itemised the produce that the chancers had taken so far. It was a rushed job, done in between serving customers throughout the anxious hour spent waiting for the scum bags to call in for this evening's pickings. But never-the-less, Mr Patel was an astute businessman and he felt confident that the long list of cigarettes, booze, Pot Noodles and various other items was as near as damn it.

"Fucking hell. They've took nearly a grand's worth of stuff of you?"

"Yes, They only took the most very expensive items. Except the Pot Noodles."

"Right, well, you lot need to pay Mr P all that money back. Plus an extra grand for all the stress you've caused him. Do you all understand?"

The pathetic looking gang all nodded and agreed to the deal, although Tommy had serious doubts that they'd keep their word. They looked as though they were all planning to leave town tonight.

"If you don't come back here every day and give at least a hundred quid to Mr Patel, I'll be coming round your houses and I'll take all your mams and dads stuff and sell it, including their cars. Then at least one of you will be going to see my mate at the hospital. Am I clear?" Tommy had that wild look in his eyes again, it was genuinely scary for everybody, even Mr Patel.

"One hundred pounds a day, for the next twenty days and then, I'll stop thinking about you all. If you miss a payment, we start again at the beginning, but with an extra grand on top. Is that completely and totally understood?"

The boys looked close to tears again. It was going to be a big and challenging task to get a hundred pounds together, every day, for twenty days. But Tommy McKinlay couldn't care less. These dickheads had shat on the wrong doorstep.

"Mr P, if they don't come in, give me a bell that day and I'll find out what the problem is. And I'll sort it out."

Finally, it seemed that Tommy was done. He walked over to the door and flicked the switch on the shutter, before keeping his hand pressed on the big red button. The grinding noise of the shutter kicked in as the huge steel curtain outside the shop began lifting slowly. Tommy gave the keys to Mr Patel and asked him to unlock the door. As soon as it was opened, the young racists walked out slowly as though it was the end of the world.

"Sincerely, thank you Tommy." Said Mr Patel, with a tear in his eye. He was relieved that the issue had been resolved without any serious harm coming to anybody.

Each time that he popped into Mr Patel's over the following few weeks, Tommy was pleased to hear that at least one member of the gang had been in every day without fail and had handed over one hundred pounds. He was pleased to learn also that each hundred pounds came with a sincere and emotional apology to Mr Patel. One thing was clear, the influence of Tommy McKinlay was a surprisingly powerful force. This fact had been proven beyond all doubt on the day of the final repayment. Tommy had told Mr Patel to inform whichever gang member that came in with the penultimate payment that every single member of the gang was required to attend a meeting with Tommy at 3pm outside the shop.

The young lads looked extremely nervous and pale as Tommy arrived a little after 5pm. "Sorry I'm late lads. Have you paid your last instalment?"

"No, its here," said Johnny, the lad who'd been dealt the most severe punishment with that knockout punch. He held out a scruffy wad of fivers, tenners and a handful of coins.

"Good. Well, go and give it to Mr Patel and ask him if he's got something for you."

Johnny looked terrified as he walked into the shop. The rest of the gang also appeared apprehensive as they stood on the pavement outside with Tommy. A couple of minutes later, Johnny reappeared holding a box.

"What's in the box?" Asked Tommy.

"Dunno. Mr Patel asked me to give it to you."

Tommy took the box and opened it. "Oh, shit, I completely forgot about this. It's the Mosque open day leaflets. I said I'd give him some help with handing them out. In fact, I could use some help. Are you lads alright to hand them out all day tomorrow in town?"

Tommy had a sarcastic look on his face as the small gang of racists realised that the slate wasn't yet clean. Tommy was planning one last act of total humiliation for them all.

"Thanks lads. Nine o' clock sharp in Rochdale bus station. Comb your hairs, I want you wearing your best clothes, shirts, ties, shiny shoes and bring a packed lunch as its going to be a long day. If any of you don't turn up, you can start paying

Mr Patel back from the start, and the amount doubles."

Tommy was laughing his head off as the young gang arrived at Rochdale bus station the following morning. They all looked very smart and presentable, as though they were due in court. Tommy handed the box of leaflets over to Johnny.

"Nice one lads. You all stay here, under these CCTV cameras, and you hand every single one of these leaflets out. And as you give them to people, you smile politely and say 'As-Salam-u-Alaikum.' Which means peace be unto you. Come on lads, lets practise. As-Salam-u-Alaikum."

The seven, petrified and thoroughly humiliated young men repeated the Islamic greeting over and over again until Tommy was happy with it. Shoppers and workers who were alighting buses gave the strange group of white lads funny glances as they passed.

"That's great, good work. Now unfortunately, summats come up and I'm not going to be able to help yous out today, but I'll pop in from time to time to see how its going. You can stop for five minutes for a piss at 1pm. Other than that, you stay right here under these cameras where my mate can keep an eye on you. Understood?"

"Yes Tommy!" Chanted the youths, desperate to get this final humiliation over and done with and hopefully, never see or hear from Tommy McKinlay ever again.

"As-Salam-u-Alaikum, lads."

Chapter Eighteen

Miller had waited at HMP Manchester almost an hour before he'd finally come face to face with the man who had requested his presence. The man who had asked for this urgent meeting had been stalling for time, apparently. Miller's stress levels were reaching their peak as he sat alone in the visiting room, being updated once every ten minutes by prison staff on McKinlay's faffing about. Each minute that passed increased Miller's tension, at the front of his mind was Clare, back at the hotel and his promise that he would be as quick as possible. Finally, a prison officer came into the room and explained that Tommy wasn't prepared to see Miller unless the conversation took place outside in the exercise yard. Miller agreed and picked up the distinct impression that the screw who was doing the negotiating with McKinlay hated the man's guts.

Tommy McKinlay is the historic prison's VIP inmate, his power and influence on the streets outside Strangeways' gigantic walls was well known and perfectly understood inside the walls as well. As a result of his status as one of Manchester's most influential gangsters, combined with his notoriety as one of Britain's hardest men, Tommy's power didn't just extend to the prison's residents. He held a good deal of power over the staff as well. If Tommy wanted the whole prison to start rioting, he was probably the only man in the establishment who could make it happen. Besides this incredible bargaining chip, every member of the prison service was acutely aware that Tommy McKinlay could have them attacked with great ease outside, in their homes or their cars, or as they went shopping with their families. As such, he enjoyed a great deal of influence over the staff and received special treatment on a daily basis.

No other member of the prison population could simply click their fingers and request a meeting, outside in the exercise yard, with one of Greater Manchester's most senior detectives. There was only Tommy McKinlay who held enough influence over the prison's governor to make such a meeting possible. And as such, DCI Andy Miller had come to the jail and waited for almost an hour before being granted an audience with Tommy McKinlay, at the location that the prisoner insisted on.

The pleasantries were kept to a minimum. McKinlay just got straight to the point.

"Thanks for coming at such short notice. So, let's get down to brass tacks. If you're wearing a wire or recording device, you'll do well to take it off and smash it up right now as the conversation that it captures will hurt you more than anybody else." Tommy was talking as though this prison yard was his office, and with so much confidence that Miller could be forgiven for thinking that he was speaking to a superior member of staff back at the police HQ.

"There's no wire, no recording. We heard the message loud and clear."

"Good. That's a sensible start. Now then, I assume you remember a local entrepreneur called Marco?"

Miller knew exactly who Tommy was talking about. Marco MacDowell, the notorious east Manchester gangster who had been shot dead at Liverpool airport by armed officers, as he tried to flee the country. It was Miller's investigation into MacDowell's activities which had led to the disturbing conclusion to his life.

"Of course I remember Marco. He was a very nasty piece of shit." Miller looked completely neutral regarding the incident.

"Oh, I agree wholeheartedly. His death was met with great appreciation by many people. Getting Marco out of the picture opened up a lot of new opportunities for a lot of people. I think its fair to say that there are a lot of serious criminals in Greater Manchester who owe you an enormous debt of gratitude."

Miller was listening and deconstructing the conversation as though he was an interpreter. Professional cons would never say anything incriminating about themselves to a police officer, so they spoke in a rather confusing third-person manner. What Miller translated from McKinlay's last comment was that Marco's death had been great news for McKinlay, and had increased his power and income dramatically, the debt of gratitude was McKinlay's. Which, if Miller was translating correctly, made things even more confusing as to what this gangster wanted with him.

"Anyway, he wouldn't have been killed if he hadn't grabbed the little girl."

"Death by cop."

Miller raised an eyebrow. "Is that your theory on what happened?"

"Oh, undoubtedly DCI Miller. Without any shadow of doubt. Marco knew he'd never again witness the breath-taking beauty of Oldham Mumps if he was never stepping foot outside of jail again, would he? I've said all along that grabbing that kid was his best chance of death by cop. So he won really. In the end."

Normally, Miller would wonder how having the top of your skull blown ten metres away from the rest of your body could ever constitute a win, but he wasn't remotely interested in the stupid logic of criminals today. He had more pressing business to attend to.

"Listen Tommy, I don't care about Marco. I just want to know what that stunt was all about this morning?" Miller had decided to cut through the crap and get to the real reason that McKinlay had requested an audience with him.

"Oh, that's a bit forward DCI Miller. All in good time." McKinlay was cool, he ended his comment with a sly grin which infuriated Miller. He'd been put through hell today, his worst fears had been messed with and McKinlay wasn't denying knowledge of it or acting coy. Indeed, he was marking his power over the conversation by deliberately toying with Miller, stamping his authority over the situation in an unmistakable manner.

Miller looked down at the floor and began counting to ten in his mind. He couldn't lose his temper, or even show his distaste. There was too much at stake. This man was threatening to harm his wife and kids, and from what Miller understood about Tommy McKinlay, he was psychotic enough to have the threat followed through.

"Now, I really need a favour." McKinlay was still

grinning. Miller's face was bright red, there was no mistaking his fury. He looked into McKinlay's eyes, desperate to hear what this was all about, finally.

"Go on."

"If somebody was sent to prison for crimes that they clearly hadn't done, crimes which could easily be pinned on other people, some of whom are deceased… Marco MacDowell being an obvious example, would you be content to look into the investigation into the supposed crimes, and build a case to prove beyond all doubt that the innocent party had been wrongfully charged?"

Miller was listening whilst also translating again. It translated quite clearly. McKinlay was saying that he wanted Miller to get him out of jail, by making up bullshit which would cast doubt on the strength of the prosecution's evidence. The unspoken part of the deal had been made clear much earlier, with the terrifying threats against his family. Miller skilfully managed to keep his emotions and his temper in check.

"Well, it would be a very difficult thing for any police officer to do…"

McKinlay started laughing loudly, as though Miller had just told the funniest joke he'd ever heard. He kept the laughter going for an awkwardly long time. Miller just stood there beside the prison walls, feeling weak and humiliated.

Eventually McKinlay spoke again. "Marco MacDowell could very easily have been named as the person responsible for a lot of crimes that certain innocent people are being accused of. It would be seen as a great triumph for the British justice system if a police officer who knew what a piece of shit Marco was, decided to prove a wrongfully accused man's innocence. A police officer who did that would be seen as a hero in many peoples eyes." McKinlay meant his eyes, and his gang's eyes. The arseholes who were still out there in the community keeping McKinlay's gangland empire running, the bastards behind today's audacious behaviour towards his family. There was absolutely no doubt about it.

"I had no involvement in your case. None whatsoever."

"Nobody said you had."

"Well... I'm just a bit confused as to why I'm being involved now?"

"Because you are a good man, a good, hard-working family man, who does the right thing. Well, most of the time."

Miller's face was heating up further, he was struggling to keep a lid on this, the veiled menace behind the words "family man" was coming through all too clear. Plus there was the rather ominous and vague "most of the time" comment to deconstruct. McKinlay had Miller right where he wanted him and both men were acutely aware of where the balance of power lay.

"So... next steps. Have a dig around, see what you can come up with, there's a pot of gold to be found here, you just need to look for it."

Miller had heard enough. He sensed that McKinlay was through and felt that it was time to wrap this up now, once and for all.

"Well, I think I understand what you've said."

"Excellent. Oh, that's great news."

"And I'll tell you now that I've been suspended from duty for personal safety reasons and my family have been moved to a place of refuge..."

"Can't stay there forever though..."

"They can stay there for enough time to get your bogey-men off the streets."

Once again, McKinlay let out a loud, exaggerated laugh.

"You seriously think you can intimidate me, Tommy? You've made a serious error of judgement." Miller had his eyes locked on McKinlay's. He wasn't backing down.

McKinlay smiled insincerely. "I know I can intimidate you DCI Miller. I know I can haunt you, I can get right there, inside your brain." The prisoner tapped two fingers at his temple, whilst staring Miller down. "I swear to God, I can take over your mind with just two words."

Miller blinked and McKinlay smiled gloatingly.

"Which two words might they be then, Tommy?"

"All in good time..."

"There's no better time than now, is there?"

"I'll let you know."

"No, fuck that Tommy. Tell me now." Despite himself, Miller sounded snappy. He was very close to losing it and it was glaringly obvious. This empowered Tommy even more and he smiled widely at the DCI.

"I'll text them to you later. I've got your mobile number. Two words which will take your fucking breath away. I hope you've not got asthma."

Miller didn't know what to say to that. He turned to the prison officer who was standing by the door on the other side of the exercise yard and signalled that he was ready to leave as he began walking. McKinlay followed him, speaking quietly as they neared the prison-officer. "Once you've calmed down from my text message, make sure you save my number. You'll need it to keep in touch, keep me up to speed with progress. But don't call before 8pm or after 2am. My phone will be up my sphincter outside those hours. I'll text you those two words that are going to make you my little puppet at about 9pm. Nice to meet you anyway, DCI Miller, especially here, with the eyes of the whole prison on us."

Miller looked up and saw that every window in every cell had at least one face at it, looking directly at him.

Chapter Nineteen

Miller was driven out of Strangeways in the ARU vehicle which had brought him down from Preston. The threat against his safety was viewed as "critical" by the higher ranks who had allowed the meeting to take place, officers such as DCS Dixon and other, senior police officials including the Chief Constable were in command of the situation.

As the police Range Rover raced out of the prison gates and through the city-centre streets, the driver was keeping an eye out for any vehicles following. He did a double-loop of the roads around Cheetham Hill just to make sure that nobody was trying to keep a tail at a distance. Content that there was nobody in pursuit, the ARU officers agreed that it was safe to proceed back to MCP HQ, where Miller would be required to meet with Dixon, and probably other senior staff members, to discuss the details of the meeting with McKinlay.

"Sorry, lads, can I request that you take me straight up to Preston? My wife is in distress and I need to go to her." Miller knew that this request was out of order, but he needed to stall for time. He had no idea what McKinlay was planning to text to him, and the last thing he needed to do was alert anybody else that he apparently had something hanging over him, until he knew exactly what it was. Miller had a very uneasy feeling about this potential threat and his gut was telling him to wait until the full picture became clearer before he showed all of his cards. People like Tommy McKinlay were notoriously hard to deal with at the best of times. Without having any clue as to which two words were powerful enough to put Miller into a precarious position, he knew that it was wise to wait and see what McKinlay had in store.

"This is ARU12 to control."

"Control receiving, over."

"Request channel change to default, over."

"Channel change to default. Go ahead on default. Over."

The ARU officer in the front passenger seat switched

channels on the radio, to one which had previously been agreed as the default. This was to frustrate any eaves-droppers who could potentially be listening over illegal police scanners, who would now need several minutes to try and figure out which of the dozens of available channels the ARU radio had defaulted to.

"This is ARU12 to control, over."

"Receiving."

"Our passenger has requested to travel direct to outset location."

"Standby over."

Miller began nibbling at a fingernail as he waited to see what control would come back and say. Dixon wasn't thick, he'd know that Miller was fobbing him off by not coming straight back to HQ to explain what had been discussed at Strangeways.

After a few seconds, the radio beeped and the controller's voice came back on the air. "Understood. Please confirm when the journey is complete and you are clear. Over and out."

Miller took his phone out of his pocket and checked the time. It was almost 8pm. McKinlay said that he would text at 9pm, so he decided to text Dixon and put him off for a little while. "Hi Sir, can't chat now, need to get back to Clare. Also, its awkward with these ARU officers around at the minute. I'll call you when I get back to the hotel and have some privacy. McKinlay seems to be trying it on, will explain more later. Andy."

The police Range Rover headed at speed away from Manchester and back towards the M61 motorway to Preston. Andy didn't participate in the idle conversations between the AR officers, he was lost in his own world, trying to imagine what bullshit "two words" Tommy McKinlay imagined would be good enough fodder to blackmail him with. Miller was at a loss, but was becoming increasingly anxious to find out what McKinlay was playing at. The roads were clear and the speeding police car made good progress, reaching the Tickled Trout hotel on the outskirts of Preston within half an hour of pulling out of HMP Manchester's secure car-park. The police driver drove past the famous hotel and up the hill towards Preston city centre to ensure that he wasn't being followed, before turning the vehicle around at the roundabout and heading a mile back down the hill to the hotel which stands at a picturesque spot on the banks of the River Ribble.

"Okay Sir. We'll just do a quick sweep of the area and then you will be escorted back to your hotel room where we will hand you over to the armed officers who are already deployed."

"Thanks a lot. I appreciate your help today lads."

"Not a problem. Hope that this all gets cleared up soon enough, Sir."

"Yes, you and me both. I don't mind a bit of aggro, it goes with the job. But bringing kids and wives into it is a step too far for my liking. Cheers anyway. I owe you one."

After a minute or two, Miller's door was opened by an armed officer and he was instructed to walk quickly into the hotel entrance, which was less than five metres away from the vehicle. The DCI followed orders and rushed inside, not particularly panicked by the drama. He knew that he wasn't in any immediate danger. Tommy McKinlay wasn't going to let anything happen to him whilst he thought that Miller could be influential in getting his charges dropped and released from prison. The only thing on Miller's mind was seeing Clare and the kids and getting them away from here as soon as possible.

Miller was followed through the posh hotel by the armed officer, which turned a number of heads as he passed other residents on the corridors. Eventually, Miller reached the corridor that his room was on, and came face to face with the other AR officer by the door.

"Everything alright?" He asked of the armed policeman who was standing in front of the door.

"Yes Sir, no issues."

"Good. What's the plan for the rest of the night?"

"Our team are on 'til ten, then a nightshift team are taking over until six Sir. Beyond that, I've not been made aware."

"Okay, that's great. My wife will be reassured by this. Thanks a lot."

"Sir."

Miller pressed the key fob against the sensor, opened the door and was greeted with a disappointed look from Clare.

Chapter Twenty

A few minutes before 9pm, Miller excused himself from the frostiness of his hotel room and headed into the bathroom, muttering something about stress playing havoc with his bowels. He locked the bathroom door and sat down on the toilet seat, clutching his mobile phone in his hand. The anticipation for McKinlay's text was becoming too much now. He was desperate to know what tricks the gangster thought that he had up his sleeve. Once he knew the rules of the game, he felt that he would have a better chance of coming up with a plan of how he was going to play it. But the waiting game was driving him mad, he was desperate to understand what he was supposedly up against.

Time seemed to be standing still. Miller realised that he was stressed out, his hand was shaking slightly and he felt a tightness in his chest. He took a deep breath and held it for as long as he could, eventually letting the breath out slowly through his nose. Once he had exhaled all of the oxygen, he repeated the breathing exercise, which always worked in slowing down his heartrate in times of severe stress. A couple of minutes of this followed, and Miller felt a sense of calmness returning.

But then the phone made its familiar beep-beep noise, alerting Miller that a text message had been received. In an instant, the tension and stress returned, the tightness in his upper body felt even stronger than it had a few minutes earlier. Miller opened the text message and gasped loudly as he read the two words that McKinlay had sent. He felt the bathroom start to spin around him as his brain tried to process the information. He stared at the two words, his hand was visibly trembling as he focused on the screen. His face was heating up but a cold sweat was enveloping his face. He blinked several times as he tried desperately to process the galloping thoughts that had suddenly begun racing through his mind. The two words which had appeared had not once crossed his mind in the past hour or so as he'd tried to work out what McKinlay might be planning.

> The two words were devastating.
> The two words were "George" and "Dawson."

Chapter Twenty-One

Tommy McKinlay smiled widely as he placed his phone on his bed and looked up at the ceiling of his single occupancy cell on B Wing of Manchester's most famous prison. He knew that the text message that he had just sent would be going off like a nuclear bomb in its recipient's face. The two words that he'd text were so powerful that his complete and immediate control of the celebrated detective was guaranteed. His first job on getting out would be making sure that nobody in the Manchester City Police force would ever have the audacity to even think about arresting him again. Once Miller got him out, he would be staying out for good, and he'd be able to do whatever the fuck he wanted as well. This brief spell in jail was going to make him the most powerful criminal in the country, so he was glad it had happened. The authorities thought they'd played a blinder, but to Tommy McKinlay, it was just part of the game. The game that he would ultimately win. He was determined about that.

The thing that pissed Tommy McKinlay off more than anything was the sheer hypocrisy of the British state. As far as Tommy could tell, if you are a certain type of person, a politician or a copper or a billionaire or a member of the Royal family, you could do whatever the hell you like. But if you're just a working-class lad from Rochdale and you start making a bit of a go of things, suddenly the police and the courts are all over you like a rash, trying to uphold the illusion of law and order. Yet, if you're a paedo and you know the right people, anything goes. Being from Rochdale, Tommy knew all about Cyril Smith, who had systematically molested little boys for over thirty years whilst he was the Member of Parliament for Rochdale. He'd been driven to children's homes by his chauffeur and would spend the night there, molesting the little kids who had no parents or home to go to. The police knew all about Smith and his depravity, the staff from the care homes had contacted them to make complaints. But nothing ever came of it. West Yorkshire police had once arrested him after he'd been accused of similar crimes on their patch and the police sergeant had been contacted by a member of Margaret Thatcher's staff at 10 Downing Street, advising the police sergeant to let Cyril Smith go on his way immediately and to drop all enquiries. Soon after, Smith was knighted. It sounds like a small-town rumour, but it sadly isn't. The details of this incident, along with many more reports against Smith are well documented and can be accessed within seconds on Google. There were 144 complaints against Smith whilst he was alive, all of which were dismissed. In many cases, investigating officers were warned to leave it alone and were silenced under the official secrets act.

This was just one example, though. Tommy McKinlay had spent many, many hours researching the extraordinary corruption at the very top of British society. It amused him that the bankers who helped create the financial crash in 2008 which had resulted in around a million deaths as a consequence of the "austerity" which followed the country going bankrupt. Yet not one of these bankers had ever appeared in court or faced jail. In Tommy's view, the system was institutionally corrupt, and it came from the very highest level. It was a system so corrupt that somebody like Jimmy Savile managed to get away with sex crimes against thousands of kids over thirty or forty years, and those who attempted to expose him, including senior members of the BBC and the NHS were sacked and silenced. Most damningly, those who fixed it for Savile to continue with his depraved crimes were promoted within the BBC and the NHS. In recent times, the British Home Secretary stopped the Savile snowball from gathering any further momentum by "losing" the files that named all of the senior politicians who were said to be involved in paedophile activity at one level or another over the previous fifty years.

Yet here was Tommy, banged up, just for having the audacity to make a few bob off the back of his own initiative. The best joke of all, in Tommy's mind, was the fact that the most evil and psychotic people imaginable who lived to create misery and suffering wherever they went had been taken out of the picture thanks to Tommy McKinlay. The loss of these people was an enormous help to the police and the authorities, there was no grey area whatsoever. The whole thing was a farce. It really amused Tommy, he was past feeling angry or embittered. He had seen so much evidence of corruption that he had decided to find a way into that murky world himself.

Tommy knew that he'd beat this shitty system one way or another, it was so bent and farcical and run by such morons that he had no doubts at all that he'd be able to penetrate the dark side of British establishment quite easily. After all, all of this was being managed and controlled by the most braindead people who'd ever lived. It really made Tommy laugh that the bullshit that he'd been remanded for was only the tip of the iceberg. Most of the crimes that Tommy had been involved with over the years were a million times worse than the shite he was being charged with. The best lesson from all of this was to see just how fragile and vulnerable this corrupt system was. Andy Miller was up to his eyes in it himself and he was supposed to be the straightest dibble in the city.

It genuinely fascinated Tommy that the people who are supposed to be the upholders of the law were usually more bent and dangerous than the folk they were employed to lock up. It was this fact that inspired and motivated Tommy McKinlay every day and he was excited to play his part. It made his stay in Strangeways an absolute pleasure. The dicks at the police and the CPS all thought they'd won the pools the day they banged Tommy up on remand. He imagined them all going for pints and high-fiving one another whilst he was laughing his cock off in the big house. None of them had any idea that Tommy had allowed them just enough to get him in here, so he could pull all their strings and take his operation to the next level.

Tommy's ambitions for the future were boundless. He knew one thing for sure though, he was well on track to become the most untouchable criminal in the land, he'd soon take that crown off Prince Andrew. He lifted his phone from his bed and checked to see if Miller had replied. He laughed loudly when he saw the tiny screen was empty and started typing a new message.

"Looking forward to working with you on this. Exciting opportunities lie in store. Anyway, that's enough for today, I'll just let the gravity of the situation sink in."

Chapter Twenty-Two

Miller sat on the toilet seat, his entire career in the police service was flashing past his eyes as he tried desperately to process the magnitude of McKinlay's text message. His very first thoughts centred around denial, his mind tried to trick itself that McKinlay's message was a mistake, or a coincidence, or a totally fluky stab-in-the-dark. His mind was trying to reinterpret the message, trying to reason that McKinlay couldn't possibly know about George Dawson or the alarm that would be felt upon hearing the man's name. This bizarre and completely involuntary attempt at dismissal only lasted seconds, but the fact that Miller's first thoughts were to play down the seriousness of the situation shocked him greatly. It wasn't long before these peculiar, irrational thoughts subsided and the full weight of the situation came crashing down. In a professional sense, there was literally nothing that Miller feared other than the fall-out surrounding the name that Tommy McKinlay had sent via text message.

The text notification sounded again. Miller was holding the phone by his side as he stared vacantly ahead at the shower unit. He was in no hurry to read the message, it was only going to be McKinlay, gloating after landing his explosive blow. As Miller stared straight ahead at the glass door of the shower, trying desperately to shake off the feeling of shock and impending doom, another text message sounded. Miller lifted the phone and looked at it. Sure enough, McKinlay had text, but his message was concealed by a newer one, the one which had just been received. It was from Dixon.

"Andy, phone me as soon as possible." Was all it said. Miller went to press the phone icon at the top of the message but realised before he did so that he couldn't discuss this over the phone. Not this phone anyway. If Tommy had his number, he had no idea whether the gangster had managed to get his phone tapped but he suspected that he would have done. People like Tommy McKinlay knew the right people who can make anything happen. Miller stood and opened the bathroom door quietly, trying not to disturb the twins who were both asleep on the bunkbeds by the side of the door. He sneaked across to where Clare was sitting on the double bed. She still looked stressed and worried about the day's events, the glass of Malbec that Miller had ordered for her sat untouched on the bedside table. Miller whispered as he reached his wife.

"Can I borrow your phone a minute please love?"

Clare didn't reply, she just lifted her phone off the bed and handed it to her husband.

"Cheers." Miller sat down on the bed beside Clare and opened her text messages. He started writing a text and then looked at his own phone for Dixon's number. He typed it in and checked the message covered everything.

"Sir, it's Miller, this is Clare's phone. Need to speak privately and urgently. Can you come here ASAP please? Andy."

Happy with the message, Miller clicked the send button and looked across at his wife.

"Are you alright, love?" As he said it, he knew it was a stupid question.

"Will you stop asking me if I'm alright Andy? Seriously. You're really doing my head in." She shot him an icy look. "This is the least alright I've ever been. If you ask me one more time I'm going to go and get that gun from the officer outside and shoot you in the mouth with it."

Miller looked down at the floor. He already knew that Clare wasn't alright, and he couldn't understand or explain why he kept asking her if she was. Her whole life had just been turned upside down, the kids had been threatened in the most violent manner and she wasn't allowed to go home. She was stuck in a stuffy hotel room thirty miles away from home with armed police guarding the door, forbidden from moving beyond these four walls. Clare Miller was far from alright.

"I've text Dixon, he'll be here soon and we'll come up with a plan. I know its shit Clare, but everything will be fine. Just trust me."

"I do trust you Andy. But you're not the one who's..." Clare's voice broke as she started crying. She couldn't repeat the details of this horrendous day. The adrenaline had been surging through her body earlier, the shock of everything had been absorbed by the energy and the urgency of events as they unfolded. But now, trapped in this hotel room with the kids finally asleep, the full, harrowing situation had begun replaying in her mind, the scary, confusing scenes at the school. That horrible bloke who'd been staring at her through her windscreen. The things that he'd said to her. Having to take the kids out of school with armed police guarding them. It was all replaying over and over in her mind and her nerves were shot to pieces.

Clare's phone pinged in Miller's hands. He looked away from his wife and read the message. "Okay Andy, on my way." As he read the message, Miller was reminded of the seriousness of his own situation. This nightmare that Clare was having was nothing in comparison to the shit which was thundering his way. The situation regarding Clare and the kids was awful, there was no mistake about it. But there were literally dozens of solutions to that particular situation. Miller didn't feel too stressed if problems had obvious and practical answers, so despite the intimidating nature of the situation regarding Clare and the kids, Miller was confident that there were plenty of suitable options available. He just wished he could think of a solution to the shitstorm that Tommy McKinlay was brewing. That was the real cause for concern in Miller's mind right now, but he couldn't say anything about that to Clare.

"What's Debs been saying?" Asked Miller, regarding Clare's best mate Debbie who'd been in constant conversation with his wife via phone and text since lunch-time.

"She wants to come and sit with me but I'm not sure I can face it."

"Tell her to come. I'm going to be talking to Dixon anyway, it'll do you good."

"I'm not sure, Andy."

"Come on Clare, there's no-one better to take your mind off this. Tell her to pack an overnight bag. I'll get a police car to pick her up."

Clare just stared dispassionately ahead.

"I'll ring her if you want?"

"And say what?"

"I don't know. I'll just say that you are upset and need a mate."

Clare let out a huge gust of air.

"Clare, you'd be round at hers like a shot if the shoe was on the other foot."

"Well, if you're going to be speaking to Dixon, I guess I'd better had. You've already left me here for hours on my own."

"I'm sorry, Clare…"

"Pass me my phone then, you stupid dick."

Chapter Twenty-Three

By the time Dixon had arrived at the Tickled Trout, Clare's mate Debbie was on her way in the back of a police car.

"Listen, Clare, I might be some time with Dixon. There's a lot to discuss about this situation."

"Yes, I know Andy."

"So, all I'm saying is, just try your best to chill out with Debs. I'll be working out a solution to this, so we can forget all about it. Okay?"

"Yes, Andy, whatever." Clare didn't make eye contact with her husband but he was acutely aware that he wasn't flavour of the month. He didn't blame Clare for taking her anger and frustration out on him, but it was starting to get on his tits a bit now.

"Kiss?"

Clare looked up at her husband and blew him one.

"That'll do. I'll see you in a bit. Debs can kip in there with you, I'll sort something out on the floor. See you in a bit."

"Yes, seeya."

Miller stood up from the bed and walked silently to the door. He was quite disappointed that Clare was giving him a hard time like this, but he didn't dwell on it too much as he explained to the armed officer at the door that he was going to meet DCS Dixon in the car park. It was clear from the officer's reaction that he had already been informed of this development as he nodded and thanked Miller for the update.

Miller followed the maze of corridors until he reached the stairs and raced down them two by two. He couldn't wait to share the burden of McKinlay's activities with his boss. The man whose shitty, inexcusable behaviour had led to the nightmare that Miller now faced. It was going to be a genuine relief to unload this heavy parcel of shit onto the lap of the man who'd created it.

Dixon looked nervous as Miller jogged across the car park and jumped into the passenger seat.

"Sir."

"Andy."

"We've got a problem."

"Serious?"

"About as serious as anything you can possibly imagine."

Dixon seemed uncharacteristically nervous. He knew that Miller wasn't one for exaggerating. His DCI never over-egged things, so his brief statement troubled the DCS greatly.

"Go on."

"We're pretty fucked. Sir."

Over the next fifteen minutes, Miller relayed the details of his conversation with McKinlay, stopping only briefly for a couple of minutes while he escorted Debbie up to the hotel room when the Salford division patrol car arrived.

Once Miller had finished, Dixon sat and considered the information in silence for a few minutes. Typically, the DCS sounded calm and collected as he summed up his understanding of the situation. "So, basically, McKinlay wants us to unearth some new evidence which proves that he wasn't responsible for the crimes he's been charged with?"

"Well, yes, that's the crux of it. He wants Marco MacDowell framing for them, which is simple enough to do in theory."

"But..."

Dixon's cold and calm manner had been irritating Miller for some minutes now. But his superiors blasé 'but' comment had pushed the DCI too far.

"But what?" Miller's tone was harsh and lacked respect. He hadn't quite snapped, but Dixon knew that Miller was getting close to it. He knew where this was heading now and started back-tracking slightly.

"Well Andy, all things considered, it seems to me that McKinlay needs to hear some comforting words. We'll... no, *you'll* tell him that we will comply with his demands."

"Are you taking the piss? If we agree to this, we'll never be able to shake McKinlay off. He'll have more authority over us than the fucking Chief Constable."

"I know. Listen, Andy, can you take a deep breath

please? I didn't say that we would let him out. I said we will tell him that we're working on it, while we figure out a way to contain this situation."

"Dangerous."

"More or less dangerous than McKinlay spilling the beans about George Dawson?"

"Well... its... none of this makes any sense. How the fuck does he know anything about Dawson anyway?" Miller was speaking to himself more than Dixon. It was a rhetorical question.

"There was always a risk of this Andy. We both knew it."

"No, sir. Sorry, but there was never a fucking risk of one of the north's biggest gangsters blackmailing us about George Dawson. Something is very seriously wrong here."

"In what way?"

"In the way that there are only a few people who know about what went on with George Dawson." Miller held his hand up and bent his thumb back. "One. George Dawson. Two, me," Miller bent his index finger back and continued counting on his fingers as he went through the names of the people who were fully aware of the situation. "You, Saunders, Chapman, Worthington, Dawson's daughter, Sykes' wife. That's nine people. Who else?"

Dixon didn't reply, he just exhaled loudly.

"Sir?"

"I don't know, Andy. There could be any number of people who knew that Dawson was the killer. Apparently the whole street was out when the shooting happened. They'd all known Saunders was carrying out surveillance on Dawson's address. We could be talking about hundreds of people. Potentially."

"Bollocks! Why would anybody start stirring up shit for Dawson now? They'd have been straight onto the press that day. That kind of story is worth a cheque for a million pounds, we both know that. There's more to this. And it goes deeper than some neighbour gossiping. Think about it. Somebody like Tommy McKinlay is not going to start acting like the big bollocks on the back of some innuendo. The public inquiry case we presented against Sykes was solid, it was easy to pin all of the killings on him, we had his phone tampering credentials backed up. We even had neighbours and relatives testifying against him in court. His fucking widow gave evidence. It was all sewn up. McKinlay knows something from the inside."

"What? You mean a member of the team has gone rogue?"

"Not *my* team. But potentially somebody upstairs. On *your* team."

"Bollocks Andy. Your imagination is running away here. Only a couple of senior officers were ever privy to this, the former Chief Constable and perhaps an assistant. They'd be liable to prosecution as well. It's not come from the police."

"Where, then? Who has given Dawson's name to McKinlay?"

"Andy, I don't know. But in reality, this is precisely what I warned you about."

Miller turned to his boss and stared at him, his face had turned violet in an instant. "Seriously, Sir? Are you attempting to use this as a told-you-so opportunity? You seem to forget that if you hadn't been such a snide about this case, James Ellis would still have a fucking mother."

Dixon had learnt many times that Miller had a sharp tongue on him, and that remark was a timely reminder of just how sharp and cutting it could be.

"Anyway, we both know where we stand on this. There's no point going over it again tonight. Let's focus on the really important issue."

"What's that Andy?" Asked Dixon, with a wobble in his voice. He sounded hurt from the Ellis comment. It was still a very raw wound for both men. Despite three years passing since the tragic events of that devastating summer's day in Little Lever, it didn't get any easier.

"We have all the time in the world to go over the mistakes and downright lies that led to Karen's death. But for tonight, we need to think about getting Clare and the kids out of the way until this shitstorm has passed."

"What are your thoughts, Andy?"

"My thoughts are that she travels to Jersey with her mate and the kids and stays there indefinitely until this is officially sorted. One way or the other."

"Jersey?"

"Yes. Our favourite hotel's there. It's where we had our honeymoon. It will be the perfect tonic to take her mind off the fact that a death-threat against her babies was received by their school this morning." Miller let a heavy silence hang in order to remind Dixon of the seriousness of this situation. "So I need tickets onto the earliest flight tomorrow and I need the Jersey police fully aware of the situation. My family will need their protection."

"I'm sure that we can organise all of that, Andy."

"Good. Okay, well I'll let you get on." Miller shuffled in his seat and grabbed a bunch of keys from his jacket pocket. He began unthreading a key from the ring. "This is the front door key for my house. Give it to Saunders as soon as you can and tell him to ring me on Clare's phone when he's at my house. I'll tell him where everything is, passports and stuff."

"You won't need passports for Jersey, Andy."

"We don't know which way she's going yet, do we? It might be best to go via France or Portugal, just in case one of McKinlay's team are keeping tabs on us. It's not beyond the realms of possibility, is it?"

"Given the circumstances, no. I guess not."

"You've a lot to sort out, so I'll let you get on. As soon as I know that my family are completely safe and out of harm's way, I'll start working on a way of making this nightmare go away."

Miller opened the car door and stepped out of Dixon's vehicle before crouching slightly and turning to face his boss. "Oh, and I don't want this matter discussing with anybody else, not even those I mentioned earlier. I need to tell those involved what's happening myself, in my own way and in my own time, so not a word. Okay?"

"Of course Andy, it goes without saying."

"Good. Try your best to book the Saint Brelades Bay

hotel if you can. The happier Clare is, the more I can focus on this. Finally, don't contact me again via my work phone. I'll need a new handset and number tomorrow so stick that on your to-do list. There's every chance McKinlay's people will be intercepting my messages and calls. God knows how he got hold of my mobile number or how long he's had it. Okay, I think that's all for now. See you later."

Miller stood by the hotel's doors as Dixon drove out of the car park and back towards the M6 motorway. He felt slightly bad for rubbing Dixon's face in the dogshit again over Ellis. But there was no time for dwelling on that right now. As bad as it was for all concerned, it still remained a fact that Karen Ellis would still be here today if it wasn't for Dixon's cack-handed management of the Pop case. The truth has a nasty habit of hurting, and there was nothing that Miller could do to alter the truth. He did recognise that he ought to be a little more sensitive with these kinds of things though. It was no secret that Dixon had been to hell and back over the outcome of his decisions three years ago. But all that was something Miller could feel bad about later, he had more important things to think about in the meantime.

Chapter Twenty-Four

"Alright? Kids still sleeping?"

"Hi Andy, yeah, they're snoring their heads off. You okay mate?" Asked Debbie as Miller entered the hotel room. She had a sympathetic look on her face. Clare still looked like she was struggling to come to terms with the day's events, her usual warmth was missing, she just looked lost.

"Hello again Debs. I'm getting there, just been working on some plans to help us through this."

"Well if the plans involve me and the kids staying in this hotel room again then you need to revise them!" Clare wasn't joking.

"She feels like a prisoner in here Andy." Said Debbie, backing her mate up.

"I know. I know, I bet. I've just organised for you to get away, properly away while we get this mess sorted out."

Debs smiled encouragingly and placed her hand on Clare's shoulder.

"But you're not coming?" Asked Clare, the question so loaded with anger that Debs pulled an awkward face for Miller's benefit.

"Listen, calm it a sec. I've just organised for you and the kids to stay in Jersey, indefinitely, until I can get this sorted."

"On my own?"

"No, I've thought of that. Obviously, I need to be here, but I've arranged for you to have someone with you. I thought Debs might want to come for a bit, then we can get your mum and dad out, then anything you want. Plus, I'll be coming and going as much as possible. What do you reckon Debs?"

"Well... yeah, I'm up for that. Work might not be though..."

"It'll qualify as compassionate leave Debs, leave that to me, I can pull the strings."

"What do you mean?"

"I'll ring your work and explain that you're assisting the police..."

"Wait. That makes it sound like I've been involved in something dodgy!"

"Nah, don't be daft. You'll be the talk of the place, everyone will be green with envy. I'll make sure any losses of wages are covered and that. It'll be an all expenses paid do, won't cost you a penny and I'll square it all off with your bosses. You can even take stuff from the mini-bar, then ring down and ask them to restock it! So what do you reckon?"

"Yeah, I'm up for it. Definitely."

Miller could tell that Debbie was absolutely thrilled but she was keeping a lid on it, under the circumstances.

"Clare?"

"Well, I was going to give you a mouthful if you were sending me on my own. But if Debs is coming, that's perfect." Clare smiled for the first time today.

"It's not just because it's your favourite place, love. It's also the safest place I can think of."

"Jersey?" Asked Debbie.

"Oh yes. It's safe as houses. Curtis Warren was in jail there, you know the big Liverpool drug baron?"

"Really?"

"Yes, it's not a place that you can get in or out of easily without the authorities knowing everything about you."

"Sounds great. Is Jim Bergerac still running things there?" Asked Debbie and Clare laughed loudly. It was a great sight for Miller to see the tension and fear finally subsiding.

"Seriously though. You'll be in the safest part of Great Britain, with the Jersey coppers looking after you. I'll come over as much as I can, its only an hour flight. It's the best solution to this mess."

"For now, Andy."

"Yes, yes of course. It won't be for long."

Clare looked a little brighter than she had done. She wasn't exactly doing cart-wheels but Miller could see that the announcement had brought a big sense of relief to her.

"So what the F is actually going on Andy? What was all that about today?" Debbie was dying to understand what all of this terror had been about, desperate to know why her normally outgoing and confident mate had been reduced to a bag of nerves.

"It's just bad luck really. Basically, some gangster reckons he can blackmail the police and get us to falsify some criminal charges he's facing so he'll be released from jail. All this carry-on today was just to show us that he's serious."

"Really?" It was Clare who asked, the look of shock and anger on her face left Debbie and Andy under no illusion of what she thought of the man responsible.

"Yes. He's basically set up that stunt today, scaring you and putting the school on terror alert, just so he could get a face to face meeting with me."

"Seriously?"

"Yes. Unfortunately. He was acting the Billy big bollocks as well, smirking at me and talking to me like I'm shit. The weirdest part is, it wasn't even my department that has been after him." Miller was only supplying part of the story, but neither Clare or Debbie would have ever guessed, he was very convincing.

"So why is he singling you out?" Asked Debbie.

"Well, you know. I'm kind of a big deal..." Miller waited for a laugh to his big-headed remark but it wasn't forthcoming and he felt quite stupid.

"God, the mind boggles."

"It's scary, no two ways about it – but that's what he was trying to do. Scare us into agreeing to his dickhead demands. So anyway, I've gone along with it and now he thinks everything's going his way. And as soon as you lot have touched down in Jersey, I can start making him realise that he's just made the biggest mistake of his life. One thing's for sure, he'll never try anything like this again. Nobody will."

Clare seemed captivated by her husband's explanation of this horrendous day's activities and pleased to hear that he was tackling it head-on in his usual no-nonsense style. But there was a lack of something in his voice which troubled her. She couldn't quite put her finger on it, but her husband sounded uncharacteristically nervous.

"Are you sure about this, Andy?"

"What... yes, course I'm sure about it. What do you mean?" Miller was surprised by Clare's question. It was unlike her to say something like that.

"Just, I don't know... this prisoner obviously has some connections outside the prison. Like that horrible bastard who threatened me this morning."

"Look, Clare... that little rat will be a junkie from the nearby estate. He'll have threatened you in return for a bag of spice or whatever. I'm not trying to play it down, I know it was scary and personal. But..."

"But what, Andy?"

"But, you just have to trust me. As soon as you lot are on that plane and out of the way of the slightest risk of intimidation, I'll get this sorted out properly. Okay?"

"Okay. But, another thing that's really pissing me off..."

"What's that love?"

"Am I cock-eyed?"

Chapter Twenty-Five

Tommy McKinlay saw the light green glow of his phone as he neared the end of his 100 press-ups. He continued with the last of them before springing up onto his feet. Nothing interrupted his daily fitness routines, not even a text message from the copper he had just started blackmailing.

But the message wasn't from Miller. It was from Nerd, one of his employees. "Boss, Miller hasn't used his phone since you texted him. He's had a few texts off other people, including one from his gaffer but hasn't replied to any of them so I think he's sussed that we're monitoring his number."

Tommy smiled widely. This was good and bad news, it meant that he'd definitely rattled Miller's cage, but it also meant that the ability to keep tabs on his text messages and call logs was now looking doubtful. Tommy began typing a reply on the tiny mobile phone which he kept stored in a very personal place. As the phone was so small, it was also very basic and writing text messages took a long time, each letter having to be selected from one of the number keys like in the old days. "Be a shame if we can't follow his calls and texts for now but not to worry, we're in the driving seat now. Keep me posted Nerd. TM."

Tommy checked his messages again and was disappointed to see that Miller had basically blanked his two messages. That wasn't the reaction Tommy had anticipated. He thought that Miller would be firing off all sorts of messages, starting with something along the lines of "how the fuck do you know about George Dawson?"

But never-the-less, things were going in the right direction as far as Tommy McKinlay was concerned. There was no way that the DCI would be able to wriggle his way out of this. Miller will have no option but to look into his case and cook up some new evidence which places Marco at the scene of each crime. It was going to be easy work for Miller, after all Marco had been a virtual recluse who'd spent most of his time locked away in his old mill. Sticking Marco at any crime-scene would be a piece of piss as there is literally nobody who would come forward and challenge the evidence and there certainly wouldn't be any conflicting evidence of Marco being elsewhere due to the fact that he spent ninety-nine per cent of his time hidden from the world behind his fortress walls.

Tommy decided to send one last text to Miller before turning in for the night. "Not had a reply from you yet Miller. If you've received my text messages, can you acknowledge them before things start to get out of hand?"

Once the message had sent, Tommy decided to give Miller a few minutes to respond. He passed the time doing one hundred sit-ups.

Chapter Twenty-Six

The twins had been amazing this evening, sleeping throughout the conversations and occasional laughter between Andy, Clare and Debbie. Despite the anxiety and terror that had been felt by their parents throughout this horrendous day, the kids seemed completely oblivious, thankfully. The ladies had managed to polish off a couple of bottles of plonk, which had certainly helped to relax Clare a bit. The highlight of the evening, if you could call it that, was the high-pitched laughter from Debbie, when Clare had asked, in all seriousness, if she really was cock-eyed.

But now, as the clock neared 1am, the tiredness was beginning to take over and the silences between conversations were becoming longer. Debbie and Clare were in the big double bed and Miller had thrown the spare duvet on the floor. He was glad to finally hear Clare's breathing gradually become slower and louder, a sure sign that she was almost asleep. Now, finally, Miller could enjoy some peace and quiet and try to get his head around the events of the day and more importantly, try and work out some kind of a game-plan going forwards. He'd already decided what needed to happen with McKinlay. The thought had crossed his mind earlier while Debbie and Clare were talking about Jersey and Clare was telling her friend all about the tiny British island just off the French coast. Miller had been thinking about this potential solution to his immediate problems for the past couple of hours and the longer he'd thought about it, the more sense it made.

Miller had been in touch with his right-hand man, DI Saunders using Clare's phone. Between himself and Clare they had talked the DI through the packing. Saunders eventually left the Miller household with two large suitcases packed with Clare's and the twins things for a fortnight in Jersey. Miller had told Saunders to keep this matter private until he had chance to speak to the rest of his team tomorrow at some point. By private, Saunders knew that he wasn't to utter a word about it to anybody, not even his girlfriend who was also a member of the SCIU department, DC Helen Grant.

DCS Dixon had been extremely abrupt when he'd handed the Miller's house keys to Saunders, telling the DI to communicate with Miller via Clare's mobile. Other than that, the most senior member of the SCIU team had remained tight-lipped about what was going on, so Saunders knew that whatever it was that was going on, it was something very serious indeed.

The thing which was causing Miller more concern than anything else was the mention of George Dawson. Miller had had no dealings with the man since he'd told him to drive away from Winter Hill on that hot summers evening three years earlier. In all honesty, Miller had hoped that he would never have to see or speak to him again, he'd always imagined that if he did ever see Dawson again, it would be in a Crown Court setting where both men would be facing lengthy prison sentences.

The text message that Tommy McKinlay had sent earlier was a game-changer and Miller knew that he faced little alternative but to dig the past up and go over everything again. The matter which McKinlay had brought up had come as a great shock, there was no getting away from it.

Miller had been aware of various rumours and conspiracy theories regarding the Pop case. There had been a number of online articles by amateur detectives which suggested that there was a lot more to the story than had come out in the news. And to their credit, these bloggers and online journalists were absolutely spot on. There was a hell of a lot more to the story than had ever been made public. But the details that these conspiracy theorists were seemingly unaware of were the juiciest bits. The focus of their articles were simply based on a series of things "that just didn't add up" in the Pop case. There was nothing concrete, no direct accusations or specific details as such, just vague but persistent suggestions that the man whose car had been involved in the well-publicised crash which led to the death of Acting DCI Karen Ellis had had a far greater involvement in the crimes than the police had realised.

There were some sensational accusations of ineptitude being levelled at the police. Specifically that Peter Sykes, the man who had killed himself on Winter Hill as he was about to be arrested and was later revealed to be "Pop" was apparently shopping in Manchester with his wife on the day that Pop murdered three paedophiles around the Greater Manchester area and there was CCTV footage to prove it. There were a couple of similar threads on the internet, stating that there was no way that "Pop" was working alone and that as many as five people were involved in the murderous campaign against convicted paedophiles. Another strong conspiracy theory centred around Peter Sykes' voice. A recording claiming to be the voice of Peter Sykes was uploaded onto a website called Hard Truths. It was placed alongside a recording of Pop's phone interview with Sky News. It was obvious that the recordings were of two completely different people, with different vocal frequencies, accents and pitch. The author of the post said that the variations were so different, it was like trying to compare Darth Vader's voice to Joe Pasquale's.

But as time went on, Miller satisfied himself that nobody was really taking any of these blogs seriously. It was just like any other conspiracy theory – such as the one about the IRA bombing of Manchester in 1996 being organised by the council so that they could redevelop a troublesome area of the city centre in time for the Commonwealth Games in 2002. This, the conspiracy theorists claim, is the reason that nobody was ever charged with planting the biggest truck-bomb ever seen on British soil which destroyed the city centre in two seconds. There were plenty of people pushing that conspiracy theory online and nobody was taking that one seriously, either.

Miller had endured more than a few sleepless nights over the past few years, worrying about these types of amateur news articles. It was never in question that if the truth were to come out about Pop, and Miller's handling of the aftermath, he'd be going to prison for a very long time and so would most of his team, and so would his boss if not countless other members of the British establishment.

But time continued to go on, and it transpired that no

serious news people were taking any notice of the online blogs and articles, Miller's sleeping patterns eventually returned to normal.

The overriding concern now was the mention of George Dawson's name. It had never come up before, and now that it had, it opened a myriad of problems for Miller. Once a genie like this gets out of the bottle, it's very hard if not impossible to put it back in. Never-the-less, if Miller wanted to remain a police officer, and watch the twins grow up, he knew that he had little option but to try and get that genie back in its bottle, come what may. It was going to be a big ask, but he felt that it was achievable. He just needed Tommy McKinlay out of the picture, and he needed to know who the people were who had put the fear of God into his wife. Those two matters were at the very top of Miller's to-do list as he lay on the hotel room floor, shocked and disturbed by how loudly Debbie snored.

Just as he felt that he might be able to drift off for a few hours sleep, Miller's phone lit up the room as a text message was received. It was from McKinlay, a passive-aggressive demand for a reply from the DCI.

Miller considered his options and decided that he would ignore the text and keep McKinlay guessing for tonight. He was certainly going to be receiving news from Miller, news which would not be very welcome. Miller smiled as he remembered a phrase that McKinlay had used rather cockily in the deserted Strangeways prison yard several hours earlier and repeated it quietly to himself. "All in good time, Tommy. All in good time."

Chapter Twenty-Seven

SATURDAY

Miller had set his alarm for 6am but Molly, his daughter had beaten the phone to it as she squatted down beside his head and whispered "Daddy, Daddy, Daddy," over and over again next to his ear. Miller smiled as the incessant appeal for attention continued.

"What's up Molly?" He asked, wrapping his arm around his little girl and pulling her onto his chest for a cuddle.

"Why are you sleeping on this floor?" She asked, the tone of her voice suggesting that she wasn't best pleased.

"Because Debbie's in bed with mum," whispered Miller.

"Debbie? Debbie's here?" Asked Molly, her head springing up and looking onto the bed. "Why?"

"We had a party last night!"

"A party! Daddy!" Molly didn't seem impressed and Miller laughed loudly before remembering that it was half past five in the morning.

"Why wasn't I allowed into the party?"

"You were asleep darling."

"Asleep?" Miller's six-year old looked astonished.

"Yes!"

"What was the party for?" Molly started stroking Miller's bristles on his chin, which reminded him that he had nothing to shave with.

"I'm not telling you."

"Yes. Tell me!"

"Nope. You'll tell everybody!"

"I wouldn't!"

"Promise?"

"Pinky promise." Molly held out her little finger and Miller held out his. They shook on the pinky promise.

"We were celebrating."

"Celebrating?"

"Yes, because guess what."

"What?"

"You're going on holiday!"

"Holiday?"

"Andy! Can you shut up mate? Trying to sleep." Said Debbie, in a very grumpy, hung-over voice.

Miller and Molly laughed quietly before the questions started again.

"Can I tell Leo?" She whispered.

"No, not yet darling, let's wait until he's awake, shall we?"

"Okay daddy."

"Okay Molly."

Molly started giggling and held her hands over her mouth as she did, which made Miller laugh.

"Andy! Will you pack it in?" It was Clare's voice this time. She sounded even grumpier and more hung-over than Debs.

"Moody mummy!" Said Molly, quite loudly, which made Miller and Debbie laugh, though Debbie followed it with a request.

"Ah! Don't make me laugh Molly! My head hurts!"

All of this activity had disturbed Leo who sprang out of bed and stood by his father's head. "Daddy, why are you on the floor?"

Molly replied on Miller's behalf. "Because mummy and Debbie are in the bed. Derr!"

Leo looked confused and rubbed his eyes.

"Come and give me a cuddle mate," said Miller, stretching his arms out. Leo fell onto his dad and laughed as Molly scrambled out of the way.

"Andy, seriously. What are you doing getting everyone giddy at this time of the night?"

"We're going on holiday!" Said Molly.

"Are we? Holiday?" Asked Leo, his face had lit up as though it was Christmas morning. "Yesss!" He said as he clenched his fist.

"Yes, we are. So, let's all get up and ready for the airport."

"What, now?" Asked Clare. "What time is it?"

"It's half five."

"Do we have to go now?"

"No, after you've had the brew I'm about to make you. How do you like yours Debs?"

"I'm alright thanks Andy. Just a glass of water please."

"You don't want a coffee? It'll sort your hangover out!" Miller got to his feet and opened the curtains.

"Nah, I don't use hotel kettles, thanks."

Miller stood and faced his wife and her friend. He looked confused and the twins were giggling at their dad's weird expression.

"Wait. What do you mean, you don't use hotel kettles? I think that's the weirdest thing I've ever heard in my entire life Deborah!"

The twins laughed loudly again. They loved it when their dad was being cheeky to people like this.

Debbie smiled and sat up slightly in the bed, her eyes trying to adjust to the Preston sunlight which was burning through the thick net curtains. "I saw this secret survey that a major hotel chain did. It was an anonymous honesty thing to see how their customers behaved in their rooms. It was aimed at their most frequent users. They asked all of the business people who stayed in their hotels a series of questions, you know, to try and improve the service and all that."

"Right?" Miller started filling the kettle from the bathroom sink as Debbie continued.

"So, anyway, one of the questions was, and I swear I never knew that this was a thing until I read this…"

"Go on?"

"Well, the question was, 'do you ever use the hotel kettle to boil your underwear?"

"What?" Asked Clare, who'd been trying to snooze through all of this. She sounded shocked at first but then laughed as she imagined somebody popping their knickers in the kettle.

"Honestly, that was one of the questions."

"Oh my God, what the hell?" Miller came back holding the kettle.

"Over seventy per-cent of them answered yes!"

"Aw, that's... what the..."

"I'm going to be sick! Please shut up!" Said Clare, which made the twins laugh loudly even though they hadn't been paying much attention to Debbie's story as they were gossiping amongst themselves about the wonders of going on holiday.

"But there was worse to come. The next question was one of those multi-choice ones, which asked if they did it occasionally, sometimes, often or always. They all ticked always!"

Miller just stood there holding the kettle, his mouth was wide open. Debbie and Clare laughed as he did a retch sound.

"Why would somebody do that?" Asked Clare after a few moments.

"To wash their gruds I suppose," said Miller. "It's a repugnant thing to do but I must say, its bordering on genius. The amount of times I've had to go commando after an unexpected night in a hotel..."

"Okay Andy, I think that's plenty." Said Debbie, before copying Miller's retch sound.

Clare was laughing hysterically. "It's true, he keeps an overnight bag in the boot of the car these days."

"And all the while, I could have just boiled them in the kettle and hung them on the radiator. So, just a glass of water Debs?"

"Yes please."

"Me too Andy."

Miller went back into the bathroom and ran the tap before returning with two glasses of water which he handed to his wife and her best mate.

"Cleaning your pants in a kettle though. Every day is a school day!"

Molly and Leo looked up at their dad with sad eyes.

"I thought we were going on holiday?" Asked Leo.

"Yes, don't you worry mate," said Miller as he lifted Leo up and gave him a hug. "We need to get organised, our lift is coming at half-past-six."

Chapter Twenty-Eight

At 6.30 am the Miller family were informed that the lift had arrived. Miller went outside to speak to the police driver and see what plans Dixon had organised. He was handed a sealed envelope. The handwriting instantly recognisable as Dixon's, Miller had taken the piss out of the scrawl many times over the years.

Inside the envelope was the family's itinerary for the day. Starting at 6.30am, the Millers were to be collected from the Tickled Trout and driven south to Luton Airport, where they would catch the 15.05 direct flight to Jersey. Dixon had stipulated the timings for the journey, which would be unusually longer than usual to allow for a couple of tactical "double-backs" to ensure that the vehicle was not being followed. It was highly unlikely that anybody from McKinlay's camp would even know that the Miller's had spent the night in Preston, but Dixon was clearly not taking any chances.

The double-backs were to be performed at the driver's discretion and would involve leaving the M6 southbound motorway and heading northbound before re-joining the southbound carriageway again. This was scheduled to take place at least twice so that officers in the trailing ARU vehicle could monitor all traffic following. This detail brought a huge sense of relief to Miller, who was pleased that the safety of his family was being taken so seriously by the force.

Upon arrival at Luton, the family would be greeted by armed officers from Bedfordshire police who would manage their safety until they boarded their flight under false names. The Miller's would be known as Carole, Lee and Milly Chadwick throughout this operation. Debbie was going to be known as Deidre Green for the duration. Dixon had tried to keep the kids names as close as possible to make it easier for them, along with providing a few tips on how to manage the youngsters understanding of what was required of them under their new assumed identities. Upon arrival at Jersey airport after a forty-five minute flight, States of Jersey Police officers would take responsibility for safeguarding the family. Miller was pleased to learn that there had been availability at St Brelades Bay Hotel, which was Clare's favourite place in the world. He hadn't anticipated that, the place is usually booked up all year round. The booking was for a fortnight and had the potential for extension beyond that.

Miller thanked the driver and then walked to the ARU vehicle which was parked nearby and explained that he would be down in a few minutes with his family. He felt remarkably calm as he walked back inside the hotel, the level of detail in the itinerary had really set his mind at ease regarding the safety of his family. He thanked the armed officer at the door as he entered the room.

"Right, guys, are we all sorted? Teeth brushed?"

"Yes!" Said the twins excitedly.

"What about you mummy?" asked Miller, making the children laugh loudly. "What about you Deborah?" The second question made Leo and Molly laugh even louder.

"Right, guys, I want to play a game with you, okay?" Miller got down on his knees as the twins stood before him. They looked excited to hear more about this game.

"The game is called the secret holiday game!"

The kids looked incredibly excited.

"And on the secret holiday, you have to have new, secret names. Otherwise it isn't a secret anymore and the holiday is ruined and everybody feels sad. Okay?"

Leo and Molly Miller were loving this, they nodded enthusiastically.

"Your secret name is Lee!" Said Miller, tapping his son on the head. "And I don't know what you're laughing at... Milly!"

This announcement was met with a great laugh. "Lee and Milly... Chadwick!" Once again, the kids erupted, they thought this was the funniest thing they had ever heard. "Mummy's got a secret holiday name too, do you want to know what it is?"

"Yes! Yes!" Squealed the kids, jumping up and down on the spot. Clare made an uncomfortable face which made Miller and Debbie laugh as well.

"Carole Chadwick!"

"Well, that's not too bad I suppose, could be worse." Said Clare once the twins had settled down.

"And Lee, Milly and Carole will be joined on this secret holiday by Deidre Green!"

Miller's hilarious announcement had sent the twins to another planet, they looked as though they had never heard of anything so funny in their lives before.

"Okay, well, your lift is outside so... does anybody need a wee?"

The toilet trips were all sorted out and Lee, Milly, Carole and Deidre were led out of the hotel room and into the car.

"Seatbelts on guys, thank you."

"I'm Lee!" Said Leo, throwing his head back as he laughed at the funny name he'd been given.

Miller turned to Clare and gave her a kiss. "I'll probably get over tonight, but if not, it'll be tomorrow. Okay?"

"Promise?" Said Clare, suddenly she looked quite nervous.

"I promise. Now listen, this is the safest you have ever been in your life. I just need your phone now, it's literally the only vulnerability we have."

Clare unzipped her handbag and handed the phone to her husband. "Cheers. I'll arrange for Jersey police to have a new phone waiting for you at St Brelades."

"Are we staying at St Brelades?" Asked Claire, thrilled to hear this excellent news.

"Yes, so listen, you've got a crappy day of travelling ahead, you're flying from Luton. But it'll be worth it when you're in Jersey for your tea."

"Luton?"

"Yes... sorry not sorry. It's to ensure nobody is tracking you."

"Okay... well, its better safe than sorry and all that."
"Exactly."
"Thanks love. See you tonight then, or tomorrow."
"Definitely tomorrow, if not tonight. Love you."

"Love you too."

"Love you Lee, love you Milly."

The kids laughed hysterically again, this amazing joke wasn't wearing thin yet. "Love you, Deidre."

Chapter Twenty-Nine

By the time that Miller had reached his office just after 8am, his mind was filled with urgent tasks which needed to be carried out. This was going to be an extremely busy day and he was glad that Clare and the kids wouldn't be at home tonight as it was destined to be a late one. There was no way he'd be getting to Jersey, but he'd already put the feelers out about that and Clare had seemed okay with the idea of him coming tomorrow.

Miller's first task was to phone Debbie's work and explain the situation. This would be straight-forward enough, the news story regarding Worsley Green Primary School was on the front of several national newspapers this morning, so the groundwork for explaining the situation was done. In these circumstances, MCP would be able to recompense Debbie's employer if they needed to hire a temp to fill her position. This was going to make excellent office gossip, anyway.

The angle that the morning's press had gone for was regarding the "The £1,000,000 Hoax Call" alongside arial photographs which really captured the enormity of the police presence around the school at the height of the drama. Miller thought that it was quite a sensational headline, but when he considered the cost of the police operation, with the chopper up and all of the ARU involvement, he contemplated that it might be a reasonable guess at the cost. What these newspapers never explained though was that it would have cost exactly the same amount if nothing had happened at all the previous day and every officer was sat in the canteen playing cards or arm-wrestling. But that simple, mundane fact wouldn't sell very many newspapers.

Next, he had to organise a meeting with Dixon. After that, he would need to speak to all of the team members who had been involved in the Pop case, and who, through their involvement, were also facing the potential of a lengthy prison sentence if Tommy McKinlay's information ever became public. This aspect of the day's to-do list worried him more than any other, as far as he and the team were concerned, this was ancient history. Something that they had all made a pact to never speak about again. It was destined to be a very stressful conversation.

Miller also needed to meet with the team who had brought the charges against McKinlay. He needed to explain the situation, minus the George Dawson detail, to better understand the man's gangland empire and hopefully find out who the people were who were still doing his chores in the community.

Miller got the first phone-call out of the way. Debbie's boss was trying to be a bit of a dick about everything but Miller just asked him to tell his line-manager to call him back urgently. That settled it and Debbie's boss was soon towing the line and the call was concluded with a very insincere "and please, tell Debbie that she mustn't worry about a thing." Miller had learnt a long time ago that everybody has a superior. And if you ask to speak to them, the person who is standing in your way usually bottles out there and then through fear of their own judgement being put under the microscope. It had happened too many times in Miller's work to be a coincidence and he wondered why people were so shit-scared of their bosses. If anybody asked for Miller's boss, he'd be delighted that Dixon would actually have to do something for a change, even if it was only to field a phone call.

Miller scrubbed "Debs" off his list and lifted the phone again, this time to call Dixon. Saunders breezed through the door and sat down opposite his boss and began eavesdropping on the conversation.

"Morning Sir, it's Andy. Yes, just got into the office. Thanks for sorting everything out. They're on their way to the airport. Hopefully, I'll be joining them tomorrow and sleeping over. I know. Well we need to meet up as soon as possible. I'll bring Keith with me. Okay, thanks Sir." Miller hung up and looked across the desk.

"Morning Keith."

"Sir."

"We're in with Dixon in fifteen minutes. I'll tell you all you need to know in that meeting."

Saunders looked disappointed. He preferred his news to be delivered without a moment's delay.

"In the meantime, I'd better go and give the gang an update." Miller stood and headed around the desk, knowing that Saunders would be desperate to hear what all of yesterday's, and last night's weirdness was all about. But he could see from Miller's body-language and his stubbly face that he wasn't in the mood for any mithering.

"Morning everyone," said Miller as he approached his colleagues.

"Sir!"

"Morning Sir."

"How's Clare and the kids?" Asked Rudovsky.

"Yeah, they're alright thanks Jo. Clare was a bag of nerves last night but I've managed to calm her down with Malbec, cheese and some Scooby Doo impressions. Her and the twins have gone away for a few days now while I try and sort this mess out."

"That's probably for the best," said Rudovsky.

"Any idea what's going on?" Asked Kenyon.

"I've got a vague idea, Pete. It looks like somebody is trying to go above the law and wants to try and intimidate certain police officers. There are likely to be more of these incidents in the coming days, against other officers. I'll understand more as the day progresses, I'm in with the big cheese in ten minutes so I'm sure I'll have more to tell you all later. I just wanted to thank you for your messages of support yesterday, they were much appreciated by myself and Clare. It was a very frightening day."

"No problem, Sir." Said Grant.

"The day from hell!" Said Chapman.

"I don't know what was worse. The kids being evacuated from school by an armed unit or having to sleep in fucking Preston." Miller's gentle dig at Manchester's neighbouring city received a good laugh which eased the tension slightly.

"We were all stressed out enough here, God knows what you and Clare were going through. Sky News made a meal of it, we all thought the school was going to blow up at one point." Said Worthington.

"Oh, so now it's all coming out! You lot were watching telly instead of working were you?" Asked Miller with a sarcastic grin. "No, it was shit, but I'm just glad I've got Clare and the kids out of the picture now so I can get on and put this to bed. Anyway, thanks a lot guys, I really appreciate your support. I'll keep you all in the loop but in the meantime, can you just crack on with what you're working on and I'll speak to you all later, hopefully in a bit more detail. Cheers."

Miller looked over towards Saunders. "Keith, where's my motor?"

Saunders grabbed the keys off his desk and handed them to his boss. "Usual spot. I thought we were going to see Dixon now?"

"I know, but I'll need a quick shave. I've got some overnight stuff in my boot. You wouldn't be a love and go and grab it would you while I get my shit together?"

"Here Sir," Said Kenyon, opening his desk drawer. "Have a blast on this." He handed his electric razor across the desk.

"Top man Pete. Cheers."

Chapter Thirty

Miller had skilfully managed to condense his explanation of the situation regarding McKinlay into a five-minute briefing. It wasn't too difficult as the information was being relayed exclusively for Saunders, who already knew quite a lot of the back story regarding George Dawson.

Saunders looked thunderstruck. He also looked surprisingly irritated by the shock announcement and Miller sensed that this unfortunate situation had opened old wounds that were far from healed. He allowed his DI a few moments of quiet to let the information sink in. Miller was sympathetic to the magnitude of the announcement, it was only a matter of hours since he had experienced the same sense of shock and disbelief the previous evening whilst sitting on a hotel toilet seat. Saunders was just getting to grips with this bombshell in the stuffy, formal surroundings of Dixon's office.

After a long, thoughtful pause which was respected by both of his senior colleagues, Saunders finally spoke. "So, who actually knows about this?" The DI had turned a funny shade, the colour had washed from his face.

"The only people who are aware of this situation are sitting in this room."

"Really?" Saunders glanced up at Miller and held eye-contact. "How is that possible considering the performance last night with Armed Response driving you into Strangeways, then back up to Preston?" Saunders suspected that half-truths were clouding the bigger picture.

Miller exhaled loudly. "Alright Keith. Before we go any further, lets get something straight. Okay?"

Saunders stared at his boss. There had been a lot of bad blood between them surrounding the George Dawson case. A lot of bad blood. These two had almost ended up fighting in this very office in the hours following the death of Karen Ellis, the department's acting DCI at the time of her murder three years earlier. Miller had resigned from his position just days prior to this devastating event and Saunders had blamed him for the loss of Ellis, a point-blank shooting which Saunders had witnessed. Ellis wasn't just Saunders' boss, he had been madly in love with her, living his daily life with the heart palpitations and nervous smiles of an infatuated teen who was experiencing his first love. Following Karen Ellis's death, there were several months of very strained relations between Miller and Saunders. But after a late-night heart-to-heart conversation about the whole affair, both men had agreed to respect one another's point of view on the matter and try their best to put their opinions to one side and move on. Nothing was going to bring Karen Ellis back, that was something they certainly could agree on.

"Go on," said Saunders, without any of his usual warmth. This bizarre and completely unexpected visit to a very dark place in his mind was most uncomfortable for the DI and the moisture in his eyes revealed that he still struggled with the horrors of that day.

"Me and you made a pact that we would never keep secrets from one another. Do you remember?"

Saunders nodded. Their completely unplanned, spontaneous late-night meeting three-years earlier had been a game-changer for both men. The main pledge made by both of them was to be completely open and honest about everything in the future, regardless. It wasn't as though any lies had been told by either of them, but the loss of Karen Ellis, a colleague they both loved dearly, had come about because of lies. The mess that Miller found himself in today was a direct consequence of his personal reaction to those lies. Or at least that was Saunders' understanding of the situation. There were plenty of things that the DI didn't know about George Dawson and as far as Miller had been concerned, he'd always thought that it was for the best if he didn't know.

"Well with that promise in mind Keith, I want you to feel completely assured that everything I am saying to you is the total truth. So let's keep this real. Everybody in the force is probably aware that it was McKinlay who set that stunt up at the school yesterday. It's certainly well known that I was summoned to see him last night at the Big House. Obviously, somebody in the ARU has got a big mouth and you know how far the gossip spreads once tongues start wagging. But this information regarding the text message, and the mention of George Dawson, you are the only person to hear it other than the gaffer." Miller flicked his eyes away from Saunders and fixed his gaze on Dixon. "Have you mentioned it to anybody, Sir?"

Dixon shook his head sombrely. "No, of course I have not." The DCS seemed irritated by the question.

"What about Clare? What about Mrs Dixon?" Asked Saunders, aware that both men had wives that they regularly confided in.

"This subject has never been discussed, Keith. Ever. I've told Clare that a gangster in Strangeways is trying to make me falsify evidence to get him off his trial. That's all she knows." Said Miller.

"I've not spoken to my wife, or anybody about this matter Keith. It is beyond sensitive, as I'm sure you completely understand."

Saunders nodded. But he wasn't done. "So, in the grand scheme of things, who actually knows about George Dawson?"

Miller was about to reply but Saunders cut in on his own question. "I mean obviously, we don't have the definitive numbers in Dawson's community, on Avenham Close. I'm talking about in the police."

Miller looked at Dixon who had opened his mouth. "There were certain senior police officers..."

"Who?" Pressed Saunders.

"Well, steady on Keith. I'll answer as best I can but hold your horses and let me get a word in...."

"Sir, forgive me for getting a bit nervous here, but it sounds like I'm facing a pretty lengthy prison sentence because of this absolute clusterfuck."

"It won't come to that." Said Dixon, reassuringly.

"Who knows about Dawson?" Pressed Saunders.

"The former Chief Constable, the former Deputy, the Home Secretary and beyond that, I genuinely do not know how many people within the Home Office and Whitehall. I'd be surprised if the PM wasn't fully briefed as well. But rest assured, all of these people will be aware of thousands of examples of procedural irregularity..."

"Procedural irregularity? Fuck me on a surfboard! Is that what this is called at the top table? Procedural irregularity! That's absolutely priceless!" The colour was returning to Saunders' face.

"Just a sec, Keith. Let's keep a sense of perspective here..." Miller wanted to calm the mood but Saunders still had more to say. He looked Miller deep in the eyes.

"I thought that we'd put this in a box. Honestly, for every misgiving I had about the entire shitshow, you assured me that it was ancient history. You said that it would never come up again. And here we are, some maniac in Strangeways is using it to blackmail you. I might as well just go and hand myself in at the front desk."

Miller looked hard at Dixon. "Sir, can you give us ten minutes, please?"

Dixon didn't look too pleased by the request to leave his own office, but he knew that it wouldn't be advisable to make a scene with tensions already running this high. He stood and brushed himself down with his hands. "Of course. I need to pick some files up from Vice anyway."

As soon as Dixon had closed his office door behind him, Miller wasted no time in explaining the situation.

"Listen Keith, for as much shit as you think we're in, Dixon is in it ten times deeper. Try and remember that! He's the one facing the most serious charges if this ever reaches court. Think about it, it was Dixon and the former Chief Constable who signed this whole nightmare off. We were just caught up in the aftershock. We're just the bystanders. We could blag our way out of the whole thing if we ever had to. Dixon can't. So, even though its shit, please try and keep that at the front of your mind, mate."

"The only thing that's at the front of my mind is the fact that you let a man go free, when you know he killed forty-odd people, and you publicly blamed Peter Sykes for the murders, knowing that what you were saying on live TV was complete and utter bollocks."

Miller sensed that a moment of reflection was in order.

He looked down at the floor and sighed quietly. This disagreement between the two men was deep and profound. They'd been over it several times and neither was prepared to back down from their moral high ground. Saunders had never agreed with the decision to pin all of the killings on Peter Sykes, it had never sat well with him. Miller on the other hand felt that it was perverse that the British government had practically encouraged George Dawson to go about his murderous campaign, and had told the very top tier of police officers in Greater Manchester to look the other way and leave him to it, effectively disrupting and manipulating Miller's investigations into the crimes. But Saunders didn't know anything about this aspect of the case. Miller was quite content to allow him to think that it was an ego trip that had led to Dawson being pardoned, that Miller had developed some sort of a God complex on Winter Hill. It was bollocks, but Miller had calculated that it was safer to allow Saunders to believe that, than learn the whole truth behind Karen Ellis's murder.

It had been very convenient that Peter Sykes killed himself that afternoon, it allowed Miller an opportunity to kick back against the system and give the crooks at the very top of British society a taste of their own medicine. But now of course, it all looked like it was coming back to haunt Miller. And Saunders, who literally had nothing at all to do with any of this but who was now guilty of perverting the course of justice for failing to reveal the true facts of the case. So too was Bill Chapman and Mike Worthington, the two DCs who had been present when the bowels of hell had been ripped open on Avenham Close in Little Lever.

"Listen..."

"No, Sir. You listen. I realise that I'm in this up to my eyeballs so I'm not going to be sulking about it for too long. Before we go any further, I want to remind you that I still think it was a total fuck up to let Dawson walk and I stand by that. But, I'm not a wanker. If it comes to court, I'll say that I was on that avenue because I had reason to suspect Sykes was Pop. I'll go along with the whole fairy-tale, with a cherry on top."

"Okay..."

"But from the moment Dixon walks back in here, I want both of your assurances that we will treat this whole pack of lies like one of our investigations. That we will go over every detail a million times so we can make it watertight that Sykes was the killer and that George Dawson was completely innocent. Your job will be to make sure it's one hundred-per-cent bomb-proof, with statements from witnesses including Sykes' wife, George Dawson, bags and bags of evidence, DNA from the gun, CCTV from one or two of the scenes. It needs to be perfect so that this can't ever come around again. It needs to prove beyond all doubt that whatever Tommy McKinlay is saying, it's a load of old shit. The truth is cancelled for the foreseeable."

"I've got no problem with any of that at all…"

"I didn't think you would have. But we still face a number of almighty problems."

"Chapman and Worthington, you mean?"

"Yes, amongst others."

"What are the others?"

"Dawson's confession at Horwich police station for a kick-off."

"I already covered that at the public inquiry, he made a false confession in order to act as a decoy, to buy extra time for Sykes to get away."

"But he wasn't charged with anything?"

"Because he was under immense emotional strain, he'd just been kidnapped at gun-point after seeing… well, you know what he'd witnessed. The doctors signed it off as a PTSD episode, reasoning that he was confused, emotionally and mentally and felt in so much danger, the police station was the safest place for him."

"Okay, I've had tea-bags with less holes in them than that crock of shit… but there are plenty of other problems."

"Such as?"

"The recorded interview at Horwich police station. Where is that?"

"Destroyed."

"When?"

"Do you remember Danny Simmons? Young copper at

Horwich, I've had him in a few times helping me out with a couple of jobs here and there."

"Vaguely."

"Cracking lad, you'll know him when you see him. He abandoned the interview recording after we'd left. There is no record of the audio and video. There's no record of Dawson ever entering the police station, but for the duty Inspector informing Dixon and one or two anecdotes from the coppers on duty. They'll have heard the official version a few hours later and will have come to the conclusion that Dawson was a crank, or a decoy. The officers who arrested him in the station thought he was talking shit anyway. They certainly won't be harbouring any conspiracy theories about it for the simple fact that George Dawson never looked the part. When he walked in, they thought it was Beadle's About playing a prank."

"When was the interview recording abandoned?"

"In the moments following us leaving the interview room. It was all still recording, the interview was never formally concluded and as it was deleted, it was never formally started, either."

"Tape or digital?"

"It was digital."

"And you know that this Simmons definitely deleted it?"

"Of course. I asked him to scrap the interview and throw the shit in the bin and make the room available for the next job. This was just after he'd sorted me out with a car to take Dawson back up Winter Hill."

"And you trust him?"

"Of course I do, Keith. Completely. He was a massive help that day, he organised a decoy with the media for me, so we could slip away in the car he'd sorted. Plus he wants to work here with us one day. So, Simmons isn't going to be a problem."

"Well, that's encouraging. But we still have bigger problems much closer to home, though."

"Go ahead?"

"Rudovsky and Kenyon. And Grant."

Miller looked confused. Grant hadn't worked in the

department at the time and both Rudovsky and Kenyon had been off sick. Rudovsky was recovering from a near-fatal knife attack while Kenyon was recovering from a hernia operation. Miller couldn't see where any of them fitted into this. "But none of them had anything to do with it."

"I know. But they are going to be asking us all about it now, while we're working every waking hour on our bullshit case, trying to keep our arses out of jail."

Miller looked down at Dixon's carpet again. He'd not considered that Saunders would want to go over the whole thing with a fine-tooth comb, nor had he considered the impact of such a tactic on the officers who'd had no prior involvement in the investigation.

"Whoah, this is a fucking nightmare, isn't it?"

Saunders spoke coldly. "It's a recurring nightmare for me, Sir."

"I know. I know, Keith."

"So, that's where we are. I'm quite prepared to work day and night on a rock-solid case that proves beyond all doubt that Sykes was the killer."

Miller sensed a but coming and nodded patiently until it arrived.

"But, our department cannot take on any more work until this is all ironed out. Not a single thing."

"Okay."

"And Rudovsky, Grant and Kenyon will have to work on the present case-load."

"And if Dixon agrees to that?"

"Well, I don't think he's got a right lot of choice, has he?"

"No. I don't suppose he has. Well, thanks for this Keith. I wouldn't blame you if you'd told me to piss off and asked for a transfer out. You'd be totally clean and well within your rights to."

"Well, I'm no quitter Sir. And even though I sincerely think you were a dick that day, I don't actually believe Karen's death was your fault. I can't for the life of me understand why you let Dawson go but that's obviously something that makes sense in your head. For the record though, quite frankly - I couldn't give a tinker's cuss about any of the paedos that he killed. So, count me in, we need to work together to make this go away and quick."

"Cheers Keith. And I totally agree that it needs to be dealt with sharpish. But while we get all of this sorted, we're going to need Tommy McKinlay out of the picture."

"Oh right. I like the sound of this. What are you thinking?"

"Let's wait for Dixon to come back and I'll share my thoughts."

Chapter Thirty-One

There was a strange mood in the SCIU department. The team had been incredibly stressed throughout the previous day, concerned about what was unfolding with Clare Miller initially, then by the threat at the twins school. It had been good to see the gaffer back in work this morning, but one or two of the team sensed that he was hiding something from them. The department's DS was the first to voice her concern about the situation.

"I can't help feeling that Miller isn't telling us everything, you know." Jo Rudovsky was staring out of the window, at the Manchester city skyline. It sounded as though she was thinking out loud.

"Totally got that impression too, Jo." DC Mike Worthington was quick to offer support for Rudovsky's theory. The other members of the SCIU team, DC Bill Chapman, DC Peter Kenyon and DC Helen Grant looked up from what they had been concentrating on. They all seemed intrigued by Rudovsky's observation, though Grant was the first to offer her support to the DCI.

"I didn't get that impression. I just thought he seemed confused and, well, a bit emotional. Slightly embarrassed, maybe? It's understandable I suppose."

"Nah, soz Helen, I've known Andy Miller a long time and there was something… I don't know exactly. But he didn't give us the full story when he came in."

"Yep. I'm with Jo," said Chapman. "I always know when Miller's being disingenuous…"

"Ooh, flipping heck! I see Bill's had his thesaurus out again last night!" Quipped Worthington.

"Dickhead! You've ruined my punchline now!" Said Chapman, without a hint of humour in his voice. He threw a paperclip at Worthington who was sitting opposite him.

"Go on Bill, what was the punchline?" Asked Kenyon.

"No, it won't work now. Will it? Another cracking joke that'll never be heard."

Rudovsky walked away from the window and opened a drawer in the filing cabinet. "Aw shit, where's the violin gone?" The oldest joke in the department received a big laugh, even from Chapman who it was aimed at.

"Well, for what its worth, I also think that Miller was hiding something," said Kenyon. "But he'll tell us everything when he's ready."

"Yeah. Stop being a nosey bitch, Jo!" Said Grant.

"Listen, nosey bitches make reasonable detectives love. You should maybe try it, hun!"

"Oooh!" Said Chapman and Worthington in unison.

"Fight! Fight!" Chanted Kenyon. After a moment or so, the frivolous mood died down.

"Anyway, all I'm saying is, I wanted the gossip off Miller and he's let me right down. I want to know what the hell was going on yesterday. It's obviously a big deal if Clare and the kids have gone away."

"It'll all come out in the wash Jo, don't worry." Said Kenyon, returning his attention to his paperwork.

"It better had do, Pete. I feel like I've missed a vital episode here."

Chapter Thirty-Two

DCS Dixon looked quite sheepish as he re-entered his office. Saunders noted that he wasn't carrying any paperwork, which led him to the conclusion that Dixon's excuse of needing to go down to vice 'anyway' was nothing more than macho bullshit because he wasn't too chuffed at being excluded from the conversation.

Miller gave Dixon a briefing on what he and Saunders had agreed on. Dixon didn't have any objections to the idea of building up a concrete argument against McKinlay's threat. It wasn't perfect by any means, but it was certainly a positive way of tackling the issue and could certainly be useful as an insurance policy. Dixon had anticipated fights and tantrums, long arguments about who was the biggest loser in the whole fiasco regarding George Dawson. It was certainly good that things were being considered in a calm and rational way.

"Which leads me on to my first important request, Sir."

Dixon looked quite nervous as he waved Miller on in his usual, cringeworthy style. The familiar hand gesture that Miller and Saunders jokingly nicknamed "the Queen's visit." But there was no humour to be found in the peculiar hand flapping today.

"Tommy McKinlay is the biggest problem we face right now. He is taking the piss out of us, well... me, having the twins' school on terror alert, sending me text messages from a phone he keeps up his arsehole, organising to have my wife threatened in the street. If he did ever manage to succeed in this blackmail attempt, well, I dread to think where it would all end."

"I know all of this Andy. I find it completely preposterous that organised criminals of McKinlay's standing can get away with these types of stunts when they're locked up. It's above and beyond my comprehension." Dixon looked as though he was about to launch into one of his completely pointless and often contradictory rants about the current state of law and order. Miller skilfully interrupted his superior and steered the conversation back on track.

"Totally agree, Sir. And so that's why I think that while

McKinlay is capable of organising the kind of activities we saw yesterday, from behind the prison walls, he needs to be controlled significantly better..."

"Andy, as you know, we have absolutely no jurisdiction in the prisons, we can't interfere with the way the prisons are run. If you are suggesting that McKinlay is moved to solitary or something, well as you know, we can only ask the question."

"No Sir. I'm a bit more ambitious than that. I'm thinking a few divisions above solitary!"

"What's that?" asked Saunders, looking equally as interested in what Miller was preparing to suggest as Dixon appeared to be.

"Well, the bottom line is, I don't think we can afford to have criminals, prisoners, any of the swamp dwellers thinking that yesterday's stunt was acceptable. I'm not just saying this just because it was my wife, and my kids. I'm pretty keen to send out a message to all of the cons. We need to say that if you're going to get that silly, then there is going to be a heavy price to pay."

"I'm not sure I follow, Andy." Both of Dixon's bushy white eyebrows were raised high on his forehead, as though they wished to prove that their host wasn't following.

"As far as I'm concerned, McKinlay's actions yesterday have completely undermined us, the police, undermined the prison, undermined the justice system. I don't think we can allow McKinlay, or any of his contemporaries to think that this kind of behaviour is acceptable."

"I wholeheartedly agree Andy, but as I say..."

"Just a sec, Sir. Hear me out. While he's walking around in prison, continuing to run his affairs on the outside, demanding an impromptu meeting with me... well, I think that's enough piss-taking. He needs taking down a peg or two or we'll be seeing a lot more of this kind of madness, we'll be playing second fiddle to every high-profile prisoner in no time."

"Totally agree," said Saunders, nodding. It was beyond simple audacity what McKinlay had been playing at over the past 24 hours or so. "What are you suggesting Sir?"

"Yes, come on Andy, step down off your soapbox. I

think you've sold Keith and I the deal, now just get on and tell us what the bloody hell it is that you are asking for!"

"Okay, but its going to need some seriously big players to make it happen and you're going to have to sort it."

"Sort what, exactly?" Dixon appeared to be losing his patience but Miller was happy with his pitch and was ready to drop the mystique.

"I want Tommy McKinlay sending down to the segregation unit at Belmarsh. Indefinitely."

"Fucking hell!" Said Saunders. "That'll take some doing!"

"Bollocks Keith. Everyone in Britain knows about the incident at my kid's school yesterday, it was the top story on Sky bloody News. We can't afford for this kind of shit to be viewed a viable option from behind bars. He needs teaching a memorable lesson."

"And what if he goes nuts, what if he starts screaming about Dawson to all and sundry?" Typically, Saunders was asking the key questions which cut right to the heart of the issue.

"He won't. Think about it. That's his only card to play. He's not going to throw it away, is he?"

"This is good, Andy. Very good. And as you say, under the circumstances, the threats Clare received and then the incident at school, followed by you being asked to speak to McKinlay in the prison yard... I think our friends in the Home Office will be very sympathetic to this request. Good suggestion."

"So, I'll leave that with you, Sir?"

"Yes. I'll report back later. I think there's enough there to warrant such a move, regardless of the Dawson angle."

"You could play that, though. If it was looking unlikely. There'll be a few twitchy bums down there as well if McKinlay's threat was mentioned."

"I agree, but I think we ought to try and keep this amongst a select few at the present time. I'm not ruling it out, Andy. I'm just cautious of ruling it in just yet... I quite like the idea of us managing this matter locally if we can."

Both Miller and Saunders appeared satisfied with that.

The fewer people who were involved, the better. The whole thing had SCANDAL written all over it in block capitals.

"In the meantime, what are the next steps?"

"I think we will need to have a chat with Mike and Bill." Said Saunders.

"Worthington and Chapman. Of course. What are you planning?" Dixon looked as though he might just be starting to relax a little as he leaned back into his chair.

"Well, Sir," Said Saunders, looking squarely at Miller. "I thought that I might go and ask them to accompany me on a job, and then we'll meet up with you and we can break the news."

"Yes, that's neat and tidy. And away from the others. Where are you thinking?"

"The canal?"

"Excellent." Miller stood and grabbed his paperwork off Dixon's desk. "I'll go straight there, tell the others I'm still up here with the boss. Nice one Keith, see you in a bit."

Dixon looked as though he was feeling a little left out. He still really missed the days when he had been Andy Miller's DCI and the young, promising detective was working swiftly through the ranks to become his DI. He saw the casual interaction between Miller and Saunders as a bittersweet reminder that his best days in the job were now a long way behind him. He cleared his throat and spoke, if only to try and feel a little involved at the cutting edge.

"See you later Andy. And hopefully, when you get back, I'll have good news regarding a little surprise for Tommy McKinlay."

"Yes. Nice one Sir. That bastard needs a good bump down to earth. See you later."

With that, Miller was gone. Saunders stood to follow in his gaffer's footsteps but Dixon had other plans. "Just take a seat a minute longer please, Keith."

Saunders did as he was told but it was clear from the expression on his face that he was concerned about this unusual turn. He very rarely spent time alone with Dixon and he felt that the way the DCS had just mentioned this additional word after Miller had left the room was a little peculiar.

"Sir?"

"Firstly, I'd like to thank you for being so gracious regarding all of this. It must have come as a terrible shock." Dixon was rarely personable with Saunders, his usual bearing was best described as "standoffish" so this came as quite a surprise.

"Okay, well, thank you Sir. There's not a lot else I can do though, is there?"

"Well, I don't believe that, Keith. You are an exceptional officer, you've achieved DI rank at a ridiculously young age and your detection rate is second to none."

Saunders began blushing and looked down at the floor. He felt very awkward and Dixon sensed it and kept the uneasy silence hanging a little longer than was absolutely necessary. "You could quite easily tell myself and Andy to stick it where the sun don't shine and take your rank to any division in the MCP. Or even to another constabulary."

"Well, thanks, Sir. But I'm quite happy where I am, in the elite! Well, I will be again, once we've got all this out of the way."

"That's the spirit. That's why you are so good at your job Keith, positivity! I don't think I can recall an occasion where I've seen anything but total optimism and a can-do attitude from you."

Saunders smiled awkwardly again. He wanted to ask Dixon if all this was going to end with a blow job and a Chinese but he kept that thought to himself.

"Anyway, I'm very grateful for your bearing in this uncomfortable matter. And I know Andy will be the most grateful."

"Sir."

"Now, let's keep this between ourselves for now, I know Andy already has a lot on his plate. But I'd like you to have a look at this file for me, and then let me know your thoughts. No rush, but I would really value your input."

Finally, Saunders began to understand what all of this was about. Dixon wanted a favour and Miller was far too busy with his own shit to help Dixon mop his workload up. Miller was always moaning about Dixon mithering him to give things a second pair of eyes. Usually, Saunders would be quite polite and accept the job, but these were not normal circumstances.

"I'm sorry Sir, but I really don't think I'm going to have any spare time to even eat my lunch, let alone anything else."

Dixon smiled and held eye contact with Saunders. "As I say, I would value your input. No rush." The DCS pushed the file marked "CONFIDENTIAL" across the desk slowly and Saunders received his first ever experience of DCS Dixon's unwitting mafia boss impression which Miller often took the piss out of. Saunders tried not to smile as Miller's ridiculous gangster accent played through in his mind. "A godda offa you caint refuse."

"Sir."

Chapter Thirty-Three

Saunders felt as though he was being watched as he walked back into the SCIU offices, even though the team were all looking down at the paperwork on their desks. There was a funny mood in the air, there was no doubt about that. He walked across to his desk, unlocked the top drawer and placed Dixon's file in there before locking it up again.

"Where's the gaffer?" Asked Rudovsky.

"He's still in with Dixon, Jo."

"What, right now?"

"Yes Jo, well he was about thirty seconds ago, when I left. Mike, Bill, can you come with me please?" Saunders grabbed his jacket off the back of his seat. The two DCs looked surprised.

"Where are you going?" Asked Rudovsky. Saunders smiled widely.

"What's got into you? Are you trying to be the new Neighbourhood Watch gimp?"

"Just wondering where you're going, Sir. That's all." Rudovsky was standing her ground. As the DS who'd been left in charge of supervising this team, she felt that she was well within her rights to ask where half of them were going.

"I need Bill and Mike to assist me with a job, Jo." Saunders gave the DS a long, cold stare, which translated a little too clearly as "fuck off with all the questions, Jo." Rudovsky received the message loud and clear and looked down at the coffee stained carpet as Saunders walked away towards the door.

Chapman and Worthington followed, shrugging at Rudovsky as they went. As soon as they had passed through the door, the DS looked across at Grant and Kenyon.

"What the actual fuck?"

"What's up Jo?" Asked Kenyon, who'd been Rudovsky's long-term partner when she was a DC.

"Keith just lied right in my face, Pete."

"What? When?"

"Just then, he said Miller was in with Dixon. Only, I watched Miller go to his car and drive off ten minutes ago. There's something really shady going on and I don't like it." Rudovsky went across to the window and watched as Saunders, Chapman and Worthington stepped across the car park and got into the DI's car. They all looked serious, with none of the usual banter taking place. "I'm really not feeling positive about any of this."

DC Helen Grant felt her face burning. This was beyond awkward, her boyfriend being talked about in this way, without the slightest attempt at disguising it. It was as though Rudovsky felt the heat from Grant's cheeks as she turned to face her.

"Has he said out to you, Helen?"

"Who?"

"Keith. Has he not told you what's going on?" Rudovsky was staring at the DC.

"Well, Jo. This is awkward. I mean, even if he had said something, which he hasn't, then I'd still be in a compromised position, wouldn't I? I mean, really, this is a shit place to be sitting right now."

"Yeah, I know, soz H. I just can't be doing with snideness. And whatever it is that's going on, it's snide as out!"

Chapter Thirty-Four

Saunders had managed to sustain small talk all the way here, he didn't want to be the one who told Chapman and Worthington what was unfolding. That was Miller's job. But it was clear that Chapman and Worthington were aware that something weird was going on. Being dragged away from their work with no explanation, and no further comment about it in the car gave the game away that something unusual was taking place.

But Saunders wasn't too fussed about the mood in the car, he knew that moods were going to be all over the place once Miller had spilt the beans about McKinlay's blackmail plot. His priority was to follow orders and meet Miller at the canal, where the DCI could explain the situation and discuss options.

"Here we are. Oh look! There's the gaffer." Said Saunders in his most sarcastic manner.

"What a coincidence!" Said Chapman.

"Small world!" Muttered Worthington.

Miller got out of his car and walked across the tiny gravel car park slowly. Upon reaching Saunders' vehicle, he opened the back door and got in. He seemed a little nervous, Chapman and Worthington picked up on it immediately.

"Alright?" Asked Miller as he got in and sat on the backseat.

"Sir."

"Alright Sir?"

"I was just thinking, whilst I was waiting for yous. The last time I got into the back of a car with you three, it was when we were investigating that factory worker who got shot in the mush."

Miller had expected a vague response from his officers and was slightly surprised that nobody acknowledged the occasion he was talking about.

"I thought we had all agreed that we were never going to speak about that case again?" Asked Worthington, looking out of the window as a canal barge juddered slowly past, its elderly helmsman looking thoroughly miserable as his wife pointed at various landmarks in the distance.

"Well, Mike, that leads me nicely onto the reason we are all reunited in Keith's car again. I'm afraid we're going to have to abandon the plan of never speaking about the Pop case again."

Another atmospheric silence filled the air. Saunders sensed that his boss needed a leg-up with this, it was going to be a difficult enough announcement without a frosty audience making things even more difficult. He decided to assist his boss in the lead up to this momentous announcement. "There's been a development."

"I had a feeling something like this was coming up," said Chapman from the front passenger seat.

"Why's that?" Asked Miller.

"Well, I don't know really. Things have just been a bit… strained. Normally, if you're asked a question, you give a straight answer. But you've seemed a bit cagey, and then when Keith marched Mike and I out of the office with no explanation, it occurred to me that it might be related to…"

"Well, your instincts are spot on detective. We've got a problem, but before I explain what it is, I need to make sure that we are all one hundred per cent that it stays exclusively amongst us four. This cannot be discussed with anybody else, under any circumstances."

Saunders, Chapman and Worthington agreed to the terms as Miller explained the position. Over the course of the next ten minutes or so, there were a number of exasperated sighs and several instances of uncomfortable fidgeting but thankfully, no interruptions. Chapman and Worthington had listened quietly to what was being said and Miller was pleased that there had been no drama.

Once he had finished explaining what McKinlay had suggested, a heavy silence hung around the car. Eventually, Worthington broke the deadlock.

"Do we think we can handle it?"

"I think we can, Mike, based on the simple premise that if anybody official ever asks any questions, we all have the same story."

"What's that, then?" Asked Chapman, leaning around to face his boss.

"The same story as always. Nothing alters. You had been told by Karen Ellis that the gunman was George Dawson but when you tried to make the arrest, you found out that it was Dawson's best mate, Peter Sykes, when he started waving a gun around. If there are any further questions, you tell the truth — that you don't know what happened after Karen was shot dead. That you all went back to HQ and were sent home on compassionate leave soon after by DCS Dixon. Any further questions after that, it's just I don't knows."

"Fucking hell. This is bad." Said Worthington.

"It's bad for me, potentially. But you lot are safe, you haven't done anything wrong."

"Well, we have, boss. Being aware that you let the real gunman walk free…"

"Bill, slow down. You don't know that. You never knew that. Just forget that altogether. Listen carefully and get it stuck in your head… you were told by Ellis that she wanted to bring Dawson in, because she felt he had information, but you have no idea what information it was or how she'd sourced it. And then it all went wrong. That's all you need to say."

"I'm not sure about this. It's fishy as fuck."

"Deep breaths Mike. Just remember that story and everything will be fine, and over the next few days, we'll be bolting extra bits on here and there to make it double rock-solid." Miller smiled reassuringly to his colleague who was sitting beside him on the backseat. Worthington looked thoroughly uncomfortable with the whole thing, which irritated Miller greatly. Things would have turned out a lot differently, and Karen Ellis would undoubtedly still have been alive if Worthington hadn't booted Sykes in the knee when he was holding a loaded gun to Karen's temple. But this was no time for recriminations or cheap shots.

"What are these extra bits that you're talking about?" Asked Chapman, surprising Miller and Saunders with how cooperative and open-minded he was being about this difficult situation which had sprung up from nowhere.

"To be confirmed, Bill. But Keith is going to be working on some extra bits and pieces which will pin another layer of guilt on Sykes."

"So to confirm... we're happy to dig the hole even deeper to protect Dawson?" Worthington sounded irritable and Miller was realising for the first time that it wasn't just Saunders who held strong feelings about the way that he'd handled the conclusion to this difficult case.

Miller managed to keep his cool and answered the rather loaded question calmly and professionally. "Well, it's not quite like that, Mike. The hole has already been dug, whether we like it or not. We can't just climb out of it now."

"I still don't understand why you let Dawson walk, boss. It was fucking insanity."

Miller took a deep breath and held it. It was better than saying what he wanted to say about the fucking insanity of kicking Sykes' knee. He felt quite disappointed that Saunders and Chapman remained quiet, silently reinforcing Worthington's point-of-view. But he could hardly blurt out his reasons for helping Dawson. Things were difficult enough without chucking a can of petrol at the candle.

"I had my reasons, Mike. That's all we need to say on the subject."

None of Miller's officers had the courage to challenge his rather dismissive explanation. A weird atmosphere gripped the interior of the vehicle, nobody really knew what to say. For the first time, Miller had an overwhelming compulsion to explain the situation, to put his side, or rather, George Dawson's side of the story across. But it was a fleeting sensation and Miller quickly came to his senses.

"Right, well. Thanks for being so good about all this. I'm really sorry that it's come up again. I'm just hopeful that we can contain it. Anyway, I'd better get on." Miller opened the car door and stepped out, walking self-consciously towards his own car.

"He can be a right dick, sometimes." Said Worthington. Neither Chapman nor Saunders commented as Miller's car sped away, the wheels throwing up a cloud of dust as he went. "I might try that excuse next time I'm late because of the roadworks on Chapel Street. Can you imagine? He'll say 'oh, Mike, you're late.' And I'll say 'I had my reasons, Sir. And that's all I want to say on the matter."

Chapman and Saunders laughed loudly, but Worthington looked out of the car window as Miller's car disappeared out of view.

"Seriously though, are we all singing from the same hymn sheet?" Asked Saunders.

"Yes, totally," said Chapman. "If anybody asks what went on, we just say that we were trying to apprehend Dawson as Ellis thought he had some information, we don't know what because we were aware that she was being secretive because she was paranoid that she was going above Dixon's head. And then Peter Sykes pulled a gun. Anything that happened before or after that, we don't know."

"That's about the size of it. You okay with it, Mike?" Asked Saunders.

Worthington exhaled loudly, he seemed a bit moody. "Yes, no problem."

"Good. Okay, let's get back to the office and obviously, if anybody asks... this discussion hasn't happened."

"Sir."

"Sir."

Chapter Thirty-Five

Rudovsky was in a mood. Everybody in the department knew it. It was very rare that the department's DS was in a mood, but when she was, it was far from subtle. A suffocating tension seemed to radiate off her. She didn't have to say anything, she didn't even have to give anybody a death-stare. It was an instinctive thing, and it made the SCIU office a very uncomfortable place to be on the rare occasions that Jo was in one of these toxic moods.

Saunders was in the office with Miller. Chapman and Worthington hadn't been back long, but the tension was so intense that every DC in the room was clock-watching, desperate to get out of here and away from this poisonous, suffocating atmosphere.

Suddenly, from out of the blue, Rudovsky asked a question which made everybody realise what all of this was about. "So, Bill, Mike. Are you going to spill the beans?"

Both of the DCs shifted uncomfortably, before thinking of a response.

"Eh. What?"

"What beans?"

"Don't piss about lads. *The* beans. Where did you go with Keith?"

"Eh... er..."

"We had to go... we were checking on something for Saunders."

"Ah, okay."

An intense frostiness filled the air as Rudovsky looked down at her paperwork. Chapman and Worthington exchanged an awkward look which she didn't see, but she could certainly sense across the desk. A minute or so passed before Rudovsky spoke again, asking another question, delivered oh-so-casually.

"What were you checking?" She looked up from her paperwork and stared at the two detectives who were sitting opposite her. It was clear from their blushes and gob-smacked expressions that she wasn't supposed to know anything about the excursion with Saunders, and most probably Miller.

"Cat got your tongues?" She asked. Both Chapman and Worthington handled this awkward, toe-curling moment spectacularly badly. But their dreadful diplomacy told Rudovsky all she needed to know. She stood, took a piece of paper out of the photocopier drawer and walked quickly over towards Miller's office. She smiled at her DCI and DI as they looked in her direction as she approached. Even now, just from the look they gave her as she approached, she knew that something seriously dodgy was going on. Rudovsky knocked politely on the door before stepping into the office, closing the door gently and sitting down next to Saunders.

"Jo." Said Saunders.

"Hi Jo, we're just in the middle of something mate… can we…"

Miller was cut short. "Anyone want to tell me what the fuck's going on?" Asked Rudovsky.

The strained, perplexed expressions that Chapman and Worthington had pulled just moments earlier were recreated brilliantly by Miller and Saunders. They were both utterly speechless.

"Fucking hell. That's exactly what Mike and Bill said as well, when I asked them. You mean to say that you are freezing me out of something, acting like snides, and you didn't even have the common-sense to think of a fucking excuse to cover for it? Jesus."

Both Saunders and Miller sat there, neither of them were able to come up with an explanation. Rudovsky held up the blank piece of paper that she had brought into the office with her.

"This is a list of all the times you two have excluded me from something in this department." She placed the piece of paper on Miller's desk and leaned back in the chair. "And now, I'm going home, and I'm not coming back into work until I've been given a full and frank explanation of why you two are treating me like a dickhead in front of the team I'm supposed to be in charge of. Put it down as leave, I'm owed fuck-knows how much anyway. Seeya." With that, Rudovsky stood up and left the office. The heavy silence which followed her out did nothing to pacify her. The fact that neither Miller nor Saunders had even attempted to reason with her, tried to explain, or even tried to take the piss and make a shit joke, really stung her. She walked across to her desk, grabbed her jacket and her phone and walked silently out of the office. It looked as though she was trying to hide her face as she walked back past Miller's office.

"Bollocks." Said Miller, staring at Saunders, hoping that his DI could think of a way out of this latest disaster.

Chapter Thirty-Six

There wasn't a great deal of conversation between Miller and Saunders as their unmarked CID car made its way across Manchester city centre. The issue with Rudovsky was playing heavily on both of their minds. If they hadn't this important appointment to attend, they'd be better fixed to tackle this crisis head on. But, there was nothing they could do just yet, this meeting was crucial. Rudovsky was going to have to wait her turn.

"Right, well I think we'd better try and cheer up if we want these lot to be helpful." Miller indicated off the main road and drove the car into the underground car park of the swish new building. He was asked for his name at the security barrier.

"DCI Miller and DI Saunders from MCP serious crimes. We've an appointment with DCI Jarvis." Said Miller into the machine. The barrier lifted up and he drove the car through.

"Never been here before." Said Saunders as Miller reversed into the first available parking space. The car park was full of police issue Vauxhall Insignias and Miller realised that his model had a slightly better spec than most of the ones the NCA staff used. This surprised him, the rumour was that all regular police departments played second fiddle to the NCA these days.

"Have you not? Oh, you'll love it, a chance to see all the toys we'll be allowed in twenty, thirty years!"

The NCA is the National Crime Agency, a relatively new national police force which has greater freedoms to investigate criminal activities nationwide rather than on a local basis, which is the limiting way that a regular police constabulary operates. The media claim that the NCA are "Britain's answer to the FBI" and they are viewed as the elite of detectives, not just by the press but by many members of the public as well.

Without the logistical constraints of only having jurisdiction within one geographical district, the NCA have been able to make incredible achievements in disrupting criminal networks which operate across numerous police force areas. For instance, the north-west of England is policed by Merseyside,

Cheshire, Lancashire, Manchester and Cumbria Constabularies. If an officer from Cheshire wanted to interview a suspect from neighbouring Manchester, a long-winded dialogue would begin between the two forces, resulting in a great deal of form filling, red-tape cutting and subsequently, delays to progress. Sadly, in the current climate of targets and budgets - this old-fashioned system of working results in a lot of CBA cases. CBA is a police acronym which means 'can't be arsed.' The CBA cases are filed away by frustrated officers who simply can't be arsed with the bureaucracy involved in trying to carry out simple tasks without hours, if not days of pointless tittle-tattle which helps nobody other than the offenders that the police were originally hoping to arrest. It causes a great deal of frustration in the modern police service.

  Communication and transport links have moved on a long way from the days when the current policing regulations were brought in. Organised criminals are no longer confined to one geographical district and this is one of the reasons that Scotland's government amalgamated the eight regional constabularies into one force. Police Scotland was formed in 2013 and much of the red-tape and bureaucracy that still plights English forces was swept away overnight.

  There are none of these barriers and obstacles standing in the way of the NCA. They can turn up anywhere they choose and arrest whoever they like. They are able to work not only nationally, but internationally on their investigations. It is these types of special abilities which puts them in a completely different league to the constabulary CID departments around the UK, a fact demonstrated by their phenomenal detection, arrest and prosecution statistics. The NCA have also been hugely successful thanks to the fact that they have cherry-picked some of the very best detectives from every constabulary in the UK since the organisation was set up in 2012. Both Miller and Saunders have been approached several times by the NCA, who offer a better pay grade system and better benefits. So far, the head-hunters haven't managed to entice either officer away from the SCIU.

  Tackling organised crime, carried out by some of the

most serious and dangerous criminals in the UK is the biggest part of the NCA's work. The NCA detectives typically work on catching and prosecuting drug dealers and their suppliers, firearms dealers, gangsters and the most unpleasant people in society. But it doesn't stop there, the NCA are also involved in major investigations into people trafficking, child porn and prostitution, child exploitation, cyber crime and counter-terrorism. The NCA operates with a staff base of almost 5,000 across the country, a figure which is rising every year as more and more traditionally localised units are absorbed into the national organisation. The suspicion amongst many police officers across England and Wales is that it is only a matter of time before the experiment in Scotland is rolled out to the south. The NCA is seen as the precursor to such a move as managing finances has become the number one concern in policing, second to tackling crime.

"So, who's this DCI we're meeting?" Asked Saunders as Miller held open the reception door for him.

"He's called Tim Jarvis, he's alright. He was at Lancashire Constabulary, he's the one who arrested Usman Amman."

"Bloody hell. That's a big collar to feel."

Miller was talking about the man who had plotted to bomb Blackburn Mall shopping centre on Christmas Eve 2015. Had Jarvis and his team not raided Amman's home address just a week before, hundreds if not thousands of lives would have been lost on the busiest day of the shopping centre's calendar.

"Hello, we're from MCP, we've an appointment with DCI Jarvis." Said Miller to the receptionist.

"What's your name?"

"DCI Miller, and DI Saunders."

"Just take a seat and I'll let him know you're here."

The two MCP officers followed the instruction and took a seat on the black leather settee. Miller commented on how comfy it was. Saunders was mesmerised by the place.

"It looks more like a posh hotel than a police station!" He said, admiring the shiny granite floor which was reflecting the modern lighting which ran off down a long corridor.

"I used to think that about our place, but they soon get tired. People soon spill coffee all over the carpets."

"That was not me."

"So you say."

"Do you know what, I wish I had done it, at least then the amount of shit I get for it would be justified!"

"It's right next your desk you fucking maniac!"

Miller and Saunders sat quietly for a few moments before a door by the side of the reception desk opened and DCI Jarvis appeared. Miller recognised him straight away.

"DCI Miller, I know your face!" Said Jarvis, extending his hand. "And you must be DI Saunders, you look familiar as well!" The SCIU officers began blushing. It was true, they were both well known faces from the regional news bulletins in the north west of England. It was one of the downsides to working in Manchester's senior CID department.

"Pleased to meet you," said Saunders.

"We have met once before, of course." Said Miller. "I was on your patch investigating the disappearance of Sergeant Knight, a couple of years back."

"Of course, yes. Christ, that was quite a case."

"You can say that again. I still have to cross my legs when I think about it."

"Yes, quite." Jarvis pulled an awkward face and Miller laughed politely. "Anyway, come on through, I've booked the board room for us. Less chance of interruptions. My colleague DS Laura Gardner is joining us. She's been the eyes and ears of the investigation you're interested in."

The three officers walked through a maze of shiny corridors before stepping into the board room. Once all of the introductions were out of the way, Miller gave a brief explanation of the problem, minus the George Dawson aspect. In concluding his overview of the situation regarding McKinlay, he explained what he wanted from the NCA officers.

"I really need your help. I need to know some more about McKinlay, his activities and crucially, any intelligence you have that might lead me to arresting the people that he has instructed to approach my wife and my children's school."

The two NCA officers looked at one another and smiled humourlessly. DS Gardner began talking. She was quite young, possibility late twenties but she had a very matter-of-fact way about her which suggested that she was much older. Miller liked her already.

"I'll cut through the crap, DCI Miller. The truth is, we know very little about Tommy McKinlay's wider network. He operates a number of smaller units and it is proving incredibly difficult to gather the intelligence on who's who. We have some ideas, and we'll be happy to pass on all of our intel to you. But the depressing truth is, we don't have any concrete evidence on his activities. He's an enigma."

"Well, I'll appreciate whatever you can give me."

"Of course, I'll be happy to. The issue we have with McKinlay is that he runs his legitimate business extremely professionally. We've combed through it all a dozen times, there's nothing to link him to any criminality at all. All of the security contracts that he has in place are legal and above-board. He has multi-million-pound deals with most of the local authorities in Greater Manchester and several in Merseyside and West Yorkshire, the footprint of TM Security Services is expanding all the time and its no secret that his ambitions are to become a national outfit. More locally, he has recently taken on new contracts with some major players such as Media City and Manchester City. Believe it or not, his firm has been hired by Manchester City Police to assist with the policing of major events on a number of occasions. On the face of it, he's a hugely successful and respected businessman. The trouble is, there is a very sinister side to him. The bad news is that it's incredibly hard to uncover anything about this side of him. I said it earlier, and I'm not trying to be a drama queen. He really is an enigma."

DCI Jarvis cut in, eager to back his officer's assessment up. "We were hopeful that now that McKinlay is on remand, one or two of his enemies might have stepped forward to help us build a solid case against him. But so far that hasn't happened. He appears to strike fear into everybody. We can't get anybody to talk. The fear of McKinlay is very real."

"But if his business is so successful, taking local

authority contracts and so on… I don't really understand why he needs to be involved in anything illegal. It sounds as though he's doing very nicely, legitimately." Miller seemed genuinely confused.

"That's an excellent question. Simple answer – greed. But if you factor in ego and reputation, I guess you'll get nearer to the answer. There was an interesting case we were looking into, it's all street rumours and legend, but here's the story as we've heard it. A senior Manchester United and England player enrolled Tommy McKinlay's security services about four or five years ago. The player was originally from Merseyside and the story goes that a well-known Liverpool gangster by the name of Eddie Francis was attempting to blackmail the player for a million quid, using threats to harm his family. The alleged incident began when the player was visiting family for a birthday party in Toxteth. Soon after, I mean literally, days later - Eddie Francis disappeared and has never been seen again. The footballer has been asked to help us with our enquiries but has refused to comment. He submitted a prepared statement in which he denies that he's never heard of Francis or McKinlay for that matter. It's all been hushed up, there was a super injunction preventing the press from reporting on the case or the interviews the footballer had with police."

"Christ!"

"But it's quite clear what happened and it seems that every crook in Greater Manchester and Merseyside knows the whole story inside out. But you try and get one of them to talk to us about it. This is why McKinlay is so successful – he allows everybody to know what he's up to so that his reputation soars and in the process, he creates even more fear which ultimately protects him. Seriously I'm not exaggerating when I say that Tommy McKinlay puts the fear of God into people, just the mention of his name changes the mood of the people we talk to. It makes life impossibly hard for any police officer who is trying to bang McKinlay up. Isn't that right, Sir?" Gardner looked at her boss and he smiled widely.

"Very hard is putting it mildly. We have between twenty-two missing persons reports which we can link back to the McKinlay empire in one way or another. We know, as police officers that there is no doubt that McKinlay or one of his employees are responsible for some very bad things happening to people. But as you know yourself, the CPS aren't interested in our case-studies or theories or our excellent intuition. So without a trace of physical evidence in any of the cases, they don't want to know. The fact that he's on remand right now is the only favour we'll ever get from the CPS. In reality, they're just as keen as us to see him banged up for good, but they need the evidence. As the clock keeps ticking and his trial creeps closer, we're beginning to panic here."

"It might sound bizarre," said Gardner. "But it's as though he's laughing at us. Laughing at the system. He's extremely good at what he does, we have to give him that."

"No. It doesn't sound bizarre at all. And that's coming from a man that Tommy McKinlay has been laughing at for the past two days."

"Sorry to butt in," said Saunders. "But what can you tell us about McKinlay's people?"

"There are two members of his staff team at TM Security who we know he has very strong relationships with. Both are on six-figure salaries. One is a partner and is employed as MD and the other is the head of IT." DS Gardner flicked through a tall pile of paperwork and pulled out a file, passing it over the table towards where Miller and Saunders were seated. "Our intelligence leads us to believe that these job titles are nonsense, and that these two individuals manage the dirty side of McKinlay's business empire. Simon Kingston, better known in the community as Kingo, 57 years old, former paratrooper, completely clean criminal record. He's the MD of the outfit and this chap, Ben Thompson is the head of IT. His nickname is Nerd. He's 32 and we believe that the IT he manages is the drugs lines, the burner phones and all the comms between the street dealers and the importers. These guys are into everything, drugs, guns, violence, counterfeit goods, you know the rest. Proving this theory is another matter altogether, these two appear to be the very top of a long and complicated ladder, with dozens if not a hundred street dealers on the bottom rung who have never met either Kingo or Nerd, or McKinlay for that matter. But they do all the work, take all the risks and the occasional shooting, stabbing or prison sentence."

"This looks like a very impressive file. Are we okay to take this?"

"Yes, that's your copy."

"Thank you."

"You're welcome. I mean, if you can get anywhere with this, you'll be heroes in a lot of people's eyes in this building!"

"Well, that's an interesting thought. I mean, McKinlay isn't my main concern right now. My principal objective is to get a hold of the people who have approached my family. What do you think are my chances of achieving that?"

The two NCA officers look at one another briefly before looking back at Miller. He took this subtle gesture to mean no chance but waited patiently for a more informed analysis.

DCI Jarvis offered his take on the situation. "Truthfully? We find that trying to pin anything on McKinlay or his network is like the Call of Duty computer game where you are shooting zombies. For every hundred zombies you destroy, there are ten thousand more following behind. In the end, you feel overwhelmed and ultimately, you lose. McKinlay's set up is like an army. His soldiers are the poorest, thickest and nastiest pieces of shit walking around this city and there are a lot of them. But they view him as a God, nobody seems to want to challenge him. What you want to do is perfectly understandable under the circumstances, but achievable?" Jarvis pulled out the three mug-shots from Gardner's file and laid them on the table facing Miller and Saunders. "In all honesty, I think you'd be better focusing your energies here, at the top of the tree, and staying out of the pond below. If you could nail something on these three, McKinlay, Nerd and Kingo, then the whole empire could be closed down overnight."

"Okay, well this has been extremely interesting. I had absolutely no idea what I was dealing with but the picture is becoming clearer."

"Just, I know it sounds incredibly patronising... but be careful. I don't want you to underestimate how dangerous these people are." DCI Jarvis had a very sincere look on his face and both Miller and Saunders sensed that he meant it. There was no escaping the fear in his eyes as he spoke. "Also, I want you to know that the files we have prepared for you remain part of the live investigation. They are for information purposes only. If you do need to engage with any of the individuals named within these pages, you will have to clear that with us first."

"Except McKinlay?" Miller appeared slightly confused.

"Naturally. You have developed your own relationship with him, at his invitation. But I do want you to be mindful that we have over a hundred officers working on this case, all of them are trying to find the end of the rainbow so that we can send McKinlay, Kingston and Thompson away for a very long stretch."

"The pot of gold? Well, I'm sure you will."

"I hope so. But in the meantime, any information that you unearth would be gratefully received."

"That's understood."

"Good stuff. It all feels rather cloak and dagger when we have to have these conversations, but we're all on the same team."

"Absolutely. No, I really appreciate your time today. It's been very helpful and I'm looking forward to getting stuck into this file." Miller gestured towards the impressive stack of papers on the desktop.

"No problem at all. I just hope that you can get this sorted out, I can't imagine the stress you're under. Finally, if you have anything you wish to discuss, any queries you might have, or if you would like to keep us up to speed on your own activities, please don't hesitate to call myself or DS Gardner, any time, day or night."

Both of the NCA officers handed their cards across the desk and Saunders took them.

"Just before you go… one thing that I should tell you," said DS Gardner. "We have learnt that Tommy McKinlay gets an enormous amount of satisfaction from winding people up. He's like a cat playing with a bird that it knows it is going to kill as soon as it gets bored. My advice to you would be to keep this at the front of your minds and try not to be distracted with anything that he does which may seem a little trivial. He has a lot of spare time on his hands and he takes great satisfaction from getting inside people's heads. That's what the school incident was about, in my view. My advice is to refuse him access to your head, because once he gets in, he'll make himself at home, just for the hell of it. He really is the very worst kind of narcissistic bully that you will ever encounter."

Chapter Thirty-Seven

Soon after the issue with Mr Patel had been resolved, the word began travelling around and Tommy McKinlay's mum's phone began ringing more and more with requests for his services. His bare-knuckle fighting was going very well at the time, he was moving quickly up the national pecking order and was attracting bigger name fights with every victory. Each new fight saw the purse increase dramatically and Tommy was getting within touching distance of the big money, the ten-thousand-pound fights. His life revolved around training and fighting and he was building up quite an extraordinary sum of cash.

Having access to a lot of cash was a complete novelty at first. The McKinlays had had nothing all their lives. Since their dad had died suddenly when the kids were small, they had been the archetypal poor, hard-luck northern family who looked like they were going nowhere. Raising her kids on a diet of No Frills beans and with wardrobes full of flea-market clothes, Tommy's mum had done her very best for her family. Wilma McKinlay was painfully thin throughout these years – the stress and grief of becoming a widow at such a young age had brought about the initial weight-loss. The years which followed, when there was seldom enough food for everyone, didn't help her to regain any of the weight. Wilma regularly missed out on having any tea through those difficult years, but the kids never went to bed with rumbling bellies and that was her over-riding concern.

As soon as Tommy started bringing home some good money from his fights, he was determined to repay his mum for all of those years of hardship. He treated her and his sisters to a fortnight's holiday in Spain with a big wedge of spends, telling them to make sure they spend every last penny having a good time and treating themselves. It was the first time that any of the McKinlays had been abroad. As soon as they were out there, enjoying the sunshine and the pool and the all-inclusive food and drink, Tommy set to work. He hired two skips which were dropped off outside the house. He worked with his mates in throwing out all the old shit, the settee, the beds, the fridge and the freezer. All the old shit that they'd had given or Wilma had bought second-hand. The washing machine that never span properly, the telly that went black and white after a couple of hours of being on. The worn-out carpets were all pulled up and launched into the skips, the shitty old cooker was chucked on top. After just a couple of hours, both of the skips were full and Tommy rang up and asked the company to fetch two more.

Over the course of the following week or so, Tommy and his mates gutted the house from top-to-bottom. Working room to room, they redecorated, laid new carpets, built new furniture and made the new beds. Brand new cupboard doors and worktops were fitted in the kitchen, a new fridge freezer, cooker and washing machine were all installed. Tommy focused his attention on the living room next, redecorating it all before unpacking the new settee, fixing up the new curtain poles and curtains. He bought a new telly which came with a video player included. The family had never had a video player before. His favourite part of all was when the Nynex engineer came to install the cable TV.

It was an exhausting couple of weeks, but well worth the effort. Wilma McKinlay was not an overly emotional woman, but her speechless, stunned, beaming reaction to the surprise after landing back from Spain made all of the hard-work and expense feel totally worthwhile. Tommy had never seen his mum look genuinely happy until that day and the sad realisation of that had a profound effect on him.

The idea to treat his mum to a holiday and a cracking surprise for when she got back had emptied his savings pot. He was glad of it, glad that he was once again penniless and had gained a real taste for money. He knew what made him tick, and he knew that blowing every penny of the stash he'd built up would make him more determined to make even more of it and build it up again, but an even bigger pile next time.

The phone calls that were coming through to Wilma's were becoming a daily occurrence. People that Wilma had never heard of were asking for Tommy. When she explained that he wasn't here at the moment, they left their numbers and begged her to ask Tommy to phone them urgently. Once Tommy did start returning the calls, out of morbid curiosity more than anything else, he quickly realised that there was a bottomless pit of cash on offer from people who needed issues similar to Mr Patel's problem solving.

Tommy enjoyed the work. It was well paid and in most cases, thoroughly rewarding to make some horrible little bastards beg for mercy in front of the people they'd been terrorising. With each new problem solved, the word went around the community and Tommy's reputation quickly became legendary across Rochdale, Oldham and many parts of the Greater Manchester area. The whole thing gathered momentum extremely quickly, such was the effectiveness of Tommy's methods of making shit people stop doing shit things. Tommy covered everything, from ridding an estate of a gang of youths who terrorised the place after dark, to making a jilted boyfriend stop stalking his ex. He got rid of skinheads who were running protection rackets in pubs and clubs, he even had one job where a copper who was bullying a young lad on his beat was dealt with. The copper left the force and moved out of the area. The success rate that Tommy was having in making problems disappear was extraordinary and business was very quickly becoming unmanageable, too many jobs were coming in and there wasn't enough time to take them all on.

Tommy's next fight was all set up and he was beginning to feel torn. He was generating so much cash from this new sideline that he was becoming distracted from his fighting. He'd feel stressed that he wasn't putting anywhere near enough training in, but if he turned work down at a thousand pounds a time – he was wracked with guilt. The answer came to him one night as he was battering the punchbag in the gym. He realised that he could easily sub-contract the jobs, pay some good lads half the fee to look after things on his behalf and it was smiles all round. Tommy could take fifty per cent of the cash just for having the reputation and success rate. The other person did the graft and earned a good wedge off the back of Tommy's name.

Tommy began making some calls and asked his most trusted sources if they knew of any "handy" lads who were looking for a bit of casual work. The term "handy lad" usually means somebody who knows how to handle themselves and wouldn't run from a fight. But when one of the hardest men in Great Britain says "handy" it transcends a few divisions higher than your standard former "cock of the school."

Fortunately, a former paratrooper by the name of Simon Kingston – better known as Kingo was in between door jobs at the time. He'd managed the doors at some of Manchester's most famous and most notorious nightclubs, one of which was famously closed down after Kingo had been shot in the leg in a drive-by shooting which miraculously missed two young girls who were queueing to get in the club. Soon after he was back on his feet, Kingo began a new job at a new club but soon realised that the old crowd from the last place were causing exactly the same problems at this place. After a bit, the same shit, different night lifestyle tends to become tedious to somebody who had served in Iraq. Dealing with wannabe gangsters, low-level drug-dealers and dicks with guns might sound exciting but the shine wears off quite quickly. Kingo was becoming bored of the clubland world and had begun looking for private security work in Qatar. These jobs were offering mad money for very little aggro.

Tommy spoke to a number of the "heads" around Manchester who worked with or knew of Kingo and the reports all came back positive. He was loyal, committed and most importantly, scary-as-fuck when he needed to be. He was supposed to be a good laugh as well. That was good enough for Tommy. Despite being quite a bit older, Kingo sounded like the ideal candidate to assist him with the endless requests for sorting horrible people out.

It seemed as though it was all written in the stars. Tommy's call to Kingo came just minutes before he was due to talk to the people in Qatar. Tommy invited Kingo down to his local gym for a chat and despite the ten-year age difference, the two men clicked straight away.

"Do you fancy doing a trial run for me tonight?" Asked Tommy, after explaining the nature of his evolving enterprise.

"Course, yeah. I'd love to."

"Buzzing. Right, let me get a shower and that and we'll get off."

Tommy explained the problem that he'd been asked to sort out as he drove his Land Rover Discovery out of Rochdale in the direction of Salford.

"So the guy we're going to see goes by the name of Danny Newton. This twat comes into the pub mob-handed every Monday and Thursday night at half-eight on the dot and picks up an envelope with a hundred quid in. He goes behind the bar, pulls him and his mates a pint, starts playing with the barmaid's tits before he necks his pint and fucks off. His mates follow him out, normally quietly but sometimes they totally fuck the place up, chucking bar-stools through the windows and all that."

"What, and the landlord's paying them for protection?"

"Yeah, I know. Total fuckwits. Wired out of their heads on coke."

"How long have they been doing this?"

"A while. I've been meaning to sort this out for weeks to be honest but I've just not had the time. Anyway, we'll get it sorted tonight and I'll get to see what you're made of."

"Nice one! I'm into the sound of this."

"Just keep your wits about you, there might be a handgun."

"Yeah, no problem at all."

Tommy was impressed. Kingo didn't flinch when the gun was mentioned. Most people who carried guns in the 90's didn't have a clue which way round to hold it. They were the sort of fuckwits who got Rottweilers which then munched holes in their legs. Tommy could tell that Kingo knew the score and he was feeling very relaxed as the Discovery neared the pub that they were going to pay a visit.

"Right, I'm gonna dump this on of these side streets. The pub's called The Staff of Life, it's halfway down this hill here." Tommy pointed down Rainsough Brow, the road which leads down to Agecroft Cemetery on the edge of Salford where the city borders with the Metropolitan Borough of Bury. "The last landlady who had it got her car torched on the car park and then got her face smashed in by these cunts, she had to have twenty-odd stitches. Obviously, the fucking brewery didn't say nowt to the new landlord about the trouble this pub gets. Snide bastards." Tommy pulled the handbrake on. "So I reckon this Danny Newton needs a fright. I think he should have a pretty bad limp for the next couple of years as well."

The conversation stopped as the two men walked down the hill and approached the pub. It was situated in quite a remote spot, a hundred yards away from the terraced houses at the top of the hill. It was one of the 1970's quick-build pubs which had sprung up all over the country as breweries bought up any old scrap of land they could find. These pubs looked like a cross between a children's home and a community centre and usually had a flat-roof section at the front, complete with a vicious alsatian which would bark at every punter that came, went or walked past. But there was no alsatian here today, just a very depressed and tired looking orange brick pub with some quite unmissable graffiti painted along the front of the building in white paint proclaiming that "Dawn Lucas is a grass."

Inside the pub, Tommy and Kingo sat out of sight of the bar area and nursed their drinks patiently. They passed the time chatting about mutual acquaintances and Kingo told his potential new boss about some of the problems Manchester city centre was experiencing in the face of guns, drugs, gangsters and corrupt police officers.

As the clock neared eight-thirty, Tommy began looking out of the window, he could hear a rowdy group but couldn't see the people responsible. It sounded like seven or eight blokes shouting and jeering and the noise was getting louder. Finally, they began walking past the window that Tommy was sitting next to. He looked away quickly. It wouldn't do if one of these racketeers recognised him. Tommy leaned around the recess which was shielding him from view and kept an eye on Terry, the pub's landlord. Tommy had agreed that the landlord would start nodding his head once Danny Newton was inside the building. Just seconds after the door opened and the noise of the group shattered the peace and quiet in the bar, Terry the landlord started nodding.

"What's up with you Terry, have you got that mad cows

disease or summat?" The man who said it was walking confidently towards the bar as his entourage laughed loudly at the remark as they followed. The man tried to lift the bar-hatch but it was locked.

"What's up with this?" He asked Terry. The man was around six-foot three, six-four and he towered over the landlord.

"Ah, you must be Danny." Said Tommy as he walked around the back of the group. "Pleasure to make your acquaintance. I'm Tommy, this is Kingo."

Danny Newton's face was a picture. He recognised Kingo from the city centre, he was well established as one of the people you don't want to fuck about with. But the guy who was talking was another level altogether, Tommy McKinlay. Rock Hard Tommy. Danny Newton had a big problem here, he couldn't lose any face in front of his lads, but he couldn't afford a confrontation with these two either. It was clear that he was thinking fast.

"Hee-yar, what's the score here. I hope yous aren't gonna just come and take this pub off us." Danny added a shit laugh on the end, trying to make it appear that this could all be sorted out reasonably. Tommy just stood there staring at him. Kingo was standing beside him, staring at the rest of the group. There were eight of them and the high-jinx mood had disappeared completely. The smell of farts was thick in the air.

"Terry, do us a favour mate, can you ask your customers to go and sit in the other room while we sort this out?"

Terry unbolted the bar-hatch and lifted it. He walked around the bar and headed to the couple of tables which had customers. They stood silently and walked through to the snug, relieved at the opportunity to get out of this terrifying atmosphere and away from the farts.

"Cheers Terry, is the fire exit locked?"

"Yes, Tommy."

"Cheers. Well go and lock the front door and then you can go in and keep the customers company in there. We'll be alright."

"Listen, what the fucks going on here..." Said Danny, his

hands out at his sides as though he was trying to dramatize his confusion.

"Oh do shut up Daniel, you big-eared malignant shit funnel." Said Tommy.

Danny just stood there, his mouth slightly open. His neck was twitching visibly as his blood-pressure reached its limit.

"What do you want me to do with these shit-cunts Tommy?" Asked Kingo who hadn't taken his eyes off Danny's entourage. They were aged between twenty and mid-thirties and every last one of them looked like they'd just got out of Strangeways judging by their crew-cut hairstyles and their grey prison complexions.

Tommy had his gaze fixed on Danny as he answered. "Tell them to take all their clothes off so we can check they're not tooled up." He tried not to laugh as he said it.

"You heard him. Throw them in a pile there." Said Kingo, pointing at the floor between Tommy and Danny. There was no debate or discussion, the young men just followed the order and started stripping off. As they stood there, in their boxer-shorts, Kingo told them to throw their pants on the pile as well. They did so, in silence.

"Oh, Tommy. That reminds me. On the way back can we stop and pick up some party sausages?"

Tommy laughed loudly, throwing his head back as he did so. Kingo's joke had come from nowhere and it had really tickled him. Danny Newton began laughing along as well, inexplicably.

"What the fuck are you laughing at, Daniel?" Asked Tommy, without the slightest hint of humour left on his face. It appeared that Danny was still deluding himself that he could blag his way out of this. He was much mistaken.

"Just the state of these fucking leppers!"

"Get your clothes off Danny and throw them on that pile you goofy cunt."

Danny sensed that there was nothing good coming back from his attempts at communicating with Tommy McKinlay. He was just staring at him, his eyes seemed dead. Danny pulled his Kickers jumper over his head and threw it on the pile, revealing a large NF tattoo on his left breast.

"Keep going." Tommy was willing Danny to say something, to start kicking off, but Danny sensed that it would be a bad move. He kicked off his trainers, unclipped his belt and dropped his jeans. Once his boxers were off, a moment of excruciating embarrassment passed before Kingo commented.

"Pickled onions as well."

Tommy's laugh was even louder this time and Kingo joined in as well, amused by how funny Tommy's laugh was. The gang of racketeers stood there, trembling with fear, their hands hiding their genitals.

"Right, so we all know why me and Kingo are here, yes?"

Danny finally submitted and gave up on the idea of trying to blag his way out of this. He nodded with the rest of the group.

"So I've come down today to make it stop. Thing is, we might be having a right laugh about it all now but this is serious stuff. Am I understood?"

The naked, thoroughly humiliated gang of wannabe gangsters nodded in silence. This included Danny who had finally wised up to the gravity of the situation.

"But I'm a fair man, so I'm going to give yous a couple of choices. We can have a ruck now, me and Kingo versus you lot. You can use any weapons you can get your hands on, bar stools, glasses, whatever you want. There's eight of yous against two of us, that's four to one so the odds are stacked in your favour. But if you choose that option, you've got to understand that me and Kingo will be proper going for it, you know what I mean? No fucking about. And we're keeping our clothes on you dodgy twats."

The gang were all listening, the trembling was becoming more and more pronounced. One of two of them had chattering teeth, the fear was so intense.

"Option two, I think you'll prefer this option, but I'm not trying to lead you here. Option two is that you all have to punch Daniel in the face so hard that you break your hand. I'll inspect your hand after you've hit him and if it isn't completely fucked, you go again."

"Yeah, that's a good idea that Tommy. A broken hand or a fight against us. I know what I'd choose if I was them, but I hope they're as thick as they fucking look and choose the fight." Kingo was really enjoying himself tonight and Tommy was very impressed with his input.

"They look like window-lickers though, to be honest with you Kingo. I mean, look at the fucking state of their leader. He's like a cross between Bugs Bunny and Prince Charles! Tell you what Danny, you look like you fell out of the ugly tree and smashed your face against every fucking branch before you landed on the motorway and got run down by the ugly truck! I heard the midwife screamed when you were born!"

"No, she resigned." Said Kingo.

"No, she fucking killed herself!" Countered Tommy.

Tommy's head flew back again as he laughed hysterically at Kingo's contribution. Danny just stood there. This big, intimidating bully who had led a reign of terror on this little pub over the past few years, who'd boasted about seeing off six landlords in eighteen months was lost for words, standing there with his flabby white belly and his tiny little cock. The bully was now getting a taste of his own medicine and he was completely demeaned in front of his fuck-wit followers.

"Cheer up Daniel, it's nearly time for the main event. So what is it going to be? A fight against me and Kingo or you all break your hands on Danny the fanny's face?"

It was clearly a tough decision and all seven of Danny's pals looked down at the floor.

Kingo intervened, keen to hurry things along. "If you want to fight, place your hand in the air right now."

None of the hands went up.

"Well there's your answer Tommy. It looks like Danny's mates all want to break their hands on Danny's kite."

"On the upside though, he'll look a lot better when his face is all smashed in! Right, you! Come here." Tommy was pointing at the lad who was nearest to Danny. "Let me have a look at your fist." The young bloke, no older than twenty-five walked nervously past the pile of clothes and up to Tommy.

After checking his fist was in good condition, Tommy explained what was happening next.

"Right, so you need to hit him so hard that you fracture your hand. Listen, it's not as easy as it sounds. Your brain will be in self-preservation mode, it'll try and make you hit him softer than you need to. But fuck your brain mate, it's a dickhead!"

The member of Danny's gang nodded his understanding.

"Go on then. You fucking cheesecake."

Danny was scared, his back was leant against the brass rail of the bar. The young lad didn't make eye contact, he just stood in front of the man that he'd feared all the time he'd known him and drew his arm back. The crunching sound of the punch was followed by a yell of pain. Tommy laughed as he realised that it was the lad who was injured, Danny had taken the punch pretty well, desperate to save some face in front of his followers.

"Let's have a look, then." Said Tommy. The young man held out his trembling hand and Tommy congratulated him. "Good work there fellah! That hand is fucked! Go and sit over there and have a good cry."

Tommy looked at the group of naked men. The fear which was etched on their faces was very rewarding to him. From a business point of view, the word of this excellent event would travel far and wide and subsequently, the phone would keep on ringing with more work. More calls from desperate people who needed help sorting out more toe-rags. Now that Kingo was on the scene and seemed so interested in being involved and that he seemed perfectly capable of doing the job made this visit to The Staff of Life a very enjoyable and pleasurable job.

The mood in the pub was becoming darker and more and more tense as Danny's lads walked over and busted their hands punching him as hard as they possibly could in the face. Tommy continued to check each fist. A couple of the lads had managed to smash their hands up on the first or second attempt. Tommy found much more enjoyment in watching the lads who had to give Danny six or seven good cracks before they managed to present a broken hand to Tommy.

As the last of the seven walked up to the bar, Danny's face was in a dreadful state. He had deep cuts above each eye, the eyes themselves were hidden by the swelling and the blood which was cascading down his face. There was a deep gash under his eye, which was oozing blood down onto Danny's chest and legs. He was trembling violently and Tommy was surprised that his legs hadn't given way yet.

"Come on, last one. Let's have a look at that fist!" Tommy checked the final hand. "Right, go on. See if you can knock the stupid fucker out. If you do, I'll let you go down to A and E with some clothes on!"

The young man looked like he had a good dig on him. He was quite well built and his arms were well developed. Judging by his physique, Tommy felt confident that this dozy looking moron was into his boxing. He was really hoping that this lad would flop Danny out, he was half way there already. The lad looked away from Danny as he punched his face with all of his strength. Tommy got his wish as Danny's head flew back, then his whole upper body fell forward and he collapsed on the floor, his chin hitting the ground last. That final, devastating punch had finally put him to sleep with a loud crunching sound.

"Nice one mate. Let's have a look at your hand." The lad held out his hand as requested. It wasn't damaged at all. "Ooh, we've got a problem here. Your hand is intact and Danny's been sparked out! I think you'll need to jump up and down on his leg and smash his kneecap off." Tommy was talking about this horrendous act of violence ever-so-casually. It was as though he was merely suggesting that this young bloke should start wearing his hair in a different style.

"No... what... that's..."

Tommy shoved the lad in the chest and the force of the push made his legs give way as he stumbled backwards over the pile of clothes in the middle of the bar area. The lad who had knocked Danny out was trying to get back to his feet. "You being lippy?"

"No... I..."

"What's your name dickhead?"

"Lee Mason."

"Well, Lee Mason, put your trainers on, there's a good lad." Said Tommy, his psychotic stare was back. The rest of Danny's racketeers were sitting on the seats opposite, paralysed with fear and feeling utterly humiliated without their clothes on. Several were looking down at the floor with their heads in their broken hands. Lee got down on all fours and started rummaging through the pile looking for his trainers.

"Hurry up, you freckly-nosed shit-beast!"

Lee put his trainers on and stood up. He looked as though he was going to burst into tears. It was comical to witness the transformation in these people. To think they had come bounding in here, full of beans just fifteen minutes earlier, excited at the prospect of extorting money from an innocent guy who was just trying to run a business. Now these horrible clowns all looked as though anxiety and depression was going to be their new state of mind for the foreseeable future.

Kingo was laughing at Lee's expression. He really was facing a monumental moral dilemma here, with his cock out on full display.

"Just jump on his knee, put all your weight into it and snap the fucker!" Said Tommy, the crazy stare was gone again and he seemed to be in a good mood once more. "Otherwise all these lot are going to break their shit hands punching your fucking lights out, you big can of tramp's piss."

Lee Mason recognised that he didn't have a great deal of choice in this. He stepped a little closer to the bar where Danny was lay unconscious and jumped on his knee, landing heavily with both feet. The disturbing click sound was louder than anybody had expected. Kingo looked away, clenching his teeth. Even Tommy had a look of distaste as he turned around and stared at the gang, all of whom looked totally appalled by the excessive violence on display.

Danny began twitching violently, then a loud, ear-piercing scream left his lips.

"Job done!" Said Tommy. "Right, fuck off the lot of yous. Leave your clothes there and if I have to speak to any of yous again, I'll come and find every single one of you and I'll make sure that both of your knees look like Daniel's."

Chapter Thirty-Eight

Jo Rudovsky was born and raised in Wythenshawe and she loved the place. It may be the biggest council estate in Europe, right next door to Manchester Airport, but it is a very dear place to her. The district has more than its fair share of scallies and ne'er-do-wells but to her, it's home and home is where the heart is. Rudovsky was doing well at work and could easily afford to move out of the area to one the posher parts of South Manchester which surrounded Wythenshawe, but she didn't want to.

Rudovsky felt indebted to this place, she had always considered it a blessing growing up here, learning all about how the drug-dealers, the blaggers, the gangsters and the knobheads operated. Seeing first-hand how victims of crime are affected, and at how woefully unfair life could be for people who weren't simply born into an easier existence. She learned how a life of crime was most often borne from necessity rather than a conscious choice. She had also gained a good idea of how the general public view the police with suspicion and distrust, and subsequently, understood the kind of policing that connected positively with the community, rather than creating animosity and conflict. Ultimately, growing up within a community like Wythenshawe, Jo Rudovsky had learnt the basic facts of life. She learnt that no matter who you are, where you are from or how much cash and stuff you've got – 95% of people are spot-on, salt-of-the-earth, kind-hearted legends. It was the 5% who cause the shit and create the trouble, fear and anguish. And by doing all that, it was this 5% who had enough power to tarnish an entire area's reputation with their shitty behaviour.

There was no question that Wythenshawe had made Jo Rudovsky the formidable detective that she is today. It was for this reason that she wanted to stay here on the gigantic estate, buying an ex-council house with her girlfriend Abby, rather than gentrifying and moving into Hale Barns or Wilmslow, the posher districts which were just a mile away in either direction.

Since leaving work so dramatically a couple of hours

earlier, Rudovsky had been home, but she had been in a shitty mood. She'd been furious that Miller hadn't called, begging her to come back to work and as a result, she was taking it out on Abby. Upon realising that she was being a total dick, she'd decided to go out and try and calm down by herself. She had no plan where to go, so just drove around the estate aimlessly, cruising past all the places that she knew so well, the Civic Centre, the youth club, her old school and the shopping precinct. But she wasn't taking in the view, her mind was consumed with this situation at work, she was fuming that she was being excluded from something and that anger was starting to turn to paranoia. What had she done? Had somebody put a complaint in about her? But who? And for what? Her mind was doing over-time, trying to think of a reason why she was being treated like this. She genuinely couldn't think of a single thing she'd done wrong, she was even sucking up to Chapman these days, despite never really liking the man. As she continued to drive around the area, past the thousands of identical, pebble-dashed houses and the gangs of kids in identical clothes and stopping to give-way to the identical buses, she was struggling to come up with a rational explanation for this unbelievable situation.

What hurt the most was that her phone still hadn't rung. That neither Miller or Saunders had tried to stop her from storming out, that Chapman or Worthington hadn't even tried to disguise the fact that they were hiding something. The not knowing what this was about, the wondering what everybody was saying about her was driving her crazy. She decided to pull her car over and ring Kenyon. He was her best mate at work, he'd be able to shed some light. She imagined that he'd have spent the whole time since she'd walked out trying to get to the bottom of things. Rudovsky looked at the clock on her dashboard, it was 5.34pm, which meant that Pete would still be driving home if he'd managed to get away on time.

"Alright, Jo?"

"Not really Pete."

"I know mate, I know. What the fuck's going on?"

"Dunno. That's why I'm ringing you. Thought you might

have an update for me?" Rudovsky's voice was uncharacteristically flat and slightly emotional.

"Not a chance mate. The mood is bloody evil in there. Bill and Mike haven't said a word since you left, Miller and Saunders went straight out a few minutes after you and haven't been back and poor Helen is sat there wondering what the fuck's going on."

"She's not the only one."

"You alright mate?"

"No Pete, I'm not. I'm really not. I'm trying to work out what the hell I've done wrong."

"You?"

"Yes."

"Why do you think it's about you?"

"It's obvious it's about me. You saw how Bill and Mike were when I asked them what was going on. Plus Saunders said Miller was still in Dixon's office when he was clearly going to meet up with those three."

"Doesn't mean it's about you, though."

"It is, Pete. I can feel it in my waters. I told Miller I was getting off until he told me what was going on and he just let me walk out without saying a word."

"Still doesn't mean it's about you, mate. Just try and chill out, you're over-thinking it. It's more likely to be about Miller's problems with this school hoax than about you. Trust me Jo, you're being a stupid neurotic bitch."

"I don't know... why would there be secrets between the gaffers and Bill and Mike?"

"Well, actually... I've been thinking about that."

"Right?"

"Well, it's probably a load of bollocks but do you remember when Karen was killed?"

"Yes Pete, obviously. Fucking hell, I couldn't go to her funeral because I was still in hospital."

"I know. And I was off after my operation. Well, if you and me and Helen aren't privy to what's happening at the moment... well, work it out. We're the only three people who weren't around at the time. And we're being shoved out in the cold on this one. I bet it's summat to do with that, you know."

"Bollocks! Really?" Suddenly, a new found energy could be detected in Rudovsky's voice.

"Well, it might explain a few things. We all know Miller isn't Bill Chapman's number one fan, but you're saying that he's cutting him in on whatever's going on. It makes sense."

"Shit the bed! You might be onto summat here, Pete."

"It seems a bit odd that Miller is having to hide his family away, then he's having secret chats with certain people. I honestly can't think of any other cases that we missed out on when we were off. This was the only one, and we've said before that there was something ultra dodgy about it all."

"Like the fact none of us are allowed to even mention it?"

"Exactly."

"So what the fuck... what happened that is so secretive?" Rudovsky's voice had lifted considerably. It was clear that she felt that her mate Peter Kenyon had found the missing piece to this puzzle.

"Well, I'm not Mystic Meg, Jo. But if you ask me, that's what's going on."

"You're right, Pete. You're right. Okay, not a word about this to anyone. Cheers, love you, bye." Rudovsky hung up and started her car's engine, feeling empowered by Kenyon's rational and well considered assessment of the situation.

Chapter Thirty-Nine

England, Scotland and Wales has 132 prisons which are staffed by almost 28,000 prison officers. At first glance, that seems like a hell of a lot of staff members, but it really isn't. Not when you consider that there are 110,000 prisoners, who are in the jails 24/7. Thousands are released daily, and just as many are arriving to start their sentences.

Looking at the figures alone, the staff are outnumbered by inmates four to one. But that's if they were working 24/7. They don't, of course. They work 8 hours, 5 days a week and have time off for holidays, sick leave and maternity / paternity time plus training courses and exams. With all of these factors considered and with the true numbers crunched down effectively, the inmates actually outnumber the staff by twelve to one on an average day. The alarming fact of the matter is that prisons have never been so full, and experienced staff numbers have never been so low. Prison officer numbers are down by dangerously low amounts, but that is only part of the problem facing the country's prisons.

In the face of ever-increasing danger of physical and mental challenges inside our prisons, at the same time as a shocking reduction in resources – a devastating amount of experienced prison staff have left the service over the past decade, many citing health and safety concerns as their reason for leaving. These experienced, skilled staff members have been replaced by younger people who don't possess the expertise to safely manage the prison population. You don't have to be Albert Einstein to work out that this is an unsustainable position, but if you needed any further evidence of the state of HMP's human resources nightmare, look no further than the 6-month retainment time average for new staff. The younger prison officers are jacking in after half a year purely because of the reality of the challenges of the role, offset by the derisory pay on offer. Why would anybody want to work in a place where people throw excrement at them, when they could earn more money delivering mail or emptying bins or driving a bus?

Britain's jails are in crisis and this is terrifying for the staff and for most of the prison inmates. It is, however, brilliant news for those prisoners who want to take advantage of the vulnerabilities in the system.

The UK's prison service has been dramatically affected by the government cuts which were introduced under the banner of "austerity" in 2010. In theory, these far-reaching cuts were designed to claw back the money lost due to the bail-outs caused by the global financial crash which occurred in 2008. But now, 10 years after the cuts were introduced and with still no end in sight for police, fire, the NHS, schools, local councils, transport and prisons, the decent staff have left and the new ones can't see the once proud role of Prison Officer as a sensible, rewarding nor affordable career choice.

What this all boils down to is chaos in the United Kingdom's jails. The prisoners know all too well that the staff are under immense pressure, and they also know that there are dozens of easy ways to cause lots of disruption, which in turn keeps them out of their cells for a while longer than the one hour they are permitted per day in most of the jails.

One example of this disruption has become a daily occurrence in every jail in the country. Prisoners are acutely aware that prison officers are not allowed to step onto the suicide prevention nets which are suspended between each landing. These gigantic nets are designed to prevent prisoners from jumping over the barrier, to meet their deaths on the cold concrete floor below. Safe in the knowledge that the staff are not permitted to step on the netting, prisoners are leaping over the barrier outside their cell doors and then use the suicide nets as trampolines, bouncing up and down, or just standing in the middle while they make demands of the humiliated staff, who can do nothing but stand behind the barrier and watch on amid the deafening noise of the other prisoners cheering, laughing and banging heavy objects against their cell doors. These types of pointless, daily incidents have forced the most experienced staff members to leave the service in their thousands over the past decade.

There are strict procedures in place for when an

incident like this occurs. The prison has to call for help from specialist teams who are trained in negotiating with the prisoners and skilled in getting them to retreat back to the safety of the landing floor. One such team of specialist officers who are tasked with these types of jobs are the Tornado team. Every prison has a Tornado team, which is comprised of the most skilled and experienced officers on duty. From the moment an incident requires their input, the Tornado Team members suspend their normal duties and scramble to their department to get kitted up in their specialist uniforms. If there is any risk of violence, this uniform consists of riot helmets, stab proof, fire-proof clothing and riot shields. In normal circumstances, the Tornado team can cope with small scale disturbances and incidents within the prison, such as a couple of lags using the suicide net as a trampoline to pass a few hours.

But if the incident is deemed more serious, the prison will call for more specialist support from the NTRG, the National Tactical Response Group. These teams are the elite "SAS" prison officers, based at two secret locations, one in the north of England and one in the south. They are on standby twenty-four hours a day, ready to leave at a moment's notice for any jail in the UK. The NTRG was set up in the months following the Strangeways riot in 1990, spearheaded by a furious government which was determined that there could never be another repeat of the outrageous activities in Manchester which saw the complete destruction of the interior of the Victorian prison and saw 47 prisoners and 147 officers injured.

The NTRG is made up of former prison officers, hand-picked from the very best staff the service has to offer. They are trained up to SAS combat standards. They train relentlessly for every possible prison disturbance scenario, from riots, fires and hostage situations to safe and effective removal of the most dangerous prisoners. Their identities are kept secret and their operational locations are also classified. They have shown on numerous occasions that they are well worth the big money which is ploughed into their department.

In 2018, these elite officers stormed Birmingham prison as a full-scale riot broke out. 500 prisoners had taken over 4 wings and it looked as though the nightmare of Strangeways was about to be repeated. But it wasn't to be. The NTRG are treated so seriously by the government that they even have a mock-up prison at each of their bases, and they train daily for these kinds of events, rehearsing for every conceivable scenario using actors who are employed as pretend, troublesome prisoners armed with everything from makeshift knives, heavy bars and fire.

This relentless schedule of training and rehearsing worked like a charm when it was put into practise during the real-life, full scale disturbance in Birmingham. The 41-strong team of elite officers worked their way through the wings, one by one and returned every single one of the 500 prisoners to their cells within a matter of hours. None of the rioters were keen to meet with the NTRG officers ever again, either.

Today, at the NTRG's secret training complex in the north of England, the training was finished for the day and the officers were sitting down to their evening meal as the emergency hotline began ringing.

"Here we go," said the commanding officer in the direction of his team as he placed his knife and fork down heavily. "It must be tea-time. So surprise surprise, we've got a job."

A couple of minutes later, he returned. "Don't panic, it's just a routine job, dangerous prisoner transfer from HMP Manchester for tomorrow morning. We can finish our tea!"

Chapter Forty

Miller looked uneasy as he pressed the doorbell at Rudovsky's house. He was quite comfortable having a confrontation with any member of his staff whenever it was required. But not Rudovsky, she could be as slippery as an eel and far too clever for her own good. It made bollocking her a major undertaking. Luckily, it was very rare that he needed to have a word with her. But he couldn't let today's outburst go unchecked. Miller recognised that he faced a big challenge here today, trying to reprimand Rudovsky whilst also trying to swerve some very tricky questions.

Abby answered the door, looking surprised to see Jo's boss standing at the step. "Flipping heck! DCI Miller! What an honour! What a privilege! Shit, where's our red carpet?" She said sarcastically, though the surprise at seeing him here was etched on her face.

"Alright Abby. Is Jo about?"

"Nah, sorry. She's gone out."

"Oh. Any idea when she'll be back?"

"No, sorry. But she text me, about half an hour ago, I didn't read it though, it'll just be an apology. She was being a proper boot when she went out, she was acting like Mariah Carey with PMT. Just hang on a sec, I'll grab my phone. Do you want to come in?"

"Cheers." Miller stepped into the house and waited politely in the hall whilst Abby went into the kitchen.

"Go through, take a seat."

Miller accepted the invitation and went into the living room, planning to sit down on the sofa. The living room was full of arts and crafts stuff. He had to move some of it to one side in order to take a seat.

"Pardon the mess, some stuff I'm getting ready for the youth club tonight." Abby looked slightly embarrassed by the state of the place as she returned, clutching her mobile phone.

"It's fine. So, you're still with the youth service? I thought Jo said you'd been laid off."

"Yeah, well... yes and no really. I'm still there, but it's voluntary now. Government cuts." Abby rolled her eyes.

"No way, what so, you're keeping it running, but for free?" Miller looked impressed.

"I'm afraid so. Someone's got to. I'm getting a bit of work in schools and with other authorities to tide me over, but the Ferrari had to be sent back."

Miller laughed. Abby had the same dry and sarcastic sense of humour as Rudovsky. "So, anyway, this text from Jo. It's about you."

"Well, I'm not surprised... we've had a falling out."

"Oh. That might explain why she was being a dick with me."

"Yes, that'll be it. Sorry Abby."

"Do you want me to read it to you?"

"Please."

"Okay. It says 'sorry for being a twat, I'm stressed about work shite and shouldn't have brought it home with me. If Miller comes round looking for me, tell him to fuck off. Tell him to fuck off as far as he can and then when he comes to the big massive sign that says you are not permitted to fuck off past here, tell him to completely ignore the sign and just keep fucking off." Abby started laughing as she finished relaying the message.

"I think she's still pissed off with me..." said Miller.

"Do you think?"

"I've come round to sort it all out. Shit."

"Well, as it goes... I think she's just pulling up outside." Abby was looking above Miller's head and out of the window. Rudovsky was parking her car on the street. "Yes, it's her. Shall I let you out of the back door?" Abby smiled warmly and Miller reciprocated as he shifted uncomfortably on the settee. Abby headed to the front door and opened it. Miller heard her whispering "Your boss is here!" and Jo replied, "I know, I saw his car, he's in my fucking space!"

Rudovsky stomped into the living room and stood facing Miller with her hands on her hips. "Well?"

"Hi Jo..."

"Right, before you two start kicking seven shades of shit

out of each other, you can both help me get this lot in the car. Then I'll be out of your hair."

Abby's rather spirited instruction knocked Rudovsky off her stride. It made sense that Abby was out of the road while she had it out with Miller, but she felt slightly embarrassed that she'd been undermined in this way. Miller looked relieved.

"Come on." Said Abby. "All this." She pointed at the tubs and piles of stuff which were everywhere. Rudovsky headed over to where Miller was sitting and picked up a few boxes. Miller followed the lead.

Five minutes later, Abby had driven off and the front room looked a lot more homely than it had done. Miller sat down again and Rudovsky stood in the centre of the room.

"I hope you've come here to tell me exactly what's going on..."

"Not quite Jo. But I have come to apologise."

"So, you're not going to tell me?"

"Well, it's not that I don't want to... It's more that it's for your own protection."

Rudovsky sat down on the armchair facing Miller.

"What's that supposed to mean?"

"Well, basically Jo, something heavy is going on. It doesn't affect you in any way..."

"Does it affect Pete?"

"No."

"Does it affect Helen?"

"No."

"So, it's got something to do with Karen?"

Rudovsky could see that she'd drawn first blood as Miller looked down and shifted in his seat, it was obvious that he was desperately trying to think of something to help him reverse out of that incriminating question which had skilfully appeared from nowhere.

"This is why suspects can't handle an interview with you Jo. You throw invisible punches..."

"Don't try and change the subject, Sir. Is it about Karen?"

Miller looked down at the floor again.

- 189 -

"Don't fuck me about, Sir. I've been going out of my mind wondering what's going on, thinking all sorts, that I'm about to be sacked. You can't mess about with people like that. It's not fair."

"No, Jo. It's not fair dragging you into something that you've got no involvement with. Something that just knowing about could put your career in jeopardy."

This comment mellowed Rudovsky's mood dramatically. Kenyon's theory had just been confirmed and the pressure had suddenly lessened considerably. She sat back in her armchair and Miller could see that she was reconsidering her attitude.

"I'm going to ask you nicely, respectfully, to just trust me on this. There is a shit-storm brewing that could see me banged up…"

"Fuck off!" The surprise on Rudovsky's face was unmistakable.

"What, past the sign that says do not fuck off past here?" Miller smiled widely, but Rudovsky ignored it. She was too interested in hearing more about this bombshell. Miller got the hint and continued. "Now, cards on the table, I could tell you all about it, right now. But the moment I did that, you'd be involved. My priority right now is firstly to protect Keith, Bill and Mike from any potential fall-out. And secondly, to try and stop this from getting out of hand. It's bad, Jo. But when I leave here, I want you to understand that I'm acting in your best interests in not telling you what has happened, or what this is about."

It was clear that Rudovsky was struggling with the vagueness of this announcement.

"It's to do with Karen?"

"About that, and a whole lot more. I can't say anything else about it. I want to, I want to give you the full disclosure, but I simply can't, Jo. Now, you can either accept that and come back to work in the morning, or I'm happy to sign you off on annual leave…"

"So something happened when Karen died, something that could see you in jail…"

"Jo!"

"Pete was off, so was I, so that's why we've been cut out..."

"Yes."

"And the thing that happened at the twins school, is that connected?"

"I can't say."

"But if it wasn't you'd say no, so that's a yes."

"Jo, you don't need to prove to me that you're a pain in the arse for suspects. But I'm not a suspect, I'm your gaffer, asking you to keep your beak out, for your own good."

Rudovsky crossed her legs on the armchair and stared at Miller. He had been a great boss to her, always supportive and had overlooked a few things in promoting her to DS. She had the greatest of respect for him. But at the same time, this was just too intriguing. She knew in her heart of hearts that what Miller was asking was impossible. Miller was the straightest copper there was, he broke the odd rule here and there, sure. But he was straight down the line when it came to right and wrong in the law. It was simply impossible for Rudovsky to consider forgetting about this, she was desperate to know what the hell was going on.

"Listen, boss."

"No, Jo. You listen, I don't want a second round. I want to leave here with you saying you respect my decision."

"Shush, this is my house, I'm in charge here."

"I quite clearly saw that Abby is in charge here, but anyway..."

"This thing, that I'm not allowed to know about. I am your way out of it."

"How the hell do you get that?"

"Okay. You've given me enough information to work most of this out. This thing at the school, Clare and the kids being sent away, the Karen element... You going into Strangeways to meet with a con... I've already learnt enough to work out that somebody is blackmailing you, something about Karen's death."

"No, wait, this is all supposition."

"No, it fucking isn't. Don't treat me like a twat boss. So

if I know this much, it's a bit unfair to leave me hanging."

"You said that you're my way out of it?"

"Yes, so, you've got two choices, you can continue being a dick with me, hiding me in the cupboard, keeping me in the dark. Or you can tell me the full story and benefit from me being involved in whatever it is you're planning to do to make this go away. One thing's for certain though, it's fucking dumb to keep me away while relying on Chapman and Worthington to pull you out of the shit. It's the shittest thing I've ever heard in my life."

"But I've already told you… it's not personal. It's something that will pull *you* into the shit. Serious shit. Jail-time shit."

"Don't care."

"What do you mean, you don't care?"

"Exactly what I just said." Rudovsky stood and unzipped her fleece, before pulling her MCP lanyard over her head. She walked across to Miller and held it before him. "Whatever the fuck is going on, I want in. And if you won't let me in, take my warrant card and my security pass now and you can start advertising for a new DS. I can't work for somebody who doesn't trust me."

Chapter Forty-One

"Keith, we need to talk, as soon as possible."

"I'm in the office if that helps, Sir?"

"No. Meet me at the canal. I'm just leaving Wythenshawe now. I'll be about twenty minutes."

"How did it go?"

"Shitly. Set off now and I'll fill you in properly, I'm not discussing this in the office or over a phone, anybody could be listening. Seeya in a bit." Miller hung up and pressed his foot against the accelerator as he drove onto the motorway.

The canal spot was Miller's favourite place to talk about things in private. He'd realised earlier today, whilst talking with Saunders, Chapman and Worthington, that he hadn't been down to that spot for ages. Now he'd needed to visit it twice in one day.

It was a secluded spot, accessible by car but off the beaten track. It was a perfect, almost tranquil setting for having long, private chats with no fear of interruption or eavesdroppers. The only people who came down here were young couples looking for a bit of privacy in their cars, but they could be quickly moved on with the flash of a police badge. Under normal circumstances, Miller would have met Saunders at Piccadilly railway station, just a few minutes walk away from the MCP HQ. He'd had many private chats here with Saunders, just walking up and down the platform over and over again until the meeting was concluded. But due to the invisible nature of McKinlay's associates, Miller was reluctant to go to any public place at this particular moment in time, at least whilst he was still unsure of who McKinlay's people were. The canal bank was perfect, if anybody was following Miller's car, or Saunders' for that matter, they'd have a half-mile drive down a little-known, deserted old lane to contend with before revealing themselves at the dead-end by the canal.

Saunders had arrived before Miller. He was sitting on the huge stone coping stones by the side of the canal, watching the sunset in the distance, admiring the view and savouring the peace and quiet when Miller's car pulled up behind his.

"Nice spot. Just need a can of lager!" Said Miller as he got out of the car and slammed the door shut. The beep-beep of his central locking fob made a couple of geese hiss on the opposite banking.

"So, what happened?"

"It's a disaster mate. She said she wants to be involved or she's jacking."

"Seriously?" Saunders exhaled loudly as he stared down into the dark water. "Another unexpected complication, eh?"

Miller groaned as he inched his frame down onto the Victorian stone-work and sat next to his DI. "Yep. She said that she can't work for somebody who doesn't trust her. Handed me her warrant card."

"Jesus."

A moment of silence passed, both men losing themselves in their thoughts. "You did tell her why you were keeping her at arms-length though?" Asked Saunders, eventually.

"Yes, course. Went over it several times. She said she's not arsed. Plus she'd worked most of it out already."

"You what? How?"

Miller spent the next five minutes going over the conversation with Rudovsky in detail, including how she had interrogated him and skilfully arrived at the conclusion that all of this was somehow about the death of Ellis. Another silence hung heavy, but for the sound of birdsong emanating from the surrounding trees. Neither Saunders nor Miller seemed compelled to shatter the peace, both were again lost in the peacefulness. Finally, Saunders had gathered his thoughts and launched into his assessment of the situation.

"Okay, it sounds like we've got no choice here. Jo wants in and Jo always gets what she wants. But if we agree to that, we have to work out how to keep Pete and Helen occupied and out of the loop."

"It's a nightmare." Said Miller, the stress and frustration was very clear in his voice.

"Yeah, it's a nightmare alright. But we need to come up

with a solution to the problem. This isn't really the problem, Tommy McKinlay is. Or rather, the stunt he's trying to pull is the problem. Something heavy is going to happen while he's on remand, I'll bet my life on it. He's basically put himself inside, and there has to be a reason. I'm not convinced that it's just to blackmail you."

"I know, Keith. I know. But there are so many things spinning about, I don't know where to start with any of it."

"So Jo's right. It would be a lot wiser to bring Jo on board, have her on the team than let her walk away. Our team will be fucked without her once all of this has been put to bed anyway."

"You think it's going to go away?" Asked Miller, with an unmissable tone of hope in his voice.

"I wouldn't be here if I wasn't banking on that outcome. I just wish I had a clear idea of how we get to it."

"You know something Keith? Me and you have never really spoken about this case, have we?"

"No."

Another silence descended, only there was suddenly a tension. Both Saunders and Miller were fully aware of the fact that they had hardly spoken to one another in the months after Ellis had been killed. When they had finally patched it up, it was all about looking forward and putting the wretched Pop case behind them both. The silence wasn't quite as peaceful now, but Miller filled the void. "Well, if its okay with you, mate, I'd like to tell you what happened from my perspective..."

"I'm not sure I want to know, to be honest. I think there's enough to think about."

"I'd appreciate five minutes, please?"

Saunders didn't say anything. He just focused on the hazy sunset in the distance. Miller took the silence as a green light to continue.

"I've told you bits about this. But I've never really explained the reason I let Dawson go that day. Now, I know you've always thought that it was some macho ego bullshit, and I've accepted that. Maybe it was to a certain extent, but it wasn't just about that. I've never tried to put my side of the story across to you. But under the circumstances, I think I should tell you why I did what I did. Are you comfortable with that?"

Saunders didn't say anything. He just grabbed some loose stones and began plopping them into the water below, staring at the circles that the chippings created as they penetrated the murky water.

"We were all being treated like idiots on that case. Dixon was the worst offender, but I've realised since that he was only following orders. He had no idea how it would end. I know for a fact he'd have played no part in it whatsoever if he'd had the slightest suspicion that any of his officers would be placed in danger. The fact is, the thing I've never told you... never told anybody... George Dawson was set up."

"What? Fucks sake, I don't think I want to..." There was an unmistakable anger in Saunders' voice. He resented the way that Miller stuck up for Dawson, it was the reason that this subject was so volatile between them.

"Hear me out, Keith. Please. As God is my witness you have to believe me. He was set up, by the government. It sounds fucking crazy, like I'm some flat-earther, but it's true. From the moment Dawson started killing, there were senior heads in the Home Office who knew exactly who he was, what he'd been planning, why he was doing it, I think they probably knew who he'd kill next as well. He'd spent seven years writing to them, phoning them up, campaigning for better protection for kids, starting petitions, you name it. He'd had meetings with senior politicians in Westminster, trying to change the law. He got nowhere with it, after years and years of trying. In the end, he wrote to his contacts in the Home Office and told them that he was going to sort the problem of paedophiles out himself. He warned them that he was going to start shooting them dead, one by one. He even told them that they'd get one bullet for each crime they'd been charged with."

Miller was staring down into the water as the dying light enveloped this hidden part of the city. He was so entranced by the ripples of the canal, he hadn't noticed that Saunders was staring at the side of his face.

"The government were using the whole thing as what

they call a 'kite-flying exercise' to see how the public responded. And from that point of view, they got exactly what they wanted, the pubs were full of crowds cheering the killer on, the mood was like England were playing in a World Cup final, it was unbelievable. Dixon had been instructed to make sure none of the investigating team got too close to arresting him until they were ready. Then, once all their forms were filled in and all their surveys were complete, they'd give the order to bring him in. That was the plan anyway. By the time my final request for more officers was ignored, I had finally twigged that something weird was going on, but Dixon just continued fobbing me off. That's why I resigned. As we know, Karen took over my role and had other ideas of how to catch the killer. She was desperate to make her mark so that she'd get my rank on a permanent basis. She was so desperate to apprehend the gunman, she'd stopped reporting back to Dixon because he was following his orders and frustrating everything. We both know what happened next. Anyway, all that's bad enough... but when I heard what George Dawson had been through himself, when he told me what had happened that led him on this course of action, that was when I knew that I couldn't possibly be the man who sent him down. I couldn't be the man who did the government's dirty work. I swear to God Keith, I couldn't work out who was worse, Dawson... or them. As soon as I found Sykes, up on Winter Hill, I told him that he was going to take the rap for everything, not just killing Karen, but all of the paedos as well. He was content with that, or at least I thought he was. He was so distraught at what had just happened, I've never seen remorse like it. I hope I never will again. Just after I'd sent Dawson home in Sykes' car, he blew his cranium off."

    Saunders was silent. This account of what happened had left him speechless. He knew that Miller had let Dawson go and had pinned everything on Dawson's best mate, Peter Sykes. Sykes was the man who had accidentally shot Karen Ellis, following a kick in the knee. Mike Worthington had lashed out as he lay on the ground beneath a crowd of people after being floored by Sykes. In the ensuing chaos, oblivious to the gun, Worthington had tried to break Sykes' leg. What resulted was the instant death of Ellis.

Saunders had always thought that Miller's stunt in letting Dawson go was an act of revenge against Dixon, who had inadvertently facilitated the death of Ellis. Miller's full and frank explanation of the true circumstances surrounding Dawson's let-off were shocking and quite humbling. Saunders was humbled by the fact that Miller had allowed him to go on thinking that the whole thing was a petty disagreement that had got out of hand. The story that Miller had just told for the first time changed everything and Saunders felt slightly confused and quite emotional.

"The very worst part of the whole thing, with regards to Dawson, was the way that he had been manipulated into carrying out the murders. There was no intervention, no visit from the police or MI6 or any of that. He didn't even receive a reply to his announcement. He'd had replies to every piece of correspondence, he was on first name terms with senior Home Office staff, several MPs and even a Minister. But as soon as he told them that he was going to take the law into his own hands, the communications stopped. There was no intervention whatsoever, not even an e-mail suggesting that he'd be wise to consider the consequences of such an idea. Nothing. I think they thought long and hard about how to handle this and stood back, waiting to see if he'd actually go through with it."

"Fucking hell, Sir. This is actually unbelievable."

"I know, Keith. I know. And then, they wanted to just bang Dawson up for the rest of his shit life once their graphs were drawn and their charts were filled in."

"I can't believe you've never told me any of this before."

"Well, it never really came up again. Did it? As far as I was concerned, it never would again, I thought it was ancient history. But here we are."

It was almost dark now and the air was becoming much cooler by the canal, so much so, Saunders was shivering.

"Have you heard from Dawson? Since that day, I mean?"

"Only once. He wrote me a letter, about six months

after. It was basically a thank you note, saying that there'd never be any more trouble from him. He posted it through my letterbox at home, I destroyed it straight away and I thought that was the end of that."

"You're going to have to speak to him." Saunders' voice had a hard edge to it.

"What? Why?" Miller was clearly stunned by this suggestion. This had never been on his to-do list.

"Firstly, we need to try and find out how the hell this information has got into Tommy McKinlay's hands and then work out what to do with the person who has passed it to McKinlay."

"And secondly?"

"Well, we're going to have to brief Dawson on every aspect of our work into proving that what Tommy McKinlay wants to suggest is a load of shit. We're going to have to inform Dawson of every aspect, so that any potential enquiries into this lead to a dead-end. It's the only way we can make this go away, for good."

"Shit. This is going to be tricky. Imagine if one of McKinlay's goons managed to get a photo of me with Dawson. That really would be game over."

"But it needs sorting. I'll give it some thought and we can discuss it properly tomorrow when I've got a bit of a plan."

"Okay, well, thanks for hearing me out, Keith. Means a lot."

"No trouble, Sir. I'd better go and see Jo."

"Rudovsky? Now? Why?"

"Well, I think I need to fill her in, make sure she's all fresh and raring to go in the morning."

"You think that's wise?"

"I think it's imperative, Sir. We're going to need Jo on this. Plus, what you've just told me sheds a whole new light on the whole thing."

"What are you going to say to her?"

"I think I'll just tell her everything. Then I'll ask her opinion on whether Pete and Helen ought to be informed as well."

"Jesus. Steady on, this is all starting to move a bit quick."

"I can't see any other option, Sir. We trust Pete and Helen, and Jo, don't we?"

"Of course, but…"

"But there are fuck knows how many scrotes out there in the community who know all about Dawson and are planning to use it as a blackmailing device against you. McKinlay is just the first we know about, there are probably more. I think it's time to grow a bit in confidence and believe in ourselves a lot more. If we're going to defeat this, we need the full team working on getting this back in the box. And once its back in the box, we get rid of the box, for good."

"Fucking hell, Keith…"

"Trust me, Sir. I've got your back."

Chapter Forty-Two

"Jo, I'm on my way over to yours. Are you in?"

"Alright? Oh, er no. I'm at the youth club with Abby."

"You're a bit old for that Jo, aren't you?" Saunders was quite pleased with his joke, but Rudovsky ignored it.

"What's the problem? Has Miller sent you?"

"Yes. I need to talk to you urgently. What time can you meet me?"

"Well, now if you want. Club finishes soon anyway and Abby's got the motor. Meet me at Woodhouse Park lifestyle centre, it's on Portway. I'll wait outside."

"Okay."

"Where are you now?"

"Not far, coming off the motorway. About five minutes…"

"Okay. But if you're coming because Miller has asked you to sweet-talk me and fob me off, you might as well save yourself the rest of the journey and bob off home to Helen because I've already told him, I'm either in or I'm out."

"Don't worry, we're going to shake it all about. I'll see you soon."

Five minutes later, Saunders pulled his car over outside the community centre and asked Rudovsky if she was looking for business.

"Shut up you cheeky twat. This better be good, Abby's kicking off now because she needs to load the car up on her own." Said Rudovsky as she sat in the passenger seat.

"First world problems, Jo."

"Go in and say that to her face, then."

"No."

"Shit-house. So, what's the crack then? Please don't leave, Jo. We wouldn't manage without you. You're the glue that holds us all together. Our rock! The blood in our veins." Rudovsky had adopted her manliest, grumpiest voice as she lauded herself.

"The pain in our arse more like."

Rudovsky laughed humourlessly.

"Nah, nowt like that. I've been with the gaffer since he left yours. We've had quite the chat."

"I hope you were sticking up for me... he's acting like a right dick."

"Well, to be honest, he's had no choice. And he was sticking up for you more than I was. I said you're a dick and that he should just let you go."

Rudovsky punched Saunders in the arm. "Knobhead."

"Ow. That really hurt, Jo."

"Good. I hope it bruises. Right, anyway, get on with it."

"Okay, well, I hope you've got an hour because that's how long this is going to take."

Saunders drove the car out of Wythenshawe and eventually parked up at the Airport Inn. "Let's do this over a pint in the beer garden. I love this place."

Over the course of the following hour, underneath the roar of aeroplanes taking off overhead every three minutes, Jo Rudovsky was stunned to hear the bizarre details of the Pop case.

"That is absolutely fucking insane." Said Rudovsky, as she drained her glass and tapped it to inform her DS that she wanted another. "It's like something out of EastEnders or summat."

"Brookside, more like." Saunders stood and picked up the glasses. "It's knocked me for six as well. I mean, I knew about Miller letting Dawson go and then letting Sykes take all the heat. But I didn't know anything else until tonight. Miller has kept this so close to his chest, I'm surprised he's not had a nervous breakdown."

"I know, yeah."

"Anyway, I'll be back in a minute. Same again?"

"Please, and get some crisps, I've not had my tea yet."

Rudovsky sat at the picnic bench as another plane came thundering along the runway towards the deserted beer garden before roaring off overhead. During daylight hours, this enormous beer garden is usually jammed with customers and plane-spotters attracted to this unique spot just metres away from the end of Runway 1. Fortunately tonight, the two SCIU officers had the place to themselves and could talk freely about this hugely sensitive situation. Whilst Saunders was at the bar, Rudovsky began to feel a bit guilty about the way that she had behaved towards Miller. She should have realised that it was something very serious, and not behaved like such a selfish diva about it all. She took her phone out of her pocket and wrote a text to Miller's new number.

"Soz for being a dick. See you in the morning, boss."

Soon after Saunders returned with the drinks and two packets of crisps, Rudovsky's phone lit up. Miller had sent her a single turd emoji which made her laugh out loud.

"So, going forwards…"

"Yes, office twat waffle time! I love this! Please say 'blue sky thinking' or 'reaching out' at some point. They're my current favourites."

"Okay well, I'm reaching out now, Jo. Going forwards with blue sky thinking, we need to talk about the elephant in the room."

"What's that?"

"Pete and Helen."

"Oh. Okay." This aspect of the problem hadn't dawned on the DS yet, she'd been so wrapped up in the extraordinary announcements of the past hour or so.

"Do we try and keep them occupied, or bring them in as well?"

"What are the pros and cons."

"Well, the cons first. It seems logical to keep this amongst the fewest number of people as humanly possible. Plus, this information and any activity relating to it would make the person involved liable for prosecution. That means you, too."

"What are the pros, Mr Negative?" Rudovsky took a thirsty gulp out of her glass.

"Well, the biggest one as far as I'm concerned is the fact that we reunite the team, readopt our honest, cooperative mentality and we come up with a way of beating McKinlay and ensuring that this goes away and stays away. I'm not talking about kicking it into the long grass."

"Well, I agree. We're on the same page." Rudovsky smiled widely as the twat waffle references were reintroduced to the conversation.

"So you think we should put them in the loop?"

"Yes. We don't want to throw them under the bus."

"Yes, an open-door policy, that would be pushing the envelope."

"Let's circle back. There's no I in team."

"We need to hammer this out and hit the ground running."

"One hundred and ten per cent! Let the cat out of the bag and run an idea up the flagpole. Let's think outside the box."

"Okay... okay. You win, Jo." Saunders laughed and proceeded to give his colleague a round of applause. He couldn't think of any more twat waffle. Rudovsky really was the champion of this game.

"Cool. Okay, well I'm ready for home now, if that's all. Can't wait to tell Abby all about this, she's going to shit!"

"Jo, don't even start you fucking knob."

"I'm kidding!" Rudovsky did jazz hands at her grinning face and Saunders laughed loudly, almost inhaling the lager.

"I know you're messing. But don't make me spell out how sensitive this is."

"Don't talk to me like I've got shit for brains! Seriously though, how the hell have you managed to keep this quiet with Helen?"

"Good question. I suppose it helps that she's not a nosey bastard, though."

"That's what's holding her back!" Rudovsky smiled widely, waiting for Saunders to take the bait. He declined politely by taking another sip from his pint.

"Okay, well... hopefully now you understand why the gaffer has been so secretive."

"Yeah, no, it's all good. Looking forward to tomorrow, now. Getting stuck in and sorting this out. Sounds to me like Miller did the right thing, under the circumstances."

"What, with Dawson, you mean?"

Rudovsky nodded.

"Yes, I think I agree. I didn't, until tonight, after he'd told me the full story. But yes, definitely. I'm just surprised that he hasn't been punished one way or another. It doesn't normally do to upset the top brass."

"No. But then again, it doesn't normally do to piss Andy Miller off. I think the top brass found that out the shit way!"

"True. Right, anyway, sup up. I need to get home. Got a busy day on the cards tomorrow."

Chapter Forty-Three

SUNDAY

Tommy McKinlay had been awake for a good hour before he'd heard the unusual activity outside his cell door. He hadn't slept well at all, he'd had an uneasy feeling throughout the night. He couldn't put his finger on what was bothering him exactly, but his instincts were never wrong and he trusted them implicitly. Whenever he got a bad feeling, he always listened to it and changed whatever plans he was making. His trust in his gut had led to several missed flights, numerous no-show meetings and even the absence from his eldest sister's wedding.

Earlier in his life, he'd ignored one of these premonitions and had paid the price in full. He'd lost his childhood best-friend Nev Gillespie in a car accident when they were both seventeen. Tommy and Nev had been invited along for a joyride in a stolen XR3i by one of the older lads from the estate. Tommy experienced a really weird, impulsive urge to say no, to drag his mate away from the car. He voiced his concerns but Nev was having none of it, goading Tommy as the driver revved the engine as loudly as possible. "Come on Tommy, don't be a yellow-belly chicken-shit."

Tommy had no way of realising the significance of the bad feeling until it was too late. The stolen car finished its journey just fifteen minutes later, crunched into a dry-stone wall on its side close to Hollingworth Lake. This was the first time that Tommy had really felt the "bad feeling" sensation and had been the only person travelling in the car who had managed to live to tell the tale. Nev had been thrown through the windscreen and into a field beyond the wall, the driver had died with the car's engine crushed onto his lap. It was angles, trajectories and mathematics which had saved Tommy's life, the backseat that he'd reluctantly got into was virtually the only section of car which had suffered no impact damage. Tommy somehow got away with only cuts and bruises, though the psychological scars were deep.

Since that day, he'd learnt to trust and respect these

occasional warning sensations as seriously as though it was God speaking directly to him. He was aware of countless situations he'd avoided by trusting his gut, situations where people had been shot and killed. He also recognised that he'd never know for sure how many situations he'd avoided by changing his plans whenever he'd felt that same, foreboding sensation.

It wasn't the same today, though. Tommy wasn't getting the familiar fight or flight feeling that normally resulted in an overwhelming urge to get away or to change his plans, which was handy as he was locked up in Strangeways and he wouldn't have a great many options at his disposal. But a dark sense of foreboding was bothering him, and it had been doing all night. He had a strong feeling that something shit was about to happen and the suspense was starting to trouble him. As he heard a shuffling sound outside his cell door, he realised that once again, his weird premonition thing had been spot-on.

It sounded as though there were a number of screws sneaking about on the landing outside his cell, but the sound which confirmed that something was about to kick off was the incessant sniffing of a dog coming from underneath his door. Tommy leapt up off his bed and stood facing the door. Almost immediately, the peep-hole cover was moved and Tommy saw an eye staring back at him through the tiny circular window. It looked as though some sort of visor was obscuring the screw's face. The tiny window turned black again as the cell door was unlocked and pushed open forcefully.

"What the fuck's going..." Tommy's mouth was wide open as a German Shepherd burst into the doorway and began barking aggressively, its handler using all of his strength to keep the dog stationary just a few feet into the cell. McKinlay stared at the dog, then up at the screws who were all dressed head to toe in riot gear, complete with their motorbike helmets, riot shields and armoured suits. This unflappable, former bare-knuckle champion had a look of real shock on his face. Even to him, this was intimidating and extremely concerning.

"ON THE FLOOR MCKINLAY!" Shouted one of the officers. McKinlay just stared back, the look of astonishment was completely genuine. The dog's barking was deafening and

McKinlay was inching backwards to try and gain as much distance from its snapping jaws as he possibly could. It was a futile exercise though, with each inch that McKinlay stepped back, the dog handler stepped forward, maintaining the 1.5 metre distance.

"FINAL WARNING MCKINLAY – GET ON THE FUCKING FLOOR – FACE DOWN – NOW!"

It was obvious from the expression on the prisoner's face that he was in shock. This level of aggression was unheard of as far as he was aware. He was staring beyond the dog, looking at the officers, there were five, no six facing him straight on, but he sensed that there were many others on either side of them, on the landing just outside the cell door.

Other than the dog's barking, there was an eery silence gripping Strangeways. In between the throaty, deafening barks which were echoing all around the place, McKinlay could pick out an incredible quietness in the building, something he'd never heard before. Traditionally, this time of the morning is the noisiest time of day in the prison, as all the fully energised lags bang on their doors, bantering and shouting, singing and jeering in anticipation of what the new day would bring. But not today, Tommy could tell that every cell door on the wing had ears pressed up against them, all listening to this commotion on the top landing.

"I'LL COUNT TO THREE MCKINLAY. IF YOU'RE NOT DOWN ON THAT FLOOR, THE DOG IS GOING TO TAKE YOU DOWN TO THE FUCKING FLOOR AND HE'S NOT HAD HIS BREAKFAST. ONE..."

McKinlay dropped slowly to his knees, then leaned into a press-up position. By the count of three, he was lay on his chest with his hands clasped together behind his back.

The dog handler quickly retreated as the lead officers stormed McKinlay's cell and put cuffs on him. He was told that his legs won't be restrained if he co-operates.

"Co-operate with what?" He asked, but none of the officers replied. Once cuffed, McKinlay was lifted to his feet and was held by two officers as a new face entered his cell. This officer was dressed identically to the rest but for his white helmet. All of the others were wearing navy blue ones.

"Right, McKinlay, apologies for the abrupt wake-up call. You are being transferred immediately. Okay, take him to the bus."

And with that, McKinlay was frog-marched out of his cell at the heart of a perfectly co-ordinated scrum of twenty-two riot officers who kettled him right along the landing, down the stair wells and off the wing. Within moments, he was in the back of the prison's "sweat box" van which was being driven out of HMP Manchester with police sirens blaring from the front and back. McKinlay looked out of his tiny, blackened-out window and as the truck turned left onto Bury New Road, he saw that his vehicle was being trailed by motorbike cops and an Armed Response Range Rover. He looked the other way and saw the same entourage ahead of the vehicle. Up above was the unmistakable roar of the police helicopter. Tommy McKinlay realised in that moment that his plans had just been dealt a very substantial blow.

"Fuck."

Chapter Forty-Four

"Good morning everyone." Miller seemed in a better mood than he had done the previous morning. It was almost as though the weight he had been carrying around yesterday had been lifted. He wasn't back to his best, not by a long chalk - but there was a marked improvement in his bearing and it was gladly received by the team.

It was more of a relief for the SCIU team to see that DS Rudovsky also appeared to be in better spirits than she had the previous afternoon, when she'd created a vile atmosphere before storming out halfway through the afternoon. Several staff had been dreading this shift today, so it was a welcome sight to see Rudovsky smiling while Miller was taking the piss out of her new hoody.

"No, honestly, it does. It looks like it says Fuckface."

"It says Fat Face, Sir. Shut up, you're taking the piss."

"No, it's the writing, the way it's set out. Keith, come here a sec."

Saunders stopped what he was doing at his PC and wandered wearily over to Rudovsky's desk.

"Settle something please Detective Inspector. What does that say on Jo's top?" Asked Miller.

"Fuckface."

"See! You'd better not wear that if Dixon comes down, he'll think it's aimed at him!"

"Bollocks! It says Fat Face. But if you think it..." Rudovsky stopped talking suddenly as Dixon walked into the office. She smiled sweetly at the DCS whilst covering the text on her chest with one arm. He looked straight through her.

"Andy, Keith, two minutes?" Said Dixon as he walked straight into Miller's office. The warm smile that had been on Miller's face cooled slightly as he headed across the office floor, Saunders followed right behind him. By the time they entered Miller's glass walled office, the elderly officer was sitting down facing Miller's desk. He got straight into it as the others sat down.

"I am the bearer of good news, you'll be pleased to hear. Tommy McKinlay is currently being transported south."

Miller's face lit up. "No way!"

"Yes, unfortunately for him, he's got a zero-star room booked in the segregation unit at Belmarsh. His phone has been removed from his anal passage and from what I've been informed, he was incredibly cooperative throughout the transfer. So, that's something we can tick off the list."

"Brilliant. Nice one Sir."

"Yes, that's a fantastic result," Added Saunders.

"Thank you. Obviously, I had to mention the seriousness of the situation, but fortunately, I didn't have to go as far as to mention the blackmailing aspect. We still have that up our sleeve should we need it. Extra ammo for later."

"Good. I'm chuffed with that. Gives us a bit of breathing space." Miller was visibly enthused by this news.

"How long is McKinlay going to be there for?" Asked Saunders.

"Indefinitely. At least until his trial. The senior officers that have facilitated this request are very sympathetic to the activities that he's been carrying out. This will prove to be quite a wake-up call for Mr McKinlay, I should think."

"Good."

"Between the three of us, there's a huge sigh of relief at HMP Manchester. It appears that Tommy McKinlay has been making a very real nuisance of himself in there. I get the distinct impression that the governor is going to be buying a big bottle of Champagne on the way home tonight!"

"Yes, I can totally imagine. I'm not quite at that stage yet, but I'm sure we'll get there."

"So, next steps. Where are we headed with everything?"

"Well, I'm glad you've asked me that, Sir. I've got some news of my own. I'm afraid that I have had no alternative but to furnish Keith with the details regarding Dawson."

"Oh…" Dixon did not look too impressed by this announcement. But there was worse to come.

"I mean, all of the details. The full package. Director's

cut."

There was a pause while Dixon allowed that significant information sink in. "I see."

"It's not a case of idle office gossip, Sir. But Keith was struggling to understand the situation fully. It wasn't adding up. I think it has all begun to make a bit more sense now, Keith?"

Saunders nodded enthusiastically. "Totally. Yes. It puts a whole new light on everything. A lot of blanks have been filled in."

Dixon was raging, but he knew better than to let it show. Apart from his face heating up remarkably, he appeared to take this unsettling news rather well. It made no odds either way, of course. The deed was done and nothing could change that. This was just the warm-up though. There was a moment of quiet reflection before Miller dropped the rest of the bombshell.

"The thing is, Sir..."

Dixon stared hard at Miller, he knew from that tone of voice that his DCI was about to really piss him off.

"...I'm going to tell the rest of the team as well. Today."

Dixon's face juddered as Miller's words processed in his mind. "Andy, that's..."

"It's the only way, Sir. This McKinlay situation risks splitting the team up, we almost lost Jo yesterday. She knew something was up..."

"You mean to say that Jo Rudovsky knows as well?"

Both Miller and Saunders nodded.

"What are you thinking, Sir?" Asked Miller. It was mainly out of politeness, but he was intrigued to hear Dixon's point-of-view. The DCS took a few moments before replying.

"Well I'll be brutally honest. I think it's utter madness. I thought that we had agreed that the fewer people who knew, the better?" Dixon's face was beginning to compose itself, the red rush was settling down a little.

"Agreed Sir. But things have taken a turn, haven't they? If it wasn't for somebody informing Tommy McKinlay of the details, then we wouldn't be having this conversation. We need to adapt for the terrain we're travelling."

"Is that from that positive thinking book?" Asked Saunders, trying to lighten the mood. His remark was completely ignored by Miller and Dixon who were locked in stares across the desk.

"I genuinely believe that it would be wiser to bring the team on board with it than playing stupid bastards and making them all suspicious. I mean, Rudovsky practically worked the whole thing out by herself anyway."

"How so?" Asked Dixon, his inner detective wanting to know how true this was.

"Because she's good. So, we had to tell her..."

"We?"

"Well, it was me, actually, Sir." Said Saunders.

"Jesus H Christ!" Said Dixon, exhaling loudly. "And you are serious? About planning to tell the others?"

"Next job on the list. It's for the best. I trust them all implicitly. If I don't tell them, I'm afraid we'll have a far bigger problem on our hands in the fullness of time. Resignations!" Miller smiled but Dixon blanked it.

"I feel very uneasy about this."

"Well, I think I would too on just hearing it. But trust me, Sir. I've been going over this all night in my head, over and over again. The more I think about it, the more sense it makes. What is it you've always said to me?"

"I don't know..."

"Since the first day I came working for you as a rookie detective, fresh out of uniform, you have always said that the best detectives sleep on it. You've taught me that things make a lot more sense after a few hours of reflection. I think, if you weigh it all up – you'll see that this is a very practical solution to our problem in the sense that it empowers us. If there are no dirty secrets, we can all focus on the job in hand, which is to draw a line under Tommy McKinlay's mad idea of running our department from here on in. Seriously, this is the least bad outcome."

"If I can interject, Sir," said Saunders, looking at the stressed DCS.

"Go ahead," snapped Dixon.

"Well, I must admit that hearing the full story from DCI Miller, it was a game-changer. Now that I'm fully aware of the circumstances, it has made me feel a lot more committed to the task of shutting McKinlay's plan down. And, at the end of the day, the real bad guys in all of this should be the ones worrying. Not you, Sir. Or you, Sir." Saunders made eye contact with both men as he reached his conclusion.

Dixon appeared to appreciate Saunders words. He stood and brushed himself down as though he'd just finished eating a Greggs sausage roll whilst reclining. "Very well. I'll leave you to it. Please pop up and see me later, Andy. I'd like to hear how it went."

"Sir."

"And I genuinely hope that you are making the right decision here. There's a lot at stake."

"Yes, Sir. Nobody is more acutely aware of that than I am."

Dixon marched out of the office, leaving a very low mood in his wake. Miller looked across at Saunders.

"He'll be right. He just needs to mull it over."

"Reckon?"

"Well, I hope so. Not much else he can do, is there?"

"Not really, no. Anyway, what's the plan for telling the others?"

"Good question. I've been giving this some thought..."

"Well we can't do it here. The walls have ears."

"I know..."

"I thought the canal might be the best place."

"So did I!" Said Miller triumphantly. Only he hadn't thought that at all and had been struggling to think of a suitable venue which offered complete privacy. Saunders suggestion was excellent. The canal was literally the perfect location, completely isolated but for the odd jogger or dog-walker on the pathway on the other side of the water. The occasional barge rattles through as well, but other than that – it was about as isolated as you will ever get whilst still in the shadow of Manchester city centre.

"Shall we just get this over and done with, then?" Asked Miller as he stood from his chair.

Chapter Forty-Five

As each identical car arrived at the end of the random lane by the cut, Miller had met them individually and asked all of his team members to leave their mobile phones inside their car and go and stand with Saunders.

They looked bemused more than anything as they followed the order, taking their phones out of their pockets and dumping them on the car seats. Once all of the officers were standing by the waters edge, at the very same spot that Miller and Saunders had sat at the previous evening, he walked across and joined them. It was obvious that something very weird was going on, Miller looked as though his confidence had disappeared.

"Okay guys. Shit, I feel like the shy kid being asked to the front of the class. Sorry, this feels really awkward." Miller laughed uncomfortably, but Rudovsky made eye contact and nodded him on. This discreet gesture did the trick and snapped the DCI out of his first-night nerves.

"Right, sorry, but this is mad. I just want to say, that I trust each and everyone one of you with my life." Miller looked at each of his team, holding their gaze for a second or so before moving on to the next person. They all looked concerned, as though a cancer announcement was coming. "I know I'm a cock at times, I know I piss you all off with my moods and my pedantic demands that you actually do a bit of bloody work once every Preston Guild!"

Miller's gentle dig got a mild laugh, which eased the awkwardness a little.

"Okay that's nice Sir. So can we go now?" Asked Kenyon, his cheeky question received a much bigger laugh. This was all feeling very strange, the normal, relaxed manner was gone and the whole team looked as though they were curling their toes, ever so politely.

"Nice one Pete. Struggling here to tell you something really deep and as always, you fuck it all up!" The mood became even more peculiar and one or two members looked down and concentrated on their footwear. Miller smiled affectionately at DC Peter Kenyon, he was becoming the resident joker of the group now that Rudovsky had been forced to tone herself down a bit to suit her sergeant's stripes.

"I'm only messing Sir, carry on."

"Thanks. Well, the thing is, I'm about to explain all of the mad shit that has been going on these past couple of days. And by the end of this conversation, each and every one of you will have enough information on me to step forward, arrest me, and send me down for a good twenty years."

This was news. It was written on every face, even Rudovsky's and Saunders, they were just as surprised by this announcement, shocked at the dramatic introduction. Miller had decided to avoid putting any spin on it and just got down to business, warts and all.

"I know, you're all thinking I'm winding you up, but I'm really not. You see, I did a very dodgy thing a few years back. At the very least, it would be called perverting the course of justice, but that would be a best-case scenario to be honest. I'm probably facing corruption charges, it would probably reach to aiding and abetting and conspiracy to assist a murder suspect. One thing's for certain, if what I'm about tell you became public knowledge, I'll be in my sixties when I get out, I'll have missed all of the twins best birthdays."

The expectation was intense. Miller decided to stay on track, get straight to the point and get this incredibly intimidating job done as his team stood in the sunshine by the weeds and wild-flowers on the bank of the canal.

"This situation I've found myself with, the incident with Clare and the school, its all connected. You see, somehow, news of my misdemeanour has reached Tommy McKinlay and he's decided to try and use it to blackmail me."

Miller got stuck in, telling his staff the same news that he had presented to Saunders at this very spot just fourteen or fifteen hours earlier. The whole story, the sordid, alarming truth behind the Pop story.

"Fucking hell fire!" Said Chapman, as Miller was wrapping up some ten minutes later. "How the hell did you keep all of that to yourself?" He asked. Chapman had been one of the officers on the scene, he and Worthington had been in charge of apprehending Dawson on that fateful day. The Sykes story had never seemed right, but the conversation had never come up again and the appropriate moment to raise it again never appeared. But it had certainly come up today.

"It's not been easy, Bill." Said Miller. "I found all this out in the minutes before you, Mike and Keith came into Dixon's office. What was that, an hour after it had happened?"

Chapman, Worthington and Saunders nodded sombrely. The "it" that Miller was referring to was the chaotic, mindless death of Acting DCI Karen Ellis.

"I felt I had no choice but to let Dawson go… there was literally no justifiable reason for the authorities allowing him to start killing the paedophiles after he'd given them numerous warnings of his intentions. They set him up, I thought that then and I still think it now. They allowed his campaign of murder to start, then sat back and did everything they could to make sure it continued, including placing endless obstacles in my way after putting me in charge of the investigation. I wasn't prepared to charge him, even though he'd handed himself in. I didn't think I'd be able to get into heaven if I did."

"This is actually mental." Said Kenyon, who'd been absent from work whilst this incredible case was unfolding. "I mean, not just the idea of you getting into heaven. No offence, Sir."

"How has McKinlay heard about this?" Asked Worthington.

"No idea. That's a complete mystery."

"What's he saying that he wants from you?" Asked Grant.

"McKinlay is demanding that I interfere with the case against him, falsify evidence and so on, so he walks, either at his trial, or before."

"Is this why you wanted us to leave our phones in the car?" Asked Chapman,

"Yes, Bill. Not because I don't trust any of you, but I don't trust the phones. I believe mine was being interfered with, that's why I had to get a new handset and number yesterday."

"I can't get my head around any of this at all." Said Worthington. "But thanks for opening up to us all... I must say, it shines a completely new light on the whole thing."

"Thanks Mike. I never wanted to involve anybody else, but I realised yesterday that I had run out of options. I didn't want to carry on sneaking around behind your backs. I only told Keith about this last night. As far as I was concerned, it was done and dusted, ancient history. I honestly can't believe that it's all come about."

A moment of quiet halted the conversation and it quickly became ominous. Rudovsky saw her cue to speak for the first time. "Well, Sir, I'm sure I speak on behalf of everybody when I say that you did the right thing. As if the fucking government were happy to let this guy go around the streets shooting people dead. It turns my blood cold just thinking about it, thinking that a little kid could have rode around the corner on a bike, right into it."

"I know, Jo. It's beyond my comprehension."

"It also kills me that Karen is dead because of this fucking madness."

That was a very good point, and Rudovsky's stirring conclusion gained grunts of approval from all, including Miller.

"So what's the plan?" Asked Chapman.

"Thanks Bill, well, the plan is we never mention this anywhere. If you have any questions, any at all, about this matter, I want you to be discreet and tell me that you'd like a word. Got that?"

The SCIU team members all nodded their understanding.

"That's going to have to be the way we operate for a while, coded messages and stuff like out of a shitty TV drama. If one of you says that you need a word, I'll take that to mean that you have a specific question about this case, and I'll arrange for us all to come back here where we can talk about it here, in private. Okay?"

"Sir."

"Now, if I survive the rest of the day, I'll know that my

instincts to trust you all with this were right. For now, we need to get back to the office where we can talk freely about my current situation, and Tommy McKinlay's demands. The only things that we can never talk about is the name George Dawson, or anything at all to do with the Pop case. Is that completely understood?"

"Sir."

"Absolutely, Sir."

"Brilliant. Okay, well, thanks for your time and your understanding. I'm sure we'll have this all thrashed out soon enough. But one last point I want to make..."

The detectives all looked alert.

"...If any of you ever try to use this against me when I refuse you some holiday leave, you'll bloody regret it!"

The meeting ended with a good laugh and the SCIU staff headed back to their cars. That had gone way better than Miller, or Saunders, or Rudovsky had anticipated.

"Nice one, Sir," said Rudovsky, tapping her boss on the shoulder as she headed towards her vehicle.

"Cheers Jo. Means a lot mate."

Chapter Forty-Six

Miller and Saunders headed back to HQ together. Saunders did the driving whilst Miller looked on his phone for a flight to Jersey.

"I think they took it very well."

"Who?" Asked Miller, not really concentrating.

"Well, Mike and Bill mainly. But everyone, Pete and Helen seemed to take it all in their stride."

"Yeah, I must confess, I was shitting my pants. I thought if it was going to kick off, it would be Bill and Mike causing a commotion."

"I know. I thought the same. I was all geared up for a confrontation."

"No, it did… it went well. I just wish this fucking thing would work!"

"What?"

"This app on my phone. It's showing me a flight to Jersey at four, there's a seat on it but every time I click the book now button it just does that." Miller held his phone in front of Saunders' face and demonstrated his problem.

"Two senior police officers from Manchester's serious crimes unit were arrested today for fucking about on a phone while driving…" Said Saunders in his best radio announcer voice.

"Soz Keith. But it's saying four people are trying to book now and it's making me panic."

"They all do that. I guarantee you, any flight you try and book, or even a hotel room, it says six people are looking at this right now. It's a blag, its designed to make you panic."

"Well what's the sense it that? I *am* panicking!"

"I don't know. To get you to hurry up, I suppose."

"I'm trying to hurry up but it keeps fucking crashing on me!" Miller's face was heating up.

"How many seats were left?"

"It didn't say how many, just said there is a seat available and four people are trying to book it."

"There'll be loads, seriously, its fine. Just hang-fire, it'll be a glitch at their end."

Miller exhaled loudly and looked out of the car window as the car approached the city centre. His mood worsened as he remembered that he would now have to go and see Dixon before he could get on any plane.

*****

"Ah, Andy. How did it go?" Said Dixon as Miller entered the office. The calm and friendly greeting wrong-footed the DCI slightly. He'd been anticipating a slanging match.

"Hello Sir. It went very well, considering."

Dixon raised one of his big bushy white eyebrows, encouraging Miller to tell him more.

"They were very understanding. Shocked, bewildered, but very supportive. I honestly couldn't have asked for more."

"Good, well, that's good. I'm glad it went that way. I had a terrible feeling…"

"Yes, I must admit, I was very nervous. But no, it was good. They've all got my back."

"Well lets just hope it stays that way."

"How do you mean?"

"Oh, nothing Andy. Except that you've just told a whole load of people who have absolutely no business in this!"

Miller's mouth was wide open. He was beginning to understand that he had walked straight into a trap, Dixon had deliberately made him feel at ease before sucker punching him.

It took Miller a couple of seconds to compose himself, but when he did, it was Dixon's turn to be winded.

"And you think that Tommy McKinlay and fuck-knows-who else have business in this? I thought I told you to think it over, weigh it all up. But you clearly haven't. My team are now fully aware of this, its all out in the open and I've made myself one-hundred-per-cent vulnerable to every single one of them. Do I look nervous, or scared, or agitated? No, because I trust them. The fact that you obviously don't trust me, or trust my judgement is extremely concerning. I'm not surprised at your sly comment there, but I am quite gutted that you obviously think my team are a bunch of shite-hawks."

"That's not what…"

"Do you know what, I can't even be arsed pointing out that all of this is your fuck up. From start, middle and end, you own this disaster and if you had even an ounce of decency, you'd keep that in mind and keep your trap shut while I, and the team you obviously distrust start trying to salvage this nightmare. You go on sitting in here, doing fuck all and leave us to it, like you always do."

"I think you're…."

"Couldn't give a fart what you think, Sir, I'm not in the mood for any of your bullshit. You've got a short memory, you. I gave you ample opportunities to level up with me during the Pop case. You chose not to for whatever stupid reason. If you'd have told me the truth, I would have gone along with it…"

"Would you now?" Dixon laughed theatrically, which wound Miller up even further. "I think we both know that's not true, Andy. I told you, in fact, I remember it distinctly. I told you to relax and just ride it out. I even said that there was no urgency. All the clues were there Andy, you just chose to ignore them. Please don't insult my intelligence by trying to lay all of this at my feet." Dixon held a cold, hard stare and Miller realised for the first time ever that the DCS desperately wanted some distance from the innuendo of responsibility for Karen Ellis's murder. The realisation that Dixon was keen to excuse himself and wished to drag others into the fray disappointed Miller greatly. He might have understood it if there was any room for manoeuvre, but as far as Miller was concerned, there was none. The facts were very simple, Karen Ellis was dead and the reason for that was because Dixon hadn't been truthful about the Pop situation. He was being so untruthful, so deceitful and obstructive that Ellis had gone off to try and solve the case herself, and the rest remains the biggest regret in the history of the SCIU department.

"I'm really surprised that you've said that. I'm pretty speechless to be honest…"

"Well, how do you think it makes me feel? Being blamed for the outcome of a lunatic waving a loaded gun around? Your bloody idiot DC kicking the gunman's kneecap whilst he'd holding a gun to Karen's head? And yet it is me you wish to point the finger at!"

"If you'd sat Karen down and told her, no, ordered her to stop pursuing the killer..."

"I did... I did, Andy." Dixon's face changed suddenly. His mouth was quivering and his eyes scrunched up as he started crying at his desk. It was a surreal moment. Miller had worked for Dixon for over twenty years and had never seen him cry, not like this. There had been tears when the news came through about Ellis admittedly, but this was something else entirely. Miller didn't know where to look or what to say, his anger and disgust from just a few moments earlier had given way to sympathy and he felt very confused.

Dixon grabbed a tissue and began dabbing his eyes before blowing his nose. He coughed loudly before elaborating, but despite the attempt to clear his throat, the raw emotions were clearly audible.

"I sat her in that seat right there and I told her in no uncertain terms that there was to be no arrest. I went a lot further with her than I did with you. I didn't spell it out... obviously... but I made it abundantly clear that she was not authorised to make an arrest. I told her that... I told her in the strictest manner that I could, to leave it, just get on with the paperwork. I warned her, made it clear that if she disobeyed my order, then acting DCI would be as far as her promotion chances would go." Dixon's chin began quivering again and Miller felt completely bewildered by this sensational announcement. He sat down opposite his boss and listened as Dixon continued.

"She ignored me Andy. She agreed to my orders, then just upped and left. I never saw her again. And I haven't slept through a full night since that day. So, yes, I accept that if I had told her the next part, that it was an order from the Home Office... that the whole thing was a sham, yes... she'd still be here today. But I didn't tell her that, not only because it was a wholly incredible situation to find myself in, but because I genuinely thought I'd done enough. I thought she'd got the message." Dixon's voice faltered again as he reached his conclusion. "I really wish I had. I'll go to my grave wishing that I had… I've… I'm seeking professional help for the mental health problems this is causing me. Yes, I know, it's not the done thing to discuss such matters. But my counsellor keeps telling me that I did not shoot Karen. He keeps reminding me that if I'd had the slightest inkling that Karen was pursuing the gunman behind my back, I'd have put an instant stop to it. Yes, it may sound very self-indulgent, maybe it is. But I have to draw a line somewhere Andy. I did not kill Karen, but I'm made to feel that I did and as pathetic as this phrase sounds, it's not fair." A final tear traced slowly down Dixon's cheek as he sniffed loudly as Miller sat there, completely lost for words. Dixon let out a strange noise of sadness, then blew his nose and Miller got the distinct impression that he felt slightly embarrassed by this emotional display.

Miller spoke, his voice was a lot calmer now and he sounded as though he'd lost all confidence. "Okay, well… there's not a lot I can say to that. There are a lot of ifs and buts about this whole thing. I'm sorry that you are still feeling the pain, Sir. And I apologise for my words earlier. I need to go and catch a flight to see the family now. Can we pick this up when I return?"

"Yes. Of course. I'm not trying to completely exonerate myself. That's not my intention. But you throw words around like bombs Andy, I don't think you ever stop to consider how damaging those bombs can be."

Miller felt bad. He thought that he'd had the moral high-ground as he'd launched into his blistering attack, but after hearing Dixon's heart-felt assessment of the situation, spoken from his personal point of view, he realised that he didn't know the half of it and the realisation brought with it a great deal of guilt and regret.

"Okay, well I would like to thank you for being so honest about this, Sir. I think we need to leave this for now. We should pick it up when I get back from Jersey."

"That's… thank you Andy. I just wanted you to know that… be assured that I will make amends for all of this. I don't know how, I don't know when… but I refuse to retire until I feel as though I've done something that puts this thing right."

Chapter Forty-Seven

Saunders had offered to drive Miller to the airport, reasoning that it would be a valuable time to talk. It was, in Saunders' defence. But that wasn't the main reason that he'd offered to drive his boss. He could tell that Miller's mood had dropped significantly since he'd gone up to see Dixon and he wanted to hear what had happened.

"Nice one Keith. It's very good of you. Right everyone, I'm going to see Clare and the kids and I'm hoping to go and speak to McKinlay at Belmarsh on the way back. Tell the bastard that he's cornered and that he needs to pipe down. I should be back tomorrow all being well, but in the meantime, I'll leave you in the perfectly capable hands of DI Saunders and DS Rudovsky. Please crack on with the jobs you've been allocated and hopefully, by the time I get back to the north, McKinlay will know that he's swum into treacherous waters and will be keen to swim back to the noxious sewer he emerged from!"

"Take care, boss." Said Rudovsky.

"Give Clare and the twins our love!" Added Grant.

"Cheers, Sir!" Said Chapman as the rest of the team joined in with their farewells.

Five minutes later, Miller was sitting in the passenger seat once again as Saunders drove his undercover police car through the city-centre streets.

"I take it something happened?" Said Saunders eventually, as it became clear that Miller wasn't in the mood for talking.

"Eh?" Said the DCI as though he'd been snapped out of a trance.

"You went into Dixon's office in a reasonable mood and you've come out looking as though you've dropped your wallet in a pan of sick."

"Oh... yeah, sorry Keith. We had a bit of a row."
"Big?"

"Well, I don't know. No, not bad, just... I don't know, he said a few things that I have never given much consideration to. I feel like a bit of an arse to be honest."

"Well if its any consolation, most of us have known that you're an arse for quite a while now."

Miller didn't laugh, he didn't even acknowledge the attempt at banter. He just stared right ahead through the windscreen as Saunders swerved a pot hole. "What the hell do they spend the road tax on?" He said, to himself mainly.

"Nuclear bombs, HS2, Foreign Farm subsidies." Said Miller flatly. "And what about that skip the Arts Council funded in Brighton? Ninety-five grand to dump a skip with a few yellow lights around it!" Miller laughed humourlessly at the absurdity of it all.

"I can beat that. I read that Stoke Council spent half a million on redundancy packages and then asked all the staff to come back a month later because they hadn't realised what they all did!"

Both men laughed, not just at the types of things that public money is wasted on, but how Saunders' throwaway comment about one of Greater Manchester ten zillion pot-holes had totally knackered up his subtle attempt to find out what had been said in Dixon's office. The DI attempted to steer the conversation back on track.

"So, have you and Dixon made up or is it going to be a bit awkward for a bit?" It wasn't a particularly subtle segue.

"No... its," Miller breathed in deeply and exhaled loudly. "It's a tricky one. Just how I wanted to offload some dark shit to you last night... Dixon's just done the same on me. Only, he's made me feel really shit about some of the things I've said to him about Karen's death."

"Fucking hell! What did he say exactly?"

"It's not so much what he said, it was more the way he said it. He basically gave me a list of reasons why its unfair to blame him for what happened and... on reflection... he's right."

"Shit."

"Yes, that's as good a word as any. But anyway, I'm feeling like a complete tosser now but I think it was good that we had that talk. It's given me a new perspective on things. No, not a new perspective, that's wrong. It's given me a completely different perspective and I'm gutted that I can't unsay the things that I've said to him."

"I see. Sounds pretty awkward."

"You don't know the half of it. But I'll have a nice pint at the airport and send him a grovelling and profound text message."

"Yeah, I got one of them the other week off Jo! We'd had a blazing row about that Dickinson Road arson job. Big, shouty argument where she was losing her shit about a line of enquiry that hadn't been followed up. I got home, opened a beer and started calming down, started watching a bit of telly and chilling out."

"Yeah?"

"Yes, then my phone lights up. Text message off Jo. I thought she'll be wanting to start all over again, I debated for a minute or two about whether to read it or not. Anyway, curiosity got the better of me so I started reading it. I was surprised, it was a very calm, ever-so-polite, to-the-point explanation about why she'd been so pissed off. I was reading it thinking bloody hell, this is a pleasant surprise. That was until I read the very last sentence…"

Miller started laughing in expectation. "Go on…"

"She'd put 'Anyway, I just wanted you to know that's why I was so frustrated earlier and as you can see from what I've just written above, I'm right and you're wrong!"

Both men laughed loudly at the audacity of the department's DS. She was worth her weight in gold but there were times when she could drive you insane.

"That's quality! You've been trolled there mate! Aw that's really cheered me up!" Said Miller. "She's a bloody maniac that lass!"

Chapter Forty-Eight

100 miles from the UK and 14 miles from Normandy in France, the tiny island of Jersey is just nine miles by five miles in size. Known to islanders as "The Rock" this wonderful little place is steeped in tradition, history and culture. What it lacks in size, it certainly makes up for in charm and stature. Not quite British and not quite French, Jersey is a very unique place that has an unmistakable charm which makes it such a desirable place for the super-rich to live. And you will have to be rich if you fancy moving here, an individual with no links to the island would not be considered for permanent residency unless they had five million in the bank, or earned a minimum of £625,000 per year and can prove that this income is sustainable. So, most people can scratch a move to Jersey off their to-do list, unless they wanted to work in one of the many service jobs which are generated by the medical, educational and tourism industries. By far the biggest employers on the island are the financial institutions who employ almost a quarter of all workers on the rock. Banking and finance is big here, thanks mainly to the island's independent financial nature which is more commonly referred to as an "off-shore tax haven."

Jersey is unique in almost every way. It is not British, it is not European either, but it is treated as an EU member state for the purpose of free trade in goods. Jersey looks after all of its own affairs through its own parliament, from tax and law to running its public services. However, the island is a British Crown Dependency like Guernsey and the Isle of Man and enjoys the knowledge that the UK is responsible for defending its shores, should the need ever arise.

Indeed, the need did arise for the UK to defend the Channel Islands. Quite famously in July 1940, the Nazi's took over the islands. They occupied Jersey for five years until the end of the second world war, viewing their audacious invasion as a golden opportunity to defend the French coast as well as making their first footstep on British soil. Britain saw the occupation as a distraction tactic and basically let them get on with it, safe in the knowledge that the German forces were attempting to divert the British soldiers away from the job of defending Britain against a Nazi invasion. The decision to ignore the occupation was unpopular with the islanders, who felt they'd been left high and dry as Swastikas appeared on flagpoles all over the island. But turning a blind eye to the invasion proved to be the correct course of action. British troops arrived in their thousands to liberate the islands of Jersey, Guernsey, Alderney and Sark and the Nazis left the Channel Islands ceremoniously in 1945, handing them back in the dying days of the Second World War. Every islander was out in the streets to celebrate the Union Jacks replacing the Nazi flags all across the islands.

Andy and Clare Miller love this place. They came here a lot for holidays, particularly before the twins arrived. Clare had holidayed here as a kid and had introduced the charms of Jersey to Andy not long after they had got together and he had fallen just as deeply in love with the place. For Andy Miller, Jersey is the only holiday destination where he really feels that he can switch off. He has never really understood the reasoning behind it, whether it's the fact that it is basically just a rock in the English Channel and is completely isolated from home or whether it's down to something else entirely.

But as his plane touched down and the tyres screeched loudly beneath him, he knew that it was highly unlikely that this flying visit to the island would do much to relax him this time around. It would be a fucking miracle if it did, he thought as the pilot slammed the brakes on and brought the aircraft to a dramatic halt.

Miller was met on the tarmac by armed officers from States of Jersey Police. They quickly briefed him on their security detail regarding his family before driving him the five minute journey down the road to St Brelades Bay, the most stunning beach on the island and the location of Jersey's most celebrated hotel where Clare and the kids were staying and where he was scheduled to spend the night.

An excitement built up within him as the police car pulled up outside the whitewashed 77 room luxury hotel. This place always looked cheerful, and as he and the police officers said farewell and he stepped outside the vehicle, Miller began to feel that familiar sense of relaxation washing over him. Under the circumstances, it felt bizarre, almost perverse.

"Must be the Jersey air," he muttered to himself as he made his way up the steps and into the hotel reception, desperately trying to remember his checking-in name. God, it felt like weeks ago that he had shared this information with the kids. Miller was shocked when he realised that it was only the previous day.

Chapter Forty-Nine

Tommy and Kingo had agreed the basic terms of their business relationship on the way back to Rochdale after sorting out the problems at the Staff of Life. The agreement was quite simple, Kingo was at liberty to take anybody with him on a job, but any costs he incurred would be met out of Kingo's cut. If ever the police had any reason to speak to either of them about one of the jobs, the only response was to be "no comment." This is standard practise for criminals today, but back in the mid 1990s, it wasn't such a popular tactic as police officers would trick their interviewees into believing that a no comment interview would act as an admission of guilt to the jurors when the case in question reached the courts.

Tommy explained that there was enough work available to see him out earning every single night of the week and that he'd be looking at £500 cash per job. If he took them all, then he would be earning around 10k per month, cash in hand. That sounds a lot now, but at the time it was worth a lot more, a nice house cost £70,000. An average house in Greater Manchester, a two-bedroom terraced was around £20,000 in the mid 90's. Kingo was keen to get involved in property so his commitment to this opportunity was sealed with a hand-shake as Tommy's Land Rover Discovery pulled up outside Kingo's house.

The USP of the operation was to make sure that people's problems went away, or they got their cash back. They couldn't advertise the service in the Yellow Pages or on KEY 103, but the word-of-mouth testimonies from satisfied customers travelled fast through the networks of pub landlords, private landlords and business owner groups.

This was 25 years ago, and the initial arrangement was supposed to last for a few months whilst Tommy honoured all of the enquiries he'd received and concentrated more time and energy on his training for upcoming fights. But the two men have continued to work together ever since, taking advantage of the never-ending need for private justice. The more the government, police and the courts softened up on law and order, the busier Tommy and Kingo became. Greater Manchester is a huge place, with a population of almost 3 million – so there was never any shortage of issues which people needed sorting out. There were jobs like the racketeering at The Staff of Life, and Mr Patel's. But there were plenty of domestic issues which needed sorting. There were hundreds of abusive husbands who needed removing from houses and relationships, similarly hundreds of teenagers who were going off the rails and needed some stern help in getting back on track – even if this involved some "tough-love." There were stalkers, burglars, sex abusers, loan-sharks, you name it, whatever problems people encountered, they could rely on Tommy McKinlay to fix them. The failure of the police to keep the streets safe had become an incredible business opportunity. Fathers of daughters in abusive relationships thought nothing of the £1000 fee to get rid of her abuser. Parents of kids who were heading down the wrong path also saw the cost as an investment into their child's future. Literally everybody was happy, none more so than Tommy McKinlay who didn't really have to do much more than buy a mobile phone and employ somebody to answer the calls who would then pass the details to Kingo. In no time at all, Kingo was sorting two, three, sometimes four issues out each day.

The business enterprise took off very quickly, the police heard whispers about the newly emerging TM Security and were very keen to look the other way. The kinds of people that TMS were dealing with were the lowest of the low so there was no desire whatsoever to infringe on the work that TMS was carrying out. Within just a couple of years of operation, Manchester's police canteens were full of officers laughing and joking about the local toe-rags who had relocated to other parts of the country after a visit from a member of TMS' staff, in most cases due to the unrecoverable level of humiliation that McKinlay or Kingo, or one of the other security officers had doled out. The sudden disappearance of local shit heads intrigued a great many community police sergeants. PNC searches on their regulars revealed that they had now, very quickly become nuisances for other constabularies around the UK and not a single officer in Greater Manchester had any complaints about this revelation.

The police couldn't really give TMS an award for flushing out the metropolitan city's worst arseholes, but they were all extremely pleased about the existence of the security firm and certain unofficial rules were relaxed to accommodate the continued growth of the enterprise.

Despite the fact that so many scumbags were running away from their home city, the workload continued to increase. It seemed that Greater Manchester had a limitless supply of arseholes in the 1990s. The company's promise of complete satisfaction or your money back was bolstered further with the proud announcement that nobody had ever come back for their cash. Things were going remarkably well, Tommy's fighting was his number one priority again whilst Kingo managed to build a team of like-minded, reliable and most importantly, hard-as-fuck bastards to join the team. By the third year of the official incarnation of TMS, the company had moved into a town-centre building and had leased a fleet of vehicles which were emblazoned with the TMS branding, which at first glance looked like police vehicles. A business manager was employed and new contracts were won, in the more traditional sense of security work. Late night patrols, night watchmen, shopping centre and town centre patrols were contracted by most of the councils in the Greater Manchester region as news of their effectiveness in driving away troublemakers had by now reached the top floors of all of the town halls in the ten metropolitan boroughs which make up the Greater Manchester region. Wigan, Bolton, Bury, Salford, Manchester, Stockport, Trafford, Tameside, Oldham and Rochdale councils had all placed contracts in TMS' hands, albeit by varying degrees. By year six, TMS was taking on long term contracts in the neighbouring shires of Merseyside, Lancashire and Cheshire and Tommy and Kingo had each netted a million pounds in profit from the enterprise, whilst acquiring a staff base exceeding fifty employees.

Tommy McKinlay was not surprised to see a million pounds in his bank account. From that very first taste of money, when he'd done his mum's house up, he knew that he'd developed an insatiable appetite for it. He was extremely grateful to Kingo for his hard work and commitment to building up the business and gave him a 49% share of the company and promoted him to managing director as a thank you for his hard work, determination and friendship.

But a hunger for more money was ever present. Tommy was thinking about the next million, and then the next one after that and then trebling all of that. The sky was the limit. TMS began taking on contracts which were becoming riskier, but were worth significantly larger sums of money. These deals were a lot different to terrorising the Z list gangsters, the Poundshop racketeers and the wife-beater jobs which had built the company up.

These new deals involved people disappearing forever, not just up or down the West Coast mainline. Drug-dealers were becoming much more sophisticated in the early 2000s. Communication technology had been revolutionised over the previous decade, even schoolkids now had mobile phones and any that didn't were bullied. The internet was still in its infancy but despite its tender years, the web was now in every house and despite the five minutes it took to connect to the web through a dial-up modem that sounded like it had had a dodgy curry, it completely changed the way that the drug supply industry operated.

The new, sophisticated drug dealers were a different breed to the previous generation of gun-obsessed, pit-bull assisted alpha males. They were more interested in profit and loss, than stabbing and shooting. Suddenly, drug-dealers were finding that they could operate in much more professional ways than they ever could before thanks to mobile phones, e-mails and internet sites such as Myspace. The new drug dealers didn't want to be bogged down with the hassle or expense of vast armies of knuckle-headed hard-men in three-quarter length black leather coats with sovereign rings on every finger. Now, in the dot com era, if you knew the right people and you had the finance - you could arrange for a competitor or a trouble-maker to be assassinated and their drugs confiscated as easily as you could order an extra-large donner kebab and two cans of diet Coke.

The new, emerging aspect of TMS' services were

extremely secretive, but it heralded a new direction for the company which would inevitably involve murder, guns, drugs and turf-wars but most importantly as far as Tommy and Kingo were concerned, even more money. This was an exciting opportunity for the two men, the "legitimate" arm of the company would continue to grow under the leadership of the business development manager, whilst this new service's profits would dwarf the significant sums which had been generated already. Things were looking up, when they had never been looking down.

Chapter Fifty

"Daddy!" Shouted Molly as Miller walked up the stairs of the hotel. Leo was running right behind her.

"Hello, Milly! Hello Lee!" He said as the giddy six-year olds launched themselves off the top step and into their father's arms. They were still finding their secret holiday names amusing by the looks of things.

"Daddy!" Said Leo, clinging onto his father as though he hadn't seen him for years.

"Are you alright? Having a nice time?" Asked Miller, feeling slightly emotional by this warm and energetic welcome.

"We saw you getting out of the police car! Mummy said we can come and see you!" Said Molly, just in case her dad was wondering why they were wandering around this posh hotel unattended.

Miller put the twins down and walked up the last few steps that remained. They scrambled down from their father's hold and grabbed his hands before leading him the rest of the way. He was pleasantly shocked to see that they pulled him to the right, which meant that the hotel suite was at the front of the hotel, which ultimately meant that there would be a sensational view of St Brelades Bay just beyond the windows.

Leo used the fob to open the hotel door and looked extremely proud to be in charge of such a responsibility as he stood on his tip-oes. The door clicked and he pushed it confidently. Miller was beaming, his heart was melting at this cute little thing. His smiled once again as the hotel suite was revealed.

"Knicky Knacky Nora! This is a bit of alright isn't it?" He said as he wandered in, chucking his overnight rucksack on the first bed he came to. Clare and Debs were sitting on the veranda, admiring the view as the sun was beating down.

"Ah, hello stranger!" Said Clare as Miller approached for a kiss.

"Hello Carole!" Said Miller after the short embrace.

"Where's mine?" Asked Debs.

"I've told you! I got a dose last time we had a snog!"

Clare and Debbie laughed as Miller stood up straight and admired the view.

"Bloody hell, you did alright with this didn't you?" Miller was looking out at the scene opposite the veranda, arguably the most picturesque beach on the island, with white sands and turquoise water just beyond the gently swaying palm trees. This little slice of heaven was all framed by a stunning 500 year old church to the right, and the rocky contour of the coast line to the left. The added bonus of this charming location is the sunset, which drops right into the sea at the centre of this strikingly beautiful spot.

"It's even better that its free! All thanks to the British taxpayer!" Said Clare whilst holding up her wine glass. Debbie clinked her own glass against Clare's and Miller laughed. It seemed that they'd been thanking the taxpayers a lot, the gesture looked very well-rehearsed.

"I'm well jealous! We've never managed to get a bay view room before, have we?"

"No, Clare was telling me earlier that you're a tight-wad!" Said Debbie, which made her friend laugh loudly.

"We sat here and had a glass of wine watching the sunset last night Andy. I swear to God, I could feel all the stress lifting. It was magical. It was incredible, it really was."

Miller placed his hand on his wife's shoulder and squeezed lightly. He was thrilled that she had managed to shake off the terrors she'd experienced a couple of days earlier.

Leo appeared on the veranda holding a bottle of beer from the mini-bar. "Here you go, Daddy, room service!" He said, once again looking extremely proud and important.

"Aw thank you mate!" Said Miller as he took the bottle. "Er, just a minute! Have you been drinking some?" Asked Miller with a suspicious look in his eye.

"Daddy! The lid's still on silly!" Said Molly and the twins laughed loudly.

"Oh yes. Well you can never be too sure. Everyone knows that Lee likes a drink!"

The twins laughed wildly again as Miller grabbed a seat

between Carole and Deidre. "Right, well, I better start relaxing and enjoying myself. I'm headed back in the morning!" Miller grabbed the corkscrew off the table and flicked the lid off his bottle before sitting back in the chair.

"Is that all we get of you?" Asked Debbie as Clare looked out across the bay as the ferry to Portsmouth headed slowly towards the horizon.

"For now, I'm afraid. But I think the promise of coming back to this place will give me plenty of inspiration to get a hurry on, so I can come and stay for a bit longer!" Said Miller, taking a thirsty gulp from his bottle. He smiled as the twins stood on either side of him, hugging each side of his chest and he wondered how it was possible that he felt like a man without a care in the world.

"I love this place!"

Chapter Fifty-One

MONDAY

Miller was feeling slightly nervous about the meeting with Tommy McKinlay. Not because of anything that the prisoner might do, Miller was aware that his meeting with McKinlay would be in the most secure part of the most secure prison in the UK. There would be a six-inch thick plate of bullet-proof glass between him and his would-be blackmailer. He knew that he was not at risk of physical confrontation.

The nervousness that he felt was simply about the pressure he was under to make sure that his performance was confident and powerful, that his response to this gangster was enough to make McKinlay back down and realise that he had crossed the line and crossed the wrong person. The apprehension was due to the pressure he was under, this was plan A and there wasn't a plan B. Miller really couldn't afford to step a foot wrong.

Several lines had been rehearsed in Miller's head, some impressive replies to McKinlay's inevitable questions. But as the final steel door slammed shut behind him and he finally came face to face with Tommy McKinlay, a rare sense of fear hit him in the guts and he could feel his face heating up.

McKinlay was sat down behind the glass, he was staring coldly at Miller and despite the solid glass which separated the two men, it was still incredibly intimidating. Miller knew as he sat down and coughed nervously, that he needed to get his act together and take the man facing him off whatever pedestal he had subconsciously placed him on.

"Tommy."

"DCI Miller." The stare was almost psychotic. But Miller didn't blink and got straight down to business, launching the conversation with one of the lines he'd prepared earlier.

"So, it looks like I'm going to have a to do bit more travelling in order to speak to you."

"Yes."

That cutting response derailed Miller's plans for

progress. He'd anticipated a furious rant from McKinlay, which would open up the conversation and provide him an opportunity to stamp some authority on proceedings. As that simple reply seemed to echo around the room, Miller felt that he might just have under-estimated his opponent and was thinking fast about how to get back on track. He decided to go forward with another prepared line.

"You must realise by now that you've fucked up, Tommy."

McKinlay was emotionless as he replied, his steely gaze still fixed on Miller.

"I was going to say exactly the same thing to you."

Miller was straight in with a reply, he felt that just one second of hesitation might reveal a weakness and he wasn't prepared to allow McKinlay to sense the slightest bit of power over these proceedings.

"Can't really see it myself Tommy. You were running Strangeways, you had more power than the Governor in there. And everybody was happy to leave you to it. But it's a familiar story isn't it? You got a bit too big for your boots and now you've lost everything. Banged up in Hell marsh, a complete nobody in isolation in the grimmest prison in the land and with zero chance of being able to knobble any of these screws. How the mighty have fallen!"

McKinlay just stared through the glass, there was no response whatsoever, not a blink or a twitch. The gangster just stared back at the policeman as though he was watching something really shit on telly but couldn't be bothered changing the channel. Miller guessed that this staring contest was an attempt at intimidation but it wasn't working, in actual fact this cliché gangster bullshit was somehow empowering him.

"So, anyway, let's get down to business. How long you stay here depends on you, and your general attitude going forwards. But a word to the wise Tommy, you thinking you could start giving me shit and get away with it was the dumbest move you ever made." Miller was starting to relax, his mind wandered back to the way McKinlay was behaving in the prison yard, talking to the DCI like he was a nobody.

"You done?" Asked McKinlay, as though Miller was a mere distraction.

"No Tommy. Not finished yet, I'll let you know when I have. I've been speaking to a lot of people about you. One of the DCI's from the NCA who charged you was telling me that you're very smart. He said that you are so sharp that if I stand too close to you, I'll cut myself! I've yet to see any evidence of that myself. You see Tommy, you Lording it up in Strangeways, acting like the dogs bollocks, it was pretty dumb."

"Is that so?" The prisoner grinned sarcastically and the sight of this was incredibly empowering as it meant that Miller had finally penetrated McKinlay's cold exterior with a good hit.

"You know its right. Deep down."

McKinlay laughed loudly, looking up at the double-lined steel caged ceiling above him. Miller took great encouragement from this laugh, as it lacked the arrogance and conviction that the laugh in the prison yard had.

"Laugh it up Tommy. Laugh your head off that the prison let you carry on like little Lord Fauntleroy while the NCA were monitoring all the calls and texts you sent and received in Strangeways, telling them who all your contacts are, all your business associates. You've fucked it."

Tommy stared at Miller. The bullshit laughter was gone and now it was McKinlay's cheeks which were heating up.

"Then, as though you wanted to prove beyond all doubt that you're the dumbest fucking crook in the north of England, you try and blackmail me over a case that the Home Secretary personally handled. Why else do you think you've landed up in here? Talk about shitting in your own bed and then rolling over." Miller laughed loudly, blatantly taking the piss out of McKinlay's over-the-top laughter back in the yard at Strangeways. Once he'd finished, he allowed a pause to hang in the air before continuing. "I need to go back to this person who told me you were sharp and have a word!" Miller laughed loudly once again, flagrantly mocking McKinlay. He was still pissed off about the way that this bastard had intimidated Clare and as a result, he was finding all of this incredibly rewarding.

McKinlay was silent and his gaze was no longer fixed on

the DCI. It seemed that everything Miller was saying was playing heavily on the gangster's mind. This wasn't the response that Miller had anticipated and he was extremely pleased with how things were going. McKinlay had viewed Miller as his way out of jail, and now he seemed to be realising that it wasn't going to be quite as straight forward as he'd imagined. In fact, it was looking like the biggest fuck up since Gary Glitter dropped his laptop off at PC World with the note which said "do not look at the photos on the hard drive."

"The NCA needed something that could prove that the phone they have been monitoring was yours and nobody else's. Apparently there are about seventy prohibited phones in use in there. And then Hey Presto! You text me! Three times in one night. They've got my phone, they've got your messages, they've put it all together and you're fucked! The best part of it all is that you're now banged up in here and you can't tell a soul. Even if you managed to get hold of a phone, you wouldn't get a signal through these walls. They're lead-lined! Designed to block phone signals."

McKinlay blew out a loud breath and looked at the floor. It looked as though he was punching his hand, but Miller couldn't be sure as his hands were hidden beneath the counter.

"Alright, DCI Miller, I think I've heard enough."

"Do you think?"

"Well, yes. See, I know you're talking pure shit. I had over an hours warning that Tornado were preparing to raid my cell, one of the screws stuck a note under my cell door. That's why I was so accommodating towards them."

Miller sat back and listened to what McKinlay had to say, a broad grin on his face for good measure.

"I had a good chance to tell my people what was happening, an excellent opportunity to make sure that plan B was all ready to roll. So, let me ask you, did the NCA say anything about the calls and texts I made that morning?"

"I haven't asked them."

"Well I suggest that you do."

"Why's that?"

"Because they'll probably be able to figure out what's

going to happen next. That is of course if you are telling me the truth, which I strongly suspect that you are not. So off you bob, get on with the work you've been instructed to do and don't come back here again until you've got something positive to tell me about my trial. Nothing has changed."

"I won't be coming here again, Tommy. Soz mate."

"You will. You just don't know why yet."

"Oh, let me guess, because I'll be getting sent here? Oh grow up Tommy, fucking hell, how old are you?"

McKinlay scoffed at Miller's reply. "I'll tell you another thing as well DCI Miller. The next time you come down here to discuss my case, you'll bring a better fucking attitude than the one you brought with you today, I can guarantee you that. Now off you fuck. Get back to Manchester and do what you've been told to do or you will reap the whirlwind that will follow, living every day with the knowledge that you had your chance to avoid it all and you squandered it. You fucking wet wipe."

With that, McKinlay stood and walked out of view of Miller, before he started banging his fists against the thick steel door. "Come on! Come on!" Shouted McKinlay over and over again as the hammering against the solid sounding door continued.

Miller sat back in his chair and wiped the sweat from his brow. His hand was soaking, he hadn't even realised that he was sweating. He felt confused, he'd thought that this had gone his way, right up until the last few minutes when McKinlay completely disregarded the details which were supposed to put an end to this dangerous situation. It was a crushing feeling, knowing that he was back at square one, having conceded even more power to McKinlay.

"Come on! Come on!" Shouted McKinlay as he continued to hammer his fists against the solid steel door.

Chapter Fifty-Two

Nerd had not heard from Tommy McKinlay for almost 48 hours and he was becoming increasingly concerned. It wasn't unusual for Tommy to keep his phone off for a day here and there, charging the illicit phones could be hard work as chargers were few and far between. But none-the-less, it did seem quite unusual not to hear from Tommy at this particular moment in time. There was a lot planned, involving a lot of people and Tommy's input was crucial during these final stages. Yet despite countless text messages and numerous phone calls to Tommy's number, Nerd was troubled that he hadn't received a single reply.

He decided to call Tommy's right-hand man in the organisation, if only to deflect any shit that might come his way. The last thing Nerd needed was to find himself on Tommy's wrong side.

"Alright Kingo, have you heard from Tommy?"

"Alright Nerd? Nope, not heard a dicky bird. Someone said they'd heard he's been moved from Strangeways, Tornado team rushed in and took someone away apparently, dogs barking, riot gear, the full works. Rumours are flying about that it was Tommy but I've not had an official word on that yet." Kingo was the managing director of Tommy's security business, Simon Kingston. He had plenty of contacts within the prison, some of whom were mobile phone holders. One thing was certain, there was plenty of confusion regarding the whereabouts of Tommy McKinlay. Some were saying he was still in the jail, on the isolation wing, whilst others were saying he'd been released because he'd threatened to have the Governer's daughter gang-raped and then set on fire.

"When are you expecting an official update?"

"I've got somebody waiting outside the prison now, the afternoon shift will be clocking on soon. One of the screws will give us an update."

"Good. Good. I was worried that I'd pissed him off, I've sent about fifteen texts that he's blanked."

"Same goes, big nose."

"So you think he might have been moved?"

"Yeah, there's a possibility. It won't take him long to get in touch and tell us the details though and I'm sure he'll have a new phone in no time. It's just a bit frustrating at the minute though."

"I know what you mean. That's what I'm worried about."

"Don't worry Nerd. Remember that old Latin saying Quae erit dulce."

"What does that mean?"

"Everything will be sweet."

"So you think it'll be going ahead?"

"I know it's going ahead, Nerd. No matter what."

"What... Even if Tommy is out of contact?"

"Yeah. Why not? It's all sorted out, and it will be even better if Tommy is completely out of touch with anyone. It's even better proof that he's not involved."

"Yeah, yeah. I see what you mean."

"Just try not to panic. Carry on with everything, Theresa May style. Nothing has changed. Tommy hasn't let himself get banged up for fuck all. If this goes tits up, I'll guarantee you now that he will be in a mood with us. A very fucking bad mood!"

"Sound, alright Kingo. Nice one."

"Laters, Nerd."

Chapter Fifty-Three

Miller arrived in his office late in the afternoon. He'd had the day from hell and it was far from over. It had all started with an emotional farewell from Jersey, Clare had suddenly become very clingy as Miller finished his breakfast and rang a cab for the airport. The twins had picked up on their mother's sadness and it had all got a bit teary.

Then he'd had a bastard getting from Heathrow to Belmarsh, before Tommy McKinlay had ripped him a new arsehole. Then he'd had to endure a train ride with every wannabe Apprentice contestant talking ya ya ya shit into their phones at full volume with the heating cranked up to the max. In the end, he'd decided to go and sit on the floor near the toilets, out of the way, before he was tempted to strangle one of his fellow passengers.

And now he was back at work and had walked straight into his office without acknowledging a single member of the team. It was clear to the SCIU team that something had gone tits up.

"So, how did it go?" Asked Saunders as he entered Miller's office.

"Alright Keith. Oh, I dunno mate. I felt that it was going brilliantly, I was about to text you to tell you that I'd made McKinlay cry and he'd begged me for a teddy bear to take back to his cell. And then it all just went to shit." Miller exhaled loudly and folded his arms as Saunders sat down in front of his desk. It was clear that Miller's hopes of nipping this in the bud had been dashed, he looked completely depressed.

Miller talked Saunders through the meeting, and the bizarre, completely unprompted ending, with that chilling, vague warning.

"And you think that went badly, then?" Asked Saunders.

"Do you not?"

Saunders could see that his boss needed a bit of a boost. He smiled kindly as he began his work on bolstering

Miller's confidence. "Well... I don't know. I wasn't there. But from what you've described to me, it sounds like he's fuming about being fired off to Belmarsh but was attempting to play it cool. Then, it sounds like he was getting stressed with you lecturing him, and in the end, all he had left was some threatening gangland hyperbole."

"Well if it was hyperbole, he was very convincing. I'll give him that."

"Well he's not going to get a squeaky voice when he's making threats, is he? I think you're being a bit hard on yourself. And anyway, he can threaten you all he wants, Clare and the kids are safe. There's no way that he knows that they're practically in France."

"True. Oh, and I've got to live in a fucking hotel like Alan Partridge until the situation has 'de-escalated' to use Dixon's words."

"Right, well, let's de-escalate it then and get this shit-show on the road!"

"I'm all for that Keith. Any ideas where we go from here?"

"Plenty of ideas, you know me. First things first, while it's still fresh in my mind. Get onto the Governor at Strangeways, ask him if there is the slightest possibility of McKinlay being warned about the Tornado team coming for him. Also ask for the name and address of every screw who was on duty that shift, start talking about a phone call to his superiors, ask what the complaints procedure is, that kind of thing. You know how to make the right waves."

"Yes, good call. What is the name of your line manager and do you have a phone number?" Miller started making notes, smiling humourlessly as his number two started giving orders as usual.

"I think we'll find out pretty quick whether it's true or not about the tip-off. I'm pretty sure that we will find out that its bullshit, because Tornado don't even tell the Governor what's happening most of the time, they just rock up as though they're raiding the place, get in there and do their job and answer questions later. They certainly don't ring ahead and get the jail gossiping that they're on their way."

"How the hell do you know that?"

"I know a lot of things about a lot of things, Sir."

"Well, if it turns out its bollocks about being pre-warned, then we know that he's trading on bullshit. I'm much happier dealing with people who are experts at chatting shit."

"I know what you mean. Sir, have you ever heard that famous quote, what is it now.."

"What is it now? Oh, let me guess. Was that the quote by Rolf Harris after he got sent down?" Miller pulled a sarcastic face but neither he nor Saunders were really in the mood for pissing about.

"I don't know it word-for-word, but its along the lines of 'you can learn what your enemy fears most by watching how he tries to scare you.' Something like that."

"Yeah, I've heard that one Keith, I think. What's your point mate?" Miller put his feet up on the desk and began twisting his pen around in his hands.

"Well, think about it. The way in which McKinlay has managed to get under your skin. Well, I'm sure you know the saying 'two can play that game."

"Yes! Bobby Brown!"

"Stop mucking about Sir, I'm trying to help you here."

"Alright, sorry Keith. I'm being a dick."

"I know. So, McKinlay has used threats against Clare and the twins to get your attention. I mean, what other way could he have got you to agree to blue-lighting it over to Strangeways to see him at his leisure?"

It was a good question. Miller thought about it. After a lengthy pause he shook his head. "I can't think of anything."

"Precisely. Let's think about this. McKinlay has had absolutely no dealings with you, whatsoever, not even an interview up until this point. Correct?"

"Correct."

"So, it's not as if he has some axe to grind with you. Yet the way he decides to attract your attention and make you vulnerable to his invitation is to put the fear of God into you, making you think your family are at risk."

"Yes, mate, I know all this. Where are you going with this because honestly, I think my head is about to burst."

"Where I'm going is, I'm trying to point something out. If McKinlay had wanted to, he could have very easily had you thrown into the back of a transit van while you were out on your morning run. A van full of his drug-dealers and security officers could have quite easily put the same fear of God into you in that scenario. They could have kicked the shit out of you, humiliated you, videoed themselves doing weird shit to you, sexually interfering with you... chucking you in a smouldering shallow grave and..."

"Alright Keith, fucking hell fire. I get your point."

"Dousing your balls with lighter fluid and then chucking lit matches around..."

"Keith!"

"So, going back to this thing, this famous quote. Why did McKinlay decide that targeting Clare and the kid's school was going to be more effective than sexually molesting you with a traffic cone?"

"I don't know."

"Would you have agreed to McKinlay's orders if there was a van full of lunatics kicking the shit out of you?"

"I don't know. Yeah, probably. I'd have just said whatever was necessary to get out of there."

"Thought so, this proves my point. What I'm saying is, whilst McKinlay is trying to act like some cold psycho legend and attempting to scare the living shit out of you, he's inadvertently revealed his weak spot to us. Hasn't he?"

Miller was finally starting to catch Saunders' drift.

"Interesting."

"Well, interesting, yes. But more importantly, it gives us an excellent opportunity to hold a mirror up at his own fears."

"You mean... wait, I'm not exactly sure what you mean?"

"Come on Sir, keep up. He has your mobile phone number, doesn't he?"

"Yes."

"In that case, what was stopping him from giving you a

quick call on that, introducing himself, telling you what he knows about Dawson, and then telling you what he wants you to do?"

Miller's eyes widened. That was an excellent question. And the way that Saunders had asked it, he made it sound as though the incidents at the school were completely pointless.

"What I mean is, he's let in a major own goal. The world's our oyster with this. McKinlay is banged up in Belmarsh with zero contact with the outside world. He won't be able to intimidate any of the screws in there, they're used to far worse people, terrorists and billionaires with all the right connections. You've been in and tried to diffuse the situation regarding Dawson and he's doubled-down, firing you off with a flea in your ear."

"I know…"

"Well, it leaves us two options. The first is to cave in and agree to his demands, or at least make it look like you're agreeing. That was originally plan A, wasn't it?"

Miller nodded sombrely.

"Well what I'm saying is, we've been handed our plan B on a plate here. We need to round up McKinlay's nearest and dearest, his parents, his lover, his wife, his kids, his in-laws, his closest friends, the fucking milkman. Bang them up, charge them with whatever bullshit we want. And then go back to Belmarsh, pass him the photos of his loved-ones in police cars and cells, copies of newspapers covering the raids. Plonk that steaming pile of stinking shit right under his nose and show him that Bobby Brown was right."

"Fucking hell, this is good."

"All we need to do is find out who his nearest and dearest are."

"I haven't a clue on that Keith. I wouldn't have known him if he was stood next to me in the chippy before all this shite started up."

"Doesn't matter, I'll soon find out everything we need to know. If you give me the nod, I'll be able to tell you which brand of toilet roll he prefers by this time tomorrow. Then, once we know everything we need to know, we'll pull his people in, dawn raids, we'll take the press office photographer with us.

Let's humiliate them all, get the whole underclass of Greater Manchester gossiping about how badly McKinlay has fucked up and from that moment on, we'll be getting in the driving seat."

Miller's face was beginning to come alive. "I'm liking this Keith, it's bloody genius."

"It won't take long for the news to get out of Strangeways anyway, Tommy has been marched off his turf by the prison service's answer to the SAS. His reputation will be shot within days."

"This really is pretty bloody excellent, Keith! Really."

"I know. We need to send him the message that he's not quite ready to play with the big boys yet and put him off the idea of ever trying again."

"Our gangs bigger than yours!" Said Miller, smiling. It was the first time that Saunders had seen his boss looking pleased since that phone call from Clare had interrupted his team briefing four days earlier and this whole nightmare had begun. Miller didn't look like he'd won the pools, but his smile certainly gave the impression that Saunders' idea had given him a lift. He suddenly seemed alert, taking his feet down off the desk and sitting up straight. It was clear that Saunders had given him a much-needed jolt and his mind had started working overtime on this ambitious and risky, but enthralling plan to take McKinlay down a peg or two.

"It's easy to see how McKinlay has got so over-confident. If he's been receiving special treatment in Strangeways because all of the wardens are scared of what he can organise outside, then it stands to reason that he's developed a bit of a God complex. I love the idea of reversing this."

"I love it, it seems like the logical step forward. Under no circumstances can we allow McKinlay to win. We'd all be finished in the end, anyway. So even though it might seem a bit dirty, its going to have to be done."

"You think that's dirty? You should see what me and Dixon have been up to while you've been galivanting."

Miller suddenly looked distracted. "Dixon?"

"Yes. Me and him are like that these days." Saunders

held up two crossed fingers.

"What has he got you doing?"

"He's handed me the CPS file for McKinlay's trial. It's a bag of shit."

"Seriously?"

"Yes. I think he'll probably walk, the evidence against him is Rizla-thin. I've got a theory about all this."

"Bloody hell, you're full of surprises today DI Saunders!"

"I think he's planned all this, the arrest, being remanded, just so he could tap you up."

"What…"

"I'm not kidding Sir. The case against him is dog shit. It will just take one witness not turning up at court and he'll be out. And his legend status will have reached an all time high, once the word has got about that he only went in so he could knobble you and get the most senior DCI in the force in his pocket. It's a stunt, the whole thing. A charade. I'm completely convinced of it."

Miller looked slightly hurt by this incredible suggestion. He realised that he must have appeared a little dazed and felt quite vulnerable. "Is that Dixon's view as well?"

"Yes, he tricked me into reading the file, asking me for some feedback. I stayed up all night on it, it's got more holes in it than Bill Chapman's underpants. And that's what I told Dixon. He agreed, said he'd only asked me to look it over to check that it wasn't his mind playing tricks on him."

"Jesus. So all this… I'm being played, aren't I?"

"Like a fucking banjo, Sir."

"Shit. This is, I mean, you've got to hand it to McKinlay, this is quite a project he's taken on."

"With respect, Sir. The only thing that you will be handing McKinlay when all this is done and dusted - is his arse."

"You've got it all worked out, haven't you Keith?"

"Not yet. But I will have as soon as I've found out who passed on the George Dawson information. But one thing is for certain, I'm absolutely buzzing about this job, I've not felt this excited in years!"

"I can tell you're wired. Thanks, mate. I honestly don't know where I'd be without you."

"Well, there's more yet. What was it McKinlay asked you to do with regards to his trial?"

"He said he wanted me to look into the case, and basically pin all the charges on Marco. In theory, it will be quite straight forward, but it would just open up the gates to hell. If I did it, he'd be onto me every two weeks with something else, I'd be groomed into being the most corrupt copper in Britain. And as we all know, I'm as clean as a whistle."

Saunders laughed sarcastically. "Well, that's not strictly true, Sir. Or we wouldn't be in this mess…"

"Okay, one-nil there. But…"

"No, just a sec, don't interrupt me, I'm leading somewhere. So McKinlay has asked you to pin his offences on Marco, who is dead and can't answer for himself. It's got me thinking…"

"I'm dying to hear this."

"The case against McKinlay is so flimsy, I'm surprised the CPS have agreed to prosecute, let alone remand him."

"Right."

"But the Marco thing, the whole episode with him getting our team busy with the DWP attacks while he closed down his drug factory, it was bordering on genius, in a really depressing and grisly way."

"I agree. I fell for it hook, line and sinker."

"I'm pretty sure McKinlay will have been impressed as well. It has made me wonder if he is trying a similar thing, distracting the shit out of you, while something else is happening in the background."

Miller was staring at Saunders as he spoke, surprised by just how much time and effort his DI had been putting into this during the 24 hours that he had been in Jersey and London. Even by Saunders exceptionally high-standards, Miller really felt that the younger detective had been pulling out all of the stops.

"When you say something else…"

"I don't know. Nothing concrete, it's just a gut feeling at this stage. But I never ignore my gut. Something is amiss."

"Go on, I know you'll have more than just your gut, or you wouldn't have mentioned it."

"Okay, well it comes back to Marco. Why would McKinlay want to blame silly little things on a dead gangster, when there will be a dozen gangsters in the north who are perfectly alive and pose a genuine threat to McKinlay's business interests, on a daily basis?"

"That's a good question. I just thought it was convenience."

"Well, I'm not being funny Sir, but it would be a lot more convenient to get the top DCI that you are blackmailing to start taking down McKinlay's competitors. You could do a lot more damage than shift some blame onto a dead man, particularly when the case is destined to collapse anyway."

Miller was thinking hard. Saunders was talking sense, and he felt slightly stupid for not picking up on any of this himself. It was pretty bloody obvious when it was all being spelt out this way.

"Are you absolutely sure the case against McKinlay is shit?"

"Totally. If I go and get my crystal ball out, it'll show that the star witness doesn't turn up on day one, and the other witness fails to appear on day two. Day three, the trial collapses and McKinlay is driving around the city, being worshipped like a hero by every crook in every town. Day four, the witnesses who failed to show up will be paying cash for a new house each."

"Day five… he wanders in here and makes me sit where you are?"

"Yes. And sellotapes a dildo to your forehead."

"Steady…"

"But yes, it stinks, there's got to be something else going on, another layer that we haven't discovered yet."

"Well, it seems to me that there's still plenty to be getting on with here."

"Totally. Well, anyway, with your permission Sir, I'll start gathering some intelligence on McKinlay's favourite people. Once we know who he loves the most, we'll be able to start messing with *his* head and showing him that he would do well to wind his neck right in."

"Well, mate... this is really positive stuff, cheers. Permission is well and truly granted!"

Chapter Fifty-Four

"Alright Nerd?"

"Alright Kingo?"

"Yeah. Just had it all confirmed by a screw, Tommy's been moved out."

"Shit."

"Yeah. Tornado Team came in and cuffed him, stuck him in a van and fucked off somewhere. No-one knows where they've took him, looks like its top secret. This was a couple of days ago so he's not scheduled to be coming back anytime soon by the looks of things."

"Shit. Tommy won't be happy with that. I bet he's..." Nerd sounded genuinely concerned but Kingo cut him short, he didn't sound particularly fussed by the news, but he was talking fast and he sounded as though he'd been at the sniff. He became a different bloke when he was taking that shit.

"Yeah. Anyway, just thought you'd want to know that it wasn't just Tommy blanking our messages!" Kingo laughed at his observation, but it sounded completely inappropriate under the circumstances.

"How can they do that?"

"Do what?" Tommy sniffed loudly as he said it, confirming to Nerd that his suspicions had been spot on.

"Just move him out of his prison?"

"Dunno. They're probably spooked about everything, want him out of the way until they sort their shit out. Tommy's been making too many headaches in there anyway, getting on everyone's tits, the screws, the bosses, the inmates. Even the fucking rats have put in a complaint about him." Kingo laughed loudly, inviting Nerd to join in.

Nerd laughed because he knew that it was easier to laugh at a shit joke rather than try to explain why he hadn't laughed. Kingo sniffed loudly again.

"Tommy, he never knows when to shut the fuck up, does he?"

"Well, I wouldn't..."

"Don't worry though, I'm going to try and sort out a way of getting him back in Strangeways before the job happens. At least if he's there we know we can talk to him if we need to."

"Right…"

"But when I do, I'm going to tell the cunt it's the last time I'm pulling him out of the fucking holes he puts himself in. Just carry on as normal, the plan isn't going to be altered by this."

"Fucking hell. I'm starting to get a bit nervous about all this now, you know."

"It was always a possibility summat like this would happen. Dibble are trying to flex their muscles but we'll soon have them back in their box. Just crack on with your work Nerd, make sure you've got every phone tracked so we know who's where and when. Don't worry about it, we're almost at the finishing line now."

"Na, Kingo, seriously. All this is getting a bit…"

"Hoi, listen you autistic little cunt. Who the fuck do you think you're speaking to? Carry on with your instructions and don't give me any more of your lip, or I'll cut your fucking lips off your mouth and glue them to your ears with that Gorilla glue from Homebase. Silly little prick."

"I'm just… I can't concentrate properly when I'm this stressed."

"Are you still fucking talking? What are… did you say you're stressed? Fucking hell, seriously? Did you honestly just say that? Or has someone slipped a trip in my Irn Bru? Fucking stressed!"

"I just like to know what's what… this with Tommy being moved out of Strangeways, it wasn't what we were originally doing. I'm sorry Kingo, but I'm flapping."

"Shut up now Nerd, I've heard enough of your shit to last me 'til Christmas. Listen you dick, it's better that Tommy's been moved, because it can't come back on him when we've done the job. Plus, he can't cause any more fucking problems for the time being, can he?"

Nerd was trying to figure out how many contradictions Kingo was coming out with, which caused his stress levels to rise even further. Kingo clearly wasn't thinking straight if he was talking about how good it was that Tommy had been moved, but he was working on a plan to get him back in Strangeways. Of all the times people needed to keep a clear head, it was now, and Kingo was certainly not keeping a clear head.

"No, well, no, I don't suppose..."

"Right, you're doing my head in now, just get on with your work Nerd or the only stress you'll have in your life is trying to work out how to reach the porno mags when you're sitting in a wheelchair."

Chapter Fifty-Five

If anybody ever wrote a book about the issues and incidents that TM Security had been involved with throughout the years, it would probably become a best seller. Over the past quarter of a century, there had been some incredible, shocking and downright disturbing stories generated by the activities that Tommy, Kingo and the rest of the team had found themselves caught up in. Some of the tales would be hard-hitting, many of them very humorous and there are one or two which might just be a little too hard to believe.

And there would undoubtedly be a number of tales which Tommy and Kingo would prefer people not to know about, real-life tales which would never make the final draft of the manuscript. Occasionally, things went too far in this line of work. When things did go too far, Tommy and Kingo tended to put it down to the white powder that they'd inhaled and just left it at that.

One such event had taken place a couple of years earlier, a job which Tommy said "had gone a bit mad" during the drive home with Kingo by his side. But it wasn't mad, it was completely demonic and there could never be any justification for it. Describing it as "a bit mad" was completely underplaying it and denying the victims of any humanity whatsoever.

A job had come in regarding the tenant of a rented house in Droylsden. The tenant had fallen behind with his rent payments and the whole thing had spiralled badly out of control. The owner of the property was in trouble with the mortgage repayments as the tenant hadn't paid him any rent for almost a year and just ignored the door whenever anybody had tried to speak to him about the situation.

At this stage in the TMS organisation's life, a job like this would fall to a couple of the fifty-plus security officers who would act as fast-track, no-shit bailiffs who would go in and evict the tenants immediately, cutting out the six-month run around that the court reps had to contend with. A TM security team had called round at the address several times and there was never any answer at the door. As the organisation had become quite professional by this time, certain rules and laws were to be adhered to and respected, particularly when the TMS vans and staff were in plain sight of the local community.

Any of the occasional, problematic jobs like this one tended to end up on Kingo's desk and he'd either look after it himself, or he'd talk to Tommy about it. Nine times out of ten, Tommy would invite himself along for the "shits and giggles" of going back to basics. He loved the nostalgia of the early days of the TMS enterprise and he viewed the opportunity to get involved on the front-line every so often as a golden opportunity to remind the population of the north west exactly what the TM in TM Security stood for.

On this occasion, Tommy was eager to get this eviction job sorted asap so the client was satisfied with the TMS experience, particularly as the job was now nearly a month old. Maybe it was the thrill of going back out as partners again which had got the two men so excited, it was quite rare that they did any 'hands-on' stuff these days. They'd both snorted a good few lines in Tommy's Rolls Royce before they'd got out and walked around to the address which was causing difficulties for their client, and now them.

Tommy crept right up to the front room window. The telly was on and a little kid was running around inside shouting about something to do with the game he was playing. A man's voice could then be heard shouting, before a woman called back. From where Tommy was standing, it sounded as though she was upstairs and was replying to whatever it was that the man had shouted.

Tommy looked across at Kingo and gave a signal that there were people inside the house. Tommy's partner pressed the doorbell and within seconds, the noise and activity within the property ceased completely. The TV had been knocked off, and the people inside had stopped shouting and yelling around the place. Tommy looked at the car on the drive. It was a brand new BMW with all the extras.

"I bet that's why he can't pay his fucking rent!" Said Tommy, before walking back towards the front door of the three-bed semi detached house close to Droylsden town centre, just a couple of miles east of Manchester city centre. "How much do you reckon that is a month? A grand?"

"And the rest, probably two. We'll probably end up with the job of collecting the money for that fucker soon as well!"

Tommy looked irritable. He didn't like the thought of his client going around saying negative things about TMS. He took things like this very seriously. "Wait here Kingo, I'll nip round the back."

He leaned over the gate at the side of the house, found the catch and opened it. As he did so, the gate made a loud scraping noise on the flagstone path. Tommy left it half opened and approached the back door, he heard the key inside being turned quickly and the mortice bolt clicking into place. He grabbed the handle and tried to open to door but it seemed he'd arrived half a second too late. This was the kind of situation which brought Tommy the most enjoyment. Some of his staff would start getting stressed out by this sort of carry on, but to him it was something to savour. The bloke inside the house was getting himself into more and more bother with everything Tommy learnt about him. The more you did things like that with Tommy McKinlay, the harsher your punishment would undoubtedly become.

"Open the door you fucking cucumber!" Shouted Tommy, with his face pressed right up to the glass.

There was no response from inside the address.

"Last chance. Open the door."

Still nothing.

Tommy gave it a couple more seconds before turning around and looking around the back garden. It looked just like any normal family home, the rear of the property was littered with kid's toys, a swing, a garden slide. There were some football nets and a towel was laid out on the grass where somebody had been sunbathing. It made Tommy smile. These people were taking the piss, living in this house and not paying a penny in rent, but from first impressions, it looked just like any other house on any other street.

Tommy saw a stone plant pot which contained a small conifer on the patio. He picked it up and threw it through the back door window. The noise of the glass breaking and then the stone shattering on the kitchen floor was quickly replaced by the sound of the little kid, who began crying hysterically. Tommy shoved his head through the gap where the glass had been and looked into the kitchen. There was nobody about, but he thought he heard somebody telling the kid to be quiet.

"Come and open this door before I start getting cross with you."

Once again, it seemed that the occupants of the house were convinced that the stay quiet and they'll go away tactic would continue to work. But there was no chance of that happening today.

Tommy put his hand through the broken window, unlocked the door and pulled the bunch of keys out of the door lock before walking into the kitchen. A neighbour from the house next door was having a nosey through her kitchen window and Tommy smiled and waved to her and jangled the keys at her with his other hand. The gesture seemed to confuse her and she looked down at her sink and continued washing her pots.

"Come out, come out, wherever you are!" Said Tommy as he closed the kitchen door and began inspecting the damage to the back door very meticulously, purely for the nosey neighbour's benefit. Suddenly, a young bloke appeared from the doorway, clutching a baseball bat. He stood in the middle of the kitchen and he thought he looked hard.

"Get the fuck out of here now or I'm going to wrap this around your fucking head!" He said. He was only a kid, mid twenties by the looks of it, he looked like he genuinely believed this was going to do the trick.

Tommy just laughed at him.

"The fuck are you laughing at dickhead? I said get out or you'll be getting this!" The young man's eyes were wild. Tommy laughed again, replicating the first laugh perfectly so that the bloke with the baseball bat was under no illusion that Tommy was blatantly taking the piss out of him. He stepped forward and swung the bat aggressively, a loud swish noise followed it. Tommy laughed again.

"Where did you get that from? It's fucking shit."

"You better get out of my house!" He swung the bat again. Tommy stayed put with a wide smile on his face.

"No Sir. You better get out of my house. This is my house now you ugly cunt."

"You what?" The young bloke was confused. This guy who'd just smashed the back door in was seriously freaking him out, he wasn't even remotely scared of the bat.

"If you don't put that down now I'm going to take it off you and use it to break your arm in half you rotter."

The young guy stepped forward again and went to swing the bat but Tommy's patience had finally worn through. He kicked his foot behind the lad's legs and lifted them high in the air. The wannabe hard-man landed heavily on his back and Tommy laughed as all the air left his lungs. It was the unmistakable groan of somebody who was in great pain but couldn't make much fuss because they'd been badly winded.

Tommy stepped forward and pulled the bat out of the hands of his would-be attacker and spent a moment inspecting it.

"Did you make this yourself out of marzipan? Its fucking bobbins! To be honest, I think this thing will break before your arm does!"

"Don't!" Said the young man, still struggling for breath. He began wriggling, trying to get up but the pain from his landing was still overpowering him.

"What's your name sunny Jim?" Asked Tommy.

"Jason..." That was all he could manage.

"Correct! Jason Jackson. Fucking hell, your parents must having been injecting smack when they named you that! That's the laziest name I've ever heard in my life!"

Jason tried once again to sit up and managed it this time. He twisted and turned onto his knees before standing up. For the past minute or so a young child had been screaming from an adjacent room.

"What do you want?"

"Well, there's quite a list JJ! But right at the very top is for you to tell your kid to shut its fucking mouth, it's doing my head in."

"Jasmine... tell Jenna to shush while I find out what this bloke wants."

Tommy laughed loudly but Jason didn't appear to get the joke.

"Oh and Jasmine, I know you're fucking hopeless at answering your front door but will you try and see if you can do it before my colleague takes it off its hinges?" Shouted Tommy and Jenna began crying hysterically again. Despite the noise, Jasmine followed the order and opened the front door. Kingo walked in and headed straight through to the kitchen where he started laughing at the baseball bat in Tommy's hands.

"Where did you get that? Poundland?" He asked and Tommy laughed manically.

"Shit innit? This fucking joker started swinging it about. He must have thought I would of run off."

Kingo turned to Jason. "You didn't did you? Oh, that was a bit dickish!"

"I told him if he didn't stop swinging it, I'll take it off him and break his arm with it. But look at it! Couldn't break the skin on a rice pudding with this!"

Kingo took the bat from Tommy and looked at it. "Is it a rounders bat?" He asked and Tommy laughed manically once again.

"Yeah, off a snide Barbie doll from Cheetham Hill I think!"

Jason just stood there, it looked as though he was planning to do something. Kingo sensed that he was waiting to open the cutlery drawer which he was standing beside. Kingo stepped forward, gripped Jason's arm between the wrist and the elbow and smashed it as hard as he could against the edge of the fridge-freezer, snapping the young man's forearm right in the centre with a loud click noise. Jason let out a stomach-churning howl before falling to his knees and trying to clutch the compound fracture before realising that he couldn't do anything to ease the pain.

Tommy laughed manically once again as Kingo smiled at the pitiful scene before him. "Now that's how you break an arm." He said.

"You fucking cunt! I'll fucking have you for this!" Said Jason, Tears were dropping from his face and creating tiny puddles on the kitchen lino.

"He's a proper gobshite this one, isn't he Tommy?"

"I think he's a bit dim. His bird looks pretty tasty though, Kingo. She must have a thing for funny-looking losers!"

Tommy was looking down at Jason who was knelt-down with his broken arm resting against the floor.

"I'm so tempted to jump on that arm you know JJ! Tell you what mate, why don't you tell Jasmine to come in here and show Kingo how pretty she is and I won't."

"Fuck off!" Said Jason, his whole torso was trembling from the overproduction of adrenaline.

"Jasmine! Jasmine! Come here a minute love!" Shouted Tommy in a deliberately patronising voice. He got his wish, Jasmine came rushing through into the kitchen, wielding a hammer above her head.

"Get the fuck out of our house!" She shrieked.

"Fucking hell, it's like groundhog day in here, I tell you," said Tommy very cheerfully, before punching Jason's partner in the face. Jasmine stood there, shocked and confused. She'd dropped the hammer on the floor and Tommy bent down to pick it up. The crying from the young kid in the room next door was becoming intolerable.

"Right, love. You need to start packing your shit together, stick whatever you want to keep on the lawn outside while we change the locks. You've got five minutes. And tell your kid to shut up will you? I'm getting a fucking migraine." Said Kingo as he lifted the kettle and walked across to the sink to fill it up. "Where do you keep the tea-bags?"

Jasmine was just standing there, speechless with shock and terror. She couldn't understand what was going on. She and Jason had run-ins with the courts and stuff before, but this was different. These people were psychopaths and Jasmine's understanding of the laws and procedures of this country were being rewritten.

"You think you're going to get away with this? What the fuck!" Said Jasmine, seemingly unaware of how futile her words were.

"I told you she was pretty, didn't I Kingo?" Said Tommy. "Those tits look a bit fake though. Too high up."

Jasmine was muted again. These people seemed to just ignore what was being said, it seemed like they didn't give a shit.

"Yeah. Too high up and too round. Is that why you didn't pay your rent for a year Jason?" Asked Kingo. "Getting the bird some new boobies? Never mind, you can sleep under them tonight you dingbat!"

"Let's have a look then," said Tommy. "Don't ignore me Jasmine. I want to see your new titties!" Tommy's face had changed. The sarcastic, faux smile was gone and an intense stare had replaced the relaxed, care-free look on his face.

"You'd better fuck off now, I'm telling you…" said Jason, who was listening to all of this, but was facing the opposite way and as a result, couldn't see the sheer terror on his partner's face.

"Oh do be quiet Jason, you are extremely quarrelsome today!" Said Kingo and Tommy laughed loudly.

"Yeah, shut up JJ. You just look at your manky arm and keep your mouth zipped. So come on Jasmine, get your tits out! Get your…"

Kingo joined in with the once famous chant.

"… tits out for the lads! Get your tits out for the lads!"

Jasmine didn't move. She stood there, frozen to the spot, Her face was bright red, but a shade darker around her cheek where Tommy had punched her.

Without another word, Tommy stepped forward and grabbed Jasmine's top with both hands around the collar and ripped it so violently that she was flung onto the floor. As she was screaming, he knelt down on her chest and yanked her bra so hard that the front section tore in half. Jasmine was lay there on the kitchen floor with her breasts exposed, Tommy remained knelt on her chest and began touching the young woman. Her screaming had stopped now, she was just staring at Tommy, her eyes pleading with him to stop.

"I'm not usually a fan, but they're spot on them! They don't feel natural, but they don't feel dead hard. No, I'm alright with them, you've got a pair of crackers! Well done."

As the kettle continued to boil, Kingo's attention was being taken up by Jasmine and subsequently, he hadn't noticed that Jason had been inching backwards along the floor towards him. Without warning, the young man kicked out at Kingo's balls, a solid, deft kick landed almost square on. Had Kingo not reacted so quickly, Jason's foot would have connected with the gangsters most vulnerable body parts. But fortunately for Kingo, he had seen a sudden movement out of the corner of his eye and had shielded himself in time. Jason's kick connected with Kingo's upper thigh.

Tommy and Kingo laughed loudly as Jason shrieked in pain. That risky manoeuvre had obviously hurt his arm pretty badly judging by the depth of the howl which escaped Jason's lips.

"What was that meant to be?" Asked Tommy, standing up and moving away from Jason's partner. She sat up and tried to cover herself up but she wasn't having much success due to the damage to her clothing.

Tommy walked across and stamped against Jason's supporting arm at the elbow. There was a loud click and a scream as all of Jason's weight fell down onto his two badly damaged arms. This latest injury had sent the arm the wrong way at the joint. But Tommy wasn't done. He gripped Jason's t-shirt at the shoulders and hoisted him up, before throwing him across the kitchen floor where he landed in the corner near the sink and the smashed up plant pot, right on top of the glass from the back door. He was leant up against the cupboard and the washing machine, his two broken arms displaced at awkward angles before him. The howls of pain were drowning out the screams of terror from the child in the next room.

"You two never fucking learn? Do yous? Right, Jasmine, you can make it up to Kingo. In a very special way."

What followed was the most appalling thing that Jason Jackson had ever witnessed. Tommy sat next to him on the kitchen floor, forcing the young man to watch as his partner performed a sex act on Kingo, who was laughing in Jason's face throughout the ordeal. Jasmine was crying and sobbing and trying not to be sick. Once Kingo was satisfied, Tommy stood up and insisted on receiving the same treatment. He shouted at Jason to keep watching, laughing hysterically as Jason was sick in his lap, unable to do anything other than watch his partner being abused in the most unspeakable manner. Watching the event which he knew, and she knew, that their relationship would never be able to withstand.

"Hey, she's spot on her JJ!" Shouted Tommy before shouting "Yee-har!" He laughed again as Jason vomited once more, all the while the child continued screaming from the next room. Once Tommy was done, he punched Jasmine in the face again and called her a dirty fucking whore, which made Kingo laugh manically.

"Now go and get your kid and fuck off out of this house you dosser!" Said Tommy, kicking Jasmine in the backside as she rushed away. He then walked over to the back door and opened it, before lifting Jason by his broken arms and throwing him out, still screaming in agony, onto the path.

"Next time, answer the flipping door!"

Chapter Fifty-Six

TUESDAY

The previous day, Saunders had set his team the task of finding out everything that they possibly could find out about McKinlay's business life and his personal life. The business side of things wasn't the number one priority, after all, the NCA detectives had already made it clear that they had been led up dead end after dead end in trying to uncover any wrongdoing at TM Security. It appeared that he ran a very tight ship in that regard.

However, the NCA hadn't revealed very much in their file regarding McKinlay's personal affairs and this subject was now the top priority for the SCIU team. They were researching every person that Tommy McKinlay held dear. His mum, his sisters, his teenage son, his current girlfriend and his wife. Lots of interesting stuff was coming back and Saunders was feeling extremely buoyed by the speed of the progress. He felt it was time to start planning the arrests which were destined to really put McKinlay's nose out of joint.

But as he entered Miller's office with the intention of working on the foundations for the arrests, he quickly learnt that Miller had more pressing concerns.

"Sounds good Keith, good work. But…"

"Ah, bloody hell, I knew there was a flipping but coming…"

"Listen. I need to speak to Dawson, as soon as possible. This is now the number one priority. There are two principle reasons for this. Firstly, I need him to know that if he no comments any questions that are put to him, we stand a good chance of surviving this. Secondly, I need to find out who has been blabbing. If we can work that out, it gives us a stronger chance of convincing McKinlay that its bullshit. Even if I can't convince him, it would be nice to sow some more seeds of doubt in his mind. Combined with what I told him about the Home Office, it might be enough to get him to pipe down, before we reveal that his loved ones have been taken into custody. I really think this will mess his head up. Control freak loses control."

"Sounds straight forward enough." Said Saunders, trying not to dwell on this interruption to the progress he'd been excited about.

"Yeah, but it's not. We need to keep our paranoid levels on maximum. What I mean by that is we need to think like master criminals here, we need to imagine that McKinlay's people are holed up in the house opposite Dawson's. Think about it. If they managed to produce photographs of me and you walking up the drive to his house, it's game over, we'll never be able to dig ourselves out of the shit."

"Yes, good point. So, what are you thinking?"

"I'm thinking that we need a way of getting a message to him. But it can't be anybody from the police who delivers it."

Saunders began tapping his pen on his pad, a sure sign that he was thinking. A few seconds later, he looked up at Miller. "Is he on Facebook?"

"No. Already looked. At least, if he is, it's not under his given name."

"Did you not say he was living with Sykes' wife?"

"Yes. Good point! I've not checked her. What's her name, shit…" Miller was wracking his brains trying to remember the name of the woman that Dawson was now living with, albeit completely platonically as he understood it. "Margaret. That's it."

Saunders opened Facebook on his phone and searched the name. There were dozens upon dozens of Margaret Sykes. "Shit… this is a popular name on Facebook." Saunders clicked on the filter function and selected "City" before typing in Bolton. The search now returned with a single result. "Bingo." Saunders clicked the profile and showed it to Miller. "Is that her?" He asked.

"I don't know, wouldn't know her from Adam."

Saunders kept clicking, selecting Margaret Sykes's photographs. There was a man present in many of them. Saunders checked the dates, the photos with the man went back several years, the earliest was 2013. "That's not Dawson is it?" He asked. Miller took the phone and focused on the photograph before shaking his head solemnly. "It's not Sykes, either. Looks nothing like him. Dead end here I think."

"No, wait. Think about it, this was a major story… if she is on Facebook, there's a good chance she's changed her name to avoid the internet trolls and what have you. We need to know what her maiden name is, she's probably using that if she's on there."

"That'll involve a call to births, deaths and marriages."

"Bloody hell. So, a ten-year delay as well."

"Usually… but that's not very wise anyway, is it, if we're turning the paranoia up to eleven."

"No, good point."

"What about a good old-fashioned letter? Through the post? We could get it sent special delivery, next-day, signed for, fully trackable. Guaranteed delivery by 1pm. We'll know the moment it's delivered."

"I like that Keith, great shout. What do you reckon we should put in it?"

"Just an MCP compliments slip with a phone number on. Say something like 'please call this number asap.' Should do the trick."

"No. he might panic. I need to give him a clue that it's me. Something that he will link straight back to me."

"Like what?"

"Got it! I'm going to need a phone number though. Can't exactly put mine on it, can I?"

"One sec." Saunders stood and went to Miller's office door. "Anyone going to Tesco's at lunch?" He asked in the general direction of the team.

"Yeah, I am," said Kenyon.

"Cool. Stop what you're doing Pete and take an early lunch. Grab us one of those drug-dealer burner phones."

"The tenner ones?"

"Yes. And quick as you can please mate."

"And get me a packet of Cherry Bakewells. You can have one." Said Rudovsky.

Saunders went back into Miller's office and closed the door. "Right, we'll have a phone sorted soon enough. I take it you know the address?"

"Yes, well, I did. Dawson sold up and moved into the Sykes house."

"That's number 11."

Miller raised an eyebrow. "How the hell do you know that?"

"Because I spent two days on surveillance outside Dawson's. That was number 9."

"Let's double-check it on Google maps. Just to be on the safe side." Miller opened his internet browser and typed in the address, Avenham Close, Little Lever. Within seconds, Miller and Saunders had the street-view photo of the street. "Which one is it?" Asked Miller as he scrolled his mouse along the street.

"That's it, there. Zoom in on the front door."

Miller did as he was asked and the number 9 beside the door came into focus. "So, Sykes' house could be number seven, or number eleven."

"No, it's number eleven. Trust me, Sir. I was sat outside number fifteen when I was doing my obs. Dawson and Sykes kept coming and going between each-others houses all day long."

Miller reversed the street view along the avenue, before zooming in on number eleven's front porch.

"Yes, that's it."

"Sure?"

"Positive."

"We can't fuck this up."

"I know. Trust me, move along one house."

Miller did as instructed.

"Right, what number is on that one?"

Miller zoomed in once again and squinted. "Er... looks like 15 to me."

"It is. That's the house I was sat outside."

"But that doesn't make any sense. The next-door house to number eleven should be thirteen."

"Exactly. That's why I'm so confident that I'm right. There is no number thirteen on Avenham Close. It's eleven, then fifteen."

Miller looked puzzled.

"Loads of streets skip number thirteen. House-builders struggle selling them..."

"Shut up!" Miller laughed loudly, pointing at Saunders as though he was halting a prank.

"Straight up. They used to have to sell them for peanuts because people thought it was unlucky. So in the end, they just stopped doing number thirteens."

Miller didn't look convinced. "Okay, never heard of this one before but I'll take your word for it. At least it shows that you know which house it was."

"But as the paranoia level is up to maximum on this, I'll do a quick scan of the current electoral register and make sure they've not flitted."

"Yes, good idea. And I'll delete this Google search."

"Oh, one more thing."

"Yes, Columbo."

"If we're being as paranoid as we are...Well, the Post Office will have CCTV cameras. We don't want it to be possible for this letter to be traced back to us. But if it's being sent via special delivery, it'll be fully traced back to the second it's registered on the Royal Mail system."

"Of course. Good point. Any investigations would lead back to me standing there at the Post Office and I'll be caught red handed. Shit."

Miller and Saunders thought about this for a few moments. It may well have been paranoid to such a level that it was bordering on neurotic, but it was crucial to be so vigilant when the stakes were this high. Both men realised that they held a huge advantage in knowing where any potential investigators would look and what they'd be looking for.

"We can't send it in the police mailbag for the same reason." Said Saunders, clearly at a loss as to how to get around this obstacle. "It'll lead straight back to this building and it won't take too long to work out which floor."

"I know! Get Jo in here."

Saunders stood and walked across to the door once again. "Jo... got a minute?" He said loudly. Rudovsky stood and walked quickly towards Miller's office, the rest of the team had a good gawk as she went.

"Jo, we have a problem and only you can save us." Said Miller.

"Standard!" Said Rudovsky.

"Sit down a minute."

Once the problem had been explained, Miller put forward his idea. "So I'm thinking you would know a trustworthy little chav on your estate who would go in the Post Office and get the letter sent for us in exchange for a tenner?"

Rudovsky smiled widely. "Sir, I know about four thousand kids on that estate who'd do that."

"Brilliant. It is absolutely crucial that this goes in today's post so I need you to make it happen. Once we've had the talk with Dawson, the pressure will drop significantly. If this letter goes today, we could realistically have this issue dealt with by this time tomorrow."

"Yeah, cool. No problem at all. I'll find a decent kid and sort it. But call it twenty quid, you tight fisted bastard!"

Miller and Saunders laughed enthusiastically. "Okay. But make sure your decoy knows that if this ever ends up in a police interview, the guy who asked for the letter to be sent was about sixty and looked like Simon Cowell."

"Simon Cowell *is* sixty."

"Perfect then!"

"So you want the decoy to say Simon Cowell asked him to send the letter."

"No. Just some guy who looked a bit like Simon Cowell. He just said go and post this letter and come back here, give me the receipt and I'll give you twenty quid. That's all your decoy needs to say."

"No problem, Sir."

"Cheers Jo. I'll give you the letter as soon as I have a phone number. Then once you've sorted that you can get an early finish and see what jobs Abby wants you to do!"

Rudovsky raised her middle finger before leaving the office.

"Sorted!" Said Miller. "We're getting somewhere now."

Chapter Fifty-Seven

WEDNESDAY

Jo Rudovsky had been up since stupid o'clock. Abby's mate was supposed to have beeen giving her a lift to a breakfast conference on the other side of Manchester but had text to say that her car wouldn't start. It was impossible to get there on public transport at such an early hour, so Rudovsky had jumped out of bed, driven Abby and her mate around the M60 motorway, and then doubled-back home to get showered and dressed for work. "What sort of a psychopath sets up a fucking meeting at half-six in the morning, anyway?" Rudovsky asked herself, numerous times as she drove back. But she wasn't that bothered really, Abby made a lot of new contacts across the Greater Manchester youth service scene thanks to these trendy early morning meetings and they always proved to be worthwhile, often securing some paid work. It was work which was gratefully received, supplementing Abby's full-time voluntary mission in keeping Wythy youth centre running. If it hadn't been for Abby and her resolute determination to keep the club going, the building would have been boarded up a long time ago.

It was almost seven by the time she pulled the car up outside the couple's neat little former council home on Falmer Drive. Rudovsky realised that time was working against her if she was going to get into work in Manchester city centre for 8am, she still had to iron her clothes yet.

She closed the front door with the back of her foot and went through to the kitchen, plugging in the iron and switching on the kettle. As the kettle began to boil, she set up the ironing board and grabbed her shirt and trousers out of the ironing basket. Within a couple of minutes, her coffee was steaming away on the worktop and her clothes were freshly pressed on the ironing board. She unplugged the iron and headed upstairs where she turned the shower on and headed through to the spare bedroom where her music system was set-up. She grabbed an album off the top and opened the CD player drawer, before selecting the track she wanted. One minute later, with the sound of James blasting out, Rudovsky was in the shower, washing her hair, singing at the top of her voice. "Born of frustration, born of frustratioooon, woo woo woo woo." Rudovsky was patting against her mouth like a Red-Indian for the chorus bit when the music suddenly stopped. The only sound she could hear now was the water jetting out of the showerhead.

"That's weird," said Rudovsky, her first thought had been that the power had gone off, but that idea was quickly dismissed as she realised the shower was working perfectly fine. Then it occurred to her that it was an old album, she'd had it for donkey's years. Maybe it had skipped. Or perhaps she'd had it on too loud and the stereo had packed in. Whatever it was, she was pissed off as she had just been getting into that. She rubbed her face under the hot water and felt slightly irritated that her rare chance at an early morning sing-along in the shower had been cut short. She poured some shower gel on the body mop and started lathering it against herself when she suddenly got the biggest fright of her life.

"Hey, DS Rudovsky!" Said a deep, booming voice. It was a man, local accent, he sounded as though he was just a couple of feet away from her, on the other side of the shower curtain. She stared at the curtain and made out a dark silhouette behind it, illuminated by the light flooding in from behind the figure. Rudovsky felt weak, as though her legs were going to give way, her heart was suddenly thumping hard against her chest and she felt dizzy. She looked along the side of the bath to see if there was anything substantial that she could use to defend herself with. There was nothing.

"Who... who's there?" She asked, feeling totally vulnerable.

"Got a message for you. You need to tell Miller to get Tommy back home to HMP Manchester urgently. Have you got that?"

Rudovsky had turned the shower off and was standing behind the curtain, shivering through fear and adrenaline.

"I said, have you got that?"

"Ye... yes..." said the DS, feeling thoroughly ashamed of how weak and subservient her voice sounded.

"We're not messing about. I'm holding a gun about a metre away from your head. If I have to speak to you again, I'll be shooting your fucking brains out. Are we clear?"

Something snapped inside Rudovsky. She wasn't having this, in her own house, being terrorised and made to feel so vulnerable.

"I said, are we clear?" Repeated the voice.

Rudovsky ripped the shower curtain open, the speed and noise of the action seemed to make the gunman jump slightly. He stood there, the handgun was pointed straight at her face. She could only see his eyes, he was wearing a balaclava but she sensed that he looked slightly unnerved by the spectacle of this terrified, naked woman staring back at him with her mouth wide-open. Rudovsky was frozen to the spot, satisfied that the man had a gun and that it wasn't just a lie to intimidate her. She just nodded slowly. "I'll... I'll pass it on..."

"You better had do. Because if Tommy's not back up here sharpish, back in Strangeways then there's going to be hell to pay." The gunman grabbed Rudovsky's towel off the holder and handed it to her. She wrapped herself with it, suddenly feeling much more confident, despite the gun which was pointing directly at her from just a few feet away.

"I notice you've not said anything stupid like Tommy who? So that's good. It means we understand each other a hundred per cent. Tell Miller, soon as you can, get Tommy back from wherever the fuck he's sent him and things will settle down. If he doesn't do as he's told then people are going to start dying. You got all that?"

Rudovsky nodded frantically, making water fly off her head.

"He needs to be back tonight. Right, I'll leave you to finish your shower. Do you want the music putting back on?"

Rudovsky shook her head again, there was more water being dispersed, this time from her eyes.

"Tune that, by the way. Not heard that for time." The gunman lowered his arm and placed the gun by his side before turning slowly. He stopped and looked back at Rudovsky before walking casually down the stairs. A few seconds later, the back door slammed shut, sending a vibration that rattled through the whole house. Rudovsky collapsed into the bath-tub she'd been standing in, her legs had completely given way.

Chapter Fifty-Eight

"What the fuck's going on with all these sirens and shit?" Asked one member of the Wythenshawe One Facebook group.

"Loads of dibble on Falmer Drive, the whole roads shut, sounds like summat serious has gone on."

"Yeah, my sister lives on there, she said there's about a million police vans there, sniffer dogs, crime scene tape up and all sorts. Probably been a murder."

"Drugs bust, po po got nowt better to do 'til Greggs have got their doughnuts ready."

"Someone said it's at Jo Rudovsky's house, the detective woman. She's been knee-capped I think."

Wythenshawe's Facebook was going into meltdown. Rudovsky was one of the best-known small-town celebs on the estate, famous for her police work and highly respected in the local community for her commitment to the area where she had lived all of her life. She was also a big noise on the local Pride committee as well as being a familiar face on the local TV news through her work.

Finally, a comment appeared which seemed to make some sense of all of the hysteria online. "Bollocks all this on here, shut the fuck up, I've just seen Jo talking to the dibble outside her house, her boss DCI Miller is there, she's fine, looks a bit shook up and that but her knees are intact and she's not been decapitated and she's not murdered anyone and she hasn't got a bomb and a helicopter hasn't crashed in her garden you fucking shit-talking dick-wads. Summat's definitely gone on at her house though, the CSI are in and out of there in the full body suits. Hope Jo's okay, top bird!" This comment on the post had attracted the most likes and was standing at the very top of the section.

"Aw no way, is it Jo Rudovsky? She's mint. What's happened at her house? Anyone seen Abby?" Said another member of the group.

One local resident uploaded a video of the scene on

Falmer Drive. The entire cul-de-sac was jammed with police vehicles and dozens of officers were standing around waiting for instructions. The video looked as though it was filmed from an upstairs window in one of the houses opposite. The shaky-handed film-maker panned the camera around and then started zooming in on Jo Rudovsky who had an unhealthily pale complexion and was shaking violently as a few plain clothes officers were talking to her. Eventually, she was led away down the avenue and put into a police car.

"She's been caught nicking corned-beef from the corner shop again. It was three cans last week, she loves her tater-ash that one." Said one joker, but to be fair - it was one of the more believable theories that were spreading around on the popular local Facebook group.

Abby's breakfast meeting in Ramsbottom was drawing to a close when her phone kept vibrating in her pocket. She was talking to an influential person from Bury Council, trying her best to learn about some new funding streams that were being made available for areas with high deprivation. The Bury MBC person was totally convinced that Abby's work in Wythenshawe was a straight box ticking exercise and that she'd be eligible for at least two-years funding. This would cover her salary and possibly two part-time positions as well. This was the best news that Abby had heard in years, but the constant vibrating of her phone was becoming a massive distraction and was really taking the shine off the moment.

"I'm really sorry, this is like... it's genuinely the most exciting news I've heard this century! But someone keeps trying my phone so I think it must be pretty urgent. Would you mind if I...?"

"No, no, go ahead."

Abby's excited expression drained from her face as she caught sight of the text messages that neighbours and friends had been sending to her over the course of the past few minutes.

"I'm...I'm really sorry... something bad has happened... I'll, I need to go..."

Chapter Fifty-Nine

Rudovsky was sitting in the back of Miller's car. There was still a great deal of police activity on Falmer Drive, more police cars were turning up and were being sent off to do various tasks by the duty Inspector who was manning the cordon line at the end of Falmer Drive. Miller's vehicle was parked just outside the exclusion zone but this location was far from peaceful. Aside from the police activity all around, dozens of nosey neighbours were standing around gawping and gossiping with parents who found themselves caught up in the excitement whilst taking their kids to the nearby school.

"Are you alright, mate?" Asked Miller, in his most sympathetic tone.

"I fucking hate it when you do that voice, Sir."

Miller looked confused, he wasn't exactly sure what Rudovsky was talking about.

"I know you're just being nice, boss. I know it's coming from a good place, but you sound like a right patronising twat!" Rudovsky smiled but there was no humour in her voice and her eyes looked vacant. She was still shaking visibly. Miller felt completely redundant, he hated these types of situations. He preferred a hands-on role, preferred to be working on something practical. He would run through fire and jump on the roof of a speeding train to catch the bastard who'd made Rudovsky look so vulnerable and lost. He recognised that he wasn't very good at offering comfort and it didn't usually bother him, but right now he really wished he knew what to say or do to make his DS feel just a tiny little bit safer or happier. He felt useless and frustrated by the fact that he was shit in these situations.

Fortunately, Miller's blushes were saved as Rudovsky's phone started ringing. "It's Abby. I'm going to have to take this… hiya, you alright?"

Miller felt incredibly sad as he watched his colleague tearing up as her girlfriend asked her what was going on. Rudovsky is without doubt one of the ballsiest police officers he had ever worked with, she never said no to anything, she was always up for whatever was going on. It was a real shock to see her looking so vulnerable and he could feel an anger rising within him. It was an even stronger sense of outrage than he had felt regarding the stunts against his family. He tried to work out why he felt such fury and came to the conclusion that it was the nature of this confrontation that had affected him so much. With Clare and the kids, it had been words, threats. Nasty, horrible and scary, yes. But the stunt that had been pulled this morning, inside Rudovsky's home, taking advantage of her when she was at her most vulnerable. It was just too shocking to imagine. Miller considered how intimidated he would feel in the same circumstances. How humiliated and defenceless he would feel standing there on a wet, slippy surface, without any means of getting away from the gunman, and completely naked. It was the stuff of nightmares.

He listened in to Rudovsky's conversation, trying to pick up a new piece of information about the ordeal that she hadn't mentioned to him in the brief explanation she'd provided him so far on the street. There wasn't much more offered to Abby, it sounded to Miller as though this whole thing had lasted for around a minute. Possibly less. But it was clear that whether it had been a minute, or an hour, the terror of this incident was going to stick in Rudovsky's mind for a long time, most probably forever.

Miller was concerned that Rudovsky was still shaking violently, her teeth were chattering together during the moments that she wasn't talking to Abby. He managed to decipher that Abby was on her way over, somebody was giving her a lift over from Ramsbottom and she didn't expect to be very long. Miller looked out of his windscreen and saw that the local Inspector was walking towards the car from Rudovsky's house. He got out of his car as the uniformed officer approached.

"What have you got?" Asked Miller.

"Sir, the back-door was the source of entry, it was forced using a crowbar. The damage is visible from the exterior but there is no visible evidence that the door was insecure from inside the property. So if Jo hadn't had reason to open it, she'd have never have guessed. From what we can work out, the intruder has gained entry whilst Jo was out, so sometime between 6 and 7am, and has then hidden inside the house until she came back."

"Any idea where he was hiding?"

"There are a number of potential sites in the property, CSI are reviewing them all now and will be looking to examine all possibilities and hopefully find some evidence that could reveal his identity."

"How long until the house can be handed back?"

"Oh, well… good question. I think they'll be here all day, potentially until late afternoon. I've got officers doing door-to-doors in the immediate vicinity, asking if anybody saw or heard anything and appealing for CCTV footage. Most of the properties have some form of CCTV around here. I note that Jo has a system with cameras front and rear but we can't access the footage, it requires a pin number."

"No problem, I'll find that out for you." Miller stepped back a few paces and opened the rear passenger door. Rudovsky was sobbing into the phone and looked embarrassed by this sudden intrusion. He closed the door gently and turned to face the Inspector. "I'll get that to you in a few minutes, if that's okay?"

"Thanks, Sir. We've got the council CCTV operators reviewing all footage in and out of the area from 5am until 8am, it's a long-shot but we're hopeful that a vehicle might show up. Other than that, I'm afraid it's a waiting game, Sir."

"Okay, thanks for the update. I'll feed all this back to Jo when she's finished on the phone and I'll come and find you once I've got the CCTV pin."

The Inspector nodded and headed back up the cul-de-sac to Rudovsky's house.

Chapter Sixty

Saunders and Grant arrived in Wythenshawe together. Their first port-of-call was Miller's car, where they tried to offer some encouraging words to Rudovsky, who was still looking thoroughly terrified. Grant stayed in the back of the car with her as Saunders went off to find Miller.

Within minutes, Miller had given Saunders the full disclosure, from start to finish. Saunders stood close to Rudovsky's garden gate, listening silently with his hands in his pockets. Once Miller was done, he launched into his typical Q and A session.

"What's happening regarding the threat?"

"It's been handed up to Dixon, he's taking advice."

"Did Jo have any clues who the intruder was?"

"Not much. Male, well built, athletic, six-two, six-three. Blue eyes."

"And you said it was a local accent?"

"Yes South Manchester, she said, reckons he's from the estate."

"Age?"

"No clue on that, but the voice was deep. Heavy smoker, whisky drinker, she said."

"Shouldn't take too long to suss out who he is. Big lad like that, obviously closely linked to McKinlay. I've got the file on McKinlay's close associates from the NCA. It's back in the office, but I'll bet this guy is on the list."

"Yes, I thought the same."

"So, we're just waiting for Dixon to clarify our position?"

"Yes, I think he'll cave, He won't want a repeat of what happened with Karen on his conscience."

"The timing is interesting though, the fact they want McKinlay back up here tonight. Did you say that the gunman made a remark about not knowing where McKinlay was?"

"Yes, he'd said 'tell 'me' to bring him back from wherever the fuck I've taken him."

"Interesting. This guy sounds like he couldn't give a shit, so he's not going to be choosing his words too carefully. It suggests that they genuinely have no idea where we've sent McKinlay."

"Yes, I know."

"Reassuring, I guess, at least we know that the NTRG are a lot more professional than some of the screws at HMP Manchester."

"Sounds that way."

"But they need him back ASAP by the sounds of things. Tells me that whatever they are planning to do while McKinlay is banged up is about to happen. Something serious, something that can never be pinned on McKinlay for obvious reasons…"

"Like, he's inside?"

"Exactly."

"Well, either way, Keith, I couldn't give a shit right now. I'm more worried about Jo, and the safety of the rest of the team. I've never known anything like this."

Saunders nodded. It was beyond outrageous.

"What's the plan with Jo, then?"

"No idea. She's in pieces in the back of my car. Not even trying to put a brave face on it. It's fucking gutting to see."

"I know, just had a quick chat, I left Helen in the car with her. She looks traumatised."

"She is. I would be. I think she'll need a few days off… meanwhile, where the fuck are we headed with this McKinlay situation? He's got us by the balls at every turn."

"Dunno. I think it will all become clear what he's planning in the next few days. Why else would they want him back in Strangeways so urgently?"

"You're pretty convinced about all this, aren't you?"

"Completely. I thought it before, but this, it's off the fucking scale. There's got to be a very good reason for it."

Miller was suddenly alerted by the Inspector who appeared from the house and was standing by the garden gate. He introduced himself to Saunders, before turning back to the DCI. "I think you'll want to come and look at this CCTV footage, Sir."

Inside the house, one of the CSI guys was holding the remote control. As soon as Miller and Saunders arrived in Jo and Abby's living room, he pressed the play button. The camera feed from the front of the house was displayed, the camera itself was situated in the doorbell. It was dark outside, the CCTV footage was green as the night-vision mode was in operation. Within seconds of the footage starting, Jo and Abby could be seen leaving the house, walking up the path and disappearing behind the hedge which surrounds the garden. After a few seconds, the car's indicator lights flashed as the couple got in and the vehicle moved off.

"Now keep your eye on the bush in the top left corner of the screen." Said the Inspector.

Saunders and Miller felt a cold chill tingle up their spines as they watched the footage. A darkly dressed figure began standing up from a crouching position and walked slowly across the small front lawn towards the house, before disappearing down the side of the property past the doorbell camera.

"Is that everything?" Asked Miller.

"So far..."

"Just rewind that please, pause it as he passes the camera." Said Miller to the CSI officer. The footage was played again and paused as requested. The two SCIU colleagues leaned in further towards the TV screen, staring at the image of a large man who was dressed from head to toe in black clothing, his face obscured by a balaclava.

"Whoever he is, he's ex-services. I can tell their walk a mile off, straight back, shoulders up. Can you get that area around the bush searched. I doubt we'll get anything, but just in case he's left any traces, even if it's a footprint. I can't tell you how much I want this fucking bastard."

Miller turned to Saunders. "Right, I need to get off. I'm expecting an important call."

Saunders' face dropped. He'd been so wrapped up in this shocking development that he had completely forgotten about the special delivery letter which had been sent the previous afternoon. He looked at his watch.

- 297 -

"Shit."

"It's okay, I'll have time. Could do with rescheduling under the circumstances but that's not going to happen. I'll have to leave you here…"

"Yes, of course, Sir."

"Find out who came in here and put the fear of God into Jo. That's the one thing I want."

"Me too, Sir. Just before you go, tell me more about the ex-services walk you mentioned."

Miller demonstrated the gait of anybody who has served in the military for a reasonable length of time, walking up and down the living room.

"It's programmed into them Keith, they don't even realise they're doing it. Just look at me, chins up straight, shoulders are back, back is perfectly erect, no slouching whatsoever, I look very proud and confident. They have to walk around on camp like this whether they're on duty or not. After they've done about six or seven years of it, they completely forget how they used to carry themselves. So this guy, his background is in the armed services. See if anybody on your list fits that criteria."

"Sir."

Chapter Sixty-One

Miller was gutted that he'd had to leave Wythenshawe but it couldn't be helped, he had already made his plans for today and there was absolutely no opportunity to reschedule the day's diary. He had decided the previous night that he would head off to a remote spot to take Dawson's call, if and when it came. From leaving Wythenshawe, he had travelled back into town and clocked into the office and had left his mobile phone switched on in his desk drawer. Miller then breezed out of the building, timing his exit perfectly as a colleague came in, saving him from using his security fob.

Miller then caught a tram out of town. His car was parked on the staff car park, under CCTV cameras and his security fob data suggested that he was still on the premises. There was no room for complacency, and Miller was quite enjoying the distraction of thinking like a crook for a change.

Wearing a hoody pullover with the hood pulled up, Miller paid cash for his tram ticket and kept his face hidden from the CCTV cameras. The Metrolink tram took him to the Heaton Park stop on the Bury line, four miles away from the office. He spent the whole journey staring into a copy of the Manchester Evening News which he was holding up high in front of his face. Even though there was only a very tiny chance of anything going wrong, Miller was still weighing up the ins and outs of this risky operation. If any evidence tied him to any communications with Dawson, he was done for. With the stakes this high, he was prepared to put up with the odd inconvenience, like only using the burner phone once, right beside the network operator's mast. Miller knew that making a call from such close proximity to the phone-mast made it practically impossible to triangulate the phone's location. It was just in case, but Miller recognised that these levels of paranoia were crucial if he had any chance of coming out of this situation unscathed.

He really never thought he'd have any dealings with Dawson again and it was still a shock that all of this had come back and blind-sided him. He literally couldn't wait to hear that phone ring as he stood beneath the famous phone tower in the park, confident that once he'd spoken to Dawson and passed on one specific instruction, the situation would become fully salvageable. The mobile phone which Pete Kenyon had purchased the previous day would be tossed in the boating lake straight after the call. It wasn't worth the risk of keeping it. Nothing at all was being left to chance.

As Miller watched people walking aimlessly around the park, he began to feel a calmness rising within - despite the despicable activities just hours earlier at Rudovsky's house. He couldn't put his finger on why he was feeling mellow under such trying circumstances, whether it was simply because of the calming surroundings combined with the sunshine or whether it was because he felt that he was finally gaining some confidence that things were going to work out. That Tommy McKinlay was going to lose.

All he needed now was for that vague letter to be delivered and for George Dawson's curiosity to be piqued enough to make him get in his car, find a phone box and ring the number on the letter. The letter itself had been straight forward enough, short and to the point and included a very specific detail that Dawson had personally given Miller. The message had been hand-written, using a fresh piece of plain A4 paper from the photo-copier. Using gloves he'd grabbed from a CS kit, Miller had written the note using his dud hand so that the letter, it's hand-writing and the content would leave no clues as to the identity of the sender if it was intercepted. The note read, "George, we need to speak urgently about the note you found in Sarah's school-bag. There is no time to waste. Drive at least three miles from your address, find a public phone box and ring 07771 232946."

Finally, just before twelve pm, the cheap pay-as-you-go phone began ringing in Miller's hand. The telephone prefix of the incoming call was 01204, the Bolton code. Dawson had received the letter.

"Hello." Said Miller.
"Hello. Er... who is this?"
"George?"

"Yes... who's...."

"I don't want to mention my name over the airwaves but I'm sure you'll recognise my voice in a few seconds. But to give you a clue, the last time I heard from you, you'd hand-delivered a letter to my home, instructing me to destroy it after I'd read it."

"Oh, yes, well... I thought it must be..."

"We've got a significant problem. We need to meet."

There was a pause before Dawson answered, almost like the old days. "Okay..."

"But before we go any further, I need you to understand that if you are intercepted before we meet, the only thing that you can ever say to police officers is 'no comment.' Is that completely clear?"

"No comment."

"Good. Right, are you familiar with Mayfield station in Manchester?"

"No... I can't say I am..."

"It's a disused station, situated behind Piccadilly railway station, it's the most isolated place I can think of to meet. There's only one way in, through a derelict lift shaft on Fairfield Street. I will have colleagues guarding that area so we know that we are completely isolated."

"This sounds extremely..."

"Yes George, it's about as extremely as you can possibly imagine. But don't panic, I'm working out a way to resolve everything. When can you meet?"

"Well, I mean... I can be there in an hour."

"Make it two hours. Catch a train from Bolton to Piccadilly, then walk around to Fairfield Street. You'll see my officers parked by a broken old fence with some shrubs growing out of it. Just tell them that you are there to see me and they'll show you where to go. In the meantime, pass the same information to Margaret. If any police were to ever speak to you, or to her about anything, the only response you are permitted to give is no comment. The alternative is prison for the rest of your days."

"That's perfectly clear."

"You need to make sure you're not being followed. Make sure you're the last to get on the train. If you feel as though you are being followed, make sure you signal to my officers as you approach them and they'll take care of it."

"That's understood. Any idea who might be following me? Who I should be looking out for?"

"No... no... I'm just being outrageously cautious. You'll understand why when we talk."

"Okay, well, I mean this is a hell of a shock but, I'll be there."

"Good. Okay, try not to worry too much. We'll sort this. See you in two hours."

"Okay."

"Also, George... you still there?"

"Yes?"

"Just... don't try to contact me again on this number, or via conventional means. I'm going to throw this phone away now, I need you to destroy the letter and envelope that you just received."

"Understood."

Chapter Sixty-Two

DCs Bill Chapman and Keith Worthington were joined by DCs Helen Grant and Peter Kenyon in checking over the disused railway station. Mayfield station is close to the rear of Piccadilly station, Manchester's busiest railway hub which links the city with Inverness, London and the south coast as well as everywhere in between.

Mayfield railway station was built to relieve pressure on Piccadilly, providing an additional 4 platforms when it opened in 1910. But its lifespan was cut short after just 50 years, in part because of the half mile walk between platforms for certain services. Mayfield was unpopular with commuters and travellers and the station was closed in 1960 when improvements were completed at Piccadilly. It had a short reprieve when Royal Mail reopened it as a parcel depot in 1970, but only lasted until 1986 when Royal Mail abandoned rail in favour of road haulage. Mayfield Station has remained abandoned ever since, except for the occasions that it was used for the filming of gritty crime dramas such as Cracker and Prime Suspect in the 1990s. It didn't take a great deal of work to tidy up and make it look like a busy, operational railway station. Today, however, it would take a good deal of work to make it look anything like. The vandals, skateboarders and the graffiti artists have ensured that the building was past its best days.

Its future remains uncertain, but Mayfield Station is a very unique place in Manchester city centre. It is literally the only place that a person could be completely alone and incognito, whilst remaining in earshot of the endless hustle and bustle of city centre life on the streets and roads all around. Due to its age, it is probably the only place within the city centre zone which isn't observed 24/7 by CCTV cameras. Quite why it hasn't become a playground for drug-dealers and prostitutes is anybody's guess.

"It's such a weird place this, doesn't half give me the creeps!" Said Helen Grant as she walked along the disused platform with her colleague Peter Kenyon. The entire place was littered with everything from upturned railway trolleys to empty spray-paint tins, broken glass and cider bottles which were strewn amongst cinders from burnt-out bonfires. Helen Grant lives less than a five-minute walk away from this unusual place and had no idea of its existence until today.

"I was just thinking the same thing. Even the tramps refuse to live here!"

"All clear?" Asked Chapman who was standing with Worthington by the old orange brick offices and smashed-up toilets in the centre of the platform. His voice echoed all around the musty building.

"Yes, there's nobody here."

"Good. We just need to check the other platform and we can piss off out of it."

The four DCs jumped down onto the stone chippings where the rails used to be lay and headed across to the opposing platform.

"TRAIN!" Shouted Kenyon at the top of his voice, making Chapman jump out of his skin.

"You rotten bastard!" Said Chapman as Worthington and Grant laughed enthusiastically at the look of panic on the beleaguered DC's face.

"Might have been scarier if you'd laid some railway tracks first!" Said Worthington, howling at the absurdity of Chapman's reaction. This stupid prank had been just the tonic after such a disturbing start to the day at Rudovsky's.

"Fucking hell, I wish Jo had seen that!" Said Kenyon, with tears of laughter in his eyes.

"Bollocks! It's like working in a fucking primary school." Said Chapman as he scrambled up the side of the platform edge, clearly quite embarrassed by his reaction to the pratting about.

Five minutes later, they had settled down and were all agreed that the place was completely deserted. They made their way down to the underpass which stunk of decay and demolition, with delicate notes of an old public toilet and pigeon shit. Finally, they reached daylight and the dilapidated fence. They squeezed through, one at a time, back into the relative civilisation of Manchester city centre.

Miller was parked on Fairfield Street by the knackered old fence with his window rolled down. Saunders was sitting beside him in the car when the four dishevelled detectives appeared, looking pleased to be out of the abandoned railway station.

"How's it looking?" He asked, appearing surprisingly relaxed under the circumstances.

"No one around… there hasn't been since about 1990 by the looks of things, Sir." Said Kenyon.

"Good. Okay, well let's check the coast is clear and I'll disappear inside."

After a few minutes, the SCIU staff had checked the entire street and had looked around in every direction. As they came back to the car, they were all satisfied that there was nobody around.

"It's just us here, Sir. I must say, this is an awesome place to get up to something dodgy!" Said Grant.

Miller got out of his car and scrambled through the fence. "Send my visitor up when he arrives and remember – stay off radio. If you need me urgently, shout me. Cheers."

With that, Miller disappeared through the gap in the fence and the detectives got back into their unmarked police car and drove down towards the junction where they could keep an eye out for Dawson. It was 1.45pm.

*****

Just before 2pm, George Dawson came walking up towards Fairfield Street looking quite nervous and unsure of his surroundings. Despite this, he didn't really stand out. The DCs in the unmarked car only realised that it was him as he got within ten metres of them.

"Fucking hell fire. This is him…" Said Chapman.

"Christ. You're right!" Confirmed Worthington.

Grant and Kenyon looked at one another with a dumbfounded expression. This small, middle-aged man looked more like a retired Vicar. It was a big stretch to imagine him as the serial killer who had excited the entire nation just three years earlier during his chaotic two-week rampage through the streets of this city, executing paedophiles.

Worthington rolled the window down. "George?"

Dawson stopped dead in his tracks. "Yes?" He asked. Grant was instantly endeared by his gentle manner.

"Do you see the other silver Insignia half-way up the street? It's identical to this one." Asked Worthington.

Dawson looked beyond the detectives and spotted the vehicle that the man in the car was talking about. "Yes, I see it. Is that where I'm going?"

"Yes, just go there and my colleague will explain everything."

"Righto. Thank you."

With that, Dawson nodded graciously and walked slowly along the pavement. Worthington wound the window up.

"Oh my God! As if that's Pop! He's adorable!" Gushed Grant, a wide smile right across her face.

"I'm not having that." Said Kenyon. "He doesn't look like he could shoo a cat, let alone execute a paedophile!"

"Yep. That's him alright," said Chapman, seeming quite surprised by Grant's assessment of the man.

"From what Karen was saying, when we'd set off to arrest him, he was the most popular teacher in his school. It made me think about his phone calls to Sky News, and how many people out there must have known it was him. I mean, you'd know your teacher's voice if he was on the telly talking about killing paedos, wouldn't you?" Worthington was looking in his wing-mirror as he spoke, watching as Dawson crossed the road and approached Saunders, who was sitting in Miller's passenger seat. "Seriously, how many of the kids from throughout the years would have said to their parents, their husbands and wives, that the serial killer is Mr Dawson, he was our Head of Year!"

"Yeah, you never forget your teacher's voice." Said Kenyon. "I agree, there will be a lot of people out there who know that it was him, you know, who know the full story like. It was bound to have leaked out to someone like Tommy McKinlay eventually. Just goes to show you though, nobody likes a paedo."

"Nobody likes a paedo! Is that the new album by Lily Allen?" Asked Worthington, but the gag fell flat.

"This is mad, all this." Said Grant. "I followed that case, when it was happening. Minute-by-minute. I genuinely thought it was the guy who'd killed himself. I remember feeling really… God, I can't think of the word…"

"Disappointed?" Suggested Kenyon.

"No, more like… well yeah, I suppose disappointed is as good a word as any. Obviously, it all changed with the incident… with Karen being shot." Grant was choosing her words carefully. She knew that two of the people she was with had only been feet away when their boss was shot dead. The other member of the team had been big mates with Karen Ellis too.

"Yes. I can't believe Miller has managed to keep the real story to himself all this time. I'd have cracked and told someone if it was me!" Said Chapman, a hint of affection for his DCI was present in his voice as he spoke.

"Right, here we go… he's going through the fence." Said Worthington, keen to change the subject. He still blamed himself for what happened that day.

Chapter Sixty-Three

"Watch your step there, George." Miller's voice echoed through the pitch-dark underpass that George Dawson was trying to navigate. Bushes and weeds were growing out of the ground and a constant drip-dripping from the brickwork above added to the intimidating ambience. Dawson grabbed the soaking-wet wall and steadied himself. Miller's voice had given him a start.

"Oh, hello, Mr Miller." He said.

"Hello George." Miller turned on the torch function on his phone but the beam didn't really help. "This is the only dodgy bit, once you reach me, you'll be past the worst of it."

Dawson persevered with the arduous journey through the stinking subway which at one time was the main entrance to this once-bustling railway station.

"Goodness me, this place is a bit of a bind!" Said Dawson as he finally reached Miller. The DCI extended his hand for a shake, the two men were illuminated by a shaft of light coming through from the platform above. As the two men shook hands, Miller was reminded of how much he liked this man, he was a very pleasant, very gentle soul. It beggared belief what he had done at first inspection. But once you knew the full story, as Miller did, things began to take on a new perspective.

"Come on, let's get out of this rat-infested sewer!" Said Miller, turning and leading the way up the ramp towards the derelict railway station above.

"With pleasure!" Said Dawson as he followed the DCI.

"So, you must be wondering what the hell is going on?" Said Miller as the pair emerged into the daylight and onto the former platform which looked in a very sorry state today.

"Just slightly. I can only assume it's bad news. But don't worry, I'm prepared for it. I've never taken a single day for granted, Mr Miller."

"Please, George. Call me Andy."

"Of course, as you wish, Andy."

The two men sat down on an old wooden railway

trolley which had been dumped outside the parcel depot building which had a smashed up "Red Star Parcels" sign overhead and Miller told Dawson the story, starting at the beginning with the drama at his children's school. It took ten minutes, but once Miller had finally stopped talking, the anxious look that had been on Dawson's face was replaced with something else. Miller wasn't too sure what, but he was about to find out.

"Well, first of all, thank you very much for such a detailed explanation of what's been happening. I had no idea that the incident at the school was in anyway connected with me. I watched it all, of course, on television. Being a former teacher myself, well, it sent shivers up my spine. So it was all designed to start a conversation about me? How bloody senseless!"

"I know. To be honest, despite the shock. I was relieved to find out who was behind it and why. I think I'd have lost my mind if there had never been an explanation."

"No… well, it does sound rather strange what you just said, but I understand exactly what you mean."

"So. We need a way out of this, and that's why I've asked you here today."

"Well, Andy. If you've got your handcuffs on you, I'm quite happy to face my time…"

"No, no, no. It's nothing like that."

"Really?"

"No, of course not. No. I just needed to tell you what was going on and advise you of the best course of action."

"The no comment detail?"

"Yes, absolutely right. Did you pass that on to Margaret?"

"I did, she is fully aware."

"Good. Trust me, the police have absolutely nothing on you. The only way that they, okay sorry, we… the only way we could bring charges against you is if you gave evidence against yourself. If you were ever interviewed, a simple no comment reply is all you need. That includes if they asked you what you had for breakfast. No comment everything, this is absolutely crucial."

Dawson considered Miller's words for a few seconds before responding. "I see. Well, thank you... once again. I really don't know what I ever did to receive such incredible treatment from you, Andy."

"Well, that's for another time. Today, I really need to know if you have any idea who might have leaked this sensitive information to Tommy McKinlay?"

Without hesitation, Dawson replied. "Yes, I do actually."

Miller was slightly taken aback by the speed and calmness of the response. He almost strained his neck as he switched his view from the bushes which had grown along the former railway line and focused on the side of George Dawson's face.

"I'm almost certain I know who is behind this dreadful situation. I guess there's no way of proving it. But I'd bet my life on it..."

Chapter Sixty-Four

Freshers week is the most exciting time in any University student's life. The name is an American import of course, brought to these shores in exactly the same way that Black Friday, Prom nights and Halloween have been. But celebrating your first week at University by going on a week-long bender is a tradition which has been around in the UK for a lot longer than the "Freshers week" term has.

For most Uni students, this is the week that they finally reach adulthood, moving away from the family home to try their first taste of freedom and independence in a new city, surrounded by new friends who are experiencing exactly the same euphoric feelings of excitement, anticipation and optimism for the future. In order to properly celebrate this coming-of-age moment, the students get absolutely shit-faced for an entire week.

Three years earlier, Lisa Dawson had been one of those students. She'd been accepted at York University to study Veterinary Medicine. Emotionally, she was probably the most mature student to join the University that year. Her childhood had been challenging, to say the least. She had lost her sister and her mum in separate incidents within weeks when she was nine years old and had been brought up by a neurotic father who had been battling the demons of manic depression ever since. He was a good man, gentle, kind, attentive, but completely broken. For Lisa Dawson, her time at University was destined to be her fresh start, the chance to step away from her eternally over-protective dad and make her own mark on the world.

And it all started extremely well, which didn't surprise anybody who knew Lisa. Not only was she extremely bright and gifted, she was also dedicated, hard-working and a thoroughly pleasant young woman. The fact that she had done so well with her GCSEs and her A-levels, with the backdrop of such an emotionally and mentally challenging home-life was evidence of what a talented, determined and well-balanced young person

Lisa was.

When she was offered a place at York University, it was without doubt the proudest day of her father's life. The guilt that he felt regarding his depression, and what he viewed as Lisa's stolen childhood had been crippling. He was not in denial about the childhood Lisa had experienced. In some ways, the day that he dropped Lisa off at University to start her new life, was one of the worst days of his life, he felt that he had finally lost the last thread that held his beloved family together. In other ways, it was the very best day of his life. His darling daughter, the baby of the family had fought back against the most horrendous adversity at such a tender age and had won, like an Olympian. His heart was breaking and bursting with pride in equal measure and he'd had to pull over on the A59 on the way home several times to wipe away his tears and compose himself during the lonely, bittersweet drive back to Little Lever.

Lisa's first two years had gone brilliantly and she had kept the partying and the adulting to a minimum, continuing with that determination to treat the degree course as seriously as she had treated her GCSEs and her A levels. But in the third year, things began to get a little bumpy.

As these things usually happen, it was a member of the opposite sex who proved a major distraction. Ryan Ingleton, a smart, handsome 20 year-old who was studying at the nearby St John's University burst into Lisa's life at a house-party one Thursday night and he set her heart on fire. Ryan was tanned, great looking and had a smile which looked as though it had been created in Beverley Hills and had cost $20,000. He was so charismatic, confident and funny that Lisa had assumed he was gay. But she quickly realised that he wasn't, as he gravitated towards her in a stinking kitchen in one of the student-houses and didn't leave her side all night.

The pair went on their first date the following evening. It was a nerve-wracking event for Lisa. She'd seen some lads, here and there, over the years. She'd even snogged some of them. Things had never gone any further than that. But this lad was different, there was something about Ryan Ingleton that affected her in ways that she had never imagined it possible.

When she wasn't with him, she felt lost and sad. He was all she could think about, morning, noon and night. A cute smile he'd given her would replay in her mind's eye none-stop. She couldn't eat when she wasn't with him, she couldn't sleep. She couldn't study.

Lisa Dawson had fallen in love for the first time, and she was loving every miserable, ecstatic moment of the roller-coaster ride. It seemed that Ryan had fallen for her just as deeply and within weeks of that chance meeting in that rancid kitchen, the pair were seldom apart. Ryan had unofficially moved out of his student accommodation on the other side of the city and had unofficially moved into the house that Lisa was sharing with three other students.

To Lisa, studying didn't seem quite so important all of a sudden. She was learning about the other things that life had to offer and was spending the vast majority of her time in bed, with Ryan. When they weren't making love, they were making each other laugh with funny stories from their pasts or making plans for their future. The house they'd buy, the cars they'd drive, the kids they planned to have. Ryan was so beautiful that Lisa couldn't take her eyes off him, she was stunned that falling in love could have such an overwhelming and profound effect on somebody. Lisa Dawson had never experienced happiness like this.

Lisa's dad called her every night at 6pm, except on Thursdays when she was scheduled to be in lectures until 7.30pm. On Thursdays he rang at 8pm. He would ask her how her day had gone, what she had done, what assignments she had to do and whether she needed any help with anything. The phone calls generally lasted between twenty-five to forty-minutes and the conversations were the highlight of her dad's day.

Ryan, on the other hand wasn't so impressed with this daily interruption to his routine. One evening, just a few weeks after he'd moved into Lisa's room, he'd suggested that the phone call should be ignored and the couple had their first row. Lisa was furious that Ryan couldn't excuse her for a short time whilst she spoke to her dad. He called her a baby and stormed out of the house, slamming the front door as hard as he could.

Lisa took the call from her dad, but despite her best efforts, she sounded low and sad, which troubled her father greatly. He sensed that something was wrong and his anxiety levels reached fever pitch. Lisa realised that he would need a reasonable explanation as to what was going on, so told him about Ryan, and the fact that they'd had a tiff. Lisa was so sensitive to her father's neurosis that she was wise enough to hold back the detail about exactly why the pair had fallen-out. Instead of telling her dad that it was because Ryan was irritated by the daily phone-calls, she told a white lie and blamed the argument on Ryan trying to make her go to the pub instead of studying.

"Oh, try not to worry, darling. He'll soon come back with his tail between his legs. He'll realise that he hit the jackpot when he met you. Please don't be upset, it will all work itself out, you mark my words."

"I know, dad. It's just, we've never fallen out before, so its all a bit… new."

"Well there will be plenty more occasions like this. Trust me!" Her dad laughed knowingly at his remark and Lisa forced a laugh too. "I'll look forward to meeting this young man soon. I can come over and take you both for lunch at weekend, if you fancy it? How does Saturday sit with you?"

Lisa liked the idea and thanked her dad for his kindness. She wasn't feeling much better about things after the call had ended, but her dad was none the wiser, Lisa had left him feeling quite satisfied that he'd cheered her up and that his calming words had solved her problems.

As soon as she'd ended the call, she tried to call Ryan but he wasn't answering. After a dozen "Welcome to the O2 messaging service" messages, Lisa grabbed her coat off the back of her door and ran down the stairs. Within moments, she was running down the street, heading for the bus-stop. A few minutes after that, she was running through York city-centre.

It didn't take her long to find him, he was in The Stone Roses Bar, the most popular of the student pubs. Inside, the music was deafening, as always.

"Hey," she said as she approached him from behind, interrupting the shouty conversation he was having with some lads she vaguely recognised.

"Oh, hey..."

"Sorry..."

"I'm sorry, too." He said into her ear. "I think my period's due."

Lisa laughed loudly at his joke and have him a squeeze, the relief she felt was intense. "Come on, let's go for a walk. I'll try and explain why my dad's so important to me..."

Ryan finished his pint of lager, wiped his mouth and shouted farewell to his friends. Within moments, they were walking hand in hand through the picturesque streets of York.

"I know it all seems a bit... weird, with my dad and everything." Said Lisa, trying hard to set the scene.

"No, I was completely out of order. Maybe I'm a bit jealous that my parents aren't as interested in me as your dad obviously is about you." Ryan put his arm around Lisa's shoulder and she snuggled into him as they stepped along the cobbles of the historic Shambles street, with its old black and white painted timber buildings overhanging above their heads. These peculiar overhangs dated back over 500 years and were originally designed for butchers to hang their meat from, long before refrigerated display cabinets came into being.

Lisa was keen to set the record straight, and she trusted Ryan enough to tell him the reason that her and her dad are so close. She'd already told him that her mum had died, but she'd never mentioned her big sister, Sarah. Now, after the fright of falling out with Ryan, she felt it was time to explain everything, properly.

"No, you're right. It is a bit weird how close me and dad are. But there's a good reason."

"Honestly, it's fine..."

"No, please. I want to explain. I told him about you, by the way. He's excited to meet you. He said he wants to take us for a bite to eat on Saturday."

"Oh, wow... that's nerve-wracking!"

"Why? It's not... he's a good man. You'll love him."

"I know... I'm just, you know..."

"You know I told you my mum died when I was little?"

"Yes?"

"When I told you that, what did you think must have happened?" Lisa's voice had become a little distant.

"What do you mean? Like, why did I think she died?"

"Yes."

"Well I dunno. I guess I assumed it was cancer. Was it not?" Ryan sensed that this was going somewhere very serious and stopped walking. He turned Lisa to face him. Lisa had tears in her eyes as she shook her head slowly.

"She killed herself."

"Oh fu... shit, like no way!" Ryan was gobsmacked. He had no idea. Lisa had never given any hint.

"She killed herself, because my elder sister, Sarah had just killed herself."

Lisa began crying and Ryan comforted her as best he could. "I'm not... I'm not crying for me... it's shit, of course it is. But I was only a kid, I don't even remember it really. I'm crying for my dad. His whole world was destroyed." The tears continued to flow and Ryan held his girlfriend tightly, completely lost for words. He felt awful for his behaviour earlier but this announcement was taking his feelings of guilt to a different level altogether.

"My sister was abused, sexually abused by a teacher or something at school. She couldn't live with it. She killed herself, hung herself. Dad found her body."

"Oh my God, Lisa... this is horrendous."

"My mum never heard about it. She killed herself a few days later. Dad says it was because she knew, but she never wanted to hear those words. Never wanted to hear the details. He said that I was the only reason he didn't kill himself as well." Lisa's voice faltered again and Ryan held her even closer as her shoulders began heaving.

"Dad blamed himself for everything, he thought that if he had been a better father, Sarah would have spoken to him about it and everything would have been different. He just channelled everything into me, he was so over-protective, it was unreal. So, well, now that I'm here, at Uni, it's just really hard for him letting go. That's why I was such a psycho about speaking to him on the phone."

"No, Lisa, listen to me. It was me, I was being a major-league douche-bag. It's nothing to do with you, it was just me being a selfish prick."

"Well, anyway, now you know why I take it so seriously. My dad's phone call to me is literally the best part of his day. I could never just ignore it..."

"No, I know. And now I feel like the biggest arsehole in York. No, in Yorkshire. No, in the UK!"

Lisa laughed and punched Ryan playfully in the chest. "Don't feel bad, that wasn't why I told you. I just wanted you to understand. We've not got a normal father-daughter relationship..."

"I'm so sorry."

"It's alright. It's not your fault. I'm just glad you're still my friend."

"Best friend! Forever! Come here." The couple held a long, tight cuddle on that historic street, before finally releasing from each other's grip. "Come on, let's go and have a quiet pint."

The couple walked arm in arm up the street before heading into The Shambles Tavern. Lisa grabbed a table whilst Ryan went to the bar, returning a short time later with two pints of lager. Lisa sent the text message she'd been writing while he was gone.

"You were right, dad! All sorted now! Ryan said he can't wait to meet you on Saturday. Love you xxx"

"Who's that?" Asked Ryan as he placed the glasses down on the table and took his jacket off. Lisa pulled an awkward face, laughing as Ryan understood the message and raised an eyebrow. He sat down, looking a little sheepish.

"I told him that you're up for meeting him."

"Ah, okay, brilliant. What shall I wear?"

"Well, he's quite a formal guy, so you'll have to wear your suit." Lisa lifted her pint to her lips but didn't manage to drink it as she laughed loudly at Ryan's expression.

"You little cow!" Ryan laughed too, it was a relief to see his girlfriend smiling and joking again. Those tears from a few minutes earlier were dried up. But then the conversation took an unexpected turn. "Seriously, though. Going back to what you just told me…"

"Yes?"

"I'm quite interested in all this, you know. It sounds mad, but do you remember a few years ago, there was this guy on the news called Pop…"

Lisa's face started heating up. She took a thirsty gulp from her pint glass.

"He was the guy who was killing paedos…"

"Yes, I remember…"

"And my mum and dad had it on TV every day, they said that the guy, Pop, they said he would never get sent to prison, because he was doing the right thing. It absolutely fascinated me, the idea that everyone in the country was cheering on this murderer…"

"Ryan, where are you going with this?" Asked Lisa, intrigued by the comment, but also desperate to wrap this up and change the subject.

"I just wondered, you know – with everything that happened… what did your dad say about it all?"

"What, about Pop?"

Ryan nodded as he took a drink from his glass.

"He…" Lisa's face was turning bright red. "Well, he agreed with it all. As you say, everybody did…"

"Mad wasn't it? I think that was the first news story that ever interested me! I was so gutted when it all ended, when that police woman was shot. What a fucking dick! In the blink of an eye Pop went from national treasure to the biggest scum bag that ever walked the streets!"

Lisa took another huge gulp from her pint. What she said next surprised her almost as much as it surprised Ryan.

"That was my dad."

As she said it, her face changed. It was as though every muscle tensed up as her mind caught up with her mouth. The room began spinning and Lisa Dawson struggled to understand what she'd just said, or why she'd said it. She'd only had half a pint, she considered. Fuck.

Ryan was staring at her with a confused expression. "What... what was your dad?"

Lisa looked down at her hands which were lay flat on the tabletop.

"Lisa... *what* was your dad?"

She looked up from the table and met his gaze. "Pop."

Chapter Sixty-Five

"Have you got a name for me?" Asked Miller.

Dawson replied instantly. "Yes. He's called Ryan Ingleton. He comes from Manchester himself, somewhere over Oldham way. He was going out with my daughter, Lisa. It turned out that he was messing around with drugs and so on…"

"What, and Lisa had told him about you?"

"I think so. She hasn't told me that, and I haven't asked her about it."

"Okay, so what makes you think its Ryan Ingleton who has told Tommy McKinlay about you?"

"A gut thing, call it a sixth sense if you will, I just couldn't warm to him, I never trusted him. Lisa thought the world of him, but I never saw why. He was incredibly charming, quite funny, extremely well presented. He looked like he was a member of a boyband. He was wonderful towards her really, but I sensed that it was all an act. I have a good intuition for these things, you see. I got the impression that he was only after one thing from Lisa, and I thought that she was too naïve and impressionable to see it herself. It's understandable, really. He was her first boyfriend. But from the moment I met him, I sensed that he was trouble."

"In what way?"

"He was… well, it's quite difficult to explain. Within minutes of meeting him, literally minutes, he gave me the impression that he wanted me to know that he knew something. He brought up the topic of the Pop story very quickly, and I saw from the corner of my eye that Lisa nudged him under the table. It made me suspicious, it felt that it was too strange a thing to be a coincidence. I guess I knew at that moment that something peculiar was going on. And, I mean we'd only met a matter of moments earlier."

"Could you ask her now?"

"I beg your pardon?"

"Could you phone Lisa now, and ask her if your suspicions are correct? If she can confirm that she told Ryan about your campaign? It's vital that I know exactly where all of this has come from."

"Well, I mean, I could, of course I could. But it might be a bit awkward…"

Miller's voice suddenly cooled a little and his statement was delivered with an unmistakable assertiveness. "George, with all the best will in the world. Nothing is going to be more awkward than you hearing your cell door slamming shut, locking you in a tiny cell with a junkie toe-rag for twenty-three hours a day for the rest of your natural and knowing that a quick call to Lisa could have avoided it all."

Dawson understood the instruction, loud and clear.

"Get her number up but don't ring her off your own phone."

"I know it by heart, it's the only number I ever ring. It's 07739 678…"

Miller typed the number into another phone which he had pulled out of his jacket pocket. It was a similar model to the one he'd thrown into the boating lake at Heaton Park just a couple of hours earlier. He had only just registered it on the network whilst he was waiting for Dawson to appear.

"Okay, it's ringing. Tell her to write this number down and call you back urgently from a public payphone. You must not discuss this matter on her mobile in case it is being monitored. Whatever you do, do not refer to yourself as Pop."

"My…" said Dawson, shocked by how serious things were suddenly becoming.

"Hello?" Said Lisa. There was a question in the greeting, the unfamiliar number hadn't gone unnoticed.

"Hi… yes, Lisa, it's Dad."

"Dad? Hi… er… are you okay? Is this a new number?" George could tell that Lisa was spooked, he sensed that she knew that something was amiss.

"I need you to go to a call box and call me back on this number. Do not call me from your own phone. It's urgent…"

"What? Hey, is… is everything okay?" The panic in her voice now was unmistakable.

"Just… as quickly as possible please, love." Dawson

looked at the naff little phone as Miller pulled it away from him and pressed the red button, disconnecting the call. He looked at Miller and the sadness in his face made the DCI feel bad. But there was no time for that right now.

"She knows something's wrong. I never call myself Dad. And I certainly don't hang up on her!"

"Okay, well, that's good. It means that she won't waste a second in getting to a call box to find out what's wrong."

"That's a good point, I suppose." Dawson looked more stressed now than he had when he'd first arrived. This surprised Miller, that the prospect of having a confrontation with Lisa was more nerve-wracking for him than the prospect of being arrested and jailed for the deadliest killing spree in British history.

Miller handed him the phone again. "Tell me a bit more about Ryan. You say that he was involved with drugs..."

"Well, yes. At least, that was what came out in the end. Lisa was very sheltered, you see. She wasn't wise to the darker things in life."

"But something happened, something regarding drugs?"

"Yes. Ryan was beaten up rather badly. It was extremely serious, to the extent that it involved an air ambulance landing in Rowntree Park, he was airlifted to Leeds Infirmary. Lisa found out that Ryan had discharged himself within a couple of hours of waking up and he then disappeared completely. She was beside herself with worry, understandably. She managed to work out that Leeds Infirmary specialised in head injuries and came to the conclusion that he must have a very serious brain trauma. This was how she explained his lack of contact with her."

"Strewth, sounds like a stressful time?"

"Oh, it most certainly was. Lisa turned detective, in fact I think you'd have been quite proud of her!" Dawson chuckled at his wise-crack and his stress levels appeared to have dropped a little. Miller smiled politely.

"Anyway, she very quickly discovered that there was another side to young Ryan Ingleton. She'd begun asking everybody in the city if they had any idea why anybody would want to hurt Ryan. It didn't take long until she began to learn a much darker truth about her boyfriend. It all came out, the fact that he was one of the city's main drug-dealers, managing a network of runners who were selling ecstasy and cocaine to the students, as well as other things. She even went to St John's University and made some enquiries. It turned out that he wasn't even studying there. It was all a pack of lies, a cover-story which concealed the real reason why he was in the city. It was a very difficult time for her, I sometimes wonder if she is still in pain."

"Good grief! What a disgusting little slug." Miller was genuinely saddened by the tale.

"Yes, you can say that again. And obviously, this is the reason that I didn't hesitate when you asked me if I had any idea who might be behind this situation."

Miller stared down the gap where the railway lines once sat, looking out at Manchester city-centre's skyscrapers which towered above this sad little place. He considered Dawson's story for a moment before speaking.

"This all makes sense… McKinlay, the gangster who is creating problems is from that end of Manchester. Rochdale to be exact. If Ryan is from Oldham and was installed into York to sell the drugs… then ended up being beaten up so badly that the heli-meds were called out, well it's all fitting together very neatly."

"Yes, I can…"

Dawson stopped talking as the phone in his hands began vibrating. He stared at it nervously.

"I'll take this call." Said Miller, his assertiveness in full flow once again as he took the phone from Dawson's grasp. The call display showed an 01904 prefix, the STD code for York.

"Hello," said Miller without much warmth.

"Er, hello. Who's that?" Lisa sounded panicky.

Using the brand new burner phone, connected to a random landline, Miller felt comfortable to talk. He knew from experience that there was no chance of the call being monitored.

"It's DCI Miller. I'm sure you have heard of me?"

"Yes, yes, of course, but... what's going on? Where's dad?"

"I'm afraid we've got a problem, Lisa."

"What?"

"Ryan Ingleton."

This threw Lisa off track. Her primary concern upon making this call was her father's well-being. This subject matter had been confused by the voice of DCI Miller. Now the introduction of Ryan's name into the proceedings had really thrown the young woman's panicked state into a frenzy.

"What... this... sorry, but what the actual fuck is going on?" The panic gave way to anger as Lisa snapped down the phone.

"I need to know exactly what you said to Ryan about you-know-what."

There was a silence. Miller could almost hear Lisa Dawson's brain whirring down the line.

"This is important Lisa." He added.

"I told him. Okay? I didn't know...."

It was clear from Lisa's voice and from the manner in which she delivered her explanation that she was struggling to justify it now, in the cold light of day. Miller felt for her. It was a dickhead, naive thing to do, but there were much worse things in the world than a loved-up teenager confiding a family secret in her boyfriend. Miller had the details he needed, the confession and the guy's name. There was no need to bully her over it.

"It's okay, it's okay. I just needed to find out who knew about it. We're having a few issues regarding this, and now we know who has been creating the problems, it's a big help. So thanks. Whatever you do, don't mention this conversation to Ryan, it will cause untold problems for your dad."

"Well, you don't need to worry about that..."

"Okay, thanks Lisa. And obviously, you probably don't need me to say it, but I'll say it anyway. You must never, ever tell anybody about what happened."

"I know... I know that now..." Lisa was crying down the

line.

"Okay. Well don't worry, we'll fix it. I'll put you on to your dad."

Chapter Sixty-Six

Tommy McKinlay had been hammering against the solid steel door for almost two hours. His hands were swollen from the constant beating against the cold, hard surface. There wasn't actually much else to do in this cell, it was just like a police cell. The only moveable object in the place was the thin, waterproof mattress which was situated on top of the raised concrete platform which served as a bed base. The rest of the cell was completely empty and the place was having an extremely negative impact on McKinlay's state-of-mind. He was acutely aware of the fact.

The noise of the relentless banging was much louder inside McKinlay's cell. On the other side of the two-inch thick steel, it was barely audible – little more than a dull thud which was concealed from the corridor by another thick, heavy door. The designers of this segregation unit, this high security prison within a high-security prison, had thought of everything when the building work had been carried out in the late 1990s. Right near the top of their list was managing disruptive, angry, powerless inmates who would be completely frustrated by their solitary confinement within this desperately lonely and isolated place. Thus, facilitating them with anything they could use to make noise with was an absolute no-no.

Finally, one of the prison officers opened the first door and then opened McKinlay's hatch before peering in through to his cell. McKinlay was staring back straight at him and if looks could kill, McKinlay's expression would be tearing this screw's head off with its bare hands and then smashing the decapitated head against the floor a thousand times until there was nothing left but blood and sludge.

"If you don't calm down, I'll close this hatch and you can start all over again."

"I'm fucking calm." Said McKinlay with a wild, psychotic glaze in his eyes.

"Well busting your hands against this fucking door isn't really the sign of a calm person. Now you've probably realised already that we can hardly hear your noise on this side of the door. I bet you can't hear the radio I turned up so I don't have to listen to your fucking shit tantrum."

"You wouldn't have the balls to say that if you didn't have that fucking door there."

"You're probably right about that Mr McKinlay. But there is this door, and you're behind it, and that's because you've been getting up people's noses. If you ever want to get on the right side of this tank-proof door, and out of this segregation unit, you need to start thinking about how you're coming across. This kind of shit is only going to prolong your stay here. It's like slapping yourself in the face with your own shit and then moaning that you've got shit all up your face."

"Fucking hell, did you think of that one yourself?"

"No. We had a guy that used to do it. We nicknamed him Shit-head."

McKinlay's face was reaching a dangerous level of crimson. But this prison officer couldn't give a fart about that, and his contempt for the prisoner was quite blatant. There was none of the politeness and hero worshipping that McKinlay had taken for granted at HMP Manchester, but then again, none of the staff down here were worried that McKinlay's people would be knocking on their front doors and intimidating them with death threats. The staff here seemed completely free of that kind of manipulation and viewed the prisoners with blatant contempt rather than the unfettered adulation that McKinlay had become accustomed to.

Belmarsh isn't like any other part of the wider prison network. This is the most secure and meanest jail in the UK, built to deal with the very worst types of prisoners that the country has to offer. This place is designed and managed in such a way as to send a stark but organic message to every prisoner in every jail up and down the land. The message is a simple but effective one and it travels well. Behave yourself or you'll end up in Hell Marsh and you will hate every fucking second of your time there.

"What the fuck are you on about? Getting up people's noses?" McKinlay looked as though he was smirking as he brought his face right up to the hatch.

"I don't know, Mr McKinlay. That's for you to try and work out. But from what I've heard, you had it nice and cushy up in Manchester. Word is the Governor up there was coming in and tidying your cell for you. And then you went and fucked it all up for yourself and swapped the good life for this shit heap! With this knowledge, I can totally understand why you're so cheesed off but please, for goodness sake, stop taking it out on this poor door."

"Fuck off! You don't know what you're chatting about officer."

"Okay, well, I've dispensed my advice in accordance with your care plan. Quite honestly I couldn't give a fuck if you turn your hands into mince on this door. Good night!"

With that, the screw slammed the hatch shut and the deafening clang echoed all around Tommy McKinlay's empty cell. He stood there, staring at the door, realising that he hadn't achieved very much from this encounter other than wrecking his fists.

It had taken a bit of time, but it was starting to dawn on Tommy McKinlay that maybe the screw was right. Maybe he had fucked up. He'd known that there was a risk of being moved from Strangeways, that was understood and had been fully planned for. But neither Tommy or any of his team had ever envisaged him being banged up down here, completely isolated with no outside contact in the jail they use to deal with Britain's most serious and vulnerable criminals. That had never been considered, in fact, Tommy McKinlay had never even realised that the prison service could do this. He'd assumed he had all these human rights laws and policies and stuff on his side. He'd never once considered that making threats against a school full of children would automatically make him a terror suspect and would ultimately jeopardise the soft-touch rules that he thought he had on his side.

"FUCKING GET MILLER DOWN HERE… NOW!!!"

"I WANT TO SEE MILLER!" Shouted McKinlay as loudly as he could, suddenly remembering why he'd been punching the cell door for the past few hours. "TELL HIM TO GET DOWN HERE

AS SOON AS." Yelled McKinlay. But the prison staff couldn't hear him, they had turned Smooth FM back up and were humming along to a Luther Vandross number.

Chapter Sixty-Seven

Tez Walker is not the type of man that people tend to cross. He has very few enemies, largely due to the fact that people know not to annoy him. The best way to get along with Tez is to stay well away from Tez. Even the police were rumoured to avoid having any dealings with "Teflon Tez" as he was known by officers, a nickname inspired by the fact that the police had tried many times to charge him with all manner of crimes, but they just couldn't make anything stick. In the wider community, he has a number of other nicknames, including Sted Head Tez and Terence the Terrible, but nobody has ever had the poor judgement to say these names in his presence.

Six foot four and built like a brick shit-house, Tez Walker runs a boxing gym in Little Hulton, the Salford over-spill estate on the edge of the city's border where it meets with Bolton's boundary. The area is not particularly well known for much more than the stars it has produced over the years, from Paul and Shaun Ryder of the Happy Mondays, the comedian Jason Manford and former Doctor Who and Cracker actor, Christopher Eccleston.

Tez Walker's gym has been raided several times through the years, police sniffer dogs have covered every nook and cranny in the building looking for drugs, guns, sex-workers and cash. Their luck has never been in, despite lots of intelligence that Tez Walker runs his criminal empire from the upper floor of the gym which is based in an old Victorian Co-Operative building close to the Farnworth border. It is believed that Tez supplies all of the coke, smack and recreational drugs in this highly populated area which covers the west-side of Salford and the eastern side of Bolton.

Although it is a generally accepted rule that Tez Walker is a man who is best avoided, five males in dark hooded jackets were hiding in the shadows down the side of the doctors building opposite, waiting for Tez to leave his gym for the night. His black Range Rover sport with the registration plate TE 2 was parked outside the building, all four tyres had several nails pressed against the rubber, front and back. It was raining quite heavily, which was good news for the five men who were waiting patiently behind the industrial bins, their eyes transfixed on the glow from the office lights on the upstairs floor.

*****

Naseem Ahmed has previously served time in prison for drugs offences, but he has been a constant source of frustration for police who know that he is the principal supplier of class A drugs in the Tameside area of Greater Manchester. They just can't prove it, despite spending years and many hundreds of thousands of pounds in trying to get this ruthless drug dealer off the streets.

Nas has been so successful in his drug supplying career that he purchased the number plate 1 NAS from the former world champion boxer, Prince Naseem Hamed for an undisclosed sum. The 34 year-old man from Oldham is a well known face in the area, famed locally for his flamboyant designer outfits and for constantly having a fresh parking ticket affixed to the windscreen of his £90,000 Mercedes G Wagon, which he tends to park wherever he pleases.

Nas never touches any of the drugs that he has made his fortune from selling, in fact police believe that he never even sees them. He employs a large network of people to look after the dirty side of the business, many of whom have never met him but remain incredibly loyal as he pays them all extremely well and runs the enterprise like a legitimate business. The business is run via a complex system of burner phones and social media accounts, an enterprise which is so secretive and so well organised that it is impossible to find evidence of who is running the elaborate system which involves the bulk buying of cocaine and heroin, cutting, repackaging and distribution into smaller quantities across the eight towns area.

Internally, police officers in the East of the city have named Naseem Ahmed as the number one target they'd like to lock away, but he seems far too clever to fall into their grasp and they have little choice but to sit back and wait, hoping beyond hope that he slips up some day. That day never seems to arrive, Nas Ahmed's web and social media marketing business provides enough cover to explain his success and acts as the ultimate alibi for his day to day whereabouts and activities.

Nas usually arrives home from his office in Ashton town centre at around 9pm. He has a large detached house which he designed himself on Holmfirth Road in Greenfield, overlooking the stunning Dovestones Reservoir on the very edge of the Greater Manchester border where it meets with West Yorkshire. The property has a driveway almost a quarter of a mile long, and the building is hidden from the main road, behind huge bushes and a large electronically operated gate.

Across the road from the gate is a dry-stone wall, behind which four darkly dressed men were crouched down, keeping an eye on the entrance of Naseem Ahmed's home.

*****

South Manchester, more traditionally known as Cheshire before the Greater Manchester region was invented in 1974 contains some of the wealthiest parts of the city. The areas of Wilmslow, Marple and Altrincham are home to TV stars, Premier League footballers, retired politicians and former heads of Universities, schools and government departments as well as some of the UK's leading CEOs. The world's most successful football manager of all time, Sir Alex Ferguson lives here, too. But despite the big names and the wealth in the area, South Manchester is not immune from the drug problem which plights the rest of Britain. In fact, business in the drug trade is booming here, amongst the very richest and the very poorest.

Demand for cocaine in this region is at an all-time high. Heroin, after a dip in popularity for the previous twenty-years is making a major come-back, too. Most of these drugs are supplied by the man who fits in quite well amongst the television and sport stars and business leaders in the million-pound plus detached properties around Wilmslow.

James Parker looks just like any other respectable homeowner in the district. He is in his late thirties, good-looking, impossibly charming and immaculately well-presented. But his cover-story of being a successful investment analyst masks a much darker truth. James Parker is a major league drug dealer, responsible for supplying all of the smaller dealers who flood the streets of Wythenshawe, Heaton Moor and Stockport with the heroin, coke and crack that causes untold misery and pain for thousands of addicts and their loved ones. But you'd never guess the horrors that this man is responsible for by talking to James Parker. He would charm the socks off you as he regales you with his wonderful stories of his yacht in Abersoch Harbour and his villa in Portugal. He'd tell you about how well his children are doing at the £22,000 per year Stoneyhurst private school in rural Lancashire. You'd never guess that this utterly charming, thoroughly pleasant man was directly responsible for most of the burglaries, car thefts, muggings, robberies and violent crimes in the region, as addicts do whatever they have to do in order to get another fix of James Parker's toxic products.

Hiding in the back of a Sky TV emblazoned transit van parked close to James Parker's lavish house were three men, sitting silently, waiting patiently for an update from Nerd. The sound of the rain hammering against the roof was deafening. Just behind the van, sitting in a silver Ford Fiesta, two men were sitting with the engine running, waiting for an update on which direction James Parker would be travelling towards his address.

*****

The five men crouching behind the huge red Biffa bins remained silent as they saw the lights in Tez Walker's office go out. The windows were suddenly filled with darkness and the tension rose dramatically behind the bins.

Two minutes later, three people walked out of the main doors of the gym. Tez and two of his staff members chatted briefly as Tez locked the door and pulled the shutter down.

"Go on, get out of this rain. I'll see yous in the morning." Said Tez as he bent down to lock the shutter. His two associates ran along the road and got into a car, before pulling off onto the main road. Tez stood and walked casually towards his Range Rover, his arms typically extended at his sides as though he was carrying two invisible beer barrels. He got into his car and turned the engine on, the headlights suddenly illuminating the bins across the road.

Tez's face lit up in the vehicle as he checked his phone and a long, tense minute passed as he wrote a message before he moved the phone away and placed it on the passenger seat. As soon as he lifted the hand-brake and pulled up the clutch, the car stalled as all four tyres punctured at once. At that precise moment, the sound of gun-shots rang out all around the area as Tez's windscreen was sprayed with bullets from the Biffa bins. After a couple of seconds, all five men leapt up from their hiding place and sprinted towards the car, firing more shots into the driver's side window. They had to be sure that Tez Walker was dead, and they made absolutely sure that he was, pumping his head with bullets at point blank range.

*****

The four men standing behind the dry-stone wall in Greenfield were saturated from the relentless rain which had been falling the whole time they'd been hidden, waiting for a call from Nerd. Finally, the call came and was answered in silence.

"Okay, standby, the G Wagon is in Greenfield Village now, just leaving the Tesco supermarket. ETA is about one minute." A long silence followed before Nerd spoke again. "Okay, he's at the roundabout at The Clarence pub, yes, he's coming straight home, he's heading your way. He'll be with you in fifteen seconds."

The man listening to Nerd's commentary tapped the man next to him and gave a thumbs up. One of the figures behind the wall leapt up and vaulted over the stones before sprinting into the middle of the road, throwing a stinger device across the carriageway. As he quickly checked that it had landed correctly, he turned and ran back, leaping over and crouching down once more behind the dry-stone wall. Within seconds, all of the men heard the tyres on the G Wagon pop with loud bangs, just as Naseem Ahmed was slowing to turn into his drive.

As soon as the vehicle became stationary, just fifteen yards from his gates, the men stood from their position and began spraying the driver side window with gun-fire.

Nas Ahmed hadn't stood a chance. All of the men scrambled over the wall and fired more shots at the dead man's head, chest and face, before they ran down the hill in the direction of Greenfield for ten seconds, and getting into the vehicle they had parked up at the bottom of Hollins Lane. Within seconds, they were speeding towards Mossley. Just one minute after that, they had dumped the vehicle and transferred into another car which had been parked close to the Royal George pub, before heading left onto Huddersfield Road in the direction of Micklehurst and Stalybridge.

*****

"Here we go, Nerd's on the phone." The driver of the Ford Fiesta which was parked behind the Sky TV van, close to James Parker's home address answered the call.

"Alright, he's heading your way, he's coming towards you from the M56."

"That's cool, that's the way we've set-up."

"Okay, standby, he's about five minutes away, I'll phone you back when he's a bit nearer. Make sure you're all ready."

Nerd had been tracking both Naseem Ahmed's and James Parker's vehicles all evening with his GPS software. Tez Walker was so thick and arrogant that his murder had been the easiest one to plan, leaving his gym at the same time every night, usually alone. The plan from the very beginning had been to co-ordinate the three executions at roughly the same time. Everybody involved knew that the news of one of Manchester's major drug dealers being assassinated would spread far and wide very quickly and would subsequently hamper the opportunity to carry out any further executions for the foreseeable future. Therefore, after months of careful planning, it had been considered the best solution to do them all at the same time, or as near as damn it. Things were going exceedingly well in that regard as far as Nerd was concerned, two down and one to go. The police were still en-route to the crime-scene in Little Hulton and as far as Nerd could make out from the police radio, Naseem Ahmed's murder hadn't even been phoned in yet. James Parker was driving straight into his trap right now, it was looking like this was going to be an excellent night's work. None-the-less, the tension was heavy.

The phone rang again. "Alright Nerd?"

"Yes, okay, he's heading your way, I'm guessing he'll be on you in about 45 seconds so prepare to engage."

Without further a do, the man in the passenger seat stepped out of the car and jogged a few metres. He switched on the temporary traffic light that had been set up to remain on red, just in front of the Sky TV van. The man then jogged back and got into the car.

"Here he comes, like a fucking lamb to the slaughter!" Said the driver. Right behind his vehicle, James Parker's Porsche was slowing down and preparing to stop behind the Fiesta.

"Okay guys, his handbrake is on." Said the driver into a hand-held radio. At that moment, the back doors of the Sky van burst open and the three occupants stepped out, firing their guns through James Parker's windscreen. They kept walking, right up to his window and continued firing the shots until they reached point-blank range. It was imperative that he was dead. Satisfied that he was, the gunmen ran back to their van, jumped in, slammed the back doors and just a few seconds later, the tyres screeched and the vehicle pulled off, followed closely behind by the Fiesta. A few seconds after that, another car slowed, stopped and waited patiently behind the Porsche.

Chapter Sixty-Eight

The Salford Online Facebook group was the first place that the story appeared. A member of the page called Sue Northwood posted the following comment, along with a photograph of Tez Walker's car, which was surrounded by police cars and ambulances. At first glance it was hard to make out what the picture displayed due to the distortion of blue lights from several emergency vehicles. But on closer inspection, the shocking subject matter slowly same into focus. It was a black Range Rover with a sheet thrown over the windscreen, with several police officers looking into the vehicle from both sides. The centrepiece of this grisly photograph was the well-known registration plate TE 2.

"Can't believe what I've just witnessed as I was walking the dogs. This is right now outside Tez Walker's gym!!!"

Within seconds, the post was attracting dozens of comments, from the "OMG!" type to other user's names being tagged in the story to inform them of this momentous announcement.

"Shit. This is officially the start of World War 3!" Said one member, accompanying his comment with several "wow" emoji icons.

Very few people dared to say what they really thought, but some did and there were a handful of comments which showed very little sympathy or concern for the apparent victim of this disturbing incident.

"Hope he's dead the angin' cunt!" Said one member of the group, which attracted 57 likes and 16 laughing emojis.

"Long time coming this!!!" Said another member of the Salford Online community page.

"Weird this... I'm in another page called Wythenshawe One and they're saying another bloke's been shot dead in his car. Porsche I think. Wait, BRB I'll screen grab the post."

Beneath this, somebody added another comment.

"Fucks going on? Police have shut the main road between Greenfield and Holmfirth, apparently the same has happened there, a driver shot to death in the road!!!"

"WTF?????"

"Something's deffo going on!!!"

Within minutes, Facebook and Twitter were going bonkers with people searching for information. Newspapers and radio stations always take hours to get their stories out, which is frustrating in the "on-demand" "instant-gratification" world that we live in today. Consequently, people had learnt to just check social media for their news, finding the raw, unedited, legally questionable updates and videos within seconds. It's not just the general public who gather their news this way. The major broadcast and print journalists do too, they just have to be a lot more responsible in their reporting, checking and double-checking facts to avoid ending up in court and out of work.

By 9.30pm, there was a great deal of confusion around Greater Manchester. Plenty of footage was being uploaded to social media which showed the aftermath and road closures around the three murder scenes in the Tameside, Salford and South Manchester boroughs. But other police incidents around the city were also being reported as "murder scenes" as the hysteria surrounding the nights activities began being exaggerated and confused. Shortly before 10pm, a car-crash near Failsworth had been photographed and uploaded onto Twitter, the person who'd taken the photo had managed to take the photo in a very clever way, cropping out the other vehicle involved and focusing on the police and paramedic activity on the driver's side. Then news of another "murder" was uploaded to Snapchat, though in reality, it was a domestic incident that police were responding to in Irlam. It seemed that three separate gun murders across the city in one night wasn't quite enough for the social media addicts across the region.

Sky News had realised that something very serious was happening in the north of England and interrupted their output to report what was known at 10:10pm, complete with the yellow flash of their BREAKING NEWS banner.

"And some news which is just reaching us from Manchester this evening, it is being reported across social media that there have been a number of shootings around the city in the past hour, resulting in at least three deaths. Our north of England correspondent Paul Mitchell joins us on the line. Paul, what more can you tell us?"

"Yes, good evening Tina, that's right, I am currently on my way to the scene of one of those shootings, which took place just after nine o'clock this evening, so this was little over an hour ago. The location of that shooting was in the most surprising of places, a small, idyllic village on the edge of the Greater Manchester border called Greenfield. This is not the kind of place that one might expect to hear about a shooting of this nature. What we understand so far..."

Paul Mitchell gave a briefing to the news channel, based on what was understood of the three crime scenes, adding that there was lots of speculation that there were other unconfirmed attacks that were still to be substantiated. It was clear that Paul Mitchell was excited about this dramatic breaking news story, he was speaking quickly and energetically as he gave his initial report, fully aware that once he was on location, his face would be leading the channel's output over the coming hours.

"Manchester City Police have not released a statement about these attacks as yet, but we are expecting to hear from a senior officer in the next couple of hours. At that point, we will learn much more about this shocking night of terror on Greater Manchester's streets."

"Okay, Paul, thank you, we'll come back to you just as soon as you have reached the location of this shocking breaking news story in Greenfield, Greater Manchester."

Chapter Sixty-Nine

"Alright Keith?"

"Hi Sir. Have you seen the news?"

"No…"

"Put it on."

"What's… I'm in bed. Was about to switch myself off… why what's going on?"

"I think the reason McKinlay wanted banging up has just happened!" Saunders talked Miller through the incidents in Wilmslow, Little Hulton and Greenfield.

"Fucking hell fire!"

"Indeed. And all three of the victims are well known to us and the NCA. They're all currently on the MCP major crimes hit-lists suspected of being senior drugs suppliers and traffickers."

"Shit."

"So, I was right. This is what McKinlay has been planning all along. What better alibi can he have than being banged up in prison while all this went off?"

"Or, to be a bit more accurate, to be in a prison van under police escort from Belmarsh to Strangeways!"

"Shit, no way. So, he got his own way?"

"Yes. He certainly did. In fact, what time are we on?"

"Half-ten."

"Right, well, he'll be back now. They set off about six, they waited about trying to avoid the rush-hour. His transport was flanked by four Met police cars, six outriders and an ARU front and back."

"Jesus Christ! Taking no chances then?"

"Nope. Some of our ARUs were scheduled for joining the convoy when it reached Sandbach as well."

"Well, I doubt he'd try escaping. He's got the upper hand here hasn't he? It's all going his way."

"It does seem that way at the minute. I think we've no choice but to finalise our case files regarding you-know-who and then await the inevitable."

"Reckon?"

"Yeah. It's the only way out of this bollocks now. Let McKinlay say whatever the hell he likes to whoever will listen and then just release a statement rubbishing the claims. We're nearly there, just need to hold our nerve now. The more I'm learning about McKinlay, I think I'd rather get sent down now, than let him win."

"Bollocks."

"Yeah, probably. But he's not showing himself in a good light after that with Jo this morning, and now this."

"And the shit he's caused for your Clare and the kids."

"Yeah. But I'm getting over that now, they're having a great time. I'm more concerned about Jo at this moment in time."

"How is she? Any news?"

"You know Jo, she's alright, she's calmed down a lot and she's putting a brave face on. But there's the risk for some serious psychological damage from that. She'll start joking about it tomorrow, but I doubt she'll ever enjoy a relaxing shower again. I'm still fuming Keith, haven't calmed down all day."

"Where is she?"

"She's stopping at Abby's parents house over Didsbury way. Our maintenance contractors are fixing her house up, new doors and frames, the steel framed ones. It'll be like Fort Knox when they're done. I've put in a request for the security windows as well, just to give her some peace of mind."

"Good idea."

"I've given her the week off but I've asked the mental health team to make an intervention, get her through some counselling and stuff before she comes back to work."

"She'll be alright."

"She will when we catch the bastard that broke into her house. Any joy with that?"

"Couple of possibilities have flagged up from the NCA's database of McKinlay associates."

"Anything a bit more..."

"Don't get your hopes up too high but McKinlay's number two in the organisation, Simon Kingston fits the profile spot on."

"Kingo?"

"Yes. Former paratrooper, so he fits your ex-services criteria. He's got blue eyes as well, really vivid blue. I've been on Youtube replaying some of his clips from McKinlay's TV show. His accent is about as South Manchester as you can get. I'd love to ask Jo to check it out but I'm conscious that it might be a bit soon..."

"Yes, I agree with that. If it is him, it's going to put her right back in that shower. Hold off with that for now, let's see how she's bearing up tomoz."

"No problem."

"Is Kingo your horse then?"

"He's a favourite. But like I say, there are a few in the race. A few names in the NCA file fit the physical profile. I imagine that every name in there has been involved in this pantomime tonight."

"Well, that's not going to be our problem, I'll tell you now. If Dixon tries putting that shitshow on my desk in the morning, I'll get him in a headlock. Have a report ready for me tomorrow, anybody who fits the physical profile who has connections to McKinlay is getting lifted tomorrow."

"Nearly done, Sir."

"Nice one."

"How are Clare and the kids, by the way?"

"Great. They're loving being away, just got off the phone to Clare before you rung. She was a bit tipsy, singing Neil Diamond songs down the phone, doing my head in!"

"Good. Right, well, I'll see you in the morning..."

"Yeah, I might stick Sky News on, see what they reckon this was all about."

"Well, they won't say it, but basically, three of the city's most notorious drug-dealers are presently sat in their cars with between eighteen and twenty-seven bullet wounds in their heads, arms and chests."

"And its still pissing down with rain outside! Wouldn't fancy being the investigating officer in this. Right, good work Keith. See you tomoz."

"Night, Sir."

Chapter Seventy

The journey up north had gone without a hitch and McKinlay had been as good as gold, sitting quietly in his secure compartment as the big white "sweat box" vehicle rattled and vibrated its way up the M6 motorway, accompanied by the relentless wailing of sirens front and back keeping the fast lane clear for the VIP prisoner.

Staff on board the truck didn't hear a peep out of McKinlay, which was a very rare occurrence. Their passengers usually spend their entire journeys shouting obscenities and kicking against the internal panels which house each inmate during transportation between courts and prisons. Not today though. If you had been on board, you'd have been excused for believing that the vehicle was empty as it thundered north up the motorway, in the direction of Manchester.

Staff on board had been checking on McKinlay regularly, looking through the one-way glass partition on his door to check on his welfare. The small compartment looks a little bit like a toilet cubicle on the older trains, except there's no loo or sink, just a hard, uncomfortable seat. McKinlay was sitting there in his compartment with a satisfied grin on his face. He was feeling extremely content in the knowledge that he had won and was still very much calling the shots, despite that dickhead stunt DCI Miller had pulled in farming him out to the toughest jail in Britain. It was now time for the second part of the plan to take effect and McKinlay was working out the best way to get the wheels in motion on that, he was eager to get this job finished and start moving things forward. Sorting out the issues with DCI Miller would have to wait for the time-being.

Within minutes of arriving back at Strangeways, Tommy McKinlay was making his presence known. The screws were laying it on thick, pretending to be pleased to see him back at inmate reception. They were making shit jokes and forcing frivolity, and it all felt very staged and disingenuous. McKinlay could tell that the staff were all gutted that he was back, all scared that he might ask one of them for a favour which would be impossible for them to refuse.

"Thank God you're back Tommy, the place has been boring as fuck without you!" Was just one of the duplicitous comments that prison staff with painted on smiles were saying. Tommy held their gaze, staring at them as they tried to double-down on their insincere remarks. "Honestly, its been a nightmare without you, everyone has been jostling for position!"

McKinlay didn't say anything, he just nodded along, desperate to get through this long-winded check-in bullshit and get back on the wing so he could get on the phone and start making his arrangements.

"I hope my room's not been taken?" Said McKinlay, forcing a couple of the prison officers to look down at the floor. "I suggest that if there has been anyone else in there, you get them out right now and give the place a thorough fucking clean. I'll want a new mattress, I'm not lying on anyone else's wank. And put some bleach down the bog."

"I... I don't think anyone's been in, Tommy..."

Bullshit, thought McKinlay. But he didn't say anything. He just nodded moodily at the screw who was still doing his paperwork with shaky hands and a rigid fake smile. The prison is kicking people out early, every day, because they can't manage the volume of new inmates coming in from the courts. As if they'd left a cell empty in case its occupant came back from transfer. These screws think the lags are as thick as pig-shit.

"Seriously, mate. Stop what you're doing right now and go and check that my room's ready. I've had a long journey and I can't be arsed with any more fucking about today."

The screw looked at his colleague who disappeared silently through a door at the side of the counter. The staff at HMP Manchester had all been given plenty of warning that their star guest was on his way back up from London. The cell that McKinlay referred to as "his room" had been tossed several hours earlier and the inmate who'd been given it had caused a fuss, but soon piped down when he'd heard why he was being moved to another cell. Single occupancy cells in Strangeways are few and far between and being given one is akin to winning the lottery to anybody who is serving a lengthy sentence and can't stand the degradation of breathing in a stranger's farts for 23 hours a day.

A few minutes later, the other screw arrived back and smiled warmly at McKinlay. "It's all sorted Tommy. There *was* an inmate in there but he's been moved and it's all been sorted."

"That's okay then. Tell you what though, if those windows have been scratched again, they're going to need replacing."

Nobody had anything to say to that. The check-in desk had five staff and three inmates working and every single one of them was thinking 'who the fuck do you think you are, you horrible cunt.' But you'd never guess as they went about their work with fake positive smiles and sporadic bursts of shit banter amongst themselves.

"Right, Tommy. If you can read this and sign here, here and just down here." The screw had placed little Asterix marks on the paperwork where Tommy's signature was required. It was the most pointless contract in the world. An inmate's signature on this form basically meant that they agree to the fact that they're completely fucked and have to live here now, where the other inmates will probably beat them to within an inch of their lives for a squeeze of their toothpaste. That particular detail doesn't apply to Tommy McKinlay of course, but it does to 99% of new inmates, at least until they have established themselves within the prison community. Quite why they have to sign it three times is anybody's guess, but nobody gets into the main prison building until these types of formalities are completed. Mckinlay signed the contract before chucking the pen down on the counter.

"I want all my stuff back from when I was transferred. And I mean, all my stuff."

This demand created a sudden tension. The most senior screw on duty placated the situation. "Leave that with us, Tommy."

"As soon as." Said McKinlay, as though he was trying to be as obnoxious and difficult as possible. Everybody in the room knew that he was demanding his phone back and that this demand was a fragrant disregard for the rules and procedures.

But nobody had the bottle to laugh in his face and tell him to have a fucking word with himself. It didn't work that way with Tommy McKinlay and everybody was acutely aware of it.

Moments later, McKinlay was led through a locked gate and then frisked ever-so-lightly, before being released through the next gate which led out into the hub of the jail. The smell of bad breath, body odour and human excrement hit him straight away, he'd not missed the Strangeways aroma at all while he'd been staying in the sanitised surroundings of Belmarsh's segregation unit. It was shit to be home, but not for too much longer.

McKinlay was led by two officers back to his wing, the gates were unlocked and opened as he approached, more screws and one or two lags who were on cleaning duties extended the fake-as-fuck welcome. McKinlay just smiled psychotically as he breezed through the gate which was slammed loudly behind him. He turned around and stared at the screw on the other side of the bars, making his dissatisfaction at the noise known.

After climbing the three flights of stairs amid the sound of more fake euphoria coming from the cells, Tommy finally reached his cell and inspected the window panes, pleased to see that whoever had been in here had not participated in the usual, moronic activity of scratching the tiny glass panes for so long that you can't see out of them. Next, he looked on his bed and began rifling through the pile of items that were folded up. Fortunately for the prison staff, he spotted his mobile phone tucked away inside one of the bed sheets.

"Right, you can fuck off now. I want to get my head down." Said McKinlay to the screw, who wasted no time in closing the cell door with a gentle crunch and locking it.

Chapter Seventy-One

THURSDAY

Saunders was in the office first, just after 6am. He had done his usual trick of slipping out of bed without Helen stirring. He had grabbed his clothes and closed the bedroom door silently. He got dressed in the living room, had a quick toilet trip and brushed his teeth before leaving the flat, or "apartment" as it was fashionably called by the trendy types of people who tended to call their tea "dinner." He would nip back and have a shower later, he decided, under no illusion that the racket he made in there, knocking off shampoo bottles or slipping and crashing into the wall as he dried himself would wake Helen up and he'd be in the doghouse.

Saunders was not one for lying in bed and trying to get back to sleep if he woke up too early. He had tried that, once or twice over the years but had arrived at the conclusion that wasting time trying to get back to sleep was time he could be utilising much more productively. In the few, short minutes that he'd been awake before deciding to sneak off to work, his mind had been racing. Thoughts about Rudovsky and the incident at her house, then being reminded of the targeted attacks around the city the previous night as well as the recollection that McKinlay was back in town had all fleeted through his mind before he'd even opened his eyes. Once he had opened his eyes, he remembered that there was unfinished business with Dawson, particularly tracking down the young drug dealer Ryan Ingleton and trying to find out who else he had discussed the matter with. He and Miller also needed to work on a decoy story regarding the confession, something that would make Ryan doubt the authenticity of Lisa's story about her dad.

And all of this was on top of trying to co-ordinate the actual work he had on his desk, which was to put this 'George Dawson is the real Pop' conspiracy theory to sleep once and for all so that Tommy McKinlay and his ilk would never again try and use it as a bargaining tool. It was going to be a busy day, that was for certain, and Saunders was as enthusiastic as ever and keen to get stuck in.

As soon as he had finished stirring his coffee, he took his mug back to his desk and got to work. He suspected that Rudovsky would be awake. She dealt with stress in a similar way that he did, by developing insomnia.

"Alright Jo. You awake mate?" He wrote in a text message and sent it. Within seconds, he had received a reply.

"How did you guess lol? What's going on? Pissed the bed?"

"Nah, couldn't sleep. Thought you'd be up. Fancy a chat?"

"Yeah, give me a couple of minutes, I'm in bed with Abby, she's snoring like a man. I'll sneak down to the back yard. Let me make a brew and I'll ring you."

"Cool."

Saunders logged into the Sky News app to pass the time. Nothing new had been reported since the previous night's sensational reporting of the three gangland shootings across Greater Manchester. The only additional piece of information related to the appeal for witnesses, surprisingly MCP had teamed up with Crimestoppers in announcing a £50,000 reward for any information leading to the prosecution of any of the individuals responsible for these audacious attacks.

"Good luck with that," said Saunders humourlessly, as he checked the time of this latest update. It had been published at 4.13am, which told Saunders that some of the top brass had been working very late, or very early on this case to secure the authorisation for such a sum of money. It smacked a little of desperation and Saunders felt that it proved beyond all doubt that senior officers were desperate to get something to throw at McKinlay and his crew, in the hope that it might stick.

The phone began vibrating in Saunders' hand and the Sky News story was replaced by a photo of Jo Rudovsky. The call connect button was flashing green.

"Hi Jo." Said Saunders, as cheerfully as he could for the time of day.

"Alright?"
"Are you?"

"Nah. Not really. Still a bit raw from everything…"

"Aw, you're not still going on about that are you? Fucking hell, move on you boring bitch!"

"Shut up you little dick!"

"Nah, I'm only kidding. I bet you are… I would be."

"I'm more fucking angry now than upset. I can't believe the fucking cheek of it."

"I know. It's like there's no fear now… I mean, I know that respect went out of the window a while back but once the fear of the police is gone, we're knackered."

"You can say that again."

Saunders heard a lighter wheel flick, followed by a deep intake of breath. "You're not… have you started smoking again?" Asked the DI. The disappointment in his voice was unmistakable.

"Yeah… 'fraid so. God, I've missed these buggers! Don't think I'd have made it through yesterday without my tabs. Not keen on the packet design these days though! Gross!"

"Put it out Jo!" Saunders adopted his strictest voice and Rudovsky laughed heartily. It made the DI smile.

"So…"

"So what?"

"I spent most of yesterday trying to work out who this twat was who came in your house."

"And?"

"Well, I wanted to phone you last night but I thought it would be a bit insensitive."

"Oh I wouldn't have minded. It would have made a change from Abby's mam and dad asking me if I'm alright yet!"

"Bless them!"

"No! You don't fucking ask somebody if they're alright, yet! It's like saying 'fucking hurry up and be alright again. You're doing our heads in! I tell you, in-laws are dickheads. Whether you're gay or straight or whatever. It's a universal truth!"

Saunders laughed loudly. It wasn't so much the phrase that Abby's parents had used, Saunders was more entertained by the rant which Jo had added on the end.

"Is Abby being a help?" Asked Saunders.

"Yeah, bless her. She was pretty shook up herself, it

makes you feel totally violated when some bastard's been in your house."

"Yeah, I can imagine. Well, I've heard that the contractors have fixed the place up, you've got some new doors out of it. Miller's going to get you some new windows in as well, the sort people can't break, not even with a sledge-hammer."

"Cool. Well, that's something…"

"Yeah. Unless you lock your keys inside. Then you're absolutely snookered."

"So go on anyway, what did you want to ring me about last night?"

Saunders heard another heavy draw on the cigarette.

"Well, it's a voice-clip. I want you to listen to it and see if it sounds like the guy…"

"Send it."

"Yeah, but… I'm just worried it might freak you out. If it is him, I mean… I didn't want you reliving the moment…"

"Are you serious? I've been reliving that moment non-stop since it happened. Proper scared me that did, I can't get my head around the fact that it was less than twenty-four hours ago! It feels like a lifetime ago. I'm just so glad I didn't actually do a shit in the shower. How embarrassing would that have been?"

It was standard that Rudovsky would be trying to make light of it. Saunders laughed for her benefit but he found the situation quite strained. It really wasn't funny at all and he wanted the bastard behind this in a police van, as soon as it was humanly possible. He had a strong suspicion that the man who had broken into Rudovsky's house was Kingo.

"You sure this won't freak you out?"

"I'm already pretty freaked out, boss."

"Right. Give me two minutes. I'll fire it over on e-mail. It's only a short clip but there should be enough."

"Okay, no problem."

Five minutes later, Saunders phone began ringing again. It was Jo.

"Hello?"

"Hi boss. Yeah, that's the man who was in my

bathroom."

"Hundred per cent?"

"Hundred and ten." The sound of the cigarette lighter flicked again.

"Excellent. That's amazing news. I'll get him banged up today. Are you up for doing an identity parade?"

"What…"

That was unexpected. Saunders heard the unfamiliar sound of anxiety in Rudovsky's voice. He understood just from the way she had said that one word that she was completely uncomfortable with the idea.

"It's alright, don't worry about it…"

"Well, I mean, if I have to…"

"No. It's cool Jo. I'll think of something else…"

"I'm just. This guy really meant business. What if somebody else came… what if they killed Abby as revenge?"

This question sent a cold wave up Saunders' spine. It wasn't like Rudovsky to be melodramatic, but there was an uncharacteristic edge in her voice. The question that she'd asked, it sounded as though she really thought that it was a possibility. Under the circumstances, Saunders realised that she was right to be frightened.

"Don't worry about it, Jo. We'll sort something else…"

"Well you can't really. Can you? All you'll have is the CCTV and my ID parade. The CCTV alone will be inconclusive." Rudovsky sounded stressed and anxious. This was not what Saunders wanted.

"Just leave it with me, Jo. All I wanted to know was whether the voice fitted. At least I know I'm on the right path. I'll think of something…"

"Who is he?"

The question threw Saunders, which surprised him. He should have anticipated this question and had an answer prepared. He knew that if he told the truth, it would add another layer of fear in Rudovsky's mind. The very reason that he had transferred the Youtube video clip to audio the previous evening was to disguise who the person was. If Jo knew that it was McKinlay's number two, it would certainly spook the DS. These were powerful people with a lot of foot-soldiers at their disposal. The activities of this week had certainly confirmed that. Saunders realised this was a significant problem that he faced and he cursed himself for not preparing an answer.

"Sir? Are you there?"

"Yeah, Jo, sorry... the line dropped."

"So who's the guy?"

"Not sure." Lied Saunders. But he knew that this was not a sustainable position.

"Well... I'm getting the impression that you're lying through your teeth. But I imagine that its coming from a good place again."

"Listen, I didn't want to bother you Jo, but you've given me what I needed, a positive ID on the voice. You just try and take it easy now."

"Okay, Sir. I'll try..."

"I'll have a word with Miller and see what we can sort out. Abby's not working at the minute, is she?"

"Not paid. But she's still volunteering full time hours!"

"Okay, well I think that will have to wait for a while, we might have to get you both out of the picture for a bit, at least a few days until we get these feral bastards under control. I'll buzz you back in a few hours. In the meantime, try and get some sleep mate. And stop smoking! You'll end up talking like Deidre Barlow."

Saunders smiled as he hung up on Rudovsky, pleased that he had spoken to her and that she was okay. He was also extremely excited about the break-through regarding Kingo's voice clip. This was a game-changer. Saunders rifled through his bag and pulled out DCI Jarvis's card. He looked at the clock and wondered if the "call anytime" invitation had included twenty-past six in the morning. He decided that it definitely did as he typed the numbers into his handset and waited for the call to connect.

"Hello?" Said Jarvis, the fuck sake sound of his greeting told Saunders that 'any time' had definitely not included twenty-past-six after all. Saunders introduced himself and Jarvis seemed to brighten up a little.

"How can I help?"
"Ah, where to start…"

Chapter Seventy-Two

The national media were making a great deal of fuss about the shootings which had taken place the previous evening in Manchester. This came as a surprise to TV viewers and radio listeners in the north of England. The stuff that happens in London tends to be deemed "national" news by the network broadcasters. But the stuff that happens everywhere else is viewed as "regional." Ask any northerner if that's true, particularly when the weather is warm down south and the national news is the "unprecedented heatwave" whilst for viewers north of Birmingham, it's pissing it down as usual.

But today, the crimes on the streets of Greater Manchester the previous evening seemed to have caught the breakfast news editor's imaginations and every major network had their broadcast vehicles and reporters pitched up at all three crime scenes. The familiar wide-angled shots of a subdued looking police officer guarding a cordon line tape which was flapping in the wind was followed by the mandatory forensics tent shot, and concluded with a slow zoom-in on the detectives talking amongst themselves close to the crime scene.

The Good Morning Britain reporter appeared to be quite in awe of the attack which had taken place in the south of Manchester, explaining to viewers how the perpetrators of this shocking and grisly crime had gone to extraordinary lengths to entrap their victim with the use of a fake roadworks problem, complete with a temporary traffic light rig.

"It just goes to demonstrate how sophisticated and daring the gunmen were as they stopped at nothing to ensure that their victim was trapped, with nowhere to go."

Miller turned the TV screen off and muttered "he could have reversed, you nipple." Miller stood and looked out of his office window, his team were all working hard at their desks, the group dynamic had taken a different angle without Rudovsky and the mood seemed a little flatter in her absence. Miller wasn't sure if this flatter mood was helping them focus better. Things were nearing completion with regards the Dawson cover-up and he knew that the moment Saunders stood up from his seat and headed across towards this office, there would be plenty of compelling evidence that George Dawson was not responsible for the crimes that Peter Sykes committed using the nickname "Pop." The key part of the evidence, the Ace card had been signed off by the Home Office, via a little help from DCS Dixon. Now, it was just a case of tidying up all the straggling bits.

As soon as Miller was in receipt of all this, it was going to be all systems go. Ryan Ingleton was presently in custody at Oldham police station following his arrest in a dawn raid at his mother's address. Ingleton had been extremely forthcoming during his arrest, Miller had heard. It was an occupational hazard, all part of the job of a drug-dealer and Ingleton was so familiar with the procedures of the law due to his lifestyle choices, that Miller anticipated he would be under the impression that officers wished to speak to him about some local misdemeanour or another. He'd probably reply no comment throughout the interview and would be anticipating his release within a matter of hours, no doubt planning to grin like a Cheshire cat as he strolled out of the police station, having got one over on the law yet again. Miller was looking forward to surprising the young man later and turning his world upside down. But he couldn't do that until Saunders had given him the nod. Tensions were rising, Miller hated having a jam-packed full to-do list but none of the tools to start his work.

It was destined to be a busy old day, with the blessing of Tim Jarvis, the DCI at the NCA, Miller had instructed Rochdale Division's Inspector to organise an ARU arrest of Simon Kingston at the earliest opportunity. McKinlay's number two in the TMS organisation would be spending the next 24 hours in a police station, but hopefully much longer. Life hopefully, thought Miller as he switched his view from his staff team to the Manchester cityscape. He could lose hours gazing at this spell-binding view if he wasn't careful. He could literally stand there and feel the stress levels subside minute by minute as he took in the sights, starting at the Pennine moors at the very back of the picture and working his way towards the city, one landmark, town and building at a time. Miller was feeling stressed, and realised that the hypnotic pull of his office view was drawing him in. He snapped out of the spell, promising himself a good gaze at it all later, when his fluorescent highlighter pen had scored off all the things that were scribbled on his to-do list.

There were jobs on other people's lists too. Saunders had Miller in hysterics when he'd first arrived in the office and his DI had told him about Jarvis's early morning wake-up call. The outcome had been positive, however. Jarvis had been delighted to hear the compelling story surrounding the three shootings around Greater Manchester, and Saunders' theory on who was responsible for them. Saunders had also explained the positive voice ID that Rudovsky had provided. When all of these pieces were put together, it suggested to DCI Jarvis that Simon Kingston had broken into Rudovsky's house and demanded McKinlay's return to Strangeways just a matter of hours before the shootings. There was still lots of work to do in order to prove anything, but Jarvis could tell that this was a big bone which still had plenty of meat on it. The call ended with Jarvis committing to organising the arrests of every individual that his team had been investigating as a matter of urgency. It really was destined to be a busy day.

Miller decided to touch-base with Rudovsky and see how she was getting on. That passed ten minutes and he was pleased to hear that she was keen to take off for a couple of weeks of well-earned holiday time. Miller told her that if she text him with the details of where she and Abby wanted to go, he'd get Dixon to authorise it through expenses. It was the least he could do. The call was concluded with a sincere pledge. Miller promised Rudovsky that everything would be sorted by the time she got back, and as he said it, he was pleased at how confident he sounded about that. He had a feeling, deep-down inside him that all of this shit was coming to an end. That Tommy McKinlay was going to come out of all this looking like nothing more than a fucking pillock. Miller was even contemplating holding a news conference, and announcing the allegation on every TV and radio station, then explaining how mental his accuser was, detail by detail. That's how confident he felt about the matter coming to a positive conclusion. The idea that Miller could walk out of here, perhaps even tonight, finally free of the shackles that remained from the Pop case was a delicious proposition.

Finally, Saunders stood, walked across to the photocopier and started pressing some buttons. An excitement grew within Miller. This was it. The ducks were finally in a row. It was time to see Tommy McKinlay off for good.

Chapter Seventy-Three

Ryan Ingleton was sitting with his brief in interview room 2C at Oldham police station. He was a very smart, very good-looking young bloke. Miller wasn't used to seeing people like this one in an interview room and he wondered why a young lad with all that he had going for him would choose to go down the one-way street into the cess-pit of supplying drugs.

"Hello Ryan." Said Miller with a warm smile and a friendly manner.

"No comment." Said Ingleton, refusing to make eye-contact. His solicitor sat beside him, looking quite bored as he made notes.

"Do you know who I am?" Asked Miller.

"No comment."

"Ah, it's like that is it?"

"No com..."

"Thing is, Ryan. I've had a very shit week because of you."

Ingleton didn't look up. He knew the system, just sit there, don't create a fuss, say "no comment" to everything. That's all there was to it. "No comment."

"Fair enough, you're no commenting. But I wanted to ask you about the things you've been saying about me. Things that have caused me a major headache this week..."

"No comment."

"You see, we've managed to figure out that you have said some rather peculiar things about me to certain people. And the thing is, it's a complete mystery. For one, I don't know you, I've never had any dealings with you. For two, the things that you have been saying about me are completely bewildering..."

"No comment."

"Forgive me whilst I talk to your solicitor for a moment please Ryan. Mr Mahmood, I'd like to give you this overview of what your client has been saying about me." Miller handed over a piece of A4. The young solicitor looked intrigued by this unusual interruption to proceedings and began scanning through the document. Miller had come across Mr Mahmood once or twice before and he liked him, he was one of the more sensible duty solicitors working in the Greater Manchester area.

"As you will see from my statement, Ryan has alleged that I am involved in a very serious cover-up in which I have allowed a man who he alleges is responsible for multiple murders to be released without charge from police custody. Now, in itself, that's perfectly okay, this is a free country, we have freedom of speech etcetera. However, this issue has created a very serious problem…"

Ryan sniggered. It seemed quite involuntary, Miller didn't get the impression that the young man was being deliberately antagonistic. He just seemed genuinely amused by the comments that the DCI was making to his brief. Miller ignored the outburst and continued.

"The thing is, Mr Mahmood. I face a number of challenges as a result of this."

"Yes, I imagine you do…" Mr Mahmood looked at Miller. He had very warm, friendly eyes and his smile lit up the room.

"The problem is, this thing has got out of hand in a very troubling way. Naturally, the things that Ryan has been saying are total nonsense…"

Ryan's laugh came again and Miller revised his original theory that the first one had been down to nerves or something similar.

"Sorry to interrupt you DCI Miller. You say that these allegations are total nonsense to quote you directly. Can I ask if you have made any official representations to this effect?" Asked Mr Mahmood.

"Yes, of course. The allegations have been handed to my superior officer, Detective Chief Superintendent who has referred the matter to the PCC as per the MCP policy. I have a PCC reference number for you, it's GM221330348."

Mr Mahmood wrote the reference number down and looked quite intrigued as to where all of this was heading. The fact that this matter had been referred to the Police Complaints

Commission was a very big announcement. Ryan also began to look a little wrong-footed and sat up a tiny bit taller in his chair.

"If that's the case then I'm quite confused as to why you are involved in this investigation. The CPS guidelines quite clearly state that any officer who is referred to the CPS cannot work on any ongoing investigations relating to the matter under consideration by the PCC?" Mr Mahmood was good, he knew his stuff.

"That's absolutely true, but the circumstances of this case are quite extraordinary and time is a critical factor. As I am not here to interfere in any way in the outcome of the PPC inquiry, I am permitted to pursue this line of enquiry as there is a very serious chance of harm coming to your client."

Ryan suddenly looked as though he was beginning to take things seriously as he searched Miller's face for clues as to what this "harm" comment was all about. Mr Mahmood smiled again. It was clear that he was struggling to keep up.

"Sorry, I realise that it's confusing. Put bluntly, the allegation per say is not what we are here to discuss. That is now in the hands of the PCC and will be dealt with accordingly, and the audio file from this interview will also be supplied to them. But I'm afraid that there is something far more important which requires urgent attention."

This was an interesting remark, it was clear from the faces opposite Miller that they were desperate to understand where all of this was heading, if it wasn't about the allegations that Ryan Ingleton had made.

"So, to be perfectly clear DCI Miller – this interview is not in relation to the issue that your own manager has referred to the PCC?"

"No. The allegations which Ryan has made are completely false and frankly so extraordinary that it looks like whoever concocted this conspiracy theory and gave him this information has completely neglected to take five minutes to look at the facts from the case, they certainly haven't studied the evidence which was presented during the public inquiry and most alarming of all, the man who Ryan has claimed was actually responsible for the crimes was not even in the country for one of the two weeks whilst this was all happening. But that will all come out when the PCC complete their assessment and make their findings public."

Miller left that statement to hang in the air. He wanted Ryan to really soak up every word of it, so he was well primed for the second part of this conversation. The important part. Mr Mahmood looked down at the allegations again, seemingly quite content with Miller's explanation of the situation.

"Now, as I stated, just before Ryan laughed in such a curious manner, this has caused me a lot of personal trouble. I won't go into the details, but what I will say is that now that the individual that Ryan told these details to has realised that they are total nonsense, I'm afraid to say that Ryan is now in very serious danger."

Miller left that one to hang as well. It was clear from the pretty-boy face of Ryan Ingleton that he was beginning to treat this matter a lot more seriously.

"So, let's cut the crap. We're all big boys, so let's talk straight and see if there is a way that we can resolve this without having to send Ryan off to America on witness protection for the rest of his life. Tommy McKinlay, the man that Ryan gave this bizarre information to is now feeling deceived by Ryan. Deceived and humiliated. So what I need to do is work out a way of resolving this, as there is a very real possibility that Ryan is now in mortal danger."

Miller breathed out loudly as Ryan began to cry. The message had got through, loud and clear and Miller was extremely pleased to see that the young man was as soft as squirty cream.

"Now, what we need to do is come up with a reasonable explanation for what has gone on here, who has said what and to whom. If you genuinely believed that the information that you gave to Tommy McKinlay had come from a reliable source, then he might begin to blame the person who gave it to you. So who was it, Ryan? Who gave you this false information which has resulted in you becoming Tommy McKinlay's number one enemy? If you tell me, and I pass it on to Tommy, then we might stand a chance."

Ryan broke down completely. He knew enough about McKinlay and his people to recognise how much trouble he was in. This was clearly a bolt-from-the-blue, the young man looked petrified as he began rocking from side-to-side in his seat.

"DCI Miller. Can I request a break please?" Asked the solicitor.

"Of course. I'll just stop the tape." Miller knocked off the recording machine and the familiar, high pitched tone sounded for five seconds. He still called it a tape despite the old cassette machines being upgraded to hard-disk recorders almost fifteen years earlier. He'd been using these modern machines longer than he'd used the tapes but somehow struggled to adapt the modern terminology for the devices. Miller stood and opened the door. "I'll be right outside."

*****

The interview room door opened and Mr Mahmood popped his head out to alert Miller that Ryan Ingleton was ready to continue. Mr Mahmood looked quite surprised to see that Miller was standing right at the end of the corridor, as far away from the interview room as he possibly could. Most police officers he encountered stood as close as they could to the door, trying to eaves-drop on the conversations between the solicitors and their clients. Mr Mahmood had caught many of them, after sneaking up to the door and opening it quickly. He knew what Miller's gesture meant, it was easy to read between the lines. Miller was demonstrating that he had no need desire to earwig on this occasion, that he had absolutely no interest in what Ingleton had to say to his brief. It was a gesture which was designed to show where the balance of power lay.

"DCI Miller. We're ready to continue." Said the young solicitor and Miller walked casually along the corridor.

Once Miller had restarted the recording and got through all of the formalities once again, the recording machine was up and running and the conversation quickly began heading in a different direction.

Mr Mahmood spoke first. "DCI Miller, we thank you for

your advice today. We are grateful for the information that you have shared and we appreciate your concerns regarding my client's general welfare. But I feel that we need to clear the air here. Is my client being investigated for a particular crime?"

Miller had anticipated this and had polished his answer to the question in his head whilst standing outside on the corridor.

"At this moment in time, my overriding concern as a police officer is to protect Ryan from the impending danger that his actions have placed him in. That is my principal concern right now."

"And that is much appreciated as I have already stated. However..."

"Mr Mahmood, if you are asking me which crimes Ryan is currently being investigated for, then I can confirm that his actions have led to a number of extremely serious incidents, incidents which have resulted in one of my officers being kidnapped at gun-point in their own home as a direct consequence of Ryan's actions. As you will understand, Ryan could be charged as an accomplice for this matter as his actions led to the crime, so there would be a strong case for incitement to cause harm. Things don't usually get much more serious than that without somebody being killed, but I'm afraid that they have done on this occasion. Ryan's activities have led to the launch of a number of criminal investigations including one which is currently being looked after by officers from the counter-terrorism unit."

That was a pretty colossal answer and Mr Mahmood's bearing changed instantly. Terrorism is the most serious crime that a British citizen can be investigated for and police are automatically granted 14 days to hold a suspect who is involved in terror offences. For most other crimes, they have 24 hours. It had been obvious that Mr Mahmood was gearing up to start pushing for his client's release. He now knew beyond any shadow of a doubt that any consideration for release from custody was out of the question and that Ryan was going nowhere, quite possibly for a fortnight.

"I see."

"But as I say, that is not my biggest concern at this moment in time. I don't want to be responsible for visiting Ryan's parents and telling them that their son has been murdered… but right now, I cannot see any other conclusion to this, unless Ryan starts sharing some vital information about who is behind the information that has been given to McKinlay."

Mr Mahmood stared hard at his client who had seemed quite calm and composed since Miller had come back into the room. But he was back to the rocking and crying again now.

"So, if its okay with you guys, I think we should put a stop to the game-playing, the trying to find an easy way out of the police station, and let's start trying to work out a way of resolving this matter in a sensible and productive manner in the interests of Ryan's safety. Okay?"

There was no comment from Ingleton, nor his solicitor. Whatever plan Mr Mahmood had discussed with his client was now dead in the water, that much was abundantly clear.

"Ryan, I believe that you were viciously attacked last year in York city centre From what I've read on the police computer, you were so badly injured that you had to be airlifted to hospital due to the head injuries you sustained. Can you tell me anything about this incident? Who was behind it perhaps?"

Ingleton looked at his solicitor for guidance.

"It's worth remembering that I'm here because I want to help you. I know that I keep repeating that message, but that's literally the only reason I'm sitting here talking to you."

Ryan leaned forward and opened his mouth. He took another glance at the solicitor before he started to talk.

"Listen, I'm not fucking grassing. No way."

"I'm not asking you to grass, Ryan. I'm asking you to save your own skin here."

"I know. And I'll tell you what went on, but you keep throwing Tommy's name about as though he's just another guy on the street. It isn't like that. He's… it isn't like that. You don't realise…"

"I probably don't… and you don't have to grass on anyone. I just want to know where you got the incorrect information from."

"It's..."

"I mean, obviously, I already know where you got it from. I just wanted you to confirm it..."

"What... that's... you can't..."

"Ryan, seriously mate, you're not talking to a div. I'm the boss of the most important CID department in the city. Please, for your own sake, stop believing I'm a mug. All that's doing is slowing things down."

"DCI Miller, if you feel so confident that you know who has informed my client of this information, might I suggest that you name that individual and my client can either confirm or deny the suggestion?"

Miller dropped the niceties and leaned back in his chair. He looked pissed off with the pair sat across from him. "No. I'm not doing that. Tell you what, I think we're going to need another break. I've got a lot to do, there are a lot of other things happening right now and I really could do without this taking up so much of my time. Can I suggest that we pick this up again tomorrow?"

This dismissive response to Ryan's pissing about had finally broken the deadlock, just as Miller had anticipated it would.

Ryan started talking, an urgency was clearly audible in his voice. "Okay, okay. I got the information from Lisa..."

"Lisa Dawson?"

"Yes."

"Your ex-girlfriend?"

"Yes."

"I know. She's been interviewed under caution about this matter."

That *was* a surprise. It was written all across Ingleton's face that he was beginning to realise that he held no cards at all. He really was up shit creek without a paddle.

"I just wanted to see if you were going to tell the truth. You see, I know all about this stupid story Lisa Dawson has told you. She has told officers that she had a row with you, because you were bullying her..."

"Bullying?"

"Let me speak, please Ryan. She said that you had bullied her because she wanted to speak to her father on the phone and that you objected to this and subsequently, you both had a row."

"Yeah, but that's…"

"According to Lisa, she was desperate to make up with you, she was absolutely terrified of losing you. And she says that she concocted a story which she thought might impress you…"

"What, this is fucking insane. She told me that her dad was Pop. She said that the guy they blamed it on, she said that was a load of bollocks. And she said that you knew the real story and had let her dad go free."

Miller looked at Mr Mahmood and smiled politely, before looking back at Ingleton.

"Yes, Ryan, I know that's what she said. But that doesn't mean that it is true. I mean, it's a nice story, it would make a cracking TV series I suppose. But she only said it so that you'd leave her alone and let her talk to her dad."

"That's not how it was…she was going on about her mum killing herself. And her sister."

"So you think that she was looking for your sympathy? Trying to win you back?"

The young man thought about the question. He looked a little bit pissed off. "This is getting totally twisted about. She's chatting shit. That's not what she said…"

"Well, listen Ryan. That's her version of events. She's admitted saying this to you, and you've just confirmed that the conversation took place so at least we know where this mental story has all come from, and most importantly, why. But let's put all of that to one side and leave that for the PCC to deal with. What I'm concerned about is the danger you now face for passing on a bullshit story which Tommy McKinlay has tried to use to blackmail me and which has now resulted in my officers compiling a very long list of serious criminal charges which will be brought against him, and let's be very clear here. These charges will be brought against you also."

"I didn't know it was all bollocks! Did I?"

"Ryan, I'd like to be sympathetic, but I'm genuinely

struggling to understand why you have passed this on."

"What do you mean?"

"Did you do any research into it at all? Like, check to see if the man you claimed was supposedly responsible was even in the United Kingdom when the shootings were taking place?"

Ingleton looked down at the tabletop. "No. I didn't."

"I know you didn't. But I really bloody wish you had done Ryan, not only because I've got my officers being held at gun-point and all sorts of other stuff going on, but because you've opened up the gates of hell for yourself here." Miller exhaled loudly like a frustrated school teacher. He let a dramatic silence hang in the air for several seconds before speaking again. "Have you passed this story on to anybody else?"

"No. Course not."

"Can you tell me the circumstances of how you came to tell Tommy McKinlay this story?"

"Not on the recording."

"You mean you'd be happy to tell me off the record?"

"Yes. If it's going to make you help me."

"That's going to be awkward. Under the circumstances that the PCC are investigating this. It would put me in a bad light if there were undocumented conversations taking place regarding this matter. I'm sure Mr Mahmood would back me up on this?"

The brief nodded for Ryan's benefit.

"Well, I'm not telling you nothing on tape."

"Fine then, I'll never know. But that's neither here nor there in the grand scheme of things. McKinlay has dropped himself in so much shit, all thanks to your mad story that I'll be getting a commendation at the end of all this. It's funny how things turn out."

Ryan looked at Miller and searched the DCI's face. He was snookered and he knew it. Mr Mahmood was also studying Miller.

"Okay. Listen right, I'm not naming names. But I got robbed in York, big gang of lads. They took all the stuff I had on me..."

"By stuff, you mean the drugs that you were selling for McKinlay."

"I've not said any of that."

"But I'm quite convinced that that's what you mean. Continue..."

Ingleton rolled his eyes like an annoying teenager before remembering that he needed to clear this up.

"So, certain people were pissed off with me for getting robbed and so basically, a lot of people were after me. I was told had to pay back all the money for all the stuff that had been robbed off me."

"That's easy enough to follow."

"I discharged myself from hospital but I got gripped at Leeds train station, I was planning to fuck off to Scotland and let everything simmer down. Anyway, the people who gripped me were going to kill me. Not just because of the stuff I'd lost and the money I owed, but because they were pissed off that I was trying to get away."

"If my calculations are correct Ryan, all of this took place last August."

"Yeah."

"Which was several months before McKinlay was remanded."

Ingleton ignored the question, but Miller knew from his face that he was barking up the right tree.

"So I told the people that I had some decent information that would be useful. Next thing I knew, they drove me back here and sat me in front of the boss. And I told him what Lisa had told me. Anyway, after I'd finished he let me go, and that was that. The slate was wiped."

Miller nodded sympathetically. He knew all this already, the story and the timeline was as obvious as the nose on Ingleton's face. Miller had already worked it all out. All he had wanted to know from this bullshit interview was whether or not Ingleton had shared the information with anybody else. Miller felt confident that he hadn't. He was quite satisfied that McKinlay wouldn't have been banding it about when he thought it was going to be so useful. This was all good news. The outcome of this conversation was extremely positive, Miller had managed to convince Ingleton and his solicitor that the whole thing was nonsense, whilst securing vital information which was crucial in finding a resolution to this mess. It was quite apparent that Ryan Ingleton wouldn't be sharing this information again.

"The biggest problem we have here Ryan is your personal safety. That's the bigger picture here, nothing else matters. I know you won't say it, but I will. Tommy McKinlay and his pals are a very nasty bunch of psychopaths and they would think nothing of you disappearing forever. But I would. I don't think you deserve that, just because you got robbed and went out with a daft girl who talks a lot of shit for attention. I'm going to see if we can drop the charges, under the circumstances."

Ingleton's eyes were filling up with tears and Miller realised it was job done. "I would like you to stay here with Mr Mahmood whilst I speak to my superior officers and see what we can do regarding a safe haven for you until we work out a more permanent solution to this mess."

The tears were flowing freely now, which came as no surprise to Miller. He was just pleased that this massive piece of the jigsaw was now clicked solidly into place.

Chapter Seventy-Four

Rudovsky was feeling a little brighter now. Her thoughts were being concentrated on her holiday. There were a few logistical problems, such as packing her cossie which was back at the house. She didn't feel like going back there yet. Abby had been mithering about going home and packing but Rudovsky flatly refused and a raised tension had starting bubbling away for a bit. But other than that, she was feeling much better today.

She was surprised to see Dixon's number appear on her phone as it started vibrating on the bed. She didn't often receive a call from the Ivory Towers.

"Hello Sir!" She said in her most enthusiastic voice.

"Hello Jo. You sound rather perky, despite the circumstances!"

"Yes, well, you know... just got to get on with it. The massive bag of cocaine's helping though, thanks for sending that round!"

Dixon let out a massive laugh at Rudovsky's outrageous quip and she held the phone away from her ear slightly. The laugh sounded quite forced and fake but it still amused her enormously.

"You're a one you are!" Said Dixon, as his hysteria settled down.

"I'm only kidding Sir. How can I help?"

"I was ringing to check on how you are. Miller has told me that he's spoken to you. He says that you're off on your travels?"

"Yes, tomorrow. Not exactly sure on the details yet Sir, but I think it'll do me a bit of good to get away from Manchester for a bit..."

"Quite! I wholeheartedly agree. And just to confirm that I have signed it off, all travel, hotel and reasonable expenses will be covered by us."

"Aw, thank you, Sir."

"That's perfectly fine, Jo. But there is one tiny condition attached..."

"Right?"

"I realise that it is short notice, but I really need you to meet with a member of our Human Resources team, before you go. We have a duty of care towards you and that's something that I take very seriously. There are certain conversations that need to be had before you go. Is that okay?"

"Well, yes, of course, Sir."

"Good. Only..."

"Sir?"

"Becky from HR can only schedule in a meeting for today."

"Okay, that's not a problem. I've not got much in the diary anyway..."

"Well, I thought as much. It's just, what you've been through. It wouldn't do to put it on the shelf for a fortnight whilst you are rocking up having a holiday."

Rudovsky cringed down the phone and prevented herself from laughing at the stupid shit Dixon said when he was trying to act cool and with it like this.

"It would be good to get the ball-rolling and make sure that we, as your employers, are doing all that we can to support you after this terrifying ordeal."

Rudovsky was touched. Despite Dixon making her curl her toes, it was good of him to show that he cared. She'd had a taste of the force's excellent HR support after the stabbing which had left her in a hospital bed for several weeks. It really was reassuring to know that they gave a shit.

"When are you thinking?"

"I've spoken to Becky, she can only do two o'clock."

"Two o'clock? What, today?"

"That's right."

"Sir, you mean the two o'clock in half an hour?"

"Yes. Becky will meet you in Starbucks."

"In Didsbury?"

"Yes. I'll even ask her to bring another big bag of cocaine for you!"

This time it was Rudovsky's turn to laugh but she didn't quite manage to emulate Dixon's huge guffaw, her amusement was markedly understated by comparison.

"Okay, well, I'd better chuck some clothes on and straighten my hair. Cheers Sir."

"Oh and Jo, have a good holiday. Try and chill your beans as my granddaughter would say."

Chapter Seventy-Five

Miller arrived back at HQ with about twenty-five hours work to do, and only two or three hours within which to do it all. He was feeling the full weight of the hopelessness of his situation before he'd even reached his office door when his mobile began ringing. He was about to reject the call until he saw that it was Dixon.

"Hello Sir."

"Andy, are all of your team in the office?"

Miller paused and looked across at where his officers were working. "Everyone's here - except Jo of course, Sir. Why?"

"The chief constable wants to speak to you all, it's to do with the roll-out of his Better Together ideology strategy…"

"What? Are you kidding me on?"

"Andy, I'm really sorry. I was supposed to have organised this. I'm completely to blame, obviously… I've been a little distracted this week, what with one thing and another. But that's no excuse…"

Miller exhaled loudly, making sure that the phone's microphone picked every exaggerated second of it at full volume.

"It shouldn't take long."

"Is he coming down here?"

"No, he wants us all to meet in reception. He likes the general population of the building to see him engaging with his staff as they go about their business. That's another part of the Better Together ideology."

"Fuck me dead."

"It's at two."

"Sir, it's quarter to two."

"Yes, quite. Okay, once again please accept my profound apologies. But look on the bright side, I'm sure you'll get a lot from it!"

Dixon's weird attempt at sarcasm was badly timed. Rather than laugh, or counter with some banter of his own, Miller hung up. He dropped his bag inside his office door and walked across to where the rest of his team were working to break the news of the impending, impromptu waffle-bollocks meeting with the biggest deal in the building. As he opened his mouth to speak, Miller was fully prepared for an onslaught of abuse which would be richly deserved.

*****

"And that's the key principle behind this multifaceted objective. The world is changing fast, so fast in fact, that even if we all get our skates on, and strap a jet-pack to our backs, we'll still face a hell of a job keeping up!"

Sitting on the leather settees behind the reception desk, under the direct glare of the sunshine beating hard through the glass wall, Miller's team let out a genuine-sounding career-laugh that they could all be proud of. Even Miller joined in, although it was clear to all of his team that he was blatantly taking the piss. Miller was well known for his cynicism for all of this kind of bullshit. "Better Together" was not an exciting new directive in modern policing in Miller's view, it was just bollocks. "Better Together" was a whimsical pop song by Jack Johnson as far as Miller was concerned, and he'd bet a fiver that a CD single of that being thrown at a criminal's eyeball would be more useful in the fight against crime than this bollocks meeting which was keeping him from his work would ever be. But despite the shitness of this meeting and the appalling timing, Miller realised there was no point in sulking. Sometimes, you just have to do as you're told and get on with it, whether you like it or not. The big task now was to get through this without the chief constable realising that Miller was only here in a purely physical sense. His mind was completely switched off.

"Hundreds, if not thousands of police forces around the world have a shared interest in optimising their core strategy in the face of an ever shifting and evolving agenda driven by the principles which I intend to set out over the course of…"

Bollocks thought Miller as he glanced down at his watch and felt a massive yawn stirring deep within him, a yawn so big that he was hopeful that it didn't come out because he'd probably start giggling if it did. He suddenly felt very tired and he always got the giggles when he was feeling this strange, lethargic sensation which was nearly always powered by a shit talking management meeting. Miller glanced across at Dixon who was standing beside the chief, doing his very best to stifle a yawn himself by the looks of things.

"And that is why the Better Together strategy completely redefines our A.S.B.B.T objectives, not only at the point of delivery but in every conceivable…"

The Chief Constable was distracted by a hand-signal from his personal assistant who was sitting beside Grant on the comfy sofas. She stood and whispered something to her boss, her phone clutched by her side. The Chief pulled a funny face, as though he was mildly pissed off, but determined to remain on his best behaviour for the gophers sitting before him. He turned to Dixon and whispered something to him. Dixon's theatrical face upon hearing this whisper made Miller laugh out loud as the DCS's eyes bulged out of his head in full panto style. Miller managed to stifle his laugh with a fake cough before focusing hard on one section of the shiny floor until he'd simmered down from this wave of giddiness that was stirring inside.

A little more whispering took place before the Chief could be heard speaking at full volume again. Miller looked up from the view of the floor that he'd been concentrating on.

"My sincere apologies. An operational emergency has just come in. I'm going to have to reschedule this briefing for a later date, I'm afraid. Thank you."

With that, the Chief and his PA marched off towards the lift, he looked quite stressed. Miller looked at Dixon, who also appeared quite concerned.

"What's going on?" Asked the DCI, suddenly snapping out of his silly frame of mind and wondering what could have happened that requires the CC's urgent attention. That only ever happened when something very big had occurred.

Chapter Seventy-Six

Although Dixon insisted on staying tight-lipped "until a clearer picture emerges," the rumours had begun whirling around MCP's HQ building before the SCIU team had made it back upstairs and into the office. DCI Kev Lyons was leaning over the barrier at the top of the stairs as Miller approached, close to the door of his neighbouring Drugs and Firearms office. He seemed keen to share the gossip. According to Kev, a very serious incident had occurred in the city-centre, and every operational police officer from the closest stations had been despatched to help manage the scene.

"What's the incident?" Asked Miller with a look of concern etched on his face.

"Search me. That's just what I've been told by comms."

Miller walked up the last few steps, experiencing a range of emotions. He was concerned about this incident and hoped desperately that it wasn't anything that involved members of the public, or any members of the police family. His feelings were confused because he was also feeling chuffed that the meeting had been postponed, but mildly irritated that he would have to sit through the first bit of it all over again when it was rescheduled.

The team sat back down at their desks and began picking up where they had left off. Miller went into his office, picked up his bag from the doorway and sat down at his desk, trying desperately to think of which of the ten jobs took priority. Time was the biggest aggravator and he began scanning through his list to see which of the tasks was fighting the clock the hardest. Ryan Ingleton had been locked back in his cell whilst Miller pretended to be working on a way out of the mess he had got himself into. Miller was planning to get somebody from the team to drop him off at Preston train station, buy him an Inverness ticket and wish him well for the future. That was about as much of a care package Ryan Ingleton would be receiving, and it certainly wasn't going to be delivered by Miller, nor would it be delivered in any hurry, it could wait until tomorrow. He placed Ingleton's name at the bottom of the new list he began writing in order of priority, when his office phone started ringing.

"Andy, it's Dixon."

"Hello Sir."

"We've... there's been an incident. I'm sorry I couldn't tell you downstairs when you asked, but you had your entourage all around. But anyway, I'm telling you now." Dixon's voice sounded cold and distant and Miller sensed that something dreadful was about to be announced. He stared hard at his computer screen as he pushed the phone closer to his ear and braced himself.

"It would appear that Tommy McKinlay has been released from prison."

"What?" Miller's blood suddenly ran cold. This was the worst possible news. His mind began racing, trying to make sense of that extraordinary development.

"Yes, you heard me correctly. Within fifteen minutes of each other, the two chief witnesses who were due to give evidence against McKinlay have both approached DCI Jarvis at the NCA to tell him that they are no longer prepared to risk it. Jarvis informed the CPS who in turn filed a Discontinuance under section 23... they've dropped the case altogether."

"Holy shit..." said Miller, a cold, disturbed edge was present in his voice as he considered the implications of this colossal announcement. A discontinuance order required any remand prisoner to be released from the prison as soon as was physically possible. All of McKinley's inner-circle had been arrested on suspicion of murder today, while he'd just been let out, his case had been chucked in the bin. "This is..."

"Andy, sorry to interrupt. You see, that's not the main thrust of the update. The main part is that there has been a fatal shooting in the past half an hour, on the outskirts of Manchester city centre. It has not been officially confirmed yet, but unofficially, the victim was Tommy McKinlay."

Chapter Seventy-Seven

"You're watching Afternoon Live on Sky News and we're going to interrupt that press conference from the Prime Minister to bring you some breaking news which is just reaching us. In the past few moments, Sky sources have informed us of an incident which is currently unfolding in Manchester. It appears that another shooting has taken place in the past few moments, this means that a fourth murder has occurred in the past twenty-four hours in the city. Viewers will recall that last night, three separate murder investigations were launched following three shootings in different areas of the city at around about 9'o'clock yesterday evening. Well, our sources are informing us that there has just been another fatal shooting, this time close to the city-centre. Our north of England correspondent Paul Mitchell joins us on the line. Paul, what is the latest where you are."

"Yes, good afternoon Sarah, and what a dreadful twenty-four hours we are witnessing in Greater Manchester. I am currently on my way to the scene of this latest shooting incident in which it is believed that one man has died at the scene, this would take the number of people killed by gunfire to four."

"What more can you tell us, Paul?"

"Well, very little I'm afraid at this moment in time, but what I can say is that my sources have informed me that this incident occurred at six minutes past two this afternoon, and the attack appears to have taken place outside HMP Manchester. There are a lot of conflicting stories flying around as you will expect from these kinds of incidents, but from what I can gather from my sources, the person who has been fatally injured had just been released from HMP Manchester, he was literally still walking out of the doors when the occupants of a motor vehicle, believed to be a black motor car parked on Southall Street adjacent to the prison's main entrance, opened fire with a succession of shots, one eye-witness described the sound as similar to a machine gun. Sadly, one person was pronounced dead at the scene, there are no reports of anybody else being caught up in this shocking attack."

"Any idea who the victim was?"

"Yes, we have reasonable intelligence about that matter but we are not at liberty to report anything on that just yet, naturally a formal identification of the body has yet to be made and subsequently the victim's next of kin will have to be informed and I'm afraid that those are important procedures which must be followed. But as things currently stand, Manchester seems to be returning to its old ways, and it appears that despite the view that the gun-crime problem in this city had fallen sharply since the days when the city earned the appalling nickname 'Gunchester' in the 1990s, well it appears that gun-crimes are very much back if the shocking activities from the past twenty-four hours are anything to go by. "

*****

Twitter probably should, but doesn't follow the same reporting rules and restrictions that the traditional broadcast companies are legally bound to follow. And as a result, anybody can post anything on the social media site without first checking facts, understanding the formalities or consulting any professional standards manuals. Thanks to this "no filter" "anything goes" policy, Twitter has become the first place to turn to when a Breaking News story is announced. There's no need to wait for all the boring rules to be followed here.

On Twitter, the hashtags #McKinlayMurdered and #RIPRockHardTommy were beginning to trend in the north-west of England. Hundreds of posts had been shared and retweeted naming the victim of this latest shooting, without any consideration for the dead man's closest relatives, or the appalling way that they would learn of their loved ones passing should they stumble across it by chance.

One post was attracting the most activity, it was a very shaky video of the aftermath of the incident, recorded by a passer-by by the looks of things. In the video footage, which had been retweeted over 12,000 times already, a very disturbing incident was replayed.

Lying on the floor, just yards from the HMP Manchester gates was the body of a man, the arms and legs were twitching violently as it lay on the ground by the famous orange bricks. A voice can clearly be heard shouting "what the fuck's happened, what's happening?" as the prison gates opened and several prison officers came running out of the building. Whilst all this was happening, a car can be heard screeching away in the distance and car horns beeping loudly as the prison staff drop to their knees to assess the injuries. Soon after this, the legs and arms stopped twitching. The video footage ends soon afterwards, with a prison officer approaching the camera and standing in front of the lens. "Can you turn that…"

Chapter Seventy-Eight

The mood in The Queens was electric. Every member of the SCIU team was out, which was a rare occurrence these days. Even Rudovsky was out, the news that had come through in the past few hours had been the perfect tonic. The team all felt a renewed sense of togetherness, the events of the past six days may have been stressful and chaotic, at times very surprising - but they had worked wonders for strengthening everybody's sense of trust and belonging within the SCIU department.

As macabre as it seemed, the passing of Tommy McKinlay was something worth celebrating, if not because of the shit that Miller had been put through this week – certainly because Rudovsky could start putting that unforgettable incident behind her, safe in the knowledge that the sick bastard behind it was dead and his disciples were all off the streets now, in one fell swoop. As far as the Tommy McKinlay issue was concerned, there really couldn't have been a better outcome. Not only was McKinlay out of the picture for good, his minions in the community could no longer pose a threat either. The game was up.

It was also worth an almighty celebration for the simple reason that the biggest organised crime network in the city had been smashed to smithereens. Not only was this great news for the police and the authorities who had lost all control over these individuals, but it was also a very big deal for the SCIU. It gave the tiny, drastically underfunded department an unbelievable bragging opportunity over the hundred-plus members of the mega-funded NCA, all of whom had been working full-time in trying to get a result against McKinlay and his team for the past two years. The SCIU had only been involved with this for a matter of days and the whole TMS empire had come crashing down, never to return. Miller was on great form, reminding everybody around the table of the score. By his reckoning, it was SCIU Seventeen, NCA nil.

"I still don't even know what the hell was going on with all this, you know." Said Saunders as the giddy, high-fiving mood dipped momentarily.

"In what way?" Asked Worthington as he took a greedy slurp from his pint. The rest of the team listened intently to what was being said.

"Well, I said to the boss that McKinlay was planning something – I was pretty sure that this whole blackmail thing was a blag, designed to distract us all from what McKinlay was really planning. And I thought I had been proved right when I heard about the drug-baron shootings last night."

"What, so you don't think that now?" Asked Rudovsky.

"No, I don't think I do!" Saunders smiled as he said it, pleased that he had everyone's undivided attention.

"Come on then, Sherlock! What do you think he was planning then, before his untimely death?" Miller laughed loudly, wondering what shocking announcement was going to come out of Saunders' mouth this time. The DI very rarely disappointed.

"Well, I read the file that the NCA gave to us. It listed all of McKinlay's closest allies in there. It also contained an interview transcript with McKinlay, in which he was asked about every single name. One by one, he was asked if he employed each person, name by name. He no commented them all of course. But the point is that he knew that the NCA knew who all his people were."

"Right?" Said Grant.

"So, if McKinlay knew that the NCA already had eyes on his team... it makes me wonder if he has stitched them all up. Think about it. He gets himself banged up on a bollocks remand stretch, and while he's in there, pretends he's doing it to knobble our boss. But what if that was never his plan? What if the plan all along was to get them all sent down for murder while he's completely in the clear?"

"Wait... why would he do that?" Miller didn't look convinced, but he was certainly intrigued by what Saunders was suggesting.

"Fuck knows!"

A loud laugh filled the backroom that the team had taken over. "But, don't forget, McKinlay had twenty-four million in the bank. He might have been planning an early retirement perhaps? Maybe he thought that he couldn't trust the people in his organisation if his back was turned. Maybe he'd heard they were up to no good?"

"Nah, bollocks!" Said Chapman. "Not having that. People like that don't take early retirement."

"Well it's a theory. But if you can give me a better explanation for him organising those shootings using every name that he knew the NCA were eyeballing, I'll gladly listen!" Saunders smiled smugly as he took a swig from his beer bottle.

"Well, I think its safe to say, we'll probably never know." Said Miller. "I'm just glad the horrible bastard is not going to be our problem anymore!"

"I'll raise a glass to that!" Said Rudovsky.

"And please, don't forget to raise a glass to Dixon!" Added Miller. "I think he finally redeemed himself today."

"How do you mean?" Asked Worthington.

"You mean you haven't twigged?"

"Twigged what?"

"He organised for us all to be on the eighteen CCTV cameras in the reception area at two o'clock today. At the very same time, a certain drive-by shooting took place outside the doors of HMP Manchester."

"Fucking Norah!" Said Grant, holding her hand to her mouth.

"Oh my God!" Added Kenyon as the penny began to drop.

"Shit!" Said Rudovsky. "Dixon made me meet some young girl from HR in Starbucks at two o'clock! I sat there wondering what the hell I was doing there, she just asked me a load of shit questions about nothing!"

"Well, I can't think of any better proof that none of us lot were involved in this assassination, than the city police HQ's own CCTV system! Or in your case Jo, Starbucks!" Said Miller, holding his pint glass aloft. "But at least one thing's for sure. When this all gets investigated and the conspiracy theorists try and pin this shit on us lot, we will be able to say that the Chief Constable was spot on! We really were Better Together!

Cheers."

Epilogue

The dreams that Tommy McKinlay harboured of becoming so influential and powerful that he was effectively running the police force in Greater Manchester were never to be realised. The legend status that he had enjoyed and had actively promoted for the past quarter century had never been enough for him. As had been the case with his first taste of money all those years earlier, Tommy always wanted more. Most men would have settled for the reputation, the money and the power that Tommy had, but Tommy wanted more, always.

The sad irony is that now, Tommy isn't remembered as a legend. For somebody who had been equally feared and revered in life, his reputation in death is quite tragic. Now, he is primarily remembered for becoming too big for his boots and losing in the most extreme way that anybody can ever lose. For all of the achievements that Tommy had under his belt, and there were many, it was particularly glib that he would forever be remembered in the city as little more than a terrible gobshite who made a dick of himself trying to knobble the police. Rock Hard Tommy has been consigned to the history books as little more than a knobhead of gargantuan proportions.

From time to time, particularly on birthdays and anniversaries, Tommy's friends and family visit Strangeways prison and erect a plaque on the side of the building close to the spot where he took his last breaths. There have been several versions of this plaque already, because they have to be taken down for "health and safety" reasons. The message on the plaque reads "True Manchester Legend and Man of the People - Murdered at this spot by the state THOMAS F McKINLAY a Father, a Son, a Brother, a Lover."

"I think they'll have to order another," rhyme the prison maintenance staff each time they prise the blue steel disc from the wall. It never gets old, that one.

Keen to ensure that this never unfortunate situation came round again, Miller held a press conference to publicise, then personally denounce the absurd claims which had been made against him, although he didn't mention the source of these accusations bearing in mind the sensitivity of the timing.

George Dawson has been officially cleared of all wrongdoing with regards the Pop case. DCI Miller showed members of the press several pieces of compelling evidence which proved that Dawson was overseas for eight days whilst the murders were taking place. This has stopped the snowball from gathering any momentum before it could be pushed off the top of the hill.

Nobody knows where Ryan Ingleton is these days. He keeps a very low profile, convinced that his dynamite information was wrong. Lisa Dawson learned a very valuable lesson due to the fall-out from all of this, but her dad remains hopeful that she will learn to trust people again. Just not yet, and certainly not with the family secret.

Simon Kingston was arrested in Heywood, just a couple of minutes before McKinlay's murder. This helped to rule him out of that particular inquiry. But news of McKinlay's death, and of Kingo's arrest, was the best news that many thousands of people who had been on the receiving end of TM security's services had ever heard. From the moment the two news stories came together, the Crimestoppers line was permanently engaged as victims of the TMS empire felt confident enough to share their experiences. People like Jasmine Jackson, who wanted to speak out in memory of her man, Jason.

Jason had taken his own life, unable to accept the recurring images in his mind. Images that Tommy and Kingo had deliberately, cruelly put there, laughing all the way, all because the landlord refused to provide a gas safety check and had subsequently become locked in a disagreement that he wouldn't back away from. That's why Jason hadn't paid the rent. It was all sat there in his bank, ready to be paid the minute the check was carried out, and he'd told the landlord that, several times. "My kid and my partner live in this house. Do the safety check, and the minute I have the certificate, you'll get your rent, no mither." He'd said, on numerous occasions.

The NCA are handling the case against Kingo and the other senior TMS staff members who currently remain on remand in various prisons throughout the UK. The NCA are continuing to receive calls from people who have suffered unimaginable violence and hardship at the hands of TM Security staff members. So far the charges include numerous counts of kidnap, unlawful imprisonment, rape, gang-rape, sexual assault, ABH, GBH and murder. NCA staff are still investigating eighteen missing persons inquiries which they strongly believe will lead back to TMS. Interestingly, there are no cases of attempted murder under investigation. It seems to the investigating officers that it was all or nothing with these people.

The most macabre outcome from the NCA's investigations into TMS managed to make the national news. It wasn't the finer details of the case which attracted the attention of the media, but the travel chaos which ensued. Following a tip-off, the M6 motorway had to be closed for six days between junctions 18 and 19 at Knutsford, as engineers replaced eight upright concrete struts on two bridges which had been installed in 2017. Eight of the ten-metre tall uprights were removed and replaced, one-by-one, before being taken away for examination at a cost exceeding two-million pounds. After being dismantled by specialist engineers with pneumatic drills, it was revealed that all of the reclaimed 1.5 metre thick concrete posts contained human remains. The person who tipped off police about this grisly matter was the owner of the fabrication company which cast the posts. He is due to give evidence against Simon Kingston when the trial commences. He has been praised by the NCA's investigating team for marking the eight posts with a slightly angular pattern of finishing concrete so that they could be identified at the roadside, but would have looked perfectly normal inside the fabrication plant.

As far as the NCA are concerned, there are zero concerns regarding this forthcoming court case, the evidence against Kingo and the TMS team is overpowering, now that the threat of intimidation has gone. Whatever happens, the TMS dream is over and Simon Kingston is looking at five life sentences as a best-case scenario.

There are many conspiracies circling around online regarding the brutal death of Tommy McKinlay. The most popular and recurring one is that the police were behind the murder, that they were tipped off by prison staff that Tommy was about to be released and they went and assassinated him the moment he stepped foot outside the jail. That's a popular one. But as many people are keen to point out on these online discussions, it is logistically flawed. Tommy's release was only sanctioned by the CPS at 12.45pm. He was killed at 2.06pm, just 81 minutes later. It is argued that it's a nice idea on paper, but the police take three weeks to turn up to a crime scene in normal circumstances, so it's a bit of a stretch to think they can organise to hire a hit-man and get him to sit in a robbed car outside the prison and shoot McKinlay's heart out of his torso, in about an hour.

Other conspiracy theories speak about Tommy contacting one of his team for a lift as soon as he'd heard the news of his imminent release, and that it was an inside job, that it was one of the TMS team who killed McKinlay. But that runs out of momentum very quickly as nobody has suggested a sensible reason for that. After all, Tommy *was* TM Security, he paid the wages and attracted the contracts.

The conspiracy theory which continues to attract the most oxygen centres around one member of the senior TMS team who has not been arrested, and who appears to have disappeared completely. Ben Thompson, the man everybody at TMS knew as Nerd. Nobody seemed to know very much about him before he began working for TMS, and nobody knows anything at all about him now, as he disappeared off the face of the planet the night before Tommy's murder. Strangely, his name doesn't appear on any wanted or outstanding suspect lists.

The good thing about all of this is that it will keep all the conspiracy theorists talking for a while yet.

One thing that most people understand perfectly well is that if the state *was* involved, be that police, the NCA or MI5 or whoever... it will remain a secret for the rest of time, so there's no point in pontificating over it. After all, if successive governments can tell the police to keep quiet and look away as a predatory paedophile MP continues to molest hundreds of children over a timespan of almost forty years, then it's a reasonable guess that the government can very easily organise the murder of a man who gets a bit too cocky for his own good.

Clare Miller's friend Debbie still refuses to accept hot beverages in hotel rooms.

THE END

Printed in Great Britain
by Amazon